A TROUBLESOME WOMAN

Suzanne Downes

Country Books

Published and distributed by
Country Books
Courtyard Cottage, Little Longstone, Bakewell, Derbyshire DE45 1NN
Tel: 01629 640670
www.countrybooks.biz

ISBN 978-1-906789-58-9

British Library Cataloguing in Publication Data.
A catalogue record for this book is available from the British Library.

Printed and bound in Great Britain by
4edge Ltd, Hockley. www.4edge.co.uk

Dedication

To my friend and publisher Dick Richardson,
without whom I wouldn't be on the shelf,
and to David, without whom I would be on the shelf!

For Helen – (or is that
dear Smelly?)
Happy Christmas 2011,
Suzanne Downes
x

Aknowledgements

A word of thanks to all those kind friends who allowed me to use their names for the characters in this book – most bear no resemblance to their fictional counterparts – you can decide for yourselves which ones do!

Lisa Dunne, Diane Stafford-Naylor and her husband Rick,
Diane Towey, Alan and Yvonne Corfield,
Joanne Pooley of Melbourne, Australia, Josette Bennett,
Jan Riley (née Southworth) and her husband Dave,
my lovely Auntie, Dorothy Mason,
Pietro Bonaminio, Lisa (Jane) Wakefield, Andy Hughes,
Jane Tiplady and last but not least,
Dave Allen (not the Comedian!)

CHAPTER ONE

LIBBY – PRESENT

"I'm bored."

David folded down the top of his newspaper and glanced at his wife over it, "You're not bored. You've never been bored in your life. You just want some attention from me."

Libby grinned and dived across the room, landing plump on her husband's stomach, crushing the paper in the process, "You could be right," she said gleefully, as he groaned, "but I'm bored too. I need something to do, David. I really do. The first few weeks of freedom from a job I didn't particularly enjoy were like a holiday, but now I'm realizing that sitting around with nothing to do has limited appeal."

"Then find yourself something interesting to do," he said practically, dragging his abused paper from under her and attempting to start reading it again. She pulled it out of his hands and flung it across the room, giggling as it fluttered into chaos and he tutted with exasperation.

"Like what?"

"Well, I don't know. I've offered you a job at the garden centre and you turned your nose up at it."

"You may find greenery riveting, but I'm afraid I don't," she replied.

"You could work in the office." Her expression of contempt told him how much that meant to her, "Okay," he conceded, "so you don't want to go back into an office, what about going to college and retraining in something you do fancy?"

"But that's the problem, I don't know what I do fancy."

"Except me," he prompted.

"Except you," she agreed and kissed him. There followed a few minutes of passion but Libby refused to be distracted for long and presently she broke from his embrace and continued as though they had never been interrupted, "Seriously, what can I do?"

"I've never understood why you never followed up on the idea you had of writing a book about your family history. You can't say that isn't interesting. Especially now that your big sister is talking about taking the Allinghams to court."

"As I recall, you didn't want me to, and anyway, don't you think that's a bit close to home?" she asked, in a tone that made him think that perhaps she had already been toying with the idea herself.

He could understand her reticence. The Allinghams owned the biggest stately home in the district and his garden centre did a huge amount of business with them.

Having her sister Maddie taking them to court in pursuit of an inheritance claim from a long dead ancestress was not exactly endearing him to one of his oldest clients.

"Close to home, perhaps, but at a distance of a hundred and fifty years," he pointed out reasonably, ignoring her reference to his reluctance – like any man, he preferred not to have to explain a change of heart.

"Still, I can't see Maddie being particularly impressed if I start writing about Decima just when she thinks she has the Allinghams on the ropes."

"I suppose not, but there were other characters in the story you could investigate. Didn't you think the lawyer Brookes was interesting?"

"No, I thought he was a dreadful old bore – and let's face it, he failed to save Decima from the hangman, so why would I want to write about him?"

"Fair enough. What about the policeman? Didn't you always say he seemed to sympathize with Decima? Weren't you given his case notes? Could there be something in those?"

Libby raised herself off his chest and looked at him in amazement, "David Wright, you are a genius! I only ever read the bits that referred to Decima, but there were loads more – and the family never asked for them back."

He pushed her off the sofa and as she stood up to leave the room he dealt a well-aimed slap at her rear, "Then get to work – and stop bothering me!"

She bent and gathered his paper into a scrumpled mess which she threw at him, "Oh, get on with your reading," she said, then fled in mock terror when he rose with a bellow of pretended rage.

*   *   *

She was still smiling to herself when she reached her bedroom. She wondered briefly what she had done with all the old paperwork from the year before. She hadn't touched any of it since her Aunt Lilian's death and her own marriage to David. There had been so much to sort out at the time that she had barely had time to think about poor tragic Decima, the young woman who had turned out to be her great, great, grandmother and not her great, great Aunt as family history had suggested. The shame of an illegitimate baby had caused her father to force her to hand her baby over to her older, childless sister and Decima had never been able to prove that she had, in fact, married the father of her baby, because the license had been lost – or rather well-hidden by the groom, who was afraid that his parents would ensure the marriage was annulled should they find out about it. A complicated story which was having repercussions to the present day, for Libby's sister Maddie stood to inherit a fortune if she could prove that she was actually an Allingham, due to this hasty and secret marriage a century and a half ago.

Libby had no interest in the Allingham fortune, but she had been fascinated by the story of Decima Watkins. Poor Decima, misunderstood and rejected by her family, and faced with the loss of her reputation because of a secret marriage to a man who was subsequently killed in the Crimea. She had then been accused and found guilty of murdering three of her sisters. The hangman had ended her young life, but Libby's investigations had cast serious doubt on the verdict. The girl hadn't had much luck in her life and it had satisfied Libby's sense of justice to bring the truth belatedly forward.

She had hoisted most of the contents of a large cupboard on the landing out before she recalled what she had done with the case notes of Inspector Lazarus, the arresting officer. His compassion for his young prisoner had caused him to be taken off the case, hence Libby's lingering affection for him.

Of course they were still in the bedroom she had been occupying before Aunt Lil's death and her own inheritance of the house she now called home.

Looking around the room for the first time in months, Libby realized that this was where she wanted to be when she started writing. The view from the window was over the rocky, heather-strewn hills at the back of the house. The master bedroom where she now slept with her husband over-looked the front – an equally stunning view, but a rather more distant one, since the house stood firmly on the side of a hill, looking out over long vistas.

She took the notebooks downstairs, full of excitement, to tell David of her plans for getting rid of the guest bed and filling the room with bookshelves, a desk and a new computer. He naturally agreed to anything that he thought might buy him a little peace and quiet. He had no doubt that Libby would spend a small fortune on realizing her dream of a 'book-lined study' and would then promptly lose interest in the whole project and never mention writing again.

For once, he couldn't have been more wrong.

Within days Libby had the house upside down. A carpenter was engaged to build sympathetic shelving which would not clash with the age and atmosphere of the house.

Since talented artisans could not be had immediately due to their popularity, he was persuaded to work evenings and weekends to circumvent his other jobs by the simple expedient of offering him what David considered to be an obscene amount of money, but after all, Lil had left Libby very comfortably off – and what else was she going to spend it on?

Aged oak was the wood Libby chose and she found a stunning old desk in the most expensive antique shop in Braxton. She left the purchase of the computer to her husband and by the end of a fortnight she had a study which any writer would have found inspiring.

She hadn't wasted her time during the building work, either, but had set herself the task of reading all Inspector Lazarus' case notes, which she suddenly discovered were far from complete. The person who had donated them had obviously known about her interest in Decima Watkins and had therefore passed on only the notes referring to her case. Libby needed more – much more – if she was to fashion a novel worth reading.

There was only one solution she could think of and that was to return, cap in hand, to the police museum in Braxton, from whence she had obtained various items relating to Decima and her story. She was quite reluctant to do so, because she and Dan Gordon, the curator, had not parted on the best of terms on their previous meeting. She and Lil had decided to keep Decima's belongings and Dan had been left to explain to his bosses why one of their more sordid displays had been broken up and removed. If he was still working there, Libby couldn't imagine him wanting to be particularly helpful. Still, if she wanted to write her story, she had no choice. Gathering together a leather-bound notebook and wearing her old business suit – which had grown a little too tight, if she was honest – she drove into Braxton.

She was surprised that not only was Dan still at the museum, he also recognized her at once, "Well, I never. Libby, isn't it? I wasn't expecting to see you again. How are you?"

"I'm fine, thank you, Dan. And yourself?" She was relieved she had remembered his name, now that he had so obviously recalled not only hers, but recognized her face too. She had to be honest, if she had seen him on the street, she would have had no idea who he was, and asking a favour would have been dreadfully difficult if he knew she had banished him utterly from her memory. There was no-one less inclined to be helpful than a person who felt they had been instantly forgettable and of no importance whatsoever.

"Never better. What can I do for you? I assume you are on another quest into the past."

"As a matter of fact I am," she admitted, seeing little point in prevarication. It would only make things more awkward in the long run.

"I can only hope you're not related to any more murderers or I'll have no exhibits left." She detected a note of sarcasm despite his pleasant smile, but she decided to ignore it, "I think I can safely say that we found out I wasn't even related to one, but I'll let that pass since I need your help."

"Really? You honestly think Decima was innocent, do you? Do you have any evidence, or is that just wishful thinking?"

"I proved it to my own satisfaction, but short of digging up three graves from a hundred and fifty years ago, physical evidence is a little hard to come by."

"I can imagine it is. Presumably you've decided not to go down the exhumation route then?"

Libby hesitated for a moment. It suddenly occurred to her that her sister's law suit against the Allinghams might just end up doing that very thing. She wondered how much DNA might realistically be left in bodies buried so long ago. Hopefully she need never find out.

"No, not at present. I've moved onto pastures new, that's why I'm here."

"You intrigue me. If it's not Decima that brings you here, then who is it, may I ask?"

"Last year when I was looking into Decima's story, you were kind enough to pass on some notes written by the policeman investigating the case. His name was Inspector Lazarus, and you told me that his family had donated his old notebooks, just in the very nick of time to help me. I don't suppose you still have their details so I can get in touch myself and see if they have any more information about him?"

To her astonishment Dan Gordon began to laugh. She couldn't see that she had said anything remotely amusing, so she simply stared at him, waiting for him to pull himself together, which he did quite quickly, "Sorry about that. Look, come in the office and I'll make us a coffee. I can see I have a bit of explaining to do."

She took the only chair in the tiny room while he boiled the kettle and made them a drink.

"Okay, now what's it all about?" she asked, accepting a mug from him.

"I can see I'm going to have to admit I was a little economical with the truth last year – but I want you to realize that I had my own reasons."

"I'm listening," she said noncommittally.

"Well, for a start, it was no coincidence that the Lazarus notes turned up just in time to help you. It wasn't a stranger who donated them. It was me."

"You? You mean you pinched them from the museum?" she asked incredulously, thinking what a hypocrite he had been to complain about her own actions last year when all along he had known he was lifting museum exhibits himself.

"Most certainly not! I'm not in the habit of pinching stuff. I could send the papers to you because I'm the owner."

"Bloody hell," she gasped, light suddenly dawning, "You're descended from the man who arrested my great, great grandmother! No wonder you didn't impart that little nugget of information. Your great, great granddad sent poor old Decima to the gallows."

"Not exactly. It's not Lazarus I'm related to, but his sergeant, Tom Stonier."

"Don't split hairs," said Libby firmly, "I'd call that pretty academic. Whichever man it was, my family doesn't have much to thank yours for."

"I'd like to think you aren't going to hold it against me," said Dan, with a grin. Libby couldn't resist smiling back, "I think I could forgive you – provided I find myself in possession of the rest of Inspector Lazarus' papers."

"Oh, I can do better than that. I hold Stonier's notes too. And a diary written by his wife."

Libby looked at him open-mouthed, "That's remarkably generous of you – what's the catch?"

"No catch. You're welcome to them. I shall want them back, of course, they are, after all, family heirlooms."

"But I intended to write a book. What if I make a fortune? Aren't you going to want a cut?"

He raised a quizzical eyebrow, "I don't want to be offensive,

Libby, but do you have any idea how difficult it is to get published these days? You'll be lucky to even get your manuscript read, let alone printed. If you do find a publisher, then we'll re-negotiate. How does that sound to you?"

"Fair enough. Do you trust me, though? I could run off with your papers and deny all knowledge of you."

"You could. But I'm sure you won't. However, if it will make you feel better, I'll write out a receipt for you to sign."

"It might be wise. For both our sakes. Put something in it about shares should I make any money."

"Sixty-forty?"

"Seventy-thirty," she corrected, "After all, I'm going to be doing most of the work."

He laughed, "Fine by me. Thirty percent of nothing is just about all I'm expecting, but if I'm wrong, thirty percent is more than an agent would get – and I won't have to lift a finger."

"That's what you think," she snorted, "You are so going to earn every penny. I'll be wanting someone to help me with research."

"I should have known," he said with mock exasperation and went to his computer to compose a suitable document to seal the bargain.

CHAPTER TWO

Lazarus 1862

"Do you want another glass of ale, my friend?"

Inspector Danby Lazarus had been dozing, but this question demanded his full attention. He opened his eyes, blinking in the full glare of the midsummer sun, "Is the Chief Superintendent a Mason?" he asked.

Sergeant Stonier laughed, "I'll take that as a yes." He called towards the house and presently his wife appeared at the scullery door, wiping floury hands on her apron. Good, thought Lazarus hungrily, that means she's making a pie for after dinner.

"Getting thirsty again?" she enquired wryly, "I'll be right there – oh, and Tom, if you want any dinner, you'd better pick some carrots and a cabbage."

"Right-o." He shrugged expressively at his companion and moved off towards the vegetable patch.

Now that he was awake, Lazarus took the opportunity to look around Stonier's little kingdom. He had to admit his colleague had made a grand job of his garden, even though the raw materials had been uninspiring. The cottage was one of a row of terraces so the land attached at the back was long and narrow, though each house did have its own privy – a rare luxury when most families had to share. Even so, Stonier had managed to include a sty at the bottom for a pig, a hen run, a compost heap for whatever the porker didn't consume, several rows of lovingly tended vegetables and herbs, an old apple tree, under which Lazarus was resting, and even a bit of lawn, strung across with washing lines, ready for the morrow and washing day.

He had been well on the way to possessing a similar plot himself, until circumstances had dictated that he give up the house and take lodgings with Mrs Baker – a woman who did not live up to her name and provided him with the most basic fare for his weekly rent.

Meg Stonier reappeared holding an earthenware jug and he watched appreciatively as she strolled down the path towards him. She was a good ten years older than him, and about five younger than her husband, but she was still an attractive woman. What Tom Stonier lovingly referred to as 'a cosy armful'. She smiled at Lazarus, "You're being waited on now, Lord Muck, but you know you're washing the dishes later, don't you?"

"Wouldn't have it any other way," he grinned back, rising to his feet and holding out his glass to be refilled, "Have you time to sit for a while and enjoy the sunshine?"

"I could spare five minutes," she conceded and he offered her his seat with a bow as though she were a duchess. She laughed and pushed him playfully, "Get away with you, with your airs and graces," she said, then realized how much weight he'd lost since the last time she'd seen him, "Blood and sand, Dan! What's that Baker woman doing to you? One good gust of wind would have you off your feet!"

Things were not quite that bad, but he was thinner than he had been, "She's alright," he muttered in a half-hearted attempt at defending his landlady's reputation.

"She most certainly is not," countered Meg roundly, "Why do you stay there? You know there's always a room for you here with us."

Lazarus didn't meet her eyes, but looked down the garden to where Stonier was digging a bunch of carrots and holding them aloft to see how many he had. "It's a kind thought, Meg, but I couldn't bear it."

Meg knew exactly what he meant and she fell silent, cursing herself for her clumsiness. Of course he couldn't bear to see her and Tom happy together. It was eighteen months now since he had lost his wife in childbirth, but he seemed no nearer to getting over it than he had on the first day it happened.

She felt she had to say something, if only to cover the awkward moment, so she pulled herself to her feet and groaned with mock weariness, "Well, if you change your mind, you only have to say the word. Now I must get on – those carrots aren't going to scrape themselves."

"Is there anything I can do?"

"Certainly not, you're a guest." With that she went to collect the pickings from Tom and went back indoors.

"Any of that ale left?" asked Tom, throwing himself down on the grass beside Lazarus' chair, "A little," answered the younger man, pouring a glass.

"I'll go to 'The Old Angel' on the corner and get another gill when we sit to eat," said Tom, gratefully accepting the foaming glass and sinking half of it in one long swallow.

It was so pleasant in the sun that Lazarus was almost disappointed when Meg called them in to eat. He would have preferred to sit under the tree and eat off his knee, but Meg was never going to allow that. It was a fully formal meal, with all her best table linen, eaten in the best parlour on the hastily unfolded table with chairs brought from all over the house.

It was oddly cool in the front room of the house, with a very slight whiff of damp which spoke of a room rarely used and even more rarely heated or aired. Lazarus always found it astounding that the tradition persisted to keep one room 'for best' when space was at such a premium in the tiny cottages. Tom and Meg did not do so badly, being alone since both their son and daughter had married and moved away, but some others were cramming a houseful of children into one room, where everything went on – cooking, eating, washing – of bodies as well as clothes – and still the front room lay idle and empty, kept in case someone of worth might call. And the irony of it was, no-one ever did. If the doctor came it was because someone was at death's door and he would attend the bedside, ditto for the vicar or priest. Mill-owner's wives did not call upon their husband's employees and they were probably the nearest to gentry that anyone around here knew about.

The meal, however, made up for any lack of atmosphere. Meg had killed one of their own chickens in Lazarus' honour and when he protested at the largesse, she assured him hastily that it had stopped laying a week before and was due for the pot anyway.

It was as well that he should have enjoyed his dinner, for he was granted only half an hour to savour it, and the apple pie which followed.

A hammering at the front door had an air of urgency that made Lazarus and Stonier exchange a look of resignation tinged with interest. As policemen they both knew that a frenzied knocking on a Sunday afternoon probably heralded bad news for someone.

Sure enough Meg came back into the room bearing a note and grumbling under her breath, "Do they not know you're both off duty?"

Tom took the note from her saying rather pompously, "Now then Meg, you know as well as I do, there's no such thing as 'off duty' when there's an emergency."

"And is it an emergency?" asked Lazarus, wishing that he had a pipe to hand. Meg didn't approve of smoking indoors, especially not in her pretty, treasured parlour, but a pipe-full of good tobacco would finish that meal off nicely.

Tom read the note, raised an eyebrow and handed it silently to his superior. Lazarus swiftly perused it, then rose to his feet, "Of a sort," he answered his own question, "I'm sorry, Meg, but I must love you and leave you. Thank you for a magnificent repast."

"Must you really go?"

"I think we must."

Tom was already heading for the hall-stand to grab his and Lazarus' coats and hats.

"What you too?" asked Meg, aghast, "What on earth is it that needs the two of you?"

"Murder," said Tom tersely. Lazarus threw him an irritated glance. There were certain things one didn't mention in the presence of ladies and murder was just about the biggest taboo of all.

"Oh," remarked Meg, quite unmoved by the revelation, "Then you better get yourselves off – be sure to let me know if you are going to be very late, Tom."

"Will do."

Outside the front door, Lazarus shrugged himself reluctantly into his greatcoat. The afternoon was getting on, but it was still unbearably hot out of the shade, "Do you tell that wife of yours everything?" he enquired testily.

"More or less," said Tom stoically.

"Won't she be upset or shocked or something?"

Tom laughed, "Meg shocked? That'll be the day. She's married to a policeman, grew up with five brothers and had two children of our own – what's left in the world that she hasn't already seen or heard?" Lazarus conceded the point.

* * *

The first surprise was that the victim had been found at home and the second was that she was a woman. In Lazarus' experience, men died in the street, the pub or at work, but if a woman was murdered in her own home, she had generally been killed by her husband and with a knife or a beating. This was neither.

Mollie Waters was a milliner who lived in lodgings with an elderly lady who had been the unfortunate finder of the body.

The house was respectable enough and thankfully clean and odour-free. Lazarus had been in places that were kept like little palaces and others that gave hovels a near-run thing and he was always glad when he didn't have to cope with filth and deprivation as well as a dead body. His only objection here was the landlady, who, rather than being distressed by losing her tenant, seemed to take an unhealthy pleasure in being the centre of attention in a murder enquiry.

She led them upstairs and flung open the door of the front bedroom with a dramatic flourish, "There she is," she announced triumphantly.

Though there was, for the first time, a smell, on first viewing, Lazarus saw nothing particularly amiss in the room. Certainly the young lady was draped across the corner of the single bed, but she was fully clothed. Though there was a small pool of vomit on the floor beneath her sagging head – from whence emanated the odour, there was no sign of violence, no evidence of a struggle, no blood, no bruising. He exchanged a glance with Stonier and they entered the room together and as one checked the body, the other made a swift circuit of the room. They needed to be sure that she was dead – for if she was not, then not only was there no crime, but a doctor might be urgently required. She was cold. Death had probably occurred some time during the night or early morning, guessed Lazarus – it was barely after three and warm outside.

"When did you find her?" he asked.

"About an hour ago. I ran straight down to the police station on the corner of Henry Street. They said not to touch anything and they'd send someone over – and it took you long enough to get here," she added grimly.

"Sorry about that, madam," said Lazarus automatically, never looking towards her. He was scanning the room, taking in every detail, swiftly analysing what he saw – but nothing seemed worth notice. Almost by instinct Stonier realized that his companion was looking at him and he met Lazarus' enquiring gaze with the slightest shake of his head. His inspection of the room had given him no cause for concern either. Lazarus was puzzled. What the hell had led this old woman to suppose a murder had been committed? Nothing was amiss. Of course it was tragic that so young a person had met her death, but surely if no foul play was involved, it was merely a sad event?

"Can I ask you why you thought this was a murder, Mrs …?"

"Brown. The name's Brown. And it's as plain as the nose on your face that it's murder. For a start off, unless something was badly wrong, I'd've expected her to at least make an attempt at getting to the bowl and ewer and not soil the floor! And why would a perfectly healthy girl like her up and die, just like that?"

"Many reasons I can think of, madam. Just because someone looks healthy, it doesn't naturally follow that they are. She could have choked on her own vomit or she could have had some internal defect, perhaps of the heart, that no one knew about."

"I'd have heard her choke," countered Mrs Brown, determined not to be denied her moment of drama.

“Did you hear her being sick?” asked Stonier. He was still searching the room, peering into the wardrobe and lifting and examining items from the dressing table.

“I did.”

“But you didn’t come to her aid?” pursued Lazarus. The old woman gave him a sly, sideways glance, “That hasn’t exactly been unusual these past few weeks,” she said softly. Again the two men exchanged a look. That might very well put a different complexion on things.

“I take it she was an unmarried lady?”

“She was. And no better than she ought to be,” replied Mrs Brown with assumed piety, “You should be asking that young fellow she was seeing a few questions.”

“We’ll certainly do that,” replied Lazarus, suddenly depressed by the situation. If what the woman was saying was correct, then it wasn’t just one life that had been lost in this small, sadly bare room, but two, “Do you know his name and where we can find him?”

“No, she didn’t confide in me, but the other girls at the shop should know something. I have the address downstairs. Not that I ever went there myself. Too up-market for the likes of me.”

Stonier, who had found a small stash of beads, feathers and artificial flowers in a hat box in the bottom of the wardrobe, agreed with her. The hat shop that had employed the young lady must have been an expensive one if the quality of the frills and furbelows were anything to go by. He just hoped the items had been honestly acquired. He hated to think that Miss Mollie Waters had been light-fingered as well as unlucky. He raised a quizzical eyebrow at his companion – his tacit way of asking if the matter were to be pursued or not. Lazarus looked thoughtful, then swiftly made his decision, “If you could go down and search out that address for us madam, we’ll join you downstairs in just a moment.”

Mrs Brown was obviously reluctant to leave the scene but she shuffled off and Stonier crossed the room as Lazarus drew the cotton bedspread over the corpse. The least she deserved was a little dignity. Stonier approved of this action and showed it by laying a hand on his companion’s shoulder for a brief moment before saying quietly, "We'd better go and see if we can find a boy willing to run and fetch the doctor for us, otherwise there will be another long wait and I don't fancy drinking tea and making small talk with the old vulture downstairs."

Lazarus felt he ought to remonstrate with his subordinate for this disrespectful description of their hostess, but he couldn't in all conscience do it, for Mrs Brown did resemble a tatty bird of prey, with her hooked nose and widow's hump and her tiny, wickedly knowing eyes.

"It's Sunday, so there are bound to be several young scallywags running wild in the street, using up their one day of rest to tire themselves out."

His prediction proved to be correct. There were indeed several children sitting on a nearby doorstep, playing a complicated looking game with a handful of rounded pebbles. These appeared to be performing the same function as marbles, but evidently finances didn't run to providing the real thing.

Lazarus called the eldest of the group and the boy wandered over, the rest of them trailing after him. When they drew near enough both men were shocked to see how thin and ragged they all were. Their slow approach was neither cheek nor reluctance but sheer exhaustion. The policemen were, of course, fully aware that the war in America was affecting cotton supplies to the mills, but neither man had realized just how desperate things had become. These children had evidently not eaten a decent meal for days if not weeks.

"What's your name son?" Lazarus asked.

"Will Carter, sir."

He had originally intended to offer a couple of pennies in return for the favour, but he found himself saying, "Do you want to earn yourself a shilling, Will Carter?"

The boy's face lit up and his young followers gasped in shock at the generous offer, but his natural wariness took over and he said cautiously, "Depends." Much as he wanted to believe in miracles, he knew shillings weren't handed out by strangers for nothing.

"It's alright, son, I'm a policeman and I need you to run an errand for me. Can you read?"

"Well enough," answered the boy, mildly offended to have been asked, especially in front of his gang, who all looked up to him as the font of all knowledge.

"Good," said Lazarus, writing out the name and address in letters that could be easily read, "Now be sure and fetch this doctor and no other."

"Yes, sir," Will took the note and set off, only to stop when he realized that his faithful band were about to follow, including the smallest, who could not have been much more than two and sported a bare backside, in case of accidents, to spare his mother more washing.

"Not you lot," he said firmly, "You wait here. I'll be back soon. 'til then Jenny is in charge."

Eight year old Jenny puffed out her chest with pride and said, with an endearing lisp caused by the loss of her two front teeth, "Come on, back to the game, and I'm first, 'coz I'm in charge."

Lazarus and Stonier watched them as they went back to their 'allies' then went back inside the house to await the arrival of Dr Scattergood.

Stonier accepted a cup of tea from Mrs Brown, but waited until she left the room before asking in a low voice, "Are we calling it murder, sir?"

"I think we are calling it a suspicious death – certainly until the doctor has confirmed the cause of death, anyway."

CHAPTER THREE

Libby – Present

With a sigh of deep satisfaction Libby saved what she had written so far and allowed herself the luxury of a full stretch. She now had the first few chapters of her Inspector Lazarus novel under her belt and she was feeling fairly okay with it. She would have liked to believe it was the best prose ever written but even her presently soaring ego couldn't convince her of that. She knew when she read it over tomorrow she'd probably think it was rubbish, but she decided to go with the feeling of the moment and leave her desk feeling happy and fulfilled.

She had made the unusual, but to her, rather exciting, decision to read and write about Lazarus simultaneously, which was difficult, but ultimately gave her writing a peculiarly fresh edge. It was true to say that she was as much in the dark as to what was going to happen next and the eventual reader would be. She knew she was taking a risk because it might turn out that Lazarus never solved the case he was currently (on paper!) working on. And if that should happen, she was going to have to cobble some sort of resolution on the end of her book that would convince the reader. However, she felt confident that Lazarus was always a success and was sure enough about his genius to leave it in the lap of the gods. She had conveniently forgotten – or at least refused to acknowledge – that he had failed spectacularly to save Decima Watkins from the gallows.

Oddly enough she was getting her most insightful and human information from Tom Stonier's wife's diary. The policemen wrote businesslike and professional case notes, but Meg had obviously cared deeply about the two men in her life and confided her worries to her diaries. She wrote about the two of them becoming tired and frustrated by the obstacles placed in their way, and even about the minor fall-out that marred the first few weeks of the cases they were working on. Libby found herself being drawn more and more to Meg's observations and less towards those of Stonier and Lazarus. She realized that she was in danger of becoming too involved in the private lives of the characters and not the crimes, but what the heck! Weren't people and their foibles what made life interesting, after all?

Thinking about foibles reminded her that her sister was due for a visit the following day. The satisfied sigh was immediately replaced by an exasperated one. She and Maddie had a difficult relationship at the best of times, but since she had inherited Hill Farm and Lil's personal fortune, the veneer of sisterly affection had cracked and blistered like ancient paint on a sun-bleached beach hut.

She went downstairs to make herself a drink before bed and found that her husband had already retired. For the third time that week she had only seen him over dinner, as he was an early riser and she was working late into the evening on her project. She made a silent promise to see more of him, but didn't actually plan a time for it to happen. They'd be alright when she'd finished her book, she assured herself, stifling a yawn.

She woke the next morning to find, to her irritation, that David had risen even earlier than was his wont and was long gone. She knew that he didn't particularly like her sister, any more than she did, but she felt that a bit of moral support wouldn't have gone amiss.

She made herself a leisurely breakfast and pondered while she ate it on the idea of going upstairs and doing a little more work before the visitor was due. She hesitated for so long, weighing the possibility that she might not hear the doorbell – and wondering if that would be an altogether bad thing – that it became hardly worth leaving the sitting room. She loaded the dishwasher and did a bit of desultory dusting until Maddie arrived.

They exchanged a swiftly awkward embrace then broke free from each other with palpable relief.

"Do you want a coffee first, or shall I make lunch now?" Libby asked to cover the ensuing silence, uncomfortably aware that she had barely begun to digest breakfast.

"Oh, I rather thought we'd be eating out," answered Maddie, managing to endow the words with a wealth of emotions that only Libby was sensitive enough to pick up on. There was contempt at the very notion of a mere sandwich after her long drive, disgust at the stinginess of her hostess, who evidently wouldn't even stretch to buying a pub lunch for her only sister.

Libby hastily back-tracked, "What a lovely idea. My treat. Where would you like to go?"

Maddie beamed at having so easily vanquished her little sister, "I really fancy that nice new French place in Hanbury. It's very exclusive, but we so rarely see each other these days, we ought to make it special."

Substitute 'special' for 'expensive' thought Libby crossly, trust Maddie to get one over on her within seconds of coming through the door! It didn't bode particularly well for the rest of the weekend, but she was determined that for once she wouldn't allow her sister to wind her up. She was going to maintain a demeanour of sweet reasonableness until Monday morning if it killed her.

They ate a long and expensive lunch, during which Maddie freely indulged in the wine list whilst Libby could only watch longingly and sip ridiculously dear sparkling water. She toyed with the idea of leaving her car and taking a taxi home so that she too could have a tipple, but the thought of the fag of having to reclaim it later put her off. She couldn't be bothered – and she also couldn't be sure of keeping her temper if she indulged. All her good intentions would fly straight out of the window if she downed half a carafe of house red.

They kept to safe subjects during the meal, discussing their parents and the fact that they both now had new partners and what they thought of these two new members of the family. Libby liked them both, Maddie didn't. The whole time Libby had the vaguest sense that Maddie was holding something back and by two thirty she found out what it was. A glance at her watch and feigned surprise by the now pink-cheeked Maddie told Libby that the revelation was about to happen.

"Good gracious, look at the time. We'd better get a move on or we'll be late."

"Late for what?" asked Libby with suspiciously narrowed eyes.

"Didn't I tell you?" asked Maddie, wide-eyed with innocence, "We have an appointment to see a solicitor this afternoon. That's why I asked to come today. I felt sure I'd told you."

"No, you never told me," said Libby, striving to keep her voice even and pleasant, "Why on earth would we be seeing a solicitor?" Light suddenly dawned and she gasped, "Oh hell! Don't tell me you've had a court date for your little run-in with Brendan Tulliver?"

Maddie's sneer and dismissive wave of a hand showed her thorough contempt for the case she was facing for peppering the kneecaps of Libby's ex-boyfriend with lead shot from their Aunt's gun. In her mind Brendan deserved every minute he'd spent in surgery and she was quite confident that any jury in the land would agree with her. Libby, who was still traumatized by the attempt by Brendan to kill her and her subsequent rescue by her big sister, couldn't view the looming trial with equal *sang-froid*.

"Oh it'll be a few more weeks before we have to face that," Maddie assured her, "That's if the odious little creep actually has the bottle to continue pressing charges. I'm pretty confident that he'll back down. He's been offered an out-of-court settlement and a few months off his sentence for assaulting you. If he has any sense at all, he'll take a couple of grand and disappear."

Libby could only hope she was right, "Well, if it's not that, what is it?"

She could see that her sister was being deliberately airy, as though the appointment was of no real importance. It was this more than anything else which alerted her to the fact that on the contrary it was extremely serious, "What have you done now?" she added wearily, when no response was forthcoming.

"Nothing. What on earth do you mean by that?"

"I think my meaning is quite clear. Why are you going to see a lawyer? If it's not about Brendan, what is it about? And why do you want me to come with you?"

"Oh well, if you can't even do me a small favour like this," said Maddie huffily, "That's charming I must say. After all, I only saved your life, rescuing you from that bonkers boyfriend of yours!"

Libby raised her hands in surrender, “Okay, okay, I didn’t say I wouldn’t come. I just want to know what its all about. Is that too much to ask?”

“It’s kind of hard to explain,” said Maddie, making great display of gathering her stuff together and studiously ignoring the bill. Libby handed her credit card to a passing waitress and replied crisply, “Try!”

“It’s all dad’s fault,” murmured Maddie, struggling to find an armhole in her jacket, “Do you know, the service in here is terrible. You’d think someone would help you on with your coat.”

“Never mind that,” said Libby hastily, aware that the staff were watching and listening. The last thing she needed was to be worrying that her dinner would be spat on every time she came back here – not that she was intending it to be that often at the prices they were charging. “What has dad to do with all this?”

“He refused to follow up on the Allingham thing. I explained it all carefully to him, how it turned out that Decima Watkins had actually been married to Richard Allingham, and that their son was our ancestor. He wasn’t in the least little bit interested. Not even the Wedding License convinced him. He said it was all too long ago and too hard to prove. He said it could cost thousands going to court and we probably wouldn’t win at the end of it all.”

“And he is right,” intercepted Libby tartly, “You should leave it well alone.”

“That’s easy for you to say,” sneered Maddie maliciously, “You’re not the eldest, so its not your birthright that’s being denied – and anyway, you’ve just inherited a couple of million quid from our dear departed Aunt Lil.”

“It wasn’t anywhere near that much,” protested Libby, but she felt a pang of guilt. Her nest-egg was certainly enough to ensure that she’d never have to work again if she chose not to – Maddie couldn’t claim the same and she knew it. She quickly regained her composure however, when she realized that once again she was being manipulated by her older sister. She still hadn’t had a straight answer to her question. Talking to Maddie was like rounding up sheep. As fast as she pursued one topic Maddie meandered off onto another one and the first one disappeared from view. She needed all her wits about her to stall Maddie's habit of going off on a tangent.

"You still haven't told me why we're going to see a solicitor."

"Oh, bugger, we're going to be late," exclaimed Maddie, loudly enough for other diners to turn and look at them with open curiosity, much to Libby's embarrassment, "Come on. I'll tell you on the way over there."

'Over there' proved to be just across the market square to a lovely old Georgian building which now housed the legal firm of Morgan and Fentiman's. Libby began to see the depth of her sister's machinations. Even the venue for lunch had been carefully planned.

It was with a slight feeling of nausea that she entered the porticoed front door. This was the same firm of solicitors whom she had used herself the year before when she had been accused of the mercy-killing of Aunt Lil. Even though she had eventually been cleared she hoped she wouldn't run into anyone in there who remembered her. It was humiliating to be thought of as a cold-blooded murderer and she preferred to forget it completely.

Maddie had no such qualms. She had dismissed the incident from her mind the moment it happened and it never occurred to her that Libby might be suffering still. Maddie lived for today – she rarely bothered her head with either consequences or regrets, or indeed explanations. She had known full well that there wouldn't be time for a full discussion by the time they reached their destination and it didn't concern her at all that she was now dragging Libby, entirely unprepared, into a meeting with a man of the law.

The relief Libby felt when she realized she didn't know the man they were about to see was soon replaced by horror. As they waited to be shown into his office she had a whispered conversation with her sister – and wished she hadn't bothered.

"So, tell me quickly what this is all about?"

"Okay, in a nutshell, I wrote a nice polite letter to Richard Allingham and told him that dad and I are the real heirs to his estate and fortune and that we'd settle out of court for a substantial wad of cash."

Libby literally felt the blood drain from her face, "You didn't!

Please tell me you're winding me up."

"Never been more serious. I'm fully expecting this meeting to be the beginnings of our negotiations with the Allingham Clan."

"That's odd, because I'm fully expecting it to be the beginning of a long prison sentence for you," exclaimed Libby bitterly, "Don't you realize that sending a message like that could be construed as blackmail?"

Even Maddie had to stop and think about that one. She hesitated, then shook her head, "Nonsense! I made it quite clear we have proof."

Libby had no chance to argue further because a plump middle-aged lady invited them into Mr Dailey's office, offering them tea or coffee as they passed her. Once again Maddie took charge, "Lovely," she said with her sweetest smile, "Coffee for me – what about you, Libby?"

"Just a glass of water," croaked Libby. She had never been more scared in her life. Heaven only knew what waited for them beyond the solid oak door with it's original brass fittings.

Mr Dailey was also plump and middle-aged. He rose and smiled, "Do come in ladies, and take a seat. I presume you are the Misses Richmond?"

"Miss Richmond and Mrs Wright, actually," said Maddie, "Pleased to meet you." she shook his extended hand and Libby reluctantly followed suit.

"And you, my dear young ladies, and you. Now, if you're happy to begin, tell me more about your intriguing letter."

Maddie grinned happily, confident that she had the upper hand. Libby's heart sank. There was something far too nice about Mr Dailey. She sensed trouble and she had the strongest feeling that it was going to be up to her to rescue her sister. Something that in that moment she had no real inclination to do.

CHAPTER FOUR

Lazarus 1862

Lazarus admired Scattergood, though he wasn't entirely sure the feeling was reciprocated. The doctor was one of those men who didn't display his emotions. He treated everyone with the same good-natured contempt, feeling, no doubt, that with his superior education and many years of medical experience, he was a cut above everyone else, and did them all a huge favour by wasting his time trying to cure them of their largely self-imposed illnesses. He neither over-indulged in food nor alcohol, didn't smoke tobacco and had imposed a strict limit of four children on his wife – large families, he thought, were a vast mistake for the poor and selfishly excessive in the rich.

Several years before he had offered his services to the fledgling Braxton police-force, feeling that many a crime had gone undetected and unpunished merely because the coroner had failed to recognize foul-play when it reared its ugly head.

Lazarus recognized his talents and made no secret of his respect for them, so that his relationship with the irascible Scattergood was the envy of all the other policemen who had to deal with him.

He and Stonier waited on the front doorstep for the doctor to arrive, sipping the rather weak tea Mrs Brown had provided.

Scattergood made his entrance with his usual flair in a hired hansom cab, with his messenger boy clinging precariously to the side of the vehicle with one bare foot on the step-up and the other swinging free, a broad grin on his face at the unaccustomed ride.

He jumped down just before the cab stopped and hit the ground running, much to the vociferous admiration of his young playmates.

For once Scattergood's normally severe countenance was lightened by a broad grin at the boy's antics, "That's a likely young fellow, Lazarus, he'll go far. You should take him into your police force. You could do with a few like him. He's not had a decent meal for weeks, but if you saw the effort he'd put into running to fetch me, you'd have given him half a crown, not a shilling."

Lazarus beckoned the boy over and presented him with the promised remuneration, "Tell me again what your name is, boy."

"Will Carter, sir."

"Call at Braxton Police Station tomorrow, Will Carter and ask for Inspector Lazarus, and I'll see if I can find some tasks for you."

The boy's face was a picture of pure joy, "Yes, sir, thank you, sir. I'll be there at seven."

Lazarus gave a wry smile, "I'll be there at nine."

Will Carter ran off to share his largesse with his friends and Lazarus turned his attention to Dr Scattergood and Stonier, who were discussing the case in low voices.

"So, you think we have a murder, my friend?" asked the doctor.

Lazarus gave a non-committal shrug, "Could be. Something isn't right. Both Stonier and I think it."

"Well, two bloodhounds can't be wrong. Let's have a look at the poor unfortunate."

The two policemen stood just inside the bedroom door, whilst the doctor made a cursory examination of the body, then knelt on the floor and sniffed loudly at the pool of vomit, much to his two companions' obvious distaste.

"Umm," he vouchsafed as he rose to his feet, "Call the landlady up here, will you Stonier?"

Tom did as requested and presently Mrs Brown joined them, looking suitably cowed at the thought of having a doctor in the house, though she still had the courage to say brusquely, "I hope you noted that you were called by these two and not me! I don't want no bills for house-calls."

"This is a police matter, madam, there will be no charge to your good self. Now, do you have such a thing as a small pudding basin or something similar – preferably one that you don't want returned. I need to take the bodily evacuations of the subject and have them analysed."

She brightened considerably at the thought that she wasn't going to have to clean up the mess, "I have the very thing. I'll fetch it."

"Good – and a table knife would be useful. Before you go, did the young lady eat a mushroom omelette last night, or even early this morning?"

"What's an omelette?" asked Mrs Brown suspiciously.

"From that reply I surmise not," murmured Scattergood to his companions, then addressed himself to the woman, "It's a concoction of fried mushrooms and beaten fried eggs."

The look of disgust on her face told the gathered men that she found the very idea repulsive, "She's never had anything of the sort in my house. I do plain cooking, none of that foreign muck – and anyway, do you know the last time we had mushrooms or a fresh egg to share, certainly not to waste in that manner?"

"Could she possibly have bought and cooked one for herself?"

Mrs Brown snorted contemptuously, "Her? Cook? That'll be the day! She thought her pretty hands too delicate to turn to any sort of housework, let alone cooking." With that she went off to fetch him a bowl.

Scattergood looked thoughtful, "Well, there you have a mystery in itself, gentlemen. It's half-digested and regurgitated, but I'd swear the young lady ate a mushroom omelette. If she did – where did she acquire and eat it?"

"Does it really matter?" asked Stonier, much to Lazarus' relief. He was thinking exactly the same thing, but didn't want to be the one to ask the good doctor anything obvious.

"It matters a great deal if my supposition is correct. I'll tell you for sure later in the day."

"You think she might have been poisoned?" guessed Lazarus.

"It's not impossible – but having said that, nor is it improbable that she died of some other cause. I'll know more when I've cut her open."

"I should warn you that Mrs Brown hinted that the young lady might have been with child," supplied Lazarus, determined that should this prove to be a wild goose chase that Scattergood would not be able to accuse him of withholding vital information.

"Then that makes it even more likely that she was overcome with some affliction she could not fight off. No pregnant woman would choose for comfort to lie on her belly. And no-one lying face down ever choked on their own vomit."

The policemen both acknowledged the truth of these statements by sagely nodding their heads, but offered no further comment.

"I've arranged for the body to be collected. I'll let you know as soon as the post mortem is over."

"Surely you'll wait until tomorrow for that," ventured Stonier, trying not to betray his shock, "It is the Sabbath after all?"

"What the deuce does that have to do with anything?" grunted Scattergood, "Do you think the good Lord cares on what day I do his work? If murderers don't lay off killing on a Sunday, why should I avoid finding the devils on the same day?"

Stonier didn't have a reply for that, but Lazarus grinned, quite sure that the same argument wouldn't hold water if Scattergood tried it on a clergyman.

"I'll continue with my investigations, Doctor," he intercepted neatly, before his sergeant could dig himself in any deeper, "Even if it turns out not to be foul play, we still need to discover if the poor lass had any family who need to be informed of her demise."

"Quite right," approved Scattergood, casting the blanket back over the body.

A loud knock on the front door told them that the conveyance had arrived to cart away the body of the unfortunate Miss Waters, and the three men left the room to give access to the undertaker and his assistant. A short conversation between Scattergood and Mr Jebson at the foot of the stairs ensured that the lady would be transported to the infirmary mortuary and not the undertaker's own premises.

Stonier busied himself with gathering the relevant information from Mrs Brown, then they all followed the plain wooden box out of the house and saw it safely stowed in the covered cart that Jebson used for pauper's funerals. He could not yet be sure he was going to be properly paid for the use of his vehicle, so he certainly wasn't going to bring out the splendid black-wood rig, and fine plumed horses that usually accompanied these solemn occasions.

Word had swiftly spread and the entire street turned out to see one of their own off on her final journey. Men were in their shirt-sleeves, a few sporting waistcoats, due to the fact that it was Sunday and not only their only day off, but that most of their good jackets and even their best boots, were currently lying unused in the local pawn shop. There had been lay-offs and short-time at the mills in recent months, and that meant hardship for everyone except the pawn-broker and the tallyman. The women stood behind their men, holding their children in check so that not a sound, nor an unruly movement would disturb the peace and spoil the respect of the moment.

The few men that were wearing hats dragged them from their heads and held them at their sides until the horse had dragged away it's sorry burden, then slowly they went back inside.

"You'll let me know what happens, won't you?" asked Mrs Brown of Lazarus and for the first time since he had met her, he thought she seemed genuinely moved. It was as though the dreary clip-clop of the tired and over-heated nag, the grinding rumble of the cart wheels on the cobbled road and the silent tribute of the neighbourhood had finally brought home to her that Mollie was really dead, that a young and vibrant life had been brought to a swift and bitter end.

"I'll keep in touch," he promised, "And if you think of anything else you feel I should know about, you send young Will with a message."

She nodded sadly, "She wasn't really a bad lass, you know, just young and thoughtless."

"We were all that once," intercepted Stonier sternly. He had taken about as much of Mrs Brown's carping as he could stand.

She wiped her eyes on the hem of her apron, "That's true enough," she agreed and went back inside, looking old and defeated.

Lazarus turned to address the doctor, who was still staring down the street after the hearse, though it had long disappeared from sight, "Are you still intending to do the post mortem now, sir?" he asked diffidently. Scattergood looked suddenly depressed and he thought he might just have had a change of heart. The doctor gave himself an almost physical shake, as though to shake off the unpleasant thoughts, "Of course, of course," he said gruffly, "I'll be off now." He went to his waiting hansom and was away with a clatter of hooves and a hand lifted in farewell.

"You might as well go home to that lovely wife of yours, Tom," Lazarus informed his companion, "I'll join the doctor at the Infirmary, but there's no use in two of us being there."

"Are you sure, sir? I don't mind staying if you need me, and Meg's not expecting me back any time soon."

"No, it's fine. We can't do anything more today. The only address we have is the hat shop and that won't be open on a Sunday. We'll go there first thing in the morning."

Tom needed no second bidding. A second slice of Meg's apple pie, cold, with a sliver of crumbly Cheshire cheese and another pint of ale was calling to him, "I'll see you tomorrow then, sir," he said.

Once he was alone, Lazarus took one last look around him. The street was now deserted. All the children had been taken indoors. There would be no more play for them today. They needed to be thoroughly grounded in the customs surrounding death. It could happen any time, to any one of them, and they could do worse than learn now what it meant. No doubt there were homilies galore going on behind all those closed doors, threatening fire and damnation to those wide-eyed little sinners should they die unshriven and unrepentant like Mollie Waters and her ilk.

A glance behind him told him that Mrs Brown had drawn her curtains, as befitted the house of death. No doubt she would milk the sympathy of her neighbours for all she was worth. Her shock and misery ought to be worth a few cups of tea, and possibly even some comforting baking or a meal or two. He wished he wasn't quite so cynical, but nothing in his life so far had led him to any other conclusions than that most of mankind were out for what they could get, for whatever reason.

* * *

The infirmary was a grim building. It hadn't started out that way.

The gift of some wealthy mill-owner, it was fronted with a limestone portico of Doric columns and a huge oak front door, but it had soon become blackened by the soot of a thousand fireplaces and mill chimneys. It wasn't just it's appearance that made one full of foreboding upon entering it's portals, but the reputation it bore. It's philanthropic builder had wanted it to be a place of healing and refuge, but by it's very nature it had become the last port of call for those too ill to be cured. Always fearful of the doctor – and more especially his bill – the poor waited too long to call for help. The few that walked unaided out of that vast front door were fortunate indeed.

The mortuary was situated in the basement for privacy and a cool atmosphere, and Lazarus made his way down the stone steps with their cast-iron handrail to his least favourite corner of the vast edifice. Not that he was particularly enamoured with any other part of the place. The stench of despair was here encapsulated in a faint odour of boiled cabbage and strong soap. There were several other mysterious smells, but he preferred not to try and recognize them.

Scattergood already had Mollie Waters on the dissecting table with all the gas lamps on the walls lit and gently hissing. Their presence removed any hope of maintaining the cool atmosphere and Lazarus immediately removed his coat and hat.

The doctor draped himself in a large green apron to protect his clothes, but made no other preparation for the task ahead of him. Lazarus wanted to avert his eyes from Mollie's nakedness, but he knew he was being unnecessarily prudish. She was past caring, after all, and it was best all round if he tried to view her merely as a piece of meat. If he humanised her now, he would be lost when the doctor began to hack at the pale skin.

He managed well enough until Scattergood confirmed her pregnancy, then he felt tears burn his eyes. A tiny lost soul, never to know the feel of the sun on its face, the wind in its hair and the tenderness of a mother's kiss. God forgive whoever did this, for he would not. He wouldn't rest until someone hanged for this abomination.

Scattergood finished the task and left his assistant to sew the body back together with huge rough stitches. Sickened Lazarus turned away.

"What's your conclusion doctor?" he asked, as Scattergood joined him by the sink and began to wash the blood off his hands.

"I'll have to test the vomit to be absolutely sure, but in my professional opinion, the girl was poisoned. I'd swear the lady was fed toadstools and not mushrooms."

"Given her situation and her unmarried state, could it have been suicide?"

"It's possible," Scattergood looked thoughtful, "Anything is possible. But I think highly unlikely."

"Why?"

"Well, it's not a method I'd choose to use. Unless you know exactly what you're doing, it's too hit and miss. And very painful."

"She may not have known that."

"True enough, but you still have the problem of where and when she cooked and ate the concoction."

It was Lazarus' turn to look thoughtful, "You raise a valid point, my friend."

"I fear I do. I'll be sure tomorrow when I've force-fed a rat some of the young lady's last meal, but I think you do have a case of poisoning on your hands. Then all you have to do is find the cook and you'll find your killer."

CHAPTER FIVE

True to his word, Will Carter was waiting on the steps of the Police Station when Lazarus arrived. He looked happy and eager, which was more than Lazarus could claim. He had endured a largely sleepless night, plagued by visions of the tiny unborn child that had nestled as though sleeping in Dr Scattergood's hand. He felt haunted by lives cut short and in the cold light of the dawn he determined to change his career and find some other way to earn his crust. The trouble with his present occupation was that it both began and ended with death and he'd had his fill of it.

The one thing he had forgotten when he made this momentous decision was that he had yesterday promised young Carter a way out of his own grinding poverty. With no Lazarus, there was no job running errands for Will.

Lazarus reached into his pocket and crumpled the letter of resignation he had penned less than hour before.

"Good morning, young fellow," he said, with an admirable attempt at bonhomie, "All ready for work?"

"Yes sir," answered Will breathlessly, "You ask and I'll do it."

"Well, first things first. Have you had breakfast?"

Will looked at him as though he was speaking of some strange exotic concoction which he had never dreamed he would be allowed to taste, "Not yet."

"Then we'll put that right for a start. I just have to show my face inside and find out if Sergeant Stonier is here yet. Come on."

Sergeant Stonier was indeed inside and only too willing to respond to his boss' wink and make their usual pretence of having somewhere important to be. It was a polite, but largely pointless exercise because everyone in the station knew that the two men were going to repair to the Rising Sun and eat a hearty repast accompanied by good strong coffee, as they did every morning.

Within a few minutes the three were ensconced in the snug, the two men enjoying their hot brew, whilst the boy gave himself a milky moustache with the best drink he had ever tasted. It occurred to Stonier that the child might make himself ill gulping down a diet too rich for a stomach only used to skimmed milk and rough bread, "Take it steady, young fellow-me-lad," he cautioned, and Will grinned happily,

"I will Mr Stonier, don't you worry."

The daily ritual of breakfast was not entirely without its uses, for the two men did discuss their next move in the matter of the suspected murder of Mollie Waters. Being a caring old soul, Mrs Brown had taken no interest in her lodger whatsoever and could provide them with no personal information except the name of the hat shop where the girl had worked, so it didn't take a detective to work out that this should be their next call. Firstly, however, they needed to find some occupation for Will Carter as they could hardly drag the poorly-dressed young urchin around with them for the entire day. He was sent to the corner to buy a newspaper whilst Stonier and Lazarus had a swift conversation regarding the way his day should be spent.

Stonier, who had children of his own and had more idea than Lazarus as to how they should be utilised, suggested he take a duster and a broom to their office. To Lazarus' certain knowledge the room they shared within the police station had never been properly cleaned. They considered themselves lucky to have a room to call their own in the organised chaos that was Braxton Constabulary let alone the luxury of a cleaning woman. Usually one of the younger constables was ordered to push a grubby cloth over the desk when they were expecting a visit from their superintendent.

"Good idea – and when he's done that he can start sorting out that pile of paperwork that needs filing – I suppose he can read well enough to do that?"

"I should think so. They treat 'em hard in the mill schools, but they teach 'em well."

Will Carter went off happily to do their bidding, his belly fuller than he ever recalled, his pockets bulging with bread and cold bacon to share with his siblings later. Stonier and Lazarus set off in the opposite direction.

The hat shop was on one of the better streets in town and styled itself a 'modish emporium for ladies'. All that was beyond Lazarus – to him a hat was a hat.

It might very well have been that cavalier attitude that rubbed the manageress up the wrong way and caused her to adjust her spectacles and look down her long nose at the two men when they entered the hallowed confines of her establishment.

"Can I do something for you gentlemen? You do realize that we hold only a very small stock of gentlemen's accessories?" Her prominent front teeth made her lisp slightly and reminded Stonier of nothing more than a bad-tempered, elderly squirrel.

Lazarus looked about him. He had never seen so many forms of headgear and he was astounded. Surely a bonnet was to keep the sun off your head and the wind from disarranging your hair? What possible need could there be for this vast array of frippery? There were bonnets with flowers, ribbons, imitation fruit, predominantly cherries from what he could see. There were black bonnets with widow's veils, white bonnets for brides. They were made of straw, cotton, silk, satin and came in every colour of the rainbow. There were fussy ones and plain, feathered and ruched. He dreaded to think what the men's might look like – and he didn't intend to ask.

Lazarus showed her his official identification, which made her look even stiffer and her nose wrinkled in contempt, "A policeman? What on earth could you possibly require from me?"

"I believe you employ a young lady by the name of Mollie Waters?"

"I did, but as of this morning at nine o'clock she ceased to be a member of my staff. I warned her that one more instance of lateness or absence and she could wave goodbye to her job."

"I'm afraid I have to tell you that she won't care about that, madam," said Lazarus but he was cut off before he could expand, "Oh really?" she snapped viciously, "Been arrested has she? Or come into money?"

"Neither, madam. The young lady is dead."

That shocked her into silence, as Lazarus had known it would. He waited a few seconds to allow her to fully appreciate just how inappropriate her comments had been then he continued, "We were hoping you could furnish us with her personal details. Her landlady seemed to know nothing more than her name and where she worked."

"Yes, yes, of course," she began to walk towards the little office behind the counter and the two men followed her without being asked, "But you must tell me how it happened? She seemed perfectly healthy on Friday, in fact she was full of the joys of spring, nursing some secret assignation to her breast, no doubt. There had been enough of those in recent months."

Now that did interest the policemen and they exchanged a glance, "Is that so? Would you have any idea who she was meeting?"

The lady laughed scornfully, "I? Certainly not. I do not exchange confidences with the staff – and she certainly wouldn't have volunteered the information. One of the girls in the workshop might know something. I believe she was friendly with one or two of them – though I cautioned her against fraternizing with them. They are rather common and if she wished to make something of herself, she needed to cultivate a better class of companion."

Neither man was surprised that Mollie hadn't chosen to befriend her employer. She had a severe case of snobbery and Mollie's delicate situation would hardly have endeared her to the woman.

"Perhaps we could have a word with the young ladies?"

"You may have five minutes with them, but no more – I have a business to run and I can't afford to pay for my staff to exchange idle chit-chat with the constabulary. It's a pity you don't remember that you are servants of the community and paid out of my hard-earned taxes."

"I can assure you, madam, we're never allowed to forget it. Now the young lady's details, if you would be so kind?"

With obvious reluctance the woman took down a ledger from a shelf above her desk and flicked through the pages until she found what she was looking for.

"She had given only a mother as next-of-kin, no mention of a father. I'll write the address down for you."

"If you would be so kind. Shall we speak to the girls in the work-shop whilst you do that?"

She glowered at him, but nodded her head towards a second door which led into the back recesses of the shop.

The opulence of the front faded swiftly when they went through into a narrow passageway and thereupon into a small, noisy room, filled with at least ten girls, seated at long tables upon which were strewn all the fripperies which were so evident in the shop. The chatter slowly ceased as one by one the girls realized they were not alone. Stonier and Lazarus found themselves steadfastly observed by ten pairs of curious eyes.

"Good morning, ladies, do you think my colleague and I could have a word?"

"Pollis," snorted one contemptuously and the stares took on a distinct hint of aggression.

Lazarus was astounded that they had so swiftly pigeon-holed himself and his companion, despite the lack of a uniform, but there was evidently something that gave them away. He wished he could ask what the devil it was, for it would make under-cover work a damned sight easier if he could hide that indefinable aura that marked him down as a member of the constabulary.

"We are indeed policemen, ladies, but on this occasion we are here to impart sad news. Mollie Waters was found dead yesterday."

The chatter broke out again as they digested and discussed this shocking piece of news. Lazarus let them get the surprise out of their systems before he began his questioning again.

"We'd be grateful for any information you could give us. Her landlady seemed to know nothing about Mollie and we need to find out who she saw and where she went just prior to her death."

The buxom girl who had spoken the word 'police' with such venom had apparently appointed herself spokeswoman, for it was she who looked up through suspiciously narrowed lids and asked warily, "Why do you want to know all that stuff? Was she done away with?"

The two men exchanged a glance. Lazarus had known Stonier long enough to realize what he was thinking. They had nothing to lose and everything to gain by admitting the truth. These women were much more likely to help if they thought they might reap revenge for the killing of one of their own.

"It's possible," he said at length, "We're not positive, but she seemed healthy enough …"

"Oh, she was healthy alright," said the girl, "aside from the baby she was carrying."

"You knew about that?"

"I did. I also know the swine that gave it to her."

The astounded faces of the rest of the workers told the policemen that it was likely that she was the only one in the room who had been privy to Mollie Waters' business, so Lazarus asked her quietly to accompany them out of the room.

"Thank you for your time, ladies, you can go back to work now," he said over his shoulder as he led her away.

"What's your name, Miss?" he asked as she went ahead of them down the dark passageway.

"Eliza Dunne," she answered, "And can we make this fast? We're on piece-work in there and I'm losing money hand over fist."

"We'll not keep you any longer than we have to," Stonier assured her, "In fact we'll do you the favour of not taking you to the station to answer questions if you swear you'll tell us everything you know."

"I've got nothing to hide," she threw over her shoulder, "And I'm not afraid of that snake in the grass that seduced Mollie."

Back in the office the stiff-faced manageress looked utterly horrified by the thought that one of the workers had been allowed into the front. That was nothing to her expression of disgust when they ushered her out of the office and closed the door in her face.

Stonier offered Eliza a seat and prepared to take notes, whilst Lazarus took the big leather chair behind the desk.

"Right, Miss Dunne, begin. You say you know who Mollie's lover was?"

“Yes. It was Lawrence Crabtree.”

“Lawrence … You mean Sir Walter Crabtree’s son?” That he was doubtful of her word was obvious to Eliza because she looked mutinously at him, “Look, friend, if you are going to call me a liar, we might as well end this right now.”

“I don’t intend to give you that impression, Miss Dunne, but you have to admit it is pretty unlikely. How the devil would Mollie Waters have met with the likes of Lawrence Crabtree? Much less end up expecting his baby.”

Sir Walter Crabtree was the second largest landowner in the district, the local MP, magistrate and friend and kin of the all-powerful Lord Allingham, whose estate was almost as large and imposing as Chatsworth.

“That’s all you know,” sneered Eliza, “she did meet him and he courted her and chased her until she gave in. Then he dropped her faster than a hot coal when he found out she was expecting.”

“But how? How did their paths cross?”

“In the shop, of course. He came in to buy a bonnet – he said it was for his Ma when he set eyes on Mollie, but we all knew it was for his fancy piece – even Mollie admitted that! No woman in her fifties would have worn the saucy little hat he bought. Mollie didn’t care though. She was too swept away by the thought that he wanted to drop the other girl for her.”

“And you’re sure it really was Lawrence Crabtree? Anyone could walk in here and give a false name.” Stonier looked up from his note-taking and raised a brow. He could hear the reluctance in Lazarus’ tone and he knew the source of it. Their boss was going to be furious if they went back to the station and announced that they needed to interview the son of a Magistrate in connection with a murder. He doubted they’d be allowed to get within a mile of Lawrence Crabtree.

“It was him alright. We saw his name and address in the ledger and later Mollie showed me the crest on the letter that came from his father’s estate manager when he paid the bill.”

That settled it. They would have to ask to see that ledger and letter. If Crabtree’s name appeared then he would have to be questioned, no matter how distasteful the task.

Stonier thought that would be the end of their chat with Eliza, but it seemed something else had occurred to Lazarus.

"One more thing, Miss Dunne. When you mentioned Mollie's lover, you said that you weren't afraid of him. What made you say that? Had Lawrence Crabtree given any indication he might be violent towards Mollie?"

Eliza looked both sad and angry, "He is a snivelling little coward. He was terrified when Mollie told him she was pregnant. He said he refused to believe the child was his and she had better not go around telling such tales. He said he knew powerful people who could put a stop to any stories she might try to tell."

"Did he indeed?" enquired Lazarus grimly.

CHAPTER SIX

LIBBY – PRESENT

Mr Dailey waited until they had their drinks before he spoke again. The delay seemed to have made Maddie even calmer, but Libby was so jittery that she almost spilled her water and hastily put it down on the desk. She knew Maddie wouldn't thank her for betraying the slightest hint of nerves.

"Now ladies," he said smoothly, as the door closed behind his secretary, "What can I do for you?"

Maddie eyed him over the rim of her cup and took her time about replying, "Mr Dailey, since you were the one to call this meeting, I rather think it's up to you to tell us what your intentions are, rather than the other way around."

The smile faded. He didn't like being challenged that much was obvious. He had evidently expected a certain response and Maddie wasn't delivering, "Alright, Miss, I'll play along. You've made a couple of ridiculous assertions and I've been asked by my client to request that you desist from any further contact. They have no interest in your fairytales and have decided to end the matter as amicably as possible."

"Do you believe it's a fairytale, Mr Dailey?" Maddie was wide-eyed and deceptively pleasant. Libby inwardly cringed. Her sister was always at her most dangerous when she was calm and polite.

"I'm afraid I do. I'm aware that there has been ill-feeling between your family and the Allinghams for many years, but I find it extremely unlikely that had there ever been any physical evidence of these old stories it would have taken a hundred and fifty years for your family to produce it."

"It was well-hidden, otherwise I'm sure you're right."

He laughed, but it wasn't a warm sound, "So well hidden that it's taken five generations to find it? It's just not true, is it, Miss Richmond. The paper wasn't in Hill Farm in 1859 and it isn't there now!"

It was Maddie's turn to smile, "You're right, it wasn't at the house. But you know that for sure, don't you? Because the Allinghams told you that their thugs turned the house over in 1859 and they didn't find it."

The rush of colour to his face belied his calm demeanour, but he still denied her claims, "Dear God, woman, do you really think anyone today is even slightly interested in the happenings of the century before last?"

"They were interested enough to arrange this appointment."

"This appointment was arranged for your benefit. Richard Allingham had two choices, either warn you in a nice way that you are playing with fire, or come the heavy with you. Having met you, I rather wish he'd gone for the latter, but I'm merely his spokesman. So I'm going to say this as politely as possible, do not contact the Allingham family again or the consequences will be unpleasant."

"I see the years have done nothing to dull the Allinghams' innate sense of their own importance. They still think they hold all the power, don't they? Perhaps you'd like to see the licence?"

"I'd love to see it," he assured her, his smug smile back in place as he realized she was going to have to put up or shut up.

She pulled a piece of folded paper from her handbag and handed it to him. He opened it up, gave it the most cursory of glances then fed it into the paper shredder at the side of his desk.

Libby gasped with shock and leapt to her feet to try and reach it before it completely disappeared into the spinning blades. Maddie calmly grasped her arm and forced her back into her seat, "What the hell are you doing, Maddie?" she cried, horrified, "He's destroyed it."

"Calm yourself, Mrs Wright, it was a fake – and a very poorly produced one, if you ask me," Dailey assured her with the sort of patronising tone to his voice that made Libby long to hit him.

"Of course it was, you blustering old fool," sneered Maddie,

"How stupid do you think I am? That was a photocopy – of which I have half a dozen. The original is safely stowed – and has certainly not been left lying around where any passing thief can get hold of it."

Dailey's grimly folded lips showed that the barb had hit its mark, "You are offensive, Miss Richmond."

"And you are a disgrace to your profession! You would have shredded the real thing if I'd been insane enough to bring it along. What exactly do they call that sort of behaviour? I'm sure the Law Society would be interested in your actions. In fact I think I'll ask them! You can put the contents of that shredder into a bag for me and I'll take it with me as proof."

He tried to stare her down for a few seconds, willing her to believe that he was totally unmoved by the threat, but she showed no sign of being intimidated and he drew in a deep breath, "I apologise. That was wrong of me, but I can assure you it was only because I thought it was a fake. I can only promise you that anything that gave the appearance of being real would have been treated with respect."

Maddie's expression showed just how deeply satisfied she was that she had scared him. He was well aware that an accusation of destroying vital evidence in what might become a major court case would have been viewed in a very poor light.

"Apology accepted, but don't worry, you'll never get the chance to prove to me that you're telling the truth. The licence is currently being examined and certified as genuine by an unbiased expert."

He scanned her face intently, desperately hoping to see a crack in her armour, but Maddie was staunch.

"For the moment I have no choice but to accept that you honestly believe you have a genuine document," he murmured, his arrogance and pomposity well and truly punctured.

"I do."

"Very well, then for my own satisfaction, and so that I can report back to my clients, would you mind telling me exactly where you found it? As you evidently know, the Allinghams have been convinced for years that the marriage never took place – and your own family have similarly never brought a court case, which they surely would have done had they held this document."

Maddie glanced towards her younger sister and grinned mischievously, "Shall we tell him, sis?"

Libby became infected with Maddie's glee. She smiled back, a pale imitation of her sibling's merriment, "I think you should," she said softly.

"Very well. Mr Dailey, last year Richard Allingham made a present to my sister. It was the campaign chest that had belonged to his great, great, great Uncle. It had been handed down generation by generation to the eldest son, but not one had used it or even looked at it. Far too old-fashioned and cumbersome. It gathered dust on a shelf for over a century, owned by people who had too much other stuff for it to be of any importance. It is a lovely piece of furniture, comprising of everything a gentleman might need when away at war. It held shaving equipment, brushes and combs, bottles and jars. And in the section set aside for stationery, there was a secret drawer..."

Mr Dailey's plump cheeks grew pale as light finally dawned on what she was saying, "The Allinghams had the licence in their possession the whole time?"

"For more than a hundred and fifty years! Isn't that exquisitely funny and ironic? They had poor little Decima killed for nothing. She never admitted she had married Richard because she could not prove it and knew that his relations would drag her through the mire if she tried to convince the world that her baby was not illegitimate."

Libby spoke up with all the passion she had felt for the unfortunate Decima since the first moment her Aunt Lil had told her of the tragedy, "Do you know what I think, Mr Dailey? I think that Decima allowed her baby to be handed over to her sister not to preserve her own reputation, but to protect her son. She knew he was the true heir to the Allingham estate and if she tried to claim his birthright, Richard's father would have had no hesitation in removing him."

Dailey was appalled, "Are you suggesting that Lord Allingham would have had the child murdered?"

"Too bloody right I'm suggesting just that! He made sure Decima was hanged. He threatened the policeman who believed in her innocence and had him taken off the case. She never stood a chance. She did the only thing she could and that was to deny her baby. She knew he'd only be safe if the Allinghams thought he was born the wrong side of the blanket." She heard her own voice break at the utter unfairness of it all and was surprised to find her hand suddenly gripped comfortingly by Maddie.

"The truth is finally out, Mr Dailey. It's taken a long time, but justice is going to be done. Your clients sent you to issue a warning to me, well, now I'm warning them. This is far from over."

"How much?" said Dailey suddenly.

"I beg your pardon?"

"How much do you want?"

Maddie and Libby both stared at him, open-mouthed, not quite able to believe in the sudden capitulation.

"I'm instructed that in the event of your claim being genuine, I can offer a sum of money agreeable to both parties. Name your figure and I will convey it to my clients – reliant, naturally, on the expert opinion on the document and your own discretion."

"But Mr Dailey, this is so sudden," exclaimed Maddie with mock coyness, regaining her sense of humour.

"Let's not beat about the bush, Miss Richmond. You want money, my clients are prepared to pay for this minor irritation to go away. Name your price and don't pretend to be naive at this late date."

"I'll have to think about it. I'll be in touch. Come, Libby. Goodbye Mr Dailey. Please send my fondest regards to my cousin Richard."

They were barely out of the office door when they both burst out laughing. They could scarcely manage to stagger out past the reception desk, where the expression of complete bewilderment on the face of the secretary sent them off into further paroxysms.

"Maddie, you are a bloody lunatic," gasped Libby at last, "I can't believe we just did that!"

"I'm going to be a very rich lunatic," chuckled Maddie, "Mr Dailey has some explaining to do. He was supposed to fob us off without a penny."

Libby was suddenly sober, "I hope we're not going to regret

this," she said quietly.

"Why the hell should there be anything to regret? I'm only asking for what is rightfully mine."

"I know. But they're a powerful family. They've used their influence to get their own way before."

"Yeah, well, they'd never met me before, had they? I'm made of sterner stuff than little Decima. And let's face it, they might have got away with murder in the eighteen hundreds, but this is the twenty-first century."

Maddie looked so much like their mother at her most pugnacious that Libby was forced to grin wryly. Maddie had a point. The Allinghams were much more likely to use money to pay her sister off than to take out a contract on her. She was worrying over nothing. Decima was finally going to get justice. Her bloodline were going to take on the Allingham clan and beat them.

"I need a drink. We'll leave the car here and take a taxi home – and the booze is on you, now you're coming into an inheritance."

The sisters almost skipped back across the square and into the pub.

*   *   *

David was home and making himself beans on toast when they finally staggered through the door. He raised an eyebrow, "Have you two eaten – or did you go straight to the wine bottle?"

"Champagne, if you please," corrected Maddie, setting them both laughing again.

"I hope you didn't drive back in that state," he said calmly.

"Of course not. We took a taxi – and it cost a bomb! I won't be doing that again in a hurry."

"I wouldn't have thought you'd have much cause to – in fact I'd be very interested to know what the celebration was for."

Maddie flopped into a chair and promptly closed her eyes, "You tell him, Libs, I'm going to sleep." David was astounded when she suited action for words and began snoring gently within seconds, "Good heavens, how much have you two had?"

"A lot," Libby assured him, "But she had more than me."

"I'm not really interested in comparisons," he answered grimly, suddenly aware that there was something going on that he was pretty sure he wasn't going to like, "I'd just like a simple answer to a simple question. Why are you both drunk?"

"Oooh, get you, Mr Misery-guts! Since when did you disapprove of a few drinks? I've seen you in a worse state than this!"

"I've no doubt you have, love," he replied, trying to keep the irritation out of his voice, "But I usually have a reason and I just want to know yours."

She went to put the kettle on and as she unsteadily made a pot of coffee she gave him a potted version of the afternoon's events. It was fortunate that she was fully occupied with cups, milk and the coffee-pot because it meant that she failed to notice that his expression grew sterner with every syllable. When she ended her story she realized that he was utterly silent and at last his sombre mood broke through her drunken haze.

"What's the matter?" she said, trying not to slur over the words.

"I'm just hoping that you're pulling my leg, Libby."

"Why should I be doing that? We haven't done anything wrong. Maddie was quite right, the Allinghams do owe us – and they've even admitted that themselves now."

"They've done nothing of the kind."

"Of course they have."

"Do you have anything in writing?"

"No, but …"

"But nothing. People like that don't just give in. All you've done is show your hand and they've gone away to re-group and plan the next stratagem."

"Yeah, well, so have we."

"Oh, grow up, Libby. These people have lived powerful lives for hundreds of years. They made a lot of money and despite everything life could throw at them, they've kept it. Do you really think fools and clowns can do that?"

"You're being rather melodramatic, aren't you? What do you imagine they're going to do – take a contract out on us?"

"Oh, they're much more subtle than that, sweetheart."

If there was one thing Libby hated, it was when her husband used an endearment when they were arguing, her suppressed anger made itself manifest in the tone of intense sarcasm she used to answer him, "Really? Well, sweetheart, I'd like to know what's really bothering you, because you didn't seem at all concerned by Maddie's little tussle with the Allinghams last night."

He seemed to realize he'd gone too far and tried to lighten the mood, "You're right, I am being melodramatic. I've listened to too many of your gory tales of past injustices."

Libby was almost convinced – but not quite. David was the calmest, most laid-back man she had ever met. He simply didn't get into a flap about anything. This was so out of character that she was determined to get to the bottom of it.

"Tell me, David."

"Tell you what?"

"Tell me what's really troubling you."

He drew in a deep breath then seemed to decide that he would be straight with her, "You seem to have forgotten that Rick is a friend of mine."

"And you think I've embarrassed you?" she asked coldly.

"Not just that, Libby. You've put me in an invidious position. I introduced you to the man – and I made him feel guilty enough to present you with that bloody chest! Can't you see how all this is making me look?"

He crossed to the coffee pot and began to pour them both a drink, "I shouldn't have said anything. This is your business – and your sister's."

"Yes, well, it's too late to say that now. You've made it your business by picking a fight with me."

He came back to her and hugged her, but somehow she didn't feel any warmth in his embrace. He was trying to patch things up, but the anger wasn't really spent for either of them, "I'm sorry. I didn't mean it to turn into a fight. I just wish you had thought things through a little before acting. This is going to affect a lot of people, not just your family."

"Who? What people? What are you talking about?" She couldn't decide whether she was being particularly obtuse because of all the champagne she'd drunk or if it was him being all mysterious and obscure.

"Do you really need me to spell it out to you? Have you forgotten that I do a lot of business with Rick Allingham?"

Struck by guilt she lifted a gentle hand to his face, "Oh, David, I'm so sorry. I admit I didn't think about that aspect of things. But really, you know, we don't rely on the money from the garden centres. You could retire tomorrow on the money Aunt Lil left me."

He shook her hand off and pulled away from her, "Bloody hell, Libby, are you crazy? I'm not forty yet! I have no intention of retiring – and that money is yours. Do I look like the sort of man who'd live off a woman?"

Her mouth dropped open with shock, but within seconds the surprise and hurt turned to fury.

"I beg your pardon?" she said dangerously, "Did I hear you correctly? Living off a woman? What happened to equality all of a sudden? What became of 'for richer, for poorer'?"

"Oh, don't start quoting the marriage vows at me! You know perfectly well what I meant. I run a business – it's what I do. I built it up from nothing by my own hard work and I don't see why I should have to stand by and watch your sister ruin it because of some fanciful notion that some nineteenth century tart was really married and not just sleeping with the local lord of the manor."

She wanted to reply but every word and phrase that flitted through her churning brain would have ended with them both throwing away a marriage that, when she was sober and calm, meant the world to her. She just looked at him for one long, fulminating minute, then turned and walked away. He called after her, but she ignored him and went up the stairs.

He meant to follow her, he wanted to, but he hesitated a fraction too long and Maddie woke herself up with a pig snort and smiled blearily at him, "Did I drop off? Champagne will do that to me every time. I don't know why I drink the stuff. Where's Libby?"

"Gone to bed, I think."

"I think I'll join her. It's okay if I crash in the guest room, isn't it?"

"Fine. It's all made up. Libby has nothing better to do these days than pretend to be the perfect housewife."

She looked at him from under a quizzically raised eyebrow, "Trouble in paradise?" she asked shrewdly.

"A little," he admitted, "Mostly caused by your family."

"Oh dear, anything I can do to help?"

He could think of several things, but he realized he had already said too much, "Don't worry about it. Libby and I will sort it soon enough, thanks."

She shrugged and yawned, "She always was an awkward little so-and-so – but that's your problem now. Good night."

CHAPTER SEVEN

LAZARUS 1862

It was not easy to find Mollie Water's mother. An address was not much use when it was merely one name amongst a warren of streets, all dirty, all similarly filled with scruffy urchins and ragged women who stared at the policemen as though they were some exotic creatures from another world. It was usually uniformed officers who were sent to make arrests so Lazarus and Stonier rarely found themselves in such insalubrious surroundings.

They had wandered for twenty minutes before Stonier had the bright idea of heading for the steeple of the church they could see above the chimneys, "The vicar will know his parish – he'll be able to direct us."

Having no better plan and growing tired of asking surly women for directions, Lazarus agreed.

Apparently the Reverend Bembridge was not at home, but could be found, or so his housekeeper informed them, in the Sunday School building behind the church, overseeing the doling out of the soup from the newly instigated soup kitchen. So much hardship had been created by the loss of cotton to the mills that children and pregnant women were now being fed once a day by the more charitable amongst the reverend gentleman's flock.

The inspector found it astounding that a war half-a-world away could cause children to starve in England, yet it was true. As the blockading of the Southern States of America grew heavier, so the machinery in Northern English mills had ground to a halt. Workers were lucky if they were on half time, but most had been laid off, waiting for the civil war to end, the black slaves to be free, and the cotton mills to resume weaving and spinning. Seeing the poverty at such close quarters, Lazarus could only hope the Americans sorted out their differences sooner rather than later. Astoundingly the mill-workers actually sided with the North, even though it was they who were stopping the export of the South's cotton. They wanted an end to slavery, and they were prepared to suffer for their black brothers. When he looked around, Lazarus could only wonder at the magnitude of the sacrifice.

The fact that lines of hungry women and children were already forming told him how close to noon it was drawing. A whole morning had gone by and they had achieved next to nothing. The thought did nothing to improve his mood.

Mr. Bembridge was exactly where his housekeeper had said, but he couldn't be described as being particularly involved. Sure enough he was wandering about the room, exchanging pleasantries with the hard-working and obviously harassed ladies, but Lazarus was quick to notice that he never attempted to help in any other way. The same could not be said for another young cleric, whom Lazarus took to be Bembridge's curate. He was bouncing about the room like an over-grown puppy, playing with the children and talking to the mothers, who managed to raise a weary smile when he addressed them. The little ones clamoured for his attention and briefly forgot their hunger when he swung them high above his head and caused them to giggle and wriggle with pleasure

The policemen stood in the doorway for a few seconds, taking in the scene. One or two ladies, set apart by their crinolined skirts in silk and satin and pretty bonnets which could well have come from Mollie Water's workplace, were overseeing the making and serving of the food, but the bulk of the work was being carried out by cooks and scullery-maids, obviously loaned by generous mill-owners' wives.

It had to be admitted that the aroma wafting towards them from the huge iron pots and large copper jam pans was hardly delectable. It consisted mainly of rancid fat and musty vegetables, and another odd smell that Lazarus didn't recognize. When he whispered to Stonier for an explanation he was told it was gruel. Thus far in his life Lazarus had been lucky enough to know of gruel only as a word contained within the works of Mr. Charles Dickens. He didn't know of anyone up North who had ever made it or indeed eaten it. But here it was. He could only imagine that the rich ladies had also read Mr. Dickens and assumed that the poverty-stricken must thrive upon the stuff. From the smell he doubted even pigs would welcome it. Stonier's porker was probably having a better diet than these poor unfortunates. The thought caused him to view Mr. Bembridge with even less favour when he observed his wobbling jowls and rotund figure – apparently he was not having to go without. The prejudice grew when a small child toddled up to the man of God and tugged at his coat tails. The look of distaste on Bembridge's face as he ushered the child away and surreptitiously wiped his hand on his handkerchief lest he had picked up some lice or other contamination from the infant was enough to make Lazarus dislike him intensely. Stonier saw the expression on his companion's face and gently pulled on his arm, "Go steady, old friend. We're not here to judge, just get information." The softly spoken warning was enough to make Lazarus take a deep breath and rein in his irritation.

They walked across the room and introduced themselves to the vicar, who looked delighted to be distracted from the task in hand, "Gentlemen from the constabulary, eh? Well, well, well, and what can I do for you?"

"We are looking for a lady who lives in a street in this vicinity, sir, but have so far failed to locate the address. We hoped you might have some local knowledge."

"I know these streets as well as any, for my sins," answered Bembridge, laughing at his own wit, "The lady's name?"

Lazarus supplied the name and address, adding, "At least we assume that is her name. It was certainly her daughter's, but she might of course be widowed and remarried."

"No, no, she hasn't remarried, Mr Lazarus. I know Mrs Waters well. In fact I can direct you to her right this moment."

"She's here?" asked Lazarus in surprise.

"She is one of my stalwarts. I'll have her brought to you directly." He raised his hand to catch the attention of his curate, but Lazarus reached out and stopped him, "Is there somewhere private we can speak to her. I'm afraid we have bad news."

Bembridge dropped his bluff friendliness and adopted a grave air as befitted his position, "Oh, dear. I'm sorry to hear that. Perhaps you should tell me and leave it to me to break the sorry tidings?" Lazarus was canny enough to recognize a ruse to winkle gossip out of him and he shook his head sternly, "I appreciate the offer, sir, but my duty is clear in this matter. Mrs. Waters must hear this from myself and my sergeant."

"Then you must take her to the vicarage. I'll come with you and see that she is served tea. Doubtless she'll need it for the shock." He signalled to the curate, who came at once.

"You wanted me, Mr. Bembridge?"

"Ah, Mr. Holbrook, a favour if you would be so good. Could you find Mrs. Waters and ask her to join us?"

"Certainly Mr. Bembridge."

He was lost to sight for a few moments amongst the growing crowd, but returned very swiftly accompanied by a woman in her forties, though her sour expression made her look older, Lazarus felt. Stonier, who had so far held his tongue, murmured in Lazarus' ear, "What's your bet that he offers his support to the lady and ends up in the room when we tell her?"

"Why wager on a dead cert?" answered Lazarus, watching Bembridge walk towards the woman in order to give her warning of their presence.

She barely managed a smile as she was introduced to them, merely giving the slightest bob of a curtsey. Judging from her clothing, the policemen guessed she was working class rather than one of the ladies. It seemed she had been occupied with cooking the food rather than overseeing, for she wore a pristine white apron, so stiff with starch that it would probably have stood alone had she removed it. Lazarus thought to himself that she must bathe in starch too, so unbending and unfriendly was her demeanour.

"Shall we repair to the vicarage?" asked Bembridge and they all obediently followed, except the curate, Holbrook, who went back to playing with the children.

Lazarus waited until they were seated in the vicarage parlour and served with tea before he broached the subject of Mollie Waters and her unfortunate demise.

"Mrs. Waters, I have something of a personal nature to impart. Do you wish Mr. Bembridge to leave the room?"

"Certainly not. I have nothing to hide."

The policeman thought she might regret that decision, but he didn't like her enough to care, "Very well. I understand you have a daughter called Mollie Waters?"

"I do."

"Then I'm very sorry to have to inform you, madam, that Miss Waters was found dead yesterday morning."

She looked shocked for literally seconds before she regained her composure and said bitterly, "Well, it was only a matter of time before something bad happened to that girl. I suppose her silliness led her into some sort of an accident?"

"Not exactly, Mrs. Waters. We have reason to believe she might have been the victim of poison."

The white face was suddenly suffused with red. She leapt to her feet, "How dare you! Are you suggesting my daughter did away with herself? Never, no matter what the circumstances..."

Bembridge joined in her protests at this point, blustering on about mortal sins and Mollie being a God-fearing girl for all her faults. Lazarus raised a placating hand, "You misunderstand me, madam. There is no suggestion at the moment that the poison was self-administered. It could have been an accident or ..."

It was the vicar's turn to voice his shock, "Dear God in Heaven, you are not intimating that Miss Waters was done away with?"

"The honest truth, sir, is that at this time, we simply do not know. Our investigations are ongoing. I do need to tell Mrs. Waters one more thing."

"What is it?" asked the woman faintly, as though she could hardly bear to hear anything more.

"When the body was examined by the doctor, he found that the young lady was expecting a baby, sadly too young to have survived outside the womb, even had the mother been found in time to operate."

He watched their faces carefully for a reaction, but to his surprise, this was the one piece of information that didn't seem to shock either party.

"I take it you knew of the pregnancy, Mrs. Waters?" he asked gently. She gave the slightest nod, "She came to me last week and asked to be allowed to come home until the child was born. I consulted with Mr. Bembridge and we both agreed that Mollie needed to face up to her responsibilities and find her own way out of the mess she had created for herself. I told her that if she had been foolish enough to fall for the blandishments of a man who would take advantage of her then refuse to marry her, then she must take the consequences. Why should I have the shame and humiliation of a base-born child brought to my door?"

"I see," said Lazarus. And sadly he saw only too clearly. Mollie had been failed by everyone who should have cared for and protected her. Suddenly suicide did not seem such a remote possibility. The girl must have been at her wit's end.

He rose to his feet and Stonier did likewise, "Thank you for your time, Mrs. Waters, and please accept my commiserations at your loss. You will be informed when the Coroner releases your daughter's and grandchild's bodies for burial."

"Tell him he needn't bother. I don't have the money to bury them. They'll have to go into a pauper's grave, unless the man that gave her the child decides to stump up." Her bitterness dripped from every word like bile and Lazarus could not help but glance towards the vicar to see how he felt about this rejection of the girl even in death. His face was bland. Apparently there was no forgiveness in life or death.

Without another word Lazarus turned away from the pair and headed out of the door, closely followed by his sergeant.

In the fresh air, Lazarus drew in a shuddering breath, "Dear God, preserve me from religion if that is how they're run!" He failed to see the irony of the comment and Stonier didn't bother to point it out to him, "I think we both need a drink," he said, "Then we'll do the next dirty task of the day. Find Crabtree and tell him that his mistress and child are both dead."

The inspector had momentarily forgotten that aspect of the case. He thought he felt a headache coming on.

"Find me a pub," he enjoined Stonier, "And just this once, I'm having a whisky, middle of the day or not!"

In the end they decided to return to their own territory for the drink. The first pub they entered was full to bursting with shabby and defeated men who nursed the single pint they could afford and looked none too kindly at the strangers who trespassed. Lazarus knew he ought not judge, but he couldn't help but despise men who could still find the money for beer when their wives and children were begging for pig's slops just down the road.

Stonier carried a pint and a whisky to the corner table where they always sat.

"What's our next move, Inspector? Do you really want to confront young Crabtree? He won't take very kindly to our interference. Gentlemen like to keep these matters to themselves."

"I'm sure they do, but that's really not my concern. Either directly or indirectly that young cad is responsible for Mollie Waters' death."

Stonier frowned at this rather black and white view of a complicated matter, "I'm not sure you can make that sort of statement without getting yourself into a lot of trouble, my friend."

"Trouble? Do you think I care for that? If Crabtree had not seduced the girl, she would still be alive. How much more involved could he be? Even if she committed suicide, she did so because he deserted her."

The frown deepened, "Why are you taking this so personally, Danby?" he asked, using Lazarus' first name, a thing he seldom did during working hours, unless he was very moved or worried.

"I don't know what you mean. It's no more personal than any other case."

Sergeant Stonier knew that wasn't true. He also recalled, with painful clarity, the last time Lazarus had been so involved in a case – a case that had very nearly ended in disaster for the younger man.

"This is all about Decima Watkins, isn't it?" he asked softly. Lazarus raised his eyes to his companion's face, then lowered them again swiftly, "Decima Watkins was three years ago – over and done with."

"Three years or not, you're still blaming yourself, aren't you?"

"She was hanged, Tom, and I was her only hope." In those few words Lazarus exposed the agony he had been hiding for three long years.

"Dear God, man, when are you ever going to forgive yourself and let that girl rest in peace? You did your best for her."

"No, I didn't. At the first threat of losing my job, I stopped digging for the truth and left her to her fate."

"What more could you have done? You had a family to consider."

"Yes," said Lazarus bitterly, "And look what happened to my family! That was justice of a kind, wasn't it? I got exactly what I deserved."

Tom looked at his friend's lowered head, not able to quite believe what he was hearing, or indeed what Lazarus was hinting at without actually using the words, "Are you trying to tell me that you think that Rosa's death was somehow connected with Decima's hanging?"

Lazarus met his friend's eyes, "She haunts me, Tom. Even now I still see her in my dreams. I should have fought for her, but I took the easy way. You never met her. You don't understand how she affected people – men, especially. She had that old fool Brookes eating out of her hand. She caused an heroic soldier to throw everything away for her."

"Dan, you're worrying me. Were you in love with her?"

For the first time Lazarus laughed, "Of course not, you old fool. I was married to Rosamund."

Stonier decided not to bother pointing out that being married to one woman didn't necessarily preclude being in love with another, he simply offered his boss the only piece of advice he could, "Draw a line under it, Dan and move on to the next page. You can't keep on living in the past."

Lazarus opened his mouth to deny he was doing any such thing, but he was interrupted by the arrival of a breathless Will, who dashed in as though the hounds of hell were on his heels, "Oh, here you are, sir," he panted, "Dr. Scattergood sent me to find you and give you a message."

“Is it urgent? Does he need to see me?” asked the inspector, surprised by the boy’s haste and wondering what on earth could be so important that the doctor would send the child running for him.

“Not urgent no. And he never said he wanted to see you. He just gave me a message for you.”

Lazarus smiled. The rush was all the boy’s then and was typical of the enthusiasm he was lavishing on his new job, “Alright, sit down and catch your breath. What’s the message?”

“He said to tell you that the rat’s dead.”

Stonier and Lazarus exchanged a glance.

CHAPTER EIGHT

Back in his office Lazarus heard a name he had hoped never to come across again. A uniformed constable put his head around the door, "Ah, you're back, sir. There's a young lady waiting to see you. Asked for you personal. Name of Allingham."

Both Stonier and Lazarus looked startled. Lazarus because of the memories the name provoked, Stonier because he knew how the mention of the dreaded family would affect his friend and colleague.

"There's an Allingham asking for me?" he queried in astonishment.

"Yes, sir. Miss Allingham. She's got her maid with her."

"If she's one of the Derbyshire Allinghams she would have a maid, and probably a carriage and a footman too."

The constable failed to hear the sarcasm in his superior's tone and replied, "As to all that, sir, I wouldn't know. But she's got a maid and she's asking to speak to you in private."

Stonier could see that Lazarus was tempted to tell the young policeman to tell Miss Allingham to take her maid and go to the devil, so he intervened swiftly, "Show the young lady in, Higson, and I'll occupy the maid."

The young lady entered the office a few moments later amid a rustle of silk and a waft of perfume to find a grim-faced police inspector facing her across the expanse of a freshly polished mahogany desk.

"Good afternoon," she said nervously, wondering what she had done to deserve the stern look he gave her, "Am I addressing Inspector Lazarus?"

He executed the slightest of bows, sat down and answered curtly, "You are. May I ask the nature of your business? I don't believe we are known to each other."

He might just as well have asked outright what the devil she meant by coming to his place of work and bandying his name about with such impertinence, for his tone implied as much. She blushed rosily and stammered, "No, sir, you do not know me, but I was given your name as a gentleman who can be trusted."

"By whom?" he inquired, with no attempt to be conciliatory. It was at that point that her consciousness of her own innate worth righted itself and she was suddenly angry at his rudeness, "Might I sit down?" she asked scathingly, glaring at him. Lazarus felt his own cheeks redden slightly and trying not to let her think she had shamed him into action, he rose to his feet and came around the desk to hold a chair for her, "Please do," he said coolly.

She carefully lifted the rear of her crinoline slightly so that she could sit in the proffered seat, then because of the heat in the room, she took off her gloves, loosened the ribbons of her bonnet and fanned herself with a small, ornate fan she withdrew from her reticule, "It's very warm in here."

Without a word Lazarus went to the window and opened it so that a slight breeze stirred some papers on the tall cabinet behind him, "Now, how can I help you, Miss Allingham?"

"Before I begin, I must insist that our conversation is strictly between our two selves. It is vitally important that not a whisper of what I am about to disclose become public knowledge."

"Madam," said Lazarus, with all the dignity he could muster, "I should like you to remember that I am a public servant. I cannot possibly make any such vow until I know the nature of your request."

She heaved an exasperated sigh and snapped her fan shut with a practiced flick of her wrist, "Oh, for goodness sake! I do think I might have been warned what an utter prig you are!" As soon as the words were out of her lips, Miss Allingham realized that she had spoken too freely – her abiding fault, did Lazarus but know it. She lowered her lids and her small white teeth sank into her full lower lip as though to bite back any further incivility, but to her astonishment she heard the unmistakable sound of laughter and glanced up to find Lazarus watching her with considerable amusement.

She tried to maintain her frown and her pout, after all he had been insufferable from the very first moment she had walked through the door, but his boyish grin and warm brown eyes melted her resolve and she found herself smiling ruefully back, "I suppose I should apologize for that," she said reluctantly.

"Please don't," he replied, "It was refreshingly direct."

"Well, I must say I don't feel inclined to be sorry," she admitted.

"Then by all means stand by what you have said," he responded, "In the meantime, shall we begin again? Perhaps you would like to tell me what this is all about, and I'll promise to listen and if at all possible, I will keep your secret to myself."

"I should not ask you, but it is not my private business we are about to discuss. I am merely the messenger."

"Then I shall endeavour not to shoot you," he said, his tone a little less stern. She had a warmth and humour about her that he had not expected from a member of the Allingham clan and it reminded him how unfair it was to judge before the full facts were known.

"It concerns my young cousin, Arabella Allingham. She is a silly, flighty girl, I'm sorry to say, but her latest escapade has gone beyond what is acceptable. Should it ever come out, it would mean her utter ruin."

"And what has Miss Arabella done that is so very dreadful?" he asked, still inclined to think the whole matter rather trivial.

"She has eloped with a penniless fellow and quite broken her papa's heart."

Lazarus lifted an eyebrow. He could quite see that this would be considered scandalous in aristocratic circles, but he quite failed to see what it had to do with the Braxton Constabulary.

"She is a minx, to be sure," he admitted, "But I fail to see how I can possibly be of service. The deed is done and can only be undone by legal means. Her bereft papa must seek the aid of a lawyer and hope to have the marriage annulled."

She blushed once again and whispered, "Oh, Mr. Lazarus, if only it were that simple. No marriage has taken place. The scoundrel writes to my uncle and asks for money in exchange for the safe return of the prodigal."

"If it means that much to him, I suggest he does so. The young lady is with the man of her own free will, so it can hardly be classed as abduction."

It was evident that she was rather shocked by his callous attitude, "My dear sir, Arabella is only seventeen years old. She cannot be allowed to make such a decision. She has no knowledge of such creatures as this fellow who has used every wile to tempt her away from the safety of her family."

Lazarus doubted the flighty Miss Allingham was quite as naïve as her cousin and doting papa supposed. He also had more pressing issues, but realized he was not going to be allowed to brush this problem aside. The Allinghams all believed they had a God-given right to rule and to be obeyed. To try and argue with this young woman would be a waste of breath, so he resolved not to do so. He rose to his feet in a very obvious gesture of dismissal,

"Very well, Miss Allingham. You may tell your father that I will look into the whereabouts of Miss Arabella and make an attempt to persuade her and her young man that they would be well advised to stop playing their silly games."

She too stood, drawing her gloves on as she spoke, "Lord Allingham is not my father, Mr. Lazarus, he is my uncle and legal guardian. He is Arabella's father."

Lazarus didn't care, but he chose not to say so, merely nodding his head briefly in acknowledgment, "Very well. Is there any other information you can give me? The man's name would be helpful. As would his last known address and occupation. Even a detective must have some clues to work with."

She looked flustered, "Of course. His name is Soper. Marcus Soper. I'm afraid I have no idea where he lived or what he does for a living. I could try and find out for you."

"If you would, and in return, I will do what I can to find your young cousin and return her to the bosom of her family."

"Thank you, sir." She held out a gloved hand which he bowed over, then led her to the door, "Good day, Miss Allingham."

"Goodbye, Inspector Lazarus."

*   *   *

When he parted company with Lazarus, Stonier had guided Miss Allingham's maid into the little scullery which lay at the back of the police station and where the constables prepared the occasional cup of tea or bite to eat. Luckily the fire was lit and Stonier was able to stir the embers and put the kettle on to boil. While they waited, he asked her name and gave her his. She took a moment to weigh him up, testing her own instincts to see whether she thought his intentions were honourable. She hadn't been in service for fifteen years without learning to sort the decent men from the predators. Apparently she decided he looked safely married and happily occupied with his own wife because she smiled as she replied, "I'm Sarah Mulligan, my friends call me Sal."

"Happy to make your acquaintance, Sal," said Stonier and she grinned at the presumption.

Within a very short time Sal was settling into an old straw-seated chair and accepting a cup of tea, "Thanks, sergeant, you're a gentleman."

"My pleasure, love. Us lower orders have to stick together."

"Huh, lower orders indeed! They think they're so far above us, but they don't know how to control their daughters any more than my old pa did!"

"Oh, so that's what all this is about, is it?"

"It is."

"That Allingham lady looks a bit young to be having trouble with her children," he ventured, knowing that a direct question would elicit no response whatsoever from one so worldly wise as Sal Mulligan and so taking a more circuitous route to find out what was going on.

She laughed, "Don't be daft! She's just the go-between. Lord Allingham can't be seen entering a police station – imagine the scandal!"

"So it's Lord Allingham's daughter who is in trouble?"

"Aye, and believe me, it's no real surprise to anyone who knows her. She's always been a little madam, but she's grown too big for her boots just lately. That's the problem with the pretty ones. They start out spoilt by their papa, then get their heads turned by smooth talking cads. I could've told them ten years ago she was heading for mischief, but would they have listened to me? Not a hope in hell! Well, they're paying the price now."

"She's come home with a bellyful of arms and legs and no ring on her finger?" guessed Stonier.

"Not come home at all," corrected the maid, "she's run off with some fellow who's now demanding money with menaces. Lord Allingham's at his wit's end."

"I'll bet he is, but he should have taken more care who he allowed her to come into contact with, shouldn't he? How did a cosseted young lady manage to meet and run off with a scoundrel?"

"Oh, he managed to get himself invited to all the best parties by claiming friendship with the Crabtree lad. It seems they were at school together. He's another one that's running wild and breaking his mother's heart."

Stonier made no comment, but he found it very interesting that Lawrence Crabtree had been mentioned twice in the past couple of days – and in both cases, no good was spoken of him. Lazarus was going to be very interested in that little snippet.

"Do you know the fellow's name by any chance?"

"I do – but you'll have to ask young Mr Crabtree for any other information. Miss Arabella was canny enough to keep her interest in Marcus Soper very quiet until the moment came for flight."

Stonier heard his name called and realized that the interview with Miss Allingham must be at an end. He took Sal's cup and escorted her back into the body of the police station, where Miss Allingham awaited her. He saw the two ladies into their waiting carriage before returning to the office and Lazarus.

"It always amuses me when the upper classes try to keep their secrets, fondly imagining that their servants notice nothing and discuss less!" he said, sitting in the chair so recently vacated by Miss Allingham.

"I'll tell you what does not amuse me," Lazarus responded bitterly, "the fact that Allingham, the bastard, thinks he has me in his pocket because of what happened to Decima Watkins."

Stonier knew this was dangerous ground and attempted to mollify his companion as swiftly as possible, "I'm sure the opposite is true, that he knows you are good at your job. You were warned off then because you were getting too close to the truth. He wants you now because he loves his daughter and he knows he can trust you to be discreet."

Lazarus pondered upon this theory but it still stuck in his craw, "No, he thinks I'm afraid of his power. Well, he forgets that I had something to lose last time."

"You still do, Danby, so don't be a fool. Don't make this personal. You're a policeman and he has a problem. Leave it at that."

Lazarus knew he was right, but he could still picture Decima's white and terrified face when she realized she was doomed; that Lord Allingham wanted her dead because she had dared to fall in love with his son.

"He's playing a dangerous game. Even now I could turn on him and bring him down."

"Only by bringing yourself down too, my friend. It's not worth the price you'd have to pay. You would humiliate him more by having him forever in your debt."

This was a side to the situation that Lazarus had not considered – and if he was honest, it appealed to him, "Umm, you could be right," he admitted thoughtfully, "But I still think I have more important tasks to occupy me. I'll be looking for Mollie Waters' murderer before I turn my attention to a spoiled little Miss, who probably deserves everything that befalls her."

Stonier was not sure he agreed with this assessment of the matter. He had gleaned as much information from the maid as Lazarus had from the young lady, and he was inclined to view Soper as a rather dangerous young man.

"I understand your feelings, Dan, but Mollie is past help – and Arabella Allingham is very much alive and is little more than a child in the hands of a man who has no morals and no conscience. I know who I'd be concentrating on."

"Then you shall do so. You look for Miss Arabella, I'll chase the murderer."

This was an unlooked for development for Stonier. He and Lazarus always worked together and had done from the first moment they had been introduced seven years before. It felt like a rejection, though it should have pleased him to know how highly he was regarded by his superior. The only way he could disguise his disappointment was to adopt an attitude as cold as that displayed by the still angry Lazarus, he rose to his feet and made for the door, "Right, sir, if that's the way you want it."

Lazarus wanted to call him back and apologize but his pride stopped him. Stonier could play into the hands of the high and mighty Allingham if he wanted to, but Lazarus was never going to bow to the man who had been responsible for the hanging of an innocent and lovely young woman.

* * *

Stonier went back into the main area of the police station and found a quiet corner where he could gather his scattered wits. Lazarus was wrong about Arabella, he was sure, and he now fully intended to find her and restore her to her family, before any more damage was done. He realized he had neglected to mention the Crabtree connection, but he was so mad just at that moment that he told himself Lazarus could wait until he was good and ready to impart what he'd learned. Serve him right for being as damned near arrogant as Lord bloody Allingham.

CHAPTER NINE

PRESENT

The house was quiet when Libby woke, but that really didn't help to ease the pounding headache. She realized regretfully that the bed beside her was empty and probably had been all night – not that she would have noticed.

For a moment she considered ringing David on his mobile and apologising for the quarrel, but recalling how unpleasant he had been, she swiftly changed her mind. It was really for him to do the making up.

Downstairs she was surprised to find a note from her sister on the kitchen worktop. It seemed that despite drinking far more than Libby, Maddie had been up and making an early start back to town whilst Libby was still pushing out the zeds. The note made cursory thanks for the hospitality and assured her sister that she would be in touch before long.

That, thought Libby, is just typical of Maddie. She sweeps in like a mini cyclone, causes mayhem, then flounces off again with never a backward glance or a thought for the trouble she's caused.

Libby made herself a pot of coffee and took two painkillers, wondering how Maddie managed to drink so much then escape relatively unscathed. She hoped that her sister wasn't driving with an excess of alcohol still in her system, but there wasn't much she could do about it now.

She managed to force herself to eat some scrambled eggs on toast and began to feel a little more human. The trouble was that as the headache faded, her memory began to return. She squirmed to think of the interview with the solicitor. It was not in her nature to enjoy confrontation and she winced when she thought of the way Maddie had dealt with the situation. Her discomfiture was not helped by knowing that David too had thoroughly disapproved of Maddie's actions. She could understand his annoyance that they had put his business arrangements with Rick Allingham in jeopardy, but she still felt he should have shown more family loyalty. He had always known how much Decima Watkins had meant to her, and how strongly she had felt that the poor girl had suffered the most horrendous miscarriage of justice. For him to now side with the Allinghams was to denigrate all Decima's trials and tribulations. It wasn't as though they needed the money. Lil had left them amply supplied with cash.

She went upstairs intending to write, but she found the cursor simply flashed on an empty screen and she couldn't concentrate. The trouble was that she had reached a point in the story where she needed a bit more background information. She didn't really understand how the Victorian Police Force worked – or indeed the modern police force if it came to that. It was time for Dan at the museum to start earning his ten percent.

She did a quick calculation as to how many units of alcohol she had taken, and how many hours ago she had them and satisfied herself that she couldn't possibly still be over the limit. She knew that if Maddie were there with her she would be mercilessly teased for her fretting but she didn't care. Maybe she was a bit anal, but better that than forever regretful! Then she remembered her car was still in Braxton. It looked like she was going to have to fork out for another cab.

*   *   *

Surprisingly, Dan looked quite pleased to see her and was more than happy to give her a quick lesson in Victorian constabulary hierarchy. It began to make a bit more sense to her why Lazarus had been so concerned not to hack his Superintendent off too much. The man literally held his officers' careers in his hands. There was very little in the way of Unions in the 1860's. They were beginning to take root, but they had a long way to go before they really began to protect workers. She was stunned to realize that ordinary constables were expected to be sober and upright at all times, whether on duty or off, in uniform or in civvies. Lazarus would have a little more leeway, being an officer and in plain clothes, but even he had to be careful. Had he lost his job through misbehaviour, he could basically wave goodbye to ever getting anything else. Disgraced policemen usually ended up on the streets or in the workhouse, their meagre pensions withheld and their families disowning them. It was a pretty grim prospect whichever way you looked at it. The police were almost universally despised by the general public, who considered they were simply paid snoops for the bosses. The upper classes thought they were poachers turned gamekeepers and trusted them not at all. It was hardly surprising that they became a tight-knit fraternity, but Libby was surprised to find just how deeply that brotherhood ran.

"Of course, you realize that many of them were Masons, don't you?"

"Well, Stonier does mention that his boss is a Mason, but I thought he was something of a one-off."

"Probably not. It became so rife that it bordered upon being a scandal. There were accusations that secret signals were sent from the prisoners in the dock to judges and lawyers in the hope of a favourable outcome to a trial. That's partly why there's such a stink even today when the society is mentioned in regard to the police force."

"I'm not surprised. Life was hard enough without the suspicion that some people were receiving an unfair advantage."

"No-one still knows how true it was. It has to be admitted that there were occasionally very surprising results in trials, but by and large justice seemed to be meted out with equal ferocity to everyone who broke the law."

"From what I've been reading so far, Stonier seems to be hinting that the Superintendent was trying to stop the investigation into the Crabtree boy for a somewhat sinister reason. Do you think it's possible that he was trying to protect the family of a fellow Mason?"

Dan shrugged, "I wonder if there's any way of finding out? It is a secret society, but after so many years, I may be able to dig a little and find names for you. Leave it with me."

They did a little more research, with Dan pointing out the stuff she needed to read and Libby making copious notes, then he announced it was time to shut for the day, "If you need any more, you'll have to come back tomorrow," he said firmly, seeing the big eyes turned upon him with a pleading expression, "I'm not staying here for another minute!"

"Alright," she said reluctantly, gathering up her notebook, pen and handbag, "I don't know about you, but I could do with a drink. Do you have to dash straight home?"

"No, come on," he said promptly, "I'll let you buy me a pint – I deserve it!"

They went into Dan's favourite pub, just across the road, one of the older buildings in Braxton and oddly enough the very place that had once been frequented by Lazarus and Stonier. Libby hadn't realized it was still there and she was enchanted, looking around the place as though it were a stately home instead of a rather ordinary stone built pub, admittedly over three hundred years old, but still the same old coaching inn it had always been.

A pleasant hour passed, their conversation turning eventually from Lazarus to more personal things and for the first time in months Libby felt like a woman again. She was in love with her husband, but she had to admit that he was rather inclined to take her for granted now that they were married. How swiftly they had left romance behind and become 'pipe and slippers'. Just talking to Dan about writing, her past, her interests, her sister and the looming battle with the Allinghams had made her feel strangely energised and interesting. She was actually disappointed when he announced it was time he was making his way home for his delayed evening meal.

"Oh, Daniel, do you have to go?" she asked, with an engaging little smile.

"A, I'm starving, and B, it's not Daniel."

She looked quizzically at him, "Dan's not short for Daniel?" she said in surprise, "Then what is it short for?"

He looked less than pleased at having to admit the truth, "Danby," he answered shortly.

"Danby? Oh, my God, you're named after Lazarus and I never realized!"

"Why would you? It's not something I advertise."

"I think it's a great name," she told him, "And Lazarus is a bit of a hero of mine, you know."

"Oh, good, that makes me feel tons better about being named after a dead Policeman!"

She rose to her feet and impulsively hugged him, "Don't be such a grouch," she said, "You really are hungry, aren't you? Off you go, then. I'll probably see you later in the week. I'm inspired to do a bit more writing now I've got all this new information."

"See you around," he answered and went off smiling about the crazy woman he'd managed to find.

Libby, sensibly, had stayed on orange juice, so she went off too, to find her car and make her reluctant way back home. She realized now that she had simply been finding excuses not to go home and face David. They had a difficult conversation to have and she wasn't particularly looking forward to it.

She was, however, destined to be delayed yet again for as she made her way across the road and past the old Braxton Police Station which now housed the museum, she happened to glance up and notice a man she vaguely recognized. He caught her eye too and stopped, "Hello there," he said.

"Hello," she responded politely, "I know you from somewhere, don't I?"

"You should do."

"Sorry, the name escapes me, very rude, I know, but I'll have to admit it."

"It's Matt Piper and speaking personally, I never forget a woman I've arrested," he said with a grin. Her face fell as it all came flooding back. She was mortified and glanced hurriedly around, "Keep your voice down!" she hissed, "What will people think?"

"What people?" he asked reasonably, "There's no one around."

"Thank God for that," her response was heartfelt which seemed to amuse him even more.

"It's not as though you were guilty of anything, in the end," he added and tried to sound comforting instead of mocking.

"That's hardly the point," Libby looked severely at him, daring him to laugh out loud, "How many people do you know who've even been arrested?"

"Hundreds of 'em," he admitted apologetically and she blushed again, realising she had asked the wrong man that particular question, "Oh, you know what I mean!" she said crossly, "I don't know anyone – oh, except my ex-boyfriend – and, come to think about it, my sister too…" she trailed off, aware that she was making her point very badly.

"Well, that's three for a start – a positive criminal fraternity," he was not even bothering to hide his grin now and Libby felt the time had come to take her leave, "I'd like to say it's been a pleasure, Mr Piper, but I don't think I can. Goodnight."

"Goodnight, Miss Richmond."

"Mrs Wright, actually."

"Of course, I should have remembered. You're down on my list for a visit fairly soon."

"Why? Have I forgotten to tax my car?" she asked sarcastically, then did a hasty mental review just in case she had forgotten to do just that.

"No, but your ex's case will be coming to court in the next couple of months. I need to clarify a few points with you."

"Shouldn't that all be in the hands of my lawyer now?"

"Probably. But I've been told that there's a good chance that Brendan Tulliver is about to change his plea. Seems to think he has something new to add to his story about what happened that day."

The redness in Libby's cheeks drained away so swiftly that Matt thought she might faint and he automatically held out a hand and grasped her elbow to prevent her falling, "Are you alright?"

She shook her head, "No, I don't think I am. That has come as something of a shock to me. I thought it was all over bar the shouting."

He glanced around, "Look, why don't we go in the pub for a minute or two. You look ghastly and I don't want you fainting on me."

"No, I'll be alright. My car's just over there."

"It's none of my business, but if you take my advice, you won't drive until you feel a bit better. You don't have to have a drink, but a sit down will work wonders."

Feeling as shaky as she did, Libby decided he was right. Her legs were barely holding her up and she really doubted she could drive, "Okay. Five more minutes won't make any difference."

Matt went to the bar and came back with a pint for himself and a small brandy for her, "Medicinal," he explained as he put the glass down in front of her, "I'll arrange for a police car to take you home if it's going to put you over the limit."

"It shouldn't. I haven't had any alcohol today."

"Then drink up. It'll do you good."

She sipped the brandy and was surprised to find that she did start to feel better as the warmth flooded into her stomach.

"You might as well give me the bad news now," she said after a moment of silence, "I should have known that slippery bastard would throw more at me."

"Nothing's settled yet, Mrs Wright, so don't worry about it. I don't think now is the time to discuss it. You've obviously had a shock, and I'd really rather talk to you when you're with your husband."

"At least give me a brief outline. I won't be able to sleep for worry if you leave me on tenterhooks."

He pursed his lips, evidently reluctant to say anything at all, but fully aware that having told her half the story, he owed it to her to try and set her mind at rest.

"I don't know the full details, but the gist of it seems to be that he's insisting that your sister misinterpreted what was happening and that he's kept quiet for your sake. He's now realising that he can no longer afford to protect your reputation and has decided that he has to tell the truth."

"The 'truth' being what?" she asked tersely.

"That he wasn't trying to kill you, but that he was actually saving you after you'd tried to hang yourself."

She gasped, "The lying …" she bit back the expletives that sprang to her tongue and swallowed deeply before continuing, "I swear to you, Mr Piper, he's lying. Maddie kneecapped him because he was trying to string me up in the hope that it would look like suicide."

"I believe you, Mrs Wright, but a jury may not, I won't lie to you, I've met him and he's a smooth bugger. He could convince most people of anything. A classic conman. You're going to have your work cut out saving your sister from an attempted murder charge."

CHAPTER TEN

Lazarus 1862

The coroner held the inquest on Mollie Waters early the following morning. It should have been held within twenty-four hours, but the fact that her death had occurred – or at least was discovered – on a Sunday, had prompted a slight delay.

As he and Stonier took their seats they were both astounded to see Superintendent Gregson. It was not his habit to attend inquests – or indeed any occasion at all that he could safely avoid. They could only imagine he had a good reason and it was not very long before they discovered what it was. He stood and took the lead in the proceedings, much to the chagrin of Sir Alan Corfield, the coroner.

In his usual pompous manner he began to expound his theory that Mollie Waters' death had been of natural causes. His tone seemed to brook no argument and Lazarus realized that in putting forward an opposite view to this assertion he was about to put his career on the line. He was just preparing to stand and protest, but was saved the trouble. Dr Scattergood, it seemed, had begun to suspect something of the sort might be mooted and had made sure he was there to lay his own evidence. This in itself was unusual as the doctor, feeling, as he did, that he was already quite generous enough with his time, normally left the paperwork and the official niceties to the policemen and was as avid as the Superintendent at absenting himself from such occasions on the understanding that he was far too busy to be bothered with such onerous duties. Lazarus wondered what had gone on in the background to produce this startling event. He knew his boss and the doctor disliked each other, but this type of public battle was unheard of, at least in his experience.

Someone had wanted very much to see Mollie Waters' death

swept under the carpet – someone who had enough clout to persuade the Superintendent of Braxton Police to try and suppress evidence. Possibly it was the Superintendent himself, but Lazarus found himself hoping that he wasn't going to have to investigate his own superior officer. Fortunately Dr Scattergood was not so easily bought and he tore the Superintendent to ribbons with less thought than he would swat a fly, "Don't talk such poppycock, man," he growled as Superintendent Gregson almost ordered the coroner to dismiss the case, "the girl died of poisoning, whether by her own hand or someone else's I have no idea, but it certainly was not natural – not unless you count the fact that toadstools grow in the wild – that could, I suppose, pass for a 'natural' death."

Superintendent Gregson's jowls grew crimson with annoyance, "I think you'll find, doctor, that I am speaking. If the coroner so chooses, you shall have your chance to give your opinion – for what it is worth."

Sir Alan evidently thought it was his moment to intervene, "Thank you, Superintendent, for your valuable contribution, but I think I would like to hear from the doctor, now, if you please."

Gregson very obviously did not 'please' but he had no choice but to retake his seat and allow the doctor to take the makeshift stand and prepare to give his evidence.

"Now, Doctor, you were telling us about the death of Miss Waters," said Sir Alan, looking pointedly at the Superintendent.

"Indeed I was, sir. The young woman died of ingesting toxic toadstools."

"You are sure of this?"

"I am. I force-fed the contents of her stomach to a rat. It was dead within minutes."

The Superintendent rose to his feet, "What proof do we have as to the health of this rat? It could already have been dying."

"Sit down, sir," said Sir Alan severely, "You shall be ejected from this hearing if you speak again uninvited."

Lazarus and Stonier exchanged an amused glance as he obeyed, his face a picture of suppressed fury.

"Go on, doctor,"

"Thank you, Sir Alan. As I was saying, the death was caused by poison, and in my opinion, it is beyond the bounds of possibility that she died by anything other than foul play. Murder is the most likely cause, but it could equally be criminal negligence or suicide. For my own part I have strong doubts about the latter."

"Why is that?"

"I suggest you call the landlady to give evidence on that point, sir, but take it from me, the victim must have cooked and eaten the poison elsewhere and not at her lodgings."

"What makes you so sure?"

"The household is a poor one. Eggs and mushrooms are rare treats. And Miss Waters was no cook. I find it difficult to believe that she would have taken the trouble to kill herself by cooking toadstools in someone else's kitchen. It defies all logic."

"If the balance of her mind was disturbed?" questioned the coroner gently. He evidently wanted to give Dr Scattergood every opportunity to make his point, but he also had to explore all possibilities.

"The balance of her mind may well have been disturbed, she had, after all, found herself about to become an unmarried mother – but the owner of the kitchen? Would you allow someone to cook and eat food in your house, knowing full well they had a place of their own? No, I'm sorry. The very idea is preposterous!"

"The very idea that her death was anything other than a tragic accident is preposterous!" snapped Superintendent Gregson.

"You've been warned, Superintendent."

Gregson obviously decided he could do no more so he left the room before he could be thrown out. After his departure the giving of evidence went much more smoothly. The landlady seemed, for once, to be in awe of her surroundings and was surprisingly polite and helpful. She confirmed everything the doctor had said. Miss Waters had certainly not cooked or eaten anything in her house that fateful night.

Sir Alan called upon Inspector Lazarus to answer some questions.

"Inspector, since you are the man who will be required to investigate this case, should it be ruled 'foul play' do you feel there is sufficient evidence that the young lady met her death by a hand other than her own?"

"I fear it may be so, sir."

"In your professional opinion, is there a case to answer?"

"Yes, sir."

"And do you have any suspects in mind?"

"I do, sir, but I would be reluctant to name them here and now. It would be grossly unfair to cast suspicion before those parties had the opportunity to defend themselves."

"Quite right too," Said Sir Alan decidedly, "Very well, Inspector. I will adjourn the case for three weeks to give you time to investigate. A verdict will be forthcoming on the strength of your discoveries in that time."

"Thank you, sir."

Very shortly after that pronouncement almost everyone filed out. Sir Alan engaged in a quiet but obviously intense conversation with Dr Scattergood. Lady Corfield, who was waiting for her husband, delayed Lazarus with a gentle hand on his arm, "My dear Inspector, may I just say how much I admire what you and Dr Scattergood did just now? For you, especially, it would have been far simpler to let that young lady's death pass as an accident or even natural causes. It was quite obvious to me that Superintendent Gregson would have much preferred it that way. I hope he is not able to cause too much trouble for you."

Lazarus smiled grimly, "I suspect you hope in vain, my Lady, but thank you for your kind words."

She looked most concerned, "I should have a word with my husband, surely he can exercise some control over your superior? It would be scandalous if he should be able to damage your career when you are merely doing your job – and doing it well."

"All may yet be well, madam. The superintendent must have his reasons for his opinion and may have his mind changed if I can produce enough evidence to convince him."

"Promise me, then, that you will call upon our aid, should you need it."

"You have my word upon it."

He joined Stonier outside in the fresh air and without saying a word they made their way back to the police station.

"What next, sir?" asked Stonier, once they were back in their office. Lazarus held out his hand, "Since when have I been 'sir' when we're alone, old friend? How would it be if I apologized and agreed that young Miss Allingham needs finding and that you were entirely right to be concerned about her?"

Stonier grinned and took the out-stretched hand, "Nothing to stop us doing both jobs, Dan. I bet a lot of the same ground needs to be covered. Seems to me that there's a good chance Miss Waters was killed by one of the gentry and Miss Allingham comes from their ranks. Who knows, the two cases might even be connected." He said it as a joke, but Lazarus looked sharply at him, "You know Tom, that's not beyond the limits of possibility. This is a small town. It could be that we have a fellow who has a downer on the fair sex."

"God, I hope not," answered Tom emphatically, "I can't think of anything more blood-curdling."

"Call yourself a policeman," mocked Lazarus, and the two friends laughed, perfectly in tune once again.

To show his genuine remorse Lazarus generously suggested that they pursue the line of enquiry regarding young Miss Allingham first. In truth he had the slightest hint of misgiving now that Stonier had made his suggestion that the two cases might be related in some way. He doubted that the girl was in any danger, but just supposing Tom was right and she had fallen into the hands of a killer? He would never forgive himself if anything unpleasant now befell her. It was enough that he had to carry the guilt of failing Decima Watkins. He never intended to feel that way again.

"So, where to begin? Do we know anything about this fellow Miss Allingham ran off with, other than his name?"

Stonier fell into step beside him, "As far as I know, our Miss Allingham didn't supply much information, but her maid, Sal Mulligan, may know something. Servants always know more than they let on."

"This is going to involve a lot of leg work and knocking on doors, if you ask me. A task then, for young Constable Newhouse – he's always annoyingly enthusiastic. Let's give him something to expend his excess energy on."

Lazarus was still evidently feeling a mite cynical, thought Stonier, wondering vaguely what ailed his friend and if there might be a remedy to restore his normal good humour. He knew for a fact that Lazarus had always liked Newhouse and thought him just the sort of man they needed in the police force.

"Didn't our Miss Allingham mention a letter? We should demand to see it. There might be a postmark or some other clue to his whereabouts."

Lazarus reacted with a surly growl, "Stop calling her 'our' Miss Allingham, she's nothing of the kind!"

"I only meant to differentiate between her and the absconder," said Stonier mildly.

"Well find another soubriquet for her," advised Lazarus.

"No matter what I call her, we're going to have to interview her again," responded the older man.

"Dammit, I suppose you're right."

"You make it sound a chore, speaking to a pretty young woman," exclaimed Stonier, barely able to hide his amusement.

"Is she pretty? I can't say I noticed."

"Then you've been alone too long, my friend," said Stonier, suddenly grim, leaving his shocked companion standing on the steps as he marched into the station, oblivious of the hurt he had unthinkingly inflicted.

Lazarus followed him in but they were both fortunately distracted by the arrival of a breathless and excited Will, who obviously had news that he couldn't wait to share,

"Oh, Mr Lazarus, sir, you'll never guess what's happened," he panted, tripping over his own words in his eagerness to impart.

"Then I shan't bother wasting my time trying to do so," asserted Lazarus, "Speak out, young fellow, what's going on?"

"I've been offered another job," breathed Will, as reverently as though he were speaking of a miracle, "Think of it. Me with two jobs. My ma'll be the queen of our street."

Stonier slapped the boy heartily on the shoulder, "That's grand, lad, well done."

"It's all down to you and Mr Lazarus, sir. You sending me for a paper every morning got the fellow who sells them interested in me. He said that if the police trusted me to fetch and carry for them, I must be an honest lad. He's given me the task of selling papers for him. I'm to collect the papers every morning, sell them on the street and he'll collect the takings every Friday. For every fifty I sell, I'm to keep a shilling."

Lazarus smiled, but his eyes remained hard, "Good for you, young shaver, but I think I'll have a word with your new master. I think he can do a little better than that." He nodded towards Stonier, "Start on finding Marcus Soper, Sergeant, while I have a word in the ear of out local newspaper vendor."

Half an hour later young Will was gasping with delight at the notion that he would now be receiving a shilling for every thirty-five papers he sold and his new employer's ears were ringing with the quietly spoken threats uttered by his friendly neighbourhood policeman.

As they walked back to the station Lazarus felt impelled to offer his young protégé a few timely words of advice, "Listen to me, Will, he may have offered you a job, but be wary of that man. He's a sharp one and you need to be on your guard. You're also going to be in possession of quite a lot of money at various times. You need a place to hide it and you need to keep your wits about you. No bragging about your two jobs, or having cash in the house. You understand that, don't you?"

"I know what I'm doing, Mr Lazarus, you can rely on me, I promise."

Looking down at the bright, open face, so full of optimism for the future, Lazarus hadn't the heart to point out that it wasn't Will he didn't trust, but every other scoundrel who wandered the streets looking for just such pigeons to pluck.

CHAPTER ELEVEN

After some deliberation they decided to call on the Crabtree residence first, mainly because it was the nearer of the two properties. It took the better part of an hour to sign out the only police vehicle Braxton police possessed, then harness the horse.

"All this for a gig," muttered Lazarus when they were finally underway, "It would have been less trouble to hire a carriage from the ostler at the King's Head."

"Yes, but that would have cost you two shillings. At least this is free," pointed out Stonier crossly. He'd been the one who had filled in the forms and persuaded the recalcitrant nag in between the shafts.

Seeing the house, the policeman wondered anew at Lawrence Crabtree associating with the likes of Mollie Waters. Of course, they had only seen her as a corpse, so they had only a vague idea of how pretty she had really been, but still it seemed unlikely. The place was vast and imposing, set in its own gardens, a long gravelled drive leading to a large turning circle outside the porticoed front door. It was built of local red sandstone, the sort that darkened almost to the colour of blood when it rained, and its tall, twisted chimneys were visible above the tree line from the road. It lay on the outskirts of town. Near enough for convenience, far enough away to grant privacy and freedom from the polluted air of the manufactury which was growing with every passing year in Braxton and its neighbouring towns and villages. Once this had been countryside, pure and simple, but industrialisation was creeping into every corner of England. Fast flowing rivers that had once been useful for nothing more than water and fish were now sources of power and a means of getting rid of effluent and other waste materials, their banks were now lined with mills instead of wildflowers.

Men like Sir Walter Crabtree had of course fully benefited from all this change and had built houses that reflected their newly elevated position in society. Lazarus was fully aware that he needed to tread carefully. Those who were novices at being gentry were so much more touchy about their reputations, unlike the innate arrogance of those who were born and bred over hundreds of years of aristocracy.

"We'd better handle this carefully," he murmured to Stonier as they drew to a halt outside the front door, "Not a word about why we're here until we've established that he even knew Mollie. At the moment we have nothing more than the word of a shop-girl, plausible though she seems."

"I'll leave it to you, sir," said Tom firmly, showing he had no intention of even stepping down from the gig.

"Thanks, friend!"

Lazarus needn't have worried. He was destined to get no further than the front door. It was answered by a supercilious individual who looked down his nose at the policeman, giving the distinct impression that he thought their proper place would have been the tradesman's entrance.

"Good day, sir, can I be of assistance?"

Lazarus knew he had never met a man who had less intention of ever being of assistance.

"Good day, I should like to speak to Mr Lawrence Crabtree if he is at home."

"I'm sorry, Mr Lawrence is not at home."

"You're sure of that, are you?"

"Yes sir, quite sure."

Stonier cleared his throat and Lazarus, recognising a coded message, glanced at him. Stonier jerked his head in the direction of a low hedge, beyond which was a tennis court. Four young men, in white flannels, were playing a raucous game. When Lazarus stopped to listen, he heard several names called out, one of which was 'Lawrie'.

He turned a stern gaze on the butler, "Perhaps you'd like to go and see again if you can't find your young master?"

"By all means, but you'll find that Mr Lawrence is not at home to you."

Lazarus took out his warrant and showed it to the man, "I think he might be at home to the police."

"I can assure you, he will not. Good day, sir."

With that the door was shut in his face.

Lazarus was livid, he lifted his hand to hammer on the door, but Stonier called him away, "Don't waste your time, Danby. They'll only make a complaint to the Superintendent. There's more than one way to skin a cat."

"You think so? I'd be very interested to hear it?"

"We're off to see Miss Allingham, aren't we?"

"Yes, And?"

"And she'll know young Mr Crabtree. I'll be bound she'll help us speak to him, on the quiet like, without his pa knowing."

"You could be right, but I'm reluctant to ask for favours."

"Well, take your choice, but you'll either be asking her, or you'll be begging the superintendent for permission to interview him and I know who I'd rather approach."

"Dammit, Tom, why are you always right about everything?"

Tom grinned, "Come on, old fellow, we'll have it dark before we get back to town at this rate."

The Allinghams' was even larger and more impressive than the Crabtrees', but Lazarus had ceased to really notice the opulence, even though it took them fifteen minutes to get from the lodge at the gates to the front of the house. He now had an object in sight and he tended to be rather single-minded under those circumstances. It was for that reason that he was short and to the point when he spoke to the housemaid who answered the door, "I'd like to see Miss Allingham, if you please."

She looked flustered and nervously twisted her hands in her apron, "I'm sorry, sir, but Miss Arabella is unwell at the present time. If you'd care to wait for a moment, I'll fetch Mr Taplow."

"Who the devil is Mr Taplow?"

"Lord Allingham's butler, sir. I … I don't usually answer the door, but the family are in the garden taking tea, and Mr Taplow is waiting on them."

"I don't want to see Taplow, or anyone else. I require Miss …" he suddenly realized he had no idea of Miss Allingham's first name. He glanced towards Stonier, who shrugged eloquently. He didn't know it either.

"The young lady I require is Lord Allingham's niece."

"Oh, you mean Miss Constance? She's in the small drawing room. Who shall I tell her is calling?"

"There's no need to announce us. Miss Allingham is expecting us." Lazarus knew that on the strength of that obvious lie he would never have put a foot over the doorstep had the butler been on duty, but this little 'tweeny' had no more idea how to keep him out than a babe in arms. She sketched a hasty curtsey as she allowed them past her and into the cool and cavernous hallway, "This way, sir." Their footsteps echoed noisily as they followed her. As they passed the grand staircase Stonier nudged him and nodded his head towards one of many portraits hanging along the wall. It was a young, dark-haired man, resplendent in his army uniform – none other than the late Richard Allingham esquire, who had courted Decima Watkins – a liaison which had ended in his death on the battlefield and hers on the gallows. Lazarus looked grimly at it for the briefest of moments, then walked on.

The 'small' drawing room was four times larger than the entire downstairs of Stonier's little cottage and furnished elegantly with quality and taste. The two men exchanged another telling glance.

Constance Allingham was sitting on the cushioned window seat, her sewing lying idle in her lap, an expression of wistfulness adorning her features as she gazed out onto the lawn where a seemingly riotous game of croquet was in full swing. From their position by the door, Stonier and Lazarus couldn't quite see the players from, but they could hear the calls and laughter through the open casement, as well as the 'tock' of the wooden mallets hitting the croquet balls.

Lazarus indicated with a wave of his hand that the servant was dismissed and she scurried away, worrying now that she had done wrong in letting them enter.

"Not playing, Miss Allingham?" he asked, by way of making

their presence known. She looked towards the sound of his voice, startled, then her face relaxed when she realized who it was, "Not invited, Mr Lazarus," she replied, "As a poor relation my duty is clear, I must keep company with my poor, sick cousin."

"It is, of course, about your cousin that I call."

She rose swiftly to her feet and crossed the room, coming suddenly to her senses, "Good gracious, Mr Lazarus, you should not be here at all! My uncle would be most displeased if he knew. We are supposed to be treating this whole matter with the greatest discretion."

"Fear not. No one knows Stonier and I are here."

"But should anyone come into the house, we are undone. You must leave at once."

"But we need to speak to you. There are things we need to know if we are to progress any further with the case."

She looked anxiously towards the window and seemed relieved that the game was apparently undisturbed, "Very well, but not here. Take the road into the village and I shall endeavour to meet you there in a few minutes."

"Whereabouts?"

"There is a small tearoom by the green, run by two elderly and extremely genteel ladies, who have fallen on hard times and are forced to earn a living. I shall be there in half an hour."

The policemen allowed themselves to be ushered swiftly out of the door and into their waiting gig, "Go, quickly, please," she begged, casting nervous glances over her shoulder, "I'll not be far behind you."

As the gig sped down the drive Stonier remarked thoughtfully, "It's a bit of a rum do when a man treats his own flesh and blood like a glorified servant just because she doesn't have any money."

"No more odd than being more concerned for his own reputation than his daughter's welfare."

"Bloody funny lot the aristocracy."

Lazarus looked even grimmer than was his wont these days, "They don't amuse me, old friend."

They found the tea-room – which was actually the ladies' front room – with no trouble at all, and discovered that they were the only customers of the day. Since it had rarely been warmer, they were not really surprised by this and gladly accepted the offer of tea in the garden instead of inside.

The Misses Penney had set up a table under the shade of a large oak tree and happily buzzed around the two men, fetching tea and cakes and providing cushions for the wooden chairs. Lazarus explained they were expecting Miss Allingham to join them and the two ladies immediately went into transports of delight, exclaiming how kind and pleasant Miss Allingham always was, and how she had no airs about her at all. Stonier smiled and Lazarus grunted with a distinct lack of grace. Not every poor person could tell the difference, he remarked to Tom after their departure, between being patronised and genuine civility.

"I can't believe you're still holding it against that poor lass that she's a member of the Allingham family."

"The apple doesn't fall far from the tree," said Lazarus and helped himself to a cucumber sandwich.

"I hope one falls right on your head," muttered Stonier with a grin. Lazarus was spared having to answer by the timely arrival of Miss Allingham, rather pink in the face and wearing her riding habit.

"I came as quickly as I could," she said, a trifle breathlessly, "And I decided riding would draw less attention than asking for a carriage."

"Thank you for seeing us," replied Stonier, "Please, take a seat. Would you like some tea?"

"Oh, yes please."

There was a short delay whilst the ladies brought another cup and saucer and then they all drank tea and made short work of the sandwiches, cakes and scones which made up their repast.

Miss Allingham was on her second cup before she asked, "Well, gentlemen, what was it you wanted of me?"

"We need to see the letter sent to your uncle," answered Lazarus bluntly, "Frankly we have nothing to go on except your word that young Arabella isn't perfectly happy where she is. You've provided us with very little information on this fellow Soper, but you expect us to search the country for the pair of them. It's simply not feasible Miss Allingham."

Stonier winced slightly at the forthright way Lazarus spoke to her, but strangely she seemed not to take offence, instead frowning a little and saying reasonably, "I do see your difficulty, Mr Lazarus. My uncle is asking rather too much of you. He should have known that it was far too difficult a task for you."

Lazarus, touched on the raw by her lack of faith in his abilities, immediately retracted, "I didn't say we can't find your cousin, just that you are throwing obstructions in our path. Either you wish to co-operate or you do not."

"Very well, I will ask my uncle to give the letter to me and, if he will allow me to I will bring it to the police station tomorrow. Was there anything else?"

"Yes, as a matter of fact there is. We need you to tell us a little more about your cousin."

"What sort of things?"

"Who her friends are, who she confides in, who she trusts. If we are to find her, we need to know if there is any possibility that she told someone where she intended to go."

The colour drained from her face, "Oh, dear me, no. I can't allow you to go around asking questions like that! Where's the secrecy if you are going to blunder about asking people if Arabella ever talked about running away from home?"

Not surprisingly Lazarus took exception to the expression 'blundering about' and Stonier, seeing his face, hastily intervened, "I think you can trust us to be a little more delicate than that, Miss Allingham, but we do need to explore every avenue if we are to return the young lady to the bosom of her family swiftly and with her reputation untarnished."

She looked mollified even if Lazarus did not.

"I suppose I have no choice."

"Not if you want the girl back," growled the inspector. She looked at him, her lips folded stubbornly,

"Are you suggesting that we do not want her back?" she enquired coldly.

"You are giving a damned good impression of cold-hearted indifference," he snapped back, "Which is more important? Your uncle's pride or Arabella's safety?"

"Everything is so very clear to you, isn't it, inspector? Very black and white! It wouldn't occur to you for a moment that our discretion is as much for Arabella's sake as the family's! If this becomes common knowledge, she will lose forever any chance of making a decent match. What man would want to marry another's leavings?" She faltered into silence, fully aware that her annoyance had led her into speaking far too frankly. The cheeks that had been pale only seconds before now flooded with hot blood and she lowered her eyes, unable to meet his unwavering gaze.

There was an uncomfortable silence, broken only by the drowsy cooing of a fat pigeon in the branches above their heads.

Stonier realized that it was going to be up to him to bring both these hot-headed young people to their senses, "Evidently this warm weather is beginning to have an effect on everyone's temper. Might I suggest we have more tea and Miss Allingham can have a little think about anyone who knows Arabella well enough to have her best interests at heart."

She transferred her eyes gratefully to his face, "A very sensible suggestion, sergeant, and couched in those terms, I have just recalled the very person we need. Arabella has a godmother, Lady Diana Stafford-Naylor, whom she adores."

Lazarus looked unconvinced, "Is the young lady likely to confide such secrets to an adult – especially a woman who is meant to be her spiritual guide in life?"

Constance laughed heartily and Lazarus looked irritated, "I was not aware I had said anything amusing."

"That's because you don't know Lady Stafford-Naylor, my dear inspector. Spiritual guide, indeed! I think not. She is the most dreadful scandal-maker you're ever likely to come across – which is precisely why Arabella likes her."

"Then what on earth possessed your beloved uncle to place her in a position of importance in the life of his precious daughter?"

There was a fleeting expression of distaste on her face when he referred to her 'beloved' uncle, but she allowed it to pass, simply answering succinctly, "Money, of course. What else?"

"Hasn't he enough of that himself?"

"Have you ever known a rich man to have enough? Lady Stafford-Naylor is not only generous, she is hopelessly extravagant and her husband is as rich as Croesus. Lord Allingham hopes that a large proportion of Arabella's dowry will come directly from her godmother."

"So he turns a blind eye to her reputation?" guessed Stonier.

"Of course. Anything can be forgiven if one has money to spare."

"Exactly what sort of a scandal are we speaking of?" asked Lazarus wearily, he was beginning to find all these machinations fairly appalling. What morals did the aristocracy actually have?

"I don't gossip," said Constance stiffly.

"Of course you do. All women do," said Lazarus bluntly. She opened her mouth to furiously refute the suggestion, but Stonier laid a restraining hand on her arm, "It's not gossip, Miss Allingham, you are assisting the police with their enquiries."

She glared at Lazarus, who merely grinned infuriatingly at her, "Do go on, Miss," he said encouragingly.

"You're impossible!" she snapped at him then went on, "If you insist, Sergeant Stonier, I shall tell you." She shifted in her seat so that Lazarus was literally given the cold shoulder and she pretended not to hear his unkind snigger.

"It was all a long time ago, you understand, so I don't know the truth of half of what is said, but the rumour is that Diana was Lord Stafford-Naylor's mistress for years before his first wife died. They say she was – well, no better than she ought to be – in her youth and that he rescued her from a house of ill-repute."

"Very laudable of him," murmured Lazarus, with barely concealed amusement, mostly at Miss Allingham's obvious embarrassment. Stonier, with his usual talent for defusing awkward situations, interjected diffidently, "Forgive me for saying so, but this woman may not have been the best choice of godparent for a wilful young Miss like Arabella. It is quite possible that her tales of the past have convinced the young lady that she needs to have very little concern for the strictures of her parents."

"You could well be right, Sergeant, but it is rather late in the day to put such ideas out of her head."

"Very true. Well, where will we find Lady Stafford-Naylor?"

Constance provided them with the information, then rose to her feet, "I should be getting back. I'll be missed if I'm not careful."

"There was one more thing," said Stonier, smiling kindly at her, "If we could ask a favour of you, Miss?"

"You may ask," she answered, "As to whether I indulge you, that's another matter."

"Naturally. There is no obligation on your part."

"So long as that is clearly understood," she sniffed and threw a contemptuous look towards Lazarus, who was brushing away a noisome fly and seemed to be totally ignoring her.

"You are acquainted with young Lawrence Crabtree?"

"Lawrie? Yes, of course I am."

"Do you think you could arrange for us to have a quiet word with the young man? We have tried to see him this afternoon, but an overly-officious butler prevented us."

"I'm sure I could help with that, in fact I don't know why we didn't think of him sooner. Of course he was a friend of Marcus Soper, wasn't he?"

"We sincerely hope so, but until we've spoken to him, we can't be sure."

"I see. Well, I'll see what I can do, but surely you have the power to simply insist that he talks to you?"

"In theory, Miss, of course we do, but his father is a friend of our Superintendent and we have to tread carefully."

"Oh, there is someone in this world who holds a whip hand over you, then?" she asked sarcastically, "How very odd! I thought Inspector Lazarus was a law unto himself!"

"Not quite, Miss," answered Stonier with a grin.

CHAPTER TWELVE

PRESENT

Libby looked so shocked that Matt regretted being quite so blunt. He wished he could get her another brandy, but it hardly seemed the right thing to do, knowing that she had to drive home.

"Look, I'm sorry. I should have waited until you were with your husband before I sprung that on you. Do you want me to arrange a police car to take you home?"

"No, I'll be fine. I just thought it was going to be cut and dried. I have to admit that I didn't think Brendan would rake all that stuff up again."

Matt raised a quizzical brow, "You mean he's said things like this before?"

Libby could hear the note of doubt creeping into his voice. She was such an idiot! When would she ever learn to think before she spoke? Now he was thinking that Brendan might have a point – that he was telling the truth and she was the one who was volatile and possibly violent.

"He tried to convince my mother that I was suicidal when my aunt Lil was dying."

"Why would he do that?"

"Because he wanted to punish me for daring to leave him – and he likes playing with people's heads."

He detected the fury in her voice and immediately strove to calm her – the last thing he needed was a scene, if she really was unstable. That was the trouble with an accusation of insanity, he thought ruefully, it always brought out the worst in the victim and tended to rather prove the case, even if they were normally the most placid soul to walk the earth.

"We all know he's a classic manipulator," he admitted carefully.

"Hah! Understatement of the year," said Libby bitterly.

"Well, don't let him win by rising to it," counselled Matt, "If I were you, I'd try and put it out of my head. Wait and see what happens in court. You know that you are telling the truth, and I'm sure that will shine through when you face the jury."

She looked at him as though she couldn't quite believe how naîve he was being, "You're kidding, right? You really think I won't fall apart in court when faced with an accomplished liar and conman like Brendan Tulliver?"

"Bottom line, Libby, you can't afford to fall apart. Unless you are convincing, your sister is going down for malicious wounding at the very least."

It was harsh, but funnily enough it was just what she needed. There was too much at stake to start letting Brendan get to her. She drew in a deep breath, "You're right. I'll be okay. I'll talk to David and Maddie. We need a plan of action."

He reached out and briefly patted her shoulder, "Good for you," he said briskly, "Never let the bastards grind you down. Now, I have to go – are you sure you're going to be alright?"

"Yeah, I'm fine. Thanks, Inspector."

"No problem. I'll be out to see you in the next few days, make it all official, but suffice it to say, I'm on your side. Tulliver is a creep and we'll see that he gets what's coming to him."

He rose to his feet and Libby suddenly recalled that she could use his help with her book. A bit of insight into police work would be invaluable.

"Just before you go, can I ask you about a completely different subject?"

"Sure, what is it?"

"I've started writing a book ..."

He looked startled and retook his seat, "If it's about the case, I'd advise you very strongly against it, at least until you've been to court – and even then, I'd think twice. Tulliver could have you for libel if you word it wrongly."

She grinned at the note of mild panic in his voice – policemen certainly took the law very seriously! "Relax," she said placidly, "It's nothing to do with that – in fact it's set in the past, but I thought you could provide a bit of atmosphere. It's a murder mystery of sorts and if anyone knows about that, it's a real police Inspector."

His face took on a strange, closed expression and all friendliness suddenly evaporated, "Been listening to gossip, Mrs Wright?" he said tightly.

It was Libby's turn to look startled, "No, what do you mean? What gossip? Have I said something I ought not? I apologise if I have."

He stared at her for several long seconds before he seemed convinced that she was genuinely puzzled by his reaction. He forced a short laugh, "Sorry, you hit on a sore subject."

"No, it's me who should be sorry – and I am. Please, forget I said anything. I'll pump someone else for information."

He drew in a breath and shook his head, "It's fine. An over-reaction on my part. And though I probably can't help you with your book, I know someone who can."

"Really? Who?"

"My partner happens to be Tess Brookes."

Libby's mouth dropped open slightly, "The Tess Brookes?" she asked breathlessly, "The writer?"

"That's the one."

"Wow." Libby was horrified that she couldn't find anything more erudite to say, but she really was rendered speechless by this piece of information. Tess Brookes was one of her favourite authors and Libby was extremely serious now about her writing. The very thought of having access to someone who knew the publishing industry like Tess Brookes was an amazing stroke of luck.

"Would you really introduce me to her?"

"I'll certainly ask her if she objects to meeting you. She's pretty reclusive these days, but not a complete hermit."

Light suddenly dawned, "Didn't she have all that trouble last year, with the stalker and the horrible accident in the bath-tub?"

"She did," he said grimly, "And I wouldn't mention that to her, if you want her help."

"Of course not," Libby said fervently, then she glanced at him with a tiny knowing smile, "Is that how you met?"

"It is – but don't even think about putting that in your book!"

"I wouldn't dream of it. When can I meet her?"

"I'll be in touch," he said, "Don't count your chickens though. She's quite fragile and may not want to see anyone."

"I understand, but I'd be so grateful if you could arrange it."

"I'll do my best."

On impulse Libby leapt to her feet and grabbing Matt's arm, she planted a resounding kiss on his cheek, "Thanks, Inspector."

He pretended to frown, "Stop with the Inspector, will you? It's Matt. We might as well cut the formality since it looks like we may be seeing quite a bit of each other over the next couple of months."

"Thanks Matt." she said dutifully, and grinned happily as she watched him walk away.

* * *

David still wasn't home when she arrived but she did find a young woman sitting on the doorstep.

"Can I help?" she asked, somewhat surprised, but determined to be polite. Her visitor hastily stood up and threw away the cigarette she had been smoking, "Oh, hi. I'm looking for Mrs Libby Wright."

"You've found her – so long as you're not religious or selling something, in which case, I've never heard of her."

The girl laughed and tucked her shoulder-length, blond hair behind her ear, "Neither of the above," she said, "Actually, I'm a journalist and I was hoping you'd give me an interview."

Libby frowned in genuine puzzlement, "You want to talk to me? What on earth for? I'm not famous or indeed infamous, am I?"

"Not yet, but give us time," answered the blond with a friendly grin.

"So, what's it all about then?"

"Well, I did try and speak to your sister, but she wasn't interested."

"Ah," said Libby, truth dawning, "this is all about the Allinghams, is it?"

"In a way – but they're not talking and neither is your sister. How about you? Want to share your views with my readers?"

Libby's first instinct was to do as everyone else involved had done and send the woman on her way, but something stopped her. The reality was that if she was ever to get her book published, she would need friends in the media. She could appear to be co-operating with the journalist without ever actually giving anything important away – and who knew how useful she might be in the future? She weighed up her options for several long seconds before she jerked her head in a gesture of invitation,

"Fancy a cuppa?" she asked.

"Sure do. I've been waiting hours for you to come back, I'm parched."

"Come on, then."

It seemed to Libby that she did most of the interviewing whilst they waited for the kettle to boil. Her visitor's name was Joanne Pooley and she had been an aspiring journalist for just over three years. She was working on the local paper, but was looking for her big story that would take her off to the bright lights of London – or at least to Manchester or Birmingham anyway. She had heard about Maddie's battle with the Allinghams through a friend of a friend and she thought it was fascinating.

"Well, you know it really doesn't concern me," said Libby, handing her a mug of tea, "This is entirely Maddie and my father's affair. They are the supposed heirs – I'm the youngest and not likely to inherit unless they both pop their clogs."

"Even so, it does affect you, albeit indirectly. If Maddie is proved right, you're suddenly related to one of the richest, most powerful families in the country – how does that make you feel?"

"I hadn't really thought much about it, to be honest. I've been too busy getting on with my own obsessions."

"And what would they be?"

Libby saw no harm in telling her – in fact it could be valuable to be mentioned as a potential writer of fiction. Who knew who might read the article?

"I acquired some diaries and notes about a Victorian policeman called Danby Lazarus. Fascinating stuff – so I've been writing a novel based on them."

"Sounds brilliant," said Joanne enthusiastically, "where did you find the research material?"

Libby didn't really see any harm in telling her, but if there was one thing she had learned over the past couple of years was that what she thought of as being harmless, others seemed not to agree. She couldn't mention Dan's involvement just in case it made trouble for him with his employers at the museum. He had told Libby that the diaries were his own property, but what if he had been stretching the truth and they were actually the property of the local authority or something? She could lose him his job if she wasn't careful.

"Oh, you know, here and there," she answered vaguely.

"Ooh, secrets!" teased Joanne, "I'm obviously going to have to worm that info out of you!"

"No chance," Libby assured her with a grin, "I've learned my lesson about opening my big, fat mouth!"

"It sounds as if there's a story there too," prompted Joanne, "What on earth did you do? Cause a scandal, or just hacked a few people off?"

"You don't catch me that easily," said Libby, "let's just say that if it hadn't been for my digging, we wouldn't have even known about our connection with the Allinghams."

"Well, that's already in the public domain, so why not tell me about that?" ventured the journalist, seeming to sip her coffee with nonchalance.

Libby didn't see any harm in that story, so she began, "It all started when my Aunt Lil found out she was dying. She'd been doing the family history years before, then life, as it does, took over, and for ages and ages she was too busy raising a family and running the small-holding. I guess the reality of her own mortality made her think about things again and she invited me here to look after her, but it was really to help her finish the story. She had found out that our great, great, great Aunt had been hanged for murder ..."

"Bloody hell!" breathed Joanne, "That's quite a skeleton to keep in the family cupboard."

"You're telling me. My mother was furious that Aunt Lil had brought it all up again. She was still stinging from finding out she married into the murderous clan. She was determined to stop Lil telling the world about it. Of course that just meant I was all the more determined not to brush it under the carpet."

"Rocky relationship with your ma?" questioned Joanne sympathetically.

"It was never great, but it sank like a stone when I found out she was sleeping with my ex," said Libby bitterly. She didn't even bother to stop and reflect that such a revelation might not be the wisest thing to tell a hack. The truth was Joanne was so easy to talk to and it had been so long since she had seen her old friends that she had all too easily fallen into the trap of thinking that Joanne was being friendly for friendship's sake and not for her own agenda.

"Your ex being Brendan Tulliver?"

"Yes, the rat."

"That is quite a betrayal, kid," said Joanne, "I'm not sure which of them is the worst. It must have been devastating for you."

"I've had better days."

"I'll bet, but carry on with your story. It is fascinating. I'm surprised you're not writing about all this."

"I've been advised not to – not until the court case is over, anyway."

"Of course. The CPS wouldn't take very kindly to reading about all that in the Sunday papers, would they? Brendan is about to appear in court, isn't he, with your sister?"

"Exactly. So no mention of him, if you don't mind. Stick to me in your piece – if indeed you don't think I'm too boring to interview."

"Boring? Are you kidding, Libby? I'm gripped. Go on about the great Aunt."

Libby continued with her tale, explaining how the heir to the Allingham's met Decima Watkins when he was invited to her home by her soldier brother and how the young couple fell in love, much to the horror of both sets of parents. The Allinghams thought the Watkins were common upstarts, who were trying to grab themselves an advantageous marriage for their youngest daughter. Ironically the Watkins took the opposite stance. Decima had been rendered almost deaf by a childhood ailment, probably measles, and Mr Watkins had long decided that she should never be allowed to marry or produce possibly handicapped children. As the youngest daughter she had been treated as little better than a servant, forced to help her older siblings with their own families, and destined to be a spinster caring for elderly and infirm parents when the time came. When she attracted the attention of the rich and powerful Richard Allingham, she found no-one to take her side. Her sisters were appalled that their free nursemaid was about to top them all with marriage to the local aristocracy and even the servants thought she was presumptuous and forward.

Lord Allingham arranged for soldier Richard to be shipped off to the Crimea, and Decima was sent in disgrace to her maternal grandmother – the very house in which they were now sitting.

"So the murders actually happened here?" asked Joanne, glancing around.

"No, they owned a house in Stockport and that was where the three older sisters died. Richard had been killed – apparently whilst displaying outstanding courage. He was a VC. Secretly he was also a father – though the poor man never knew it."

"So is this where the claim on the Allinghams comes in?"

"Not quite. It was more complicated than that. Decima had a baby boy, who was taken away from her and given to her barren oldest sister to raise. Then Richard died and suddenly Decima was bereft. Whilst Richard lived, she could dream that one day he would come home and tell everyone their secret – not just the baby, but the fact that he had actually married her before leaving for the war."

"Oops," commented the journalist, light suddenly dawning, "that's where the real problems begin for the Allinghams, then. If you could prove the heir was married and had produced an heir of his own before he died, then everyone who has inherited since is out of the picture."

"Precisely. And Decima could never prove it. Richard had hidden their wedding licence before he left, knowing that if his father found it, he would destroy it and have the marriage declared invalid. I happen to know that the Lord Allingham of the time did try and find it. When he couldn't get rid of the marriage, he decided to get rid of the wife. Three of Decima's sisters died, probably of natural causes, but it gave Allingham the weapon he needed. He had friends in high places and he made sure Decima was fingered for the crimes. In fact the policeman I'm writing about now tried to get her off – and he was taken off the case and threatened with dismissal from the force."

Joanne gave a long, low whistle of appreciation, "This is riveting stuff, Libby, you know that, don't you? A family feud that's lasted, what, a hundred and fifty years?"

"Even longer than that, actually."

"So what happens now?"

"We found the licence. Maddie and my father are in the process of bringing the case to court. Heaven only knows what will happen next. In theory my dad is the legitimate heir, but whether modern law will accept the contention is a moot point."

"Oh my God, your sister is going to take on the mighty Allinghams?"

"It would seem so. Of course, she's got to face Brendan first."

"Oh, yeah, the ex-boyfriend she kneecapped. Your family is nothing if not eccentric, Libby."

Libby laughed mirthlessly, "Eccentric? I suppose that's one word for it. It's an unholy mess – and most of it is down to me. I just wanted to help my favourite aunt with a last quest before she died and I've ended up arrested for mercy killing, the victim in an attempted murder, the sister of a woman who is being prosecuted for malicious wounding and facing one of the most powerful families in the country in court, accusing them of cheating her out of her birthright."

"Put like that, it does sound unpleasant," admitted Joanne, "Tell me, what does your husband think of all this? He must wonder what sort of a family he's married into."

"Oh, he's pretty cool about it," said Libby carefully, not for anything would she hint that her marriage might be in trouble. They hadn't even made it to their first anniversary yet.

"I understand he does quite a lot of business with the current Richard Allingham. That must be awkward." Joanne sounded so sympathetic that Libby found herself answering with more candour than was strictly wise.

"He's not best pleased with Maddie, to be honest. He understands her feelings, but he does think she could have handled things more delicately. Richard is one of his oldest friends and David is sure that a quiet word in the right ears could have produced a satisfactory result without any of the publicity that is bound to ensue."

"He could be right," said the journalist doubtfully, "But frankly I really don't see how. Obviously your sister is not going to be bought off, and with a family as well known as the Allinghams, this was never going to go away quietly once it hit the courts."

"Well, we'll find out soon enough," said Libby grimly, "Maddie is not to be headed off once she gets an idea and I don't see the Allinghams handing over their estates and fortune without a fight, do you?"

CHAPTER THIRTEEN

Lazarus 1862

The vicar and Mrs Waters had tried to keep Molly's funeral quiet, but they failed spectacularly. Such was the public outcry that they were forced to rethink the Pauper's Grave and concede defeat. Molly and her baby were to have a decent sending off, despite their disapproval. The two policemen had rarely witnessed a better attended occasion. Traditionally women did not attend funerals, unless, as in this case, it was a young, unmarried woman who was being buried. The one thing that was conspicuous by its absence was the white garland, which would have been carried before the coffin of a virgin. Even in death all who knew Molly were reminded of her fall from grace.

All the girls from the hat shop and the workroom behind were there, including the frosty-faced manageress, who looked as though she was mentally reviewing just exactly how much money the business was losing. Every family who lived on the street were also represented, mostly by the women of the household, but a good sprinkling of men too – though, of course, that was because most of them were out of work or on short time. They could never have risked their jobs or the loss of wages in the old days of full employment.

Hard times were well and truly biting now. The blockade of the Southern States of America was almost completely successful and not a wisp of cotton was being exported. Mills stood still and empty all over the North of England and as a consequence the crime rate was rising rapidly. Lazarus knew it would not be very long before his superiors down-graded Mollie's murder from high importance to unsolvable. There was simply not enough proof that she had been deliberately killed for them to waste resources on her. Had it been the elusive Miss Arabella Allingham who had been done away with, then no stone would have been left unturned, but girls like Mollie Waters were ten a penny and rail against that injustice as he might, Lazarus could do nothing to change it.

By the time he had listened to the reverend Mr Bembridge's sermon. Full of fire and damnation, as he had expected, but with a barely disguised reference to Mollie's sinful existence, it made the Inspector's blood boil. He wanted to stand and roar, "Leave the poor lass in peace, can't you? Hasn't she paid dear enough for her mistakes?" Naturally he did no such thing, but the bad mood of the day before reasserted itself and a thunderous frown adorned his face long before the service was over and they were gathered at the graveside.

It was while they were there, listening to yet more hell and brimstone, that Stonier gave him a nudge and when he looked up a nod of his companion's head directed his attention to a carriage which stood on the road, just yards from where they stood. A young man's face appeared briefly at the window, but was quickly withdrawn when it became obvious he had been spotted. Evidently the order was given for the equipage to move on and before either of the policemen could approach, it was gone.

"Who do you think it was?" asked Lazarus of Stonier under his breath, not that he would have been overheard by anyone else above the impassioned bellowing of the vicar.

"I'd hazard a guess at young Mr Crabtree," answered Stonier, "And I should very much like to find out if I'm right."

"Eliza Dunne will know, if she caught a glimpse of him. Take her to one side when you get the chance. I'm going to have a word with Mr Bembridge."

Stonier raised a detaining hand, "Oh no, Danby, not a good idea. I'll take Bembridge, you see Eliza. I'm too fond of you to see you dismissed for laying a vicar out."

Lazarus laughed at his very obvious concern and asked bluntly, "Are you suggesting I can't control my temper?"

"Not suggesting it, no. I'm saying straight out. I've been watching you fulminating for the past hour and I know Bembridge is ripe for a tongue-lashing at the very least." Stonier was equally blunt, but far from amused.

"Please yourself," Lazarus shrugged and feigned indifference, but he knew his companion was right. He had never been nearer to striking anyone than he had that afternoon. The sheer hypocrisy of the entire event sickened him. According to Bembridge poor little Mollie and her unborn baby had been sent plunging into Hell, with no chance of forgiveness, no loving God, full of understanding for human frailty, no quarter given though she was more sinned against than sinning. And naturally no such punishment awaited the cad who had seduced her.

No arrangement had been made for funerary meats after the interment, so most of the company retired to the nearest pub, which conveniently lay just across the street. Lazarus went there whilst Stonier followed the vicar, the curate and Mrs Waters to the vicarage.

When he made it obvious he expected to be asked in, he was reluctantly offered a cup of tea, which he accepted with an inward sigh of regret for the pint of ale he could be enjoying if he hadn't taken on his present task.

"Is Inspector Lazarus not joining us also, Sergeant?"

"No sir, he's attending the wake organised by Miss Waters' workmates. He thinks they might have valuable information."

Bembridge raised an ironic eyebrow, "Really? I find that very difficult to comprehend. They are, after all, merely workers. What could they possibly tell the inspector that Mollie's family do not know? Or perhaps I'm being naîve. Perchance it's the ale in the beerhouse that attracts your superior?" He gave a condescending chuckle which made Stonier long to tell him that Lazarus had, in fact, signed the pledge, but honesty stopped him, "The young ladies will be able to tell the inspector with whom Mollie spent her leisure hours and that may, in turn, lead us further on."

"I hadn't realized that Miss Waters had made any of the other girls a particular friend," said the curate.

"One or two of them, I understand," said Stonier carefully, giving away no more than he had to. He had learned over the years that a loose tongue could lead to all sorts of trouble, no matter how innocuous the information, or indeed how trustworthy seemed the company.

"Since you have joined us, I assume you have some news to impart?" asked Mr Bembridge, once they were ensconced in his study and waiting for the tea tray.

"Not really, sir, but I do have some questions for you and Mrs Waters, if that is permissible."

"Certainly, sergeant, certainly. Naturally we'll do anything we can to help. A terrible business all round. Bad enough that the girl should get herself into trouble, but for a suspicion of murder to be mooted! My sympathy lies entirely with Mrs Waters, it really does. What that poor woman has had to endure, no Christian soul should ever face."

Stonier said nothing, but thought ruefully that the vicar didn't empathise enough to make his own tea and let poor Mrs Waters sit down and take her ease after her appalling day. As though he had read his mind, the curate rose to his feet when the lady entered and said brightly, "My dear Mrs Waters, please take a seat, I'll be 'mother' today!"

Stonier winced at the *faux pas* and he noticed that Bembridge did likewise, but Mrs Waters simply gave a watery smile of indulgent gratitude, "Oh, Mr Holbrook, you are so very good to me. I don't know where I should have been these past weeks without you and Mr Bembridge, I really don't."

Stonier couldn't help reflecting on people's differing views of comfort. He, for example, would have found nothing comforting in Bembridge's assertion that Mrs Waters' daughter and grandchild were condemned to spend eternity in the fiery pit, but evidently the lady felt it was a fate justly earned and suitably rewarded.

He accepted a cup of tea from the curate, glancing briefly at the honest, open young face that had barely been able to grow its first beard, "Thank you, Mr Holbrook, is it?"

"Yes, that's me."

"Judging from your comment earlier about her friends, I assume you also knew Miss Waters?" he asked, suddenly curious as to exactly how these people came into Mollie's life. Had she broken completely from her mother when she began to live her own life in her own way, or had there been some attempt to pretend that all was well and she was living what her mother would call 'respectably' in her lodging house, with her good job and future prospects assured?

"Oh, yes, I knew her. Miss Waters had been a regular church-goer until – well …"

"Until she began to fall away from the path of righteousness!" intercepted Mrs Waters, "As soon as she stopped coming to church and began to be rude and scornful of me and all I believe in, I knew she'd fallen. I knew she'd become a whore like all the others!"

Stonier was shocked by the strength of feeling, the sheer anger and bitterness in these words and he was lost as to which of the many questions crowding into his brain he should seek answers to.

"Surely 'whore' is rather harsh?" he suggested, with an embarrassed glance at the vicar. He needn't have worried, for the man of God obviously felt quite as strongly as his parishioner. The colour had mounted in his flabby cheeks and he shook his head mournfully, "Mrs Waters speaks nothing but the truth, Mr Stonier. You, as a policeman, must know that. I'll warrant you arrest these young – well, I hesitate to use the word 'women' to describe them! They are creatures of the devil, desecrating all that should be pure and good in womankind."

Stonier hesitated to admit that if he arrested one prostitute a month, that was a lot. He really didn't see Braxton and the surrounding districts as the sinks of iniquity that these three evidently did. Admittedly things had grown a lot worse since the mills had closed. Girls were forced to earn a penny or two where they could in hard times, but even so, it was scarcely on a grand scale. These were not hardened harlots, feeding a gin and opium habit, and falling about drunk on the streets, as he had heard happened in London and Manchester.

"You are using a strong word to describe your daughter, Mrs Waters, and in the present circumstances it is very important that I know the full story. At the moment one young man is very much in our minds as being the one who killed her, but that would all change if you were to confide that Mollie was in the habit of entertaining many gentlemen rather than merely one lover."

"One or many, what's the difference? It was out of holy wedlock and that's a sin," said the loving mother firmly.

"Madam, I have no interest in the morals of your daughter, they were very firmly her own business. I need to know with whom she spent her time. You seem to forget that a far greater sin was committed. The commandments include 'thou shalt not kill' as well as the nine others. Someone murdered Mollie and her unborn child."

"You don't know that for sure," she muttered mutinously, obviously not ready to forgive her child for her failings and feeling that to recognize a greater sin would be to lessen the black badness of Mollie's soul.

"No, we don't," admitted Stonier, "And we'll never find out if you don't start co-operating."

"I don't know anything about Mollie's affairs. I only know that she left home when she was sixteen after a row in which she told me she couldn't stand another moment of my religious carping. She turned up from time to time to try and give me money, but I knew where she was getting it and I told her to keep it, for much good would it do her in the end – and I was right, wasn't I?"

"If it gives you any satisfaction to know it, ma'am, yes, you were right!" Stonier finally lost his temper and told her what had been fermenting in his mind for the past week or more, "Mollie probably died because of the bad company she kept – but what a pity she felt driven to keep that company, when she ought to have been safe at home, with the people who should have loved and protected her. May God forgive Mollie for her errors, Mrs Waters, and may He forgive you for your failure as a mother."

She gaped at him and Mr Bembridge rose to his feet, his face suffused with the hot blood of righteous anger, "I think you've said enough, Mr Stonier."

"I believe you're right, Mr Bembridge. I'll see myself out!"

Holbrook followed him into the hall, "I'll try and make sure that Mr Bembridge understands that you spoke in the heat of the moment," he quietly assured the furious policeman, who looked blankly at him, "Don't bother," he snapped.

"Come now, Mr Stonier, you don't mean that. Why would you put yourself at risk for a dead woman?"

"Risk?" asked Stonier, suddenly alert. What the devil did the man mean by that comment? All sorts of vague and disquieting notions flooded into his head. Could Holbrook be trying to tell him something which he was unable to voice directly?

"Of course it's a risk annoying Mr Bembridge. If he should decide to complain about you to your Superintendent, I'm sure it would have serious consequences for your career."

He spoke so smoothly, so reasonably, that Stonier was completely disarmed. He stared at the curate for several seconds before he managed to stutter awkwardly, "Yes, yes, I'm sure you're right. Thank you, Mr Holbrook, I'd be grateful for your intervention. I allowed my emotions to get the better of me. You'll explain and apologise to Mr Bembridge and Mrs Waters for me?"

"Of course, my dear sir. Think nothing more of the matter. It has been a fraught day for us all. Poor Mollie and that innocent babe."

They were the first words of sympathy that Stonier had heard since setting foot in the house of the man of God and that thought alone depressed him. He walked away wondering where exactly the conversation had left the investigation. He was no wiser about Mollie's lovers and had unexpectedly found himself presented with a different reason for the girl's murder. Her killer may not have been trying to silence her, but punish her.

Or she may have killed herself, overcome with remorse for her fall from grace. Raised as she was by a religious fanatic, she may not have been able to live any longer with the guilt.

Added to all that, he thought ruefully, he had done exactly as he had cautioned Lazarus against and lost his temper with Bembridge and Mrs Waters. He could only hope his boss had been more successful in his dealings with the rest of the funeral party.

He needn't have worried. Lazarus, once away from the suffocating self-righteousness of the religious members of the gathering, found himself enjoying the down to earth attitude of those who were left. They wasted no time in buying a round of drinks and remembering their friend and neighbour as a real human being with failings and flaws, yes, but with talents and humour too. Eliza Dunne began to regale them all with tales of their doings in the shop, the little scraps of pleasure and fun they had managed to extract from what must have been grindingly hard work and tediously long hours. He listened to the stories and joined in the laughter for a good half an hour before he managed to coax Eliza to a seat in an alcove and begin the real business of the day in asking her a few pertinent questions.

She was a buxom lass, with hair as dark and shiny as coal and a ready smile. It was obvious that the one thing that kept her sane amongst all the madness and misery that encompassed her life was her sense of humour. Eliza could find something to laugh at no matter how bad things were, even working for the miserable Miss Soffley, who evidently was one of those women who wasn't happy unless she was moaning about something.

When presented with this assessment of her employer, she shrugged eloquently and took a deep draught of her pint of ale, "Poor woman. She can't help it if someone shoved a pole up her arse the day she was born. It might keep her upright, but it doesn't exactly make her happy."

Lazarus hid a grin, "She must make life pretty hard for you girls."

"She tries to, but so long as we keep working, there's not much she can do. She'd love to see me walk out of the door, bag and baggage, but I have the nimblest fingers in the workshop. She may be a bitter old harridan, but she's not stupid. That's how Mollie ended up in the front of the shop. God bless her, she couldn't sew a straight seam, or make a silk flower to save her life, but she could sell! Soffley knows that men like to buy from pretty young girls and women like to imagine they'll look just as good in a hat as the girl who parades around the shop in it."

"So Mollie began working in the back with you?"

"Yes, but she wasn't there for long. Soffley saw her potential, and she wasn't wrong. Mollie could sell coals to Newcastle. But she never forgot where she came from. She didn't drop all of us just because she was front of house. She was too soft with everyone – that's how she ended up in trouble. I wish I could have persuaded her not to believe the lies of that fellow who sweet-talked her into bed, but she was smitten from the very first."

"This was young Crabtree?"

"Aye, him."

"And she had no other followers?"

"Not once she'd met him. She'd had a couple of lads who wanted to walk out with her, but she wasn't interested until Crabtree came along. And sadly it wasn't his money she was interested in. He thought it was, but I could have told him, she'd have gone barefoot just to be with him, poor, stupid little fool."

Lazarus thought he'd rarely seen such a dramatic change in a face. Eliza went from smiles to unfathomable sadness in a moment. He couldn't help but reach out and pat her hand comfortingly. She smiled again, "Why, Mr Lazarus, are you flirting with me?"

"'fraid not, ma'am. I'm on duty. Tell me, did you happen to notice a carriage on the road by the graveyard earlier?"

"Indeed I did, and how that cad had the nerve to show his face, I'll never know. If it hadn't been for the solemn occasion, I'd have been leaping over gravestones and dragging him out by his bloody ears. He'd have been down the hole with the coffin, where he belongs."

Lazarus had no doubt she meant every word.

"It was him, then? You're in no doubt?"

"None at all."

"Doesn't that seem a little odd to you, 'Liza?" he barely noticed that he had slipped easily and naturally into using her first name. She was that sort of a woman, making a man feel at home and at ease, when she wanted to be accommodating. She'd take no nonsense though, he reflected with barely concealed amusement. It would be brave man who took on Eliza Dunne – or a foolhardy one.

"Odd? What do you mean? That he was stupid enough to show his face when most of the gathering were baying for his blood?"

"No, that he cared enough to come. You say that he refused to accept paternity of the child, that he threatened Mollie if she dared to try and make a claim on him, and that he was, more than likely the man who killed her, yet he showed up for her funeral. I would have thought he'd have stayed well away, safe in the knowledge that a very unpleasant incident was being finally laid to rest."

She evidently hadn't viewed the matter thus and she took another thoughtful draught of her ale,

"Put that way, it does seem out of character, but even the worst of us can have moments of regret and remorse – and there was no doubt he had been fond of her, when things were simple and he was getting his amusement for free."

"Not quite as black as you've been painting him, then?" ventured the policeman quietly.

"I never said he was evil incarnate," Eliza excused herself, "just that he fell far short when the going got tough. He should have been a man and helped Mollie out, not abandoned her."

"True enough. And maybe we're both wrong. Perhaps he was there to gloat. To see the end of as job well done."

"It's not the end though, is it Inspector?"

"Not if I have anything to do with it, Miss Dunne. If he killed Mollie I'll see him hang, son of a magistrate or not!"

She grinned and of one accord they both raised and clinked glasses, "To getting justice for Mollie," said Eliza.

"Justice," echoed Lazarus.

Stonier joined them just as Lazarus rose to go to the bar for another round, "Perfect timing, Sergeant," said the Inspector gaily, "Mine's a pint as is Miss Dunne's."

Tom threw his friend a look that fully demonstrated his lack of amusement at this sally, "I've just been to the driest do I've ever had the misfortune to attend, sir, and all to save your skin, so I think you'll find this one is on you!"

Lazarus didn't need telling twice.

CHAPTER FOURTEEN

As they passed the corner of the street both Lazarus and Stonier were surprised to hear themselves hailed by name. It was not unusual for them to have muttered imprecations thrown after them on occasion, especially after a rowdy Saturday night which had included several arrests, but this was a polite calling of their names and they stopped and looked for the source of the voice.

It was, of course, young Will Carter, an overly large cap pulled low over his eyes, and boots on his feet that must once have belonged to his father. He was barely visible above the sandwich board which carried the headlines of the day's news and a pile of papers were kept from the dirt of the street on an upturned wooden crate at his feet.

"Young Will, as I live and breath," said Lazarus heartily when he recognized the urchin, "How's business, my boy?"

"Going well, sir," answered Will proudly, "My ma is that pleased to have some money coming in, I can't tell you!"

"Your father still not working, then?" inquired Stonier. He knew Carter the elder of old and he couldn't recall the last time the man had been in full time employment. His present excuse was the downturn in cotton production, but Stonier knew the real reason was a fondness for ale. Carter's children might have no shoes to their feet, but he could always find the money for a pint.

They could barely see it beneath the shade of the cap, but Will's cheeks flushed red, "No, not at the moment, Mr Stonier. He's looking, mind, but there's not much about."

Stonier kindly pursued it no further, merely tossing the boy a penny and saying, "I'll have a copy, thanks, Will."

Will eagerly handed over the newspaper, "What about you, Mr

Lazarus?" The Inspector wanted to say that he'd read Tom's when he was done with it, but didn't have the heart. He too delved in his pocket for a penny and accepted the proffered paper.

The two men went on their way and Will turned his attention to another customer who had seen the previous purchase and thought there must be something interesting to make two men buy a copy each of the same paper.

Back in their office, Lazarus and Stonier divested themselves of their dark overcoats, worn as a mark of respect at the funeral, "Thank God that's over, I hate funerals," remarked Lazarus and Stonier grunted, "I don't know that's there's many people who like 'em!" he said tersely.

"True enough. Shall we have a cup of tea?"

"Aye, and you can make it," said Stonier; he was still having trouble shrugging off the feelings of bitterness engendered by his time spent with the vicar and the grieving mother.

"Be blowed to that," retorted Lazarus, "Call a constable in and get him to do it. I'm still feeling the effects of daytime drinking with 'Liza Dunne. She's got hollow legs, that one."

"Well, you didn't have to keep pace with her, you know."

"Of course I did. It was a matter of pride. I couldn't let myself be drunk under the table by a girl."

Stonier threw him a look of mild exasperation and went to the door and bellowed for tea.

As the inspector sat at his desk, he noticed a letter addressed to himself in a feminine hand. He tore it open without further ado and found a short missive from Constance Allingham, telling him that she had arranged for them to visit Lady Stafford-Naylor the following morning at eleven.

"Better arrange for us to have the gig again tomorrow, my friend, it looks like we're out of town once more."

Stonier heaved a sigh, "Can't these people live in more accessible places?" he asked grumpily.

"Good God, no!" returned Lazarus with deep sarcasm, "They'd have to rub shoulders with the hoi-polloi then! The further away from humanity, the better. They might crowd their workers into hovels with ten to a room, but it wouldn't do for their delicate constitutions."

Stonier didn't deign to reply.

* * *

It was a little before eleven that they drew up outside the imposing sweep of steps that led to the front door of the Stafford-Naylor residence, but Lazarus was pleased to see that Miss Allingham was already there, waiting for them. She had ridden there and looked pink-cheeked and pretty in her brown velvet riding habit and saucy little hat with a jaunty sprig of feathers. She was fastening the reins to an iron ring set into a stone post put there for the purpose.

"Good morning," she turned and greeted them with a smile. Stonier returned both the smile and the sentiment, but Lazarus merely bowed slightly, straight-faced, and, rebuffed, she lost all her sparkle suddenly.

"We're expected," she told them coldly.

"Good," said Lazarus, "Then perhaps you'd like to lead the way?"

"Certainly," she replied and swept up the steps, the train of her dress thrown carelessly over one arm, and treating the two men to a glimpse of her tightly booted ankle.

As they had been led to expect, Diana Stafford-Naylor made no attempt to hide her humble beginnings. She spoke with the same earthy tones as her servants, called them all by their first names, and generally treated everyone like a crowd of children. When Lazarus attempted to call her by her full title, she snorted with good-natured contempt, "Less of the 'my lady', young fellow, I'm Diana to my friends, among who I intend to count you before the day is out!" For once Lazarus allowed himself to be enchanted – for who would not be bewitched by so affable a character?

She insisted on helping carry out the trays of tea and alcohol to the table she had ordered set out under a giant cedar in the garden. The two policemen found themselves carrying chairs and following her lead through the French windows and down the sloping lawn.

The weather still hadn't broken, though it was less sunny and more overcast than it had been in the previous few days. Rather than cooling the air, however, this had only created a heaviness which spoke of an approaching storm, but one that was not yet ready to burst.

When she had organised everyone, told them all where to sit and poured the tea, Lady Stafford-Naylor finally sank with a chuckle into her own chair and took up her cup and saucer, "I really should learn to let the servants wait upon me, but old habits die hard."

"I imagine you are an ideal employer, Diana," said Lazarus with feeling. He had seen too many cowed and overworked drudges in service not to think she was not far from perfect.

"Oh, I don't know. We go through more butlers and housekeepers than any other household I know of. The younger servants love to work for me, but their superiors seem to feel I allow too much laxity and apparently that makes it impossible to run a tight ship. I've tried to explain that I don't want a ship, but a home, but it cuts no ice!"

Lazarus laughed and the others joined in, even Constance managed to shake off her previous chagrin and smile in a pale imitation of his amusement. She secretly wished he would laugh more often. It changed his whole demeanour. Probably due to the nature of his job, he tended to be stern and harried most of the time – or at least that had been her impression – perhaps on reflection that mood was simply reserved for her. He certainly seemed to hold her in the deepest contempt, which cut her to the quick, since she could find no reason for it.

"Now, Inspector, enough about me. Constance tells me you wanted to ask about young Arabella?"

"I did, madam. And since you have been told that much, may I enquire if you know the full story?"

"That the little minx has run off, you mean? Yes, I'm fully aware. Allingham knows better than to try and pull the wool over my eyes – and he trusts me to be discreet when called upon."

"Good, then I may speak freely."

"Of course."

"I'm sure I can assume that you do not know of Arabella's whereabouts. Even if she were to swear you to secrecy, you could not, in all conscience, allow her parents to worry themselves in such a cruel way."

"If I knew where she was, my friend, I'd follow and drag her back by her hair," Lady Stafford-Naylor assured him grimly, "I'll not have her throw herself away on some no-account bounder who's only after her money. Arabella is horridly spoiled, but her pedigree is impeccable. I've known poverty and it's no way of life for a gently-reared girl. She's facing a life of misery with Marcus Soper, but she's too young and foolish to know it. He seems a bright prospect now, but when money flies out of the door, love flies out of the window! She'll be worn-out and dragged down before she reaches her mid-twenties."

"I think they both expect to be financed by her father," said Lazarus in a measured tone which gave no hint of his feelings about this state of affairs.

"She'll learn that a man like that would have to be financed by King Midas himself. He'll run through her money – and everything else she has to offer – faster than she can produce her first baby. And believe me, there will be babies, one after another, because that's the way he can keep control of her."

No one could produce an argument to gainsay her. They all knew she was right. Arabella thought she knew what she was doing, fondly imagined her paramour was wrapped around her little finger, that he worshipped the ground she walked upon. She would learn the hard way that he loved no one but himself.

"Very well, we can safely say that you were not taken into Arabella's confidence, but there is always the possibility that she let slip some clue that you have overlooked. When was the last time you saw her?"

Lady Stafford-Naylor frowned as she recalled the occasion, "Just the day before she disappeared. The little imp came calling and wheedled some money out of me. She said she wanted to buy a gift for her papa and that was why she couldn't ask him. I should have known she was up to mischief, she's never in her life given a thought to anyone else."

"Did she say why she wanted the gift, or where she intended to purchase it?"

"As a matter of fact she did. I think it was probably the elaborate story she concocted that convinced me she was telling the truth. Apparently she had accidentally broken a favourite ornament of her father's and he was, in her words, really angry with her for the first time in her life. It was that which had shocked her into realising that she had better make reparation."

Lazarus turned to Miss Allingham, "Had she broken anything?"

"Not as far as I'm aware," she answered truthfully, "And I think the whole household would have known had Lord Allingham been as annoyed as Arabella was suggesting. He is not a man who keeps his feelings to himself," she gave the slightest shiver as she recalled her uncle's furious outbursts. Lazarus appeared not to notice, but Stonier felt suddenly sorry for her. She must live a strange and frightening life, dependant as she was on the whims and will of a man who was not only irascible, but, as the two policemen knew to their cost, ruthless in the extreme.

"Where did she say she intended to go to buy the replacement?" asked Lazarus.

"She said she couldn't think that she could find anything similar anywhere nearer than Manchester and I warned her most strongly that if she intended to travel that far, she must ask permission and be sure to take her maid with her. She laughed and promised that she would not go alone."

"Well, she kept that promise at any rate," said Stonier emphatically, "She didn't go alone."

"Don't remind me," begged Lady Stafford-Naylor with a shudder.

"Tell me, is Arabella basically a truthful girl? If she was going to lie, would she root the deception in some twisted form of the truth, or would she happily lie through her teeth?"

Both ladies looked at Lazarus in surprise, "You think she might actually have gone to Manchester, Inspector?"

"Possibly – or she might have gone in entirely the opposite direction and merely mentioned the city to throw dust in the eyes of her pursuers. Which do you think it is?"

"I think she's gone to Manchester," said Lady Stafford-Naylor decidedly, "You are right, Mr Lazarus, she's many things, but she's a bad liar and she knows it."

"I agree," said Miss Allingham, "Arabella has never had to explain herself, she's always been fully indulged. She would find it hard to fool people who know her well. And she may have had the slightest tinge of regret for what she was about to do. It might have made her feel a little less deceitful to tell her godmother where she was going, albeit in a round about way."

"Well, it's something, but it doesn't narrow things down much. Manchester is a big place. We need a little more detail. I'm afraid out last hope may be with young Crabtree, but he's proving rather elusive and I'm not in any position to insist that he speaks with us."

Lady Stafford-Naylor looked puzzled and Constance quickly outlined the difficulty Lazarus was encountering with his Superintendent and the Crabtree family. She raised a quizzical brow, "But, Inspector, there could be no fault find with you if you were to run into Mr Crabtree at a social event and chat with him there?"

Lazarus smiled with very little humour, "Naturally not, madam, but the likelihood of my being invited to a gathering which included Mr Crabtree would be remote, to say the least."

"Nonsense," she told him roundly, "Having met you I'm quite satisfied that you know how to conduct yourself. It would give me the greatest pleasure to see you here on Saturday evening for a small soiree I'm holding. I like to be surrounded by young people, having no children of my own, and I quite often arrange these little parties so that I can indulge my little hobby of matchmaking. The parents have no objection, being fully aware that I have a discerning eye and cannot be fooled by charlatans. Mr Crabtree will find himself in your company whether he likes it or not!"

This was an unexpected development and Lazarus opened his mouth to protest, but the lady waved her hand in instant dismissal, "You must come too, Mr Stonier, and pray bring your wife – for I know, simply by looking at you, that you must have a wife!"

Tom grinned, "She'd be honoured, my lady."

"Not at all," she said graciously, adding, "Now, Constance, how can we get you here? I realize that you are ostensibly caring for your 'sick' young cousin at the moment."

The younger woman tried to hide her disappointment at having to miss the party, "Don't fret about me, Lady Diana. My uncle will not countenance my absence. He is trying too hard to create the illusion that Arabella is confined to her sick bed."

"Your uncle will do as he's told," said Lady Diana firmly, "My carriage will be sent this evening to remove Arabella to my husband's villa on the seafront at Lytham. The sea air will be most efficacious for her rapid recovery."

"He'll never agree," breathed Constance, quite bedazzled by the older woman's effrontery.

"He'll have no choice. And he'll recognize the logic of the plan when I explain it to him. One cannot go on forever pretending to a houseful of servants that a bed contains a young woman when it very obviously does not! He's a bigger fool than I thought if he imagines there is a single soul living in that house who is not fully aware of the situation."

Stonier could have told her that at least one of the servants knew everything, but he said nothing. There was no need. Lady Stafford-Naylor was canny and Miss Allingham knew it and trusted her completely.

Lazarus rose to his feet, "We shall leave you ladies to finalise your plans, but I have to add my voice to Lady Stafford-Naylor's. Arabella needs to be removed from her father's house in pretence as well as in fact. If Lord Allingham really wants this to remain a secret, the fewer people who find out about her absence the better."

The policemen left the two women working out how exactly they could pretend to remove the 'sick' Arabella from the house without causing too much of a stir of interest amongst the staff. Constance suggested that she thought Sally would agree to don Arabella's dressing gown and permit herself to be bundled into blankets and carried out of the house and into a waiting carriage. It would not be the best of disguises, but it would suffice to create the illusion that the young mistress was leaving the house.

"Good," said Diana, "I shall write a note now that you must hand to your uncle, telling him that I'll not take no for an answer. He can't expect you to sit in an empty bedroom for God knows how long, pretending to care for a sick Arabella. If it goes on much longer it's going to cause it's own minor scandal. How does he think it will look if his only daughter is sick unto death and confined to bed for weeks on end and he doesn't even bother to call in a doctor?"

"He'll be so angry," murmured Constance fearfully, "Do I have to deliver the letter?"

"Don't be such a baby," said Diana briskly, but she softened when she realized that her companion was genuinely worried, "Does he really treat you so ill, my dear?"

Constance shook her head, "He tries, Lady Diana, really he does, but he is not an accommodating man. He expects his orders to be obeyed without question and he rants furiously when he is thwarted. He is always sorry afterwards, but by then it is too late." She shuddered and closed her eyes briefly, "I do so hate people who shout and rave. You cannot conceive how horrifying I find his temper."

"Oh, I think I can imagine it," said Diana wryly, "I've lived long enough and wildly enough to have experienced most things, my love."

"I suppose you think I'm a dreadful coward."

"Not at all. We all have our little foibles."

They were silent for a moment, then Diana looked piercingly at the younger woman, "Tell me something, Constance,"

"What?" asked Constance.

"You like the Inspector, don't you?"

The rosy blush in her cheeks gave her away, though she swiftly tried to deny it, "I hardly know the man – and I have to say he's always quite unpleasant to me."

"He still intrigues you?"

"It doesn't matter whether he does or not. My uncle has other plans for me. I'm not free to like anyone – and especially not someone who so obviously dislikes me, though I have no idea why."

"I suggest you ask him, my dear," said Diana with admirable

logic.

"I could not do any such thing," asserted Constance, aghast at the very thought, "And what would be the point? I should very probably hear something I don't want to know."

"On the contrary, you might hear something very nice."

Constance picked up her gloves and rose to her feet, "You really are incorrigible, Diana," she said mildly and took her leave.

CHAPTER FIFTEEN

With flushed cheeks and brightly sparkling eyes Meg accepted the news that she was to attend a soiree at the country home of Lady Diana Stafford-Naylor with ill-concealed excitement. Since neither her husband nor Lazarus wanted to go to a dance, dressed up like a couple of toffs, they could hardly be expected to share her feelings.

"What shall I wear?" she asked breathlessly.

"A dress?" suggested Lazarus unhelpfully. She slapped him playfully, but with considerable force, just to teach him a lesson, "Watch your step, Danby, or you'll be accompanying me to the shops to buy the dress!" He threw up his hands in surrender, "Dear God, anything but that!"

"Does that mean I have to go?" ventured Tom timidly. He knew better than to antagonise an excited woman, but he didn't want to spend a wearisome afternoon trailing after his wife around various shops either.

"Oh, neither of you has to go, if it's going to be such torture for you!" she snapped back, but there was a good-natured exasperation at the root of it, so both men knew they were off the hook.

"You couldn't pick up evening dress for Lazarus and I while you're out and about, could you, sweetheart?" asked Stonier with a grin. Meg's mouth dropped open at his sheer nerve, but she couldn't help but laugh when the shock had worn off, "You really are the giddy limit," she told her husband, "Let me get my tape so I can measure you both – but you can take each other's inside leg!"

She bustled off to find her sewing box and Lazarus turned on his companion, "I hope you're joking about the evening dress," he said with horror in his voice.

"Of course I'm not, you fool! What did you expect to wear to a ball given by an aristo? Thank your stars this isn't forty years ago, you would be in satin knee-breeches."

"Bloody hell!" muttered Lazarus, "Why did I have to get dragged into this pantomime?"

"Murder and kidnap," answered Stonier grimly.

The Inspector could hardly argue with that summation of the situation.

In the event, for a surprisingly small amount of money, Meg managed to hire evening suits for the two men and buy herself a silk gown that Tom declared made her look like a duchess. She didn't bother to tell him that she had picked it up for a song at the second-hand market in Braxton and had to work all night unpicking the seams and making it fit her slightly more rounded figure than its original owner.

Stonier managed to make his frock coat look ordinary, so stocky was he and determined to be his usual self, but Lazarus was transformed. Meg had always secretly thought him a good-looking man, but he carried off the pristine shirt, stiff collar and black bow-tie like a real gentleman. The trousers she had found for him were light grey and fastened under the instep of his shoes; coupled with the dark frock coat he looked taller than his usual five ten. She had to admit that he outshone the bucolic Stonier with absolutely no trouble whatsoever – whether he wanted to or not.

The evening sun was casting long shadows by the time they arrived at Stafford Manor and it seemed the party was well underway. The house was alight with huge branches of candles and immense oil lamps. Music drifted through the open windows along with the hum of conversation and the occasional ripple of feminine laughter or a huge guffaw from some well-fed and wined male.

Meg grew uncharacteristically shy, "Oh, Tom, I don't think I can go in there! They'll all be rich and sophisticated. They'll look down their noses at me."

"Just let 'em try!" her husband said gruffly, "Anyway, why should they? You look as good as any one of them – and your manners will almost certainly be better, if my experience of the 'upper classes' is anything to go by."

Lazarus could see that this assurance had done nothing to ease her fears, so he took her hand and squeezed it comfortingly, "Come on, old girl, we'll enter the lair together – and I promise we'll stay no longer than we have to if you are not enjoying yourself."

She smiled wanly at him, "Thank you, Danby," she whispered, "Come on, then, let's get it over and done with."

She need not have worried, Lady Stafford-Naylor had enough wit to surround herself with those who either genuinely liked her, or who were too in awe of her elevated position to be open with their snobbery. The Inspector and his party caused barely a glance of interest when they entered the house and Constance Allingham had made a point of being there to greet them, aware that they would know only herself and the hostess.

She led Meg to an alcove at the side of the ballroom which contained a comfortable settee and she despatched the men to fetch drinks and a plate of delectable nibbles to tempt Meg's appetite.

It could not be expected that Lazarus would concentrate on enjoying himself when he knew his quarry was in the vicinity. He followed Stonier quietly enough towards the refreshments, but his eyes darted this way and that, seeking out the young Crabtree. Stonier had allowed himself to be swept away by Meg's excitement and had more or less forgotten their true purpose in being there. His eyes lit up when he was offered champagne and he barely noticed when Lazarus disappeared from his side.

He merely took up a tray and loaded it with plates of food and cups of punch to take back to his wife and Miss Allingham.

Lazarus thought he had heard a bray of laughter that reminded him of the voices he had heard drifting from the tennis courts a few days before. Single-mindedly he went off in search of the owner, little caring that he was supposed to be giving at least the illusion of being merely a guest.

Crabtree was in a small room next to the ballroom, surrounded by other young bucks of a similar age and class to himself. He was drinking whisky from a crystal tumbler and seemed to be trying to persuade his friends to sneak off to the billiard room, to play and indulge in cigars and more whisky.

"You know Lady S don't like us to leave the ballroom this early, old chap," protested a particularly tall, thin fellow, who was evidently growing faster than his tailor could contend with for his knobbly wrists were sticking out from his too-short cuffs, "We have to show the girlies a good time first. No games until after midnight, that's the rule."

Crabtree snorted, "Oh dash it all, Ceddie, you know I can't bear these pampered fillies ..."

"No, Mr Crabtree, your taste runs to rather more common stock, doesn't it?" intercepted Lazarus, not particularly loudly, but with a penetrating tone which brought their full attention to him. Colour flooded into Crabtree's face, "Who the hell are you?" he blustered aggressively, "Do you make a habit of barging into other people's conversations?"

"Damned rude, if you ask me," added one of his other friends and was rewarded with a withering glare from Lazarus that had the effect of stilling his tongue.

"Nobody did ask you," said Lazarus smoothly, "And nobody is interested in your opinion, so why don't you make yourself scarce whilst I have a little chat with Crabtree."

Since they were all of them from a class more used to ordering than being ordered their initial reaction was to argue with this stranger but some instinct for self-preservation managed to force its way through the fog of alcohol and arrogance and slowly, one by one, they slunk away, only too glad that the older man wanted the unfortunate Crabtree and not themselves.

He made to follow them, but the inspector held out a detaining hand, "Not so fast, sir. We haven't had a word yet,"

"Go to the devil," muttered Crabtree, "I don't even know who the hell you are, so what could I possibly have to say to you?"

"I'm so sorry, did I not introduce myself?" Lazarus asked, with blistering sarcasm, making Crabtree grow a shade redder, "My name is Inspector Lazarus of Braxton Constabulary."

The colour drained from the boy's face as if a vein had been opened, "What do you want with me? I've never heard of you in my life before."

"Really? That's odd, because I left a very specific message with your father's butler asking that you contact me urgently."

"Did you? How remiss of him to neglect to deliver it."

"That was unfortunate, but there's no harm done, since I have now fortuitously run into you here."

"Well, I can't imagine how you think I can help you, inspector, but whatever it is you require, I hardly think this is the time and place. I shall endeavour to call on you next week perhaps, now if you'll stand aside …"

"Nice try, boy, but I think not. You see, you have a nasty habit of disappearing – or should I say hiding? – whenever I need to speak to you."

"I don't know what you're talking about. I told you, I never even heard your name before now."

"If you say so, but I think we'll have our chat here – unless of course, you'd prefer me to arrest you in front of all these good people and take you to Braxton Police Station?" Naturally Lazarus knew that he dared do no such thing. Even trying to speak to the boy had brought down the wrath of his superintendent upon his head – but Crabtree didn't know that, so all he needed to do was keep his head and brazen it out, hoping the young man would be intimidated.

Crabtree knew when he was beaten, "Damn you, what is it then? Ask your questions, blast your eyes."

"Would you like to tell me where I can find Marcus Soper?" Was it his imagination, or did the young man look almost relieved to hear the question? He was relaxing too soon, did he but know it. Mollie Waters would be the next item on the agenda.

"Marcus Soper? Never heard of him. It's really not your day, is it, Inspector?" Crabtree grinned maliciously.

"Oh, I can see that I really am going to have to ask you to accompany me to the police station. Your lamentable memory is evidently going to need a night in the cells to help it recover," said Lazarus, reaching into his pocket and producing his handcuffs, which he dangled in front of the startled eyes of the younger man.

"Let me think, damn you! Oh, Marcus Soper – of course, I vaguely recall the fellow now. Had ideas above his station, that one.

We had to cut him in the end. He was sniffing around young ladies whom he had no right to know."

"He's done rather more than sniff, hasn't he, Crabtree, as you well know."

"You really do speak in riddles, don't you, my good fellow?"

"You want me to speak more plainly, sir? Very well, Marcus Soper has absconded in the company of a young lady whose father would pay dearly to have returned to the bosom of her loving family. It's my intention to find the pair of them before the reputations of the lady and her kin are permanently stained. I know Soper to be a friend of yours and I expect you to tell me where I can find him."

"And why would I do that?"

"Because if you don't I will do everything in my power to make life very difficult for you – starting with arresting you on some trumped up charge that will embarrass you and incense your father."

"You can't do that," blustered the boy, but he was evidently rattled.

It was Lazarus' turn to display a malicious grin, "Oh, you really have no idea how the real world works, do you my boy? Shall we talk about Mollie Waters now?"

"Never …"

"Never heard of her?" interrupted the inspector quietly, "then why did you attend her funeral? Why does her friend say that you were the father of her unborn child? And most importantly of all, why did you kill her?"

Crabtree's mouth dropped open and he gasped desperately for air. For a moment Lazarus feared he had gone too far and that the boy was going to die of a seizure right there in front of him. He guided him to a chair and swiftly loosened his cravat and the high collar which seemed about to choke him, "You can't be seriously suggesting …" the boy managed to croak, his eyes pleading with the policeman.

"You are the tennis player, as I recall, and now the ball is in your court, Mr Crabtree. Tell me what I want to hear and perhaps I'll believe you when you swear you never murdered that poor young lass."

"I never harmed a hair on her head," muttered Crabtree, after he took a long pull at the glass of spirits in his hand.

"You didn't offer a scrap of help either did you? You took your pleasure then left her to take the consequences. Even if you didn't kill her, her demise was mightily convenient for you – how do you think a jury would view your behaviour? If they don't hang you, they'll send you to gaol for a good few years. Honest citizens take a very dim view of seducers and cowards." He needed to say no more. Crabtree began to talk fast and breathlessly.

"Marcus Soper will be in Stockport. He has relatives there and he always said that's where he'd go if he needed to get out of Braxton in a hurry."

"The address?"

"That I really don't know, I promise you. I just know his great Aunt works in Christy's hat factory."

"Her name?"

"I don't know that either. I've told you everything I can. Marcus isn't a fool. He doesn't blabber his business to one and all."

"Very well. That'll do for the moment."

"Thank you, Inspector," said Crabtree, with real gratitude in his now humbled tone, "And you believe that I never hurt Mollie, don't you?"

"I never said that, Mr Crabtree. I'll be speaking to you again about Mollie Waters, but this is neither the time nor the place. You'll come to Braxton Police Station on Monday morning at ten thirty and you can convince me then that you had nothing to do with her death."

He walked away leaving the young man pale and sweating in his chair. He was satisfied now that he would be able to find Soper and the Allingham brat, but his instincts about Crabtree were playing him false. He had been so sure that the seducer had also been the murderer, but suddenly he was not so confident. Frankly the boy seemed to not be intelligent enough to have committed the crime. He was a typical young buck, full of swagger, interested only in the latest fashions and riding in a neck-or-nothing style that would only give him a fifty-fifty chance of attaining maturity. He would have quite happily bedded Mollie, he would have panicked when she told him she was with child; he might even have lost control and bashed her over the head with a poker when she broke her news – but to plan and execute such a cold-blooded murder as this one had been? Lazarus thought not.

* * *

Finding themselves alone when Lazarus and Stonier went off to find refreshments, Constance and Meg exchanged polite conversation for a few moments. Meg was feeling a little intimidated by the lavish setting in which she found herself and Constance could think of nothing to say that wouldn't be interpreted as patronising by the policeman's wife. It was only when a dance began and the music soared above the hum of conversation that Meg gasped joyfully, "I do hope Tom will agree to dance this evening. He does so hate it and I never attend dances these days."

"That's a shame. But I'm sure your husband will not disappoint you, Mrs Stonier."

"Please call me Meg – and I wouldn't be too sure about that. He and the Inspector are here on police business and I doubt they'll allow themselves any fun at all."

Constance digested this in silence, watching the dancers with a wistful look on her face, she too had been hoping to dance the evening away. "May I ask you a question, Meg?" she said at length.

"Of course."

"It may of course be my imagination, but I can't help feeling that Inspector Lazarus dislikes me and I cannot for the life of me fathom why he should."

Meg, who knew full well why Lazarus treated the young woman with such utter contempt, was uncomfortable with the question and attempted to deflect attention, "I don't suppose it's a question of dislike – he's merely doing his job. Feelings don't come in to it, do they?"

"I suppose not – but he gives me the oddest sensation when I speak to him. Indifference I could understand – as you say, I'm nothing to him but another case, yet he seems to take delight in offending me and since I have been given the task by my guardian of liaising with him, I wish our association could be a little less confrontational."

Her tone was so plaintive that Meg's tender heart ached for her and she could have cheerfully knocked some sense into the obstinate Lazarus' head. She glanced sideways at her companion and saw her watching the colourful scene before her as the young people swept past them, the frou-frou of the silken dresses audible because they were so close. She looked unhappy and Meg found herself confiding in her, though she knew Lazarus would prefer her not to mention his past, "You mustn't take things personally. Lazarus has nothing against you, but the name you bear holds bitter memories for him."

Constance turned to look at her, "He hates me merely because I'm an Allingham?" she asked in surprise, "But what connection can there possibly be? I have no wish to sound impertinent, but he hardly mixes in the same social circles as the Allinghams. Where can this enmity have originated?"

"There was a case, three or four years ago now. Lazarus has never forgiven Lord Allingham for his part in bringing a young and lovely woman to the gallows."

Miss Allingham looked suitably shocked, "But who was she? Was the Inspector related to her?"

"Good gracious no," laughed Meg, and proceeded to give a shortened version of the tragic story of Decima Watkins and how she and the Allingham heir Richard had fallen in love, "Of course, it was never going to be allowed to blossom, this mismatched love affair. Lord Allingham was horrified that his son and heir wanted to take a commoner to wife. He sent Richard to the Crimea, where he died a hero. As for Decima, she had a baby which was taken from her. When three of her sisters died unexpectedly, it was easy enough to accuse her of poisoning them. Lazarus was convinced of her innocence, but he stood no chance of proving it in the face of the power wielded by the Allingham family. Decima hanged and Lazarus has never forgiven himself for not saving her."

"It sounds as though he were a little in love with Decima himself," offered Constance tentatively.

Meg was saved from having to reply by the arrival of her husband bearing two cups of punch, which he handed to the ladies, "Where's the Inspector?" he asked, surprised not to see his friend in their company.

"I thought he was with you," answered his wife.

"No. He wandered off the moment I went to fetch the punch. Ah, well, no doubt he'll be back when it suits him."

It seemed to Constance Allingham that Inspector Lazarus did most things to suit himself.

"Sergeant Stonier, your wife was just expressing a desire to dance, I do hope you are not going to refuse so minor a request?"

Stonier immediately offered his hand to his spouse, "Nothing would give me greater pleasure," he stated with more gallantry than truth. Meg blushed rosily and threw a grateful smile in Constance's direction before being swept off into the throng.

Lazarus chose this moment to return and looked surprised to see Miss Allingham sitting alone,

"Where is everybody?" he asked in the clipped tone he usually reserved just for her. She tried not to look upset, but it was hard. She was growing weary of being a scapegoat for the sins of her uncle.

"Dancing," she answered in a voice quite as sharp as his own.

"Astounding!"

"Why is it so astounding?" she enquired sharply, "Surely dancing is what one does at a ball?"

"We're here to work, Miss Allingham, not to socialise."

"Then why not take yourself off and do just that," she snapped, "I might have a chance of attracting a partner if you don't hang about me, looking like a ferocious guard dog."

His frown deepened, "I'm not stopping you from dancing with whomsoever you choose," he returned brusquely.

"I can assure you, you most certainly are!"

The arrival of Lady Stafford-Naylor prevented this exchange from descending into an extremely childish and unseemly quarrel. She had an unerring instinct for preventing discord as well as a talent for match-making and had observed the cross faces from across the room.

"You are not dancing, Mr Lazarus? Tut, tut, that I cannot allow. I insist that you behave as all the other guests would and try to look as though you are enjoying yourself. I put myself to considerable inconvenience to aid your case, the very least you can do is avoid abusing my hospitality." Her words were delivered with a kindly smile, which took the sting away, but Lazarus was left in no doubt that she meant every word. If he wanted her to continue to help him, he was going to have to do her bidding.

He bowed slightly to her, then turned to Constance, "Might I have the pleasure of this dance, Miss Allingham?"

"No, you may not! I will not dance with a man who has been ordered to endure my company. Go and find some other lady to offend with your boorishness!"

Lady Stafford-Naylor snapped her fan open just inches from the end of Constance's nose, making her jump violently, "Manners, Miss! A lady never refuses a dance. On your feet now!"

With obstinately folded lips Constance did as she was bid and accepted Lazarus' proffered hand, "I'll dance, but you can't make me enjoy it!" she muttered mutinously.

She was acutely aware of his hand in the small of her back, the closeness into which they had been forced, she kept her eyes lowered, sensing his gaze upon her face, amused, but also vaguely puzzled, "You seem a little out of sorts this evening, Miss Allingham," he said as they began to waltz.

"Do I?" she answered bitterly, "I wonder why that might be?"

"Surely nothing I have said or done?" he remarked, one eyebrow raised, as though daring her to agree.

She allowed herself to look up at him, her expression stormy, "You really do have to be jesting!" she said, her breath almost taken away by his determined refusal to accept any fault for their current difficulties, "You have been nothing but rude and dismissive since the first moment we met, though I have tried to be conciliatory and now I find I am denigrated merely because I had the misfortune to be born an Allingham …"

The way a muscle twitched in his tightly clenched jaw told her that she had said too much. Tears started into her eyes, "Let me go," she whispered, "Take me to the far side of the room and let me go. I cannot bear to offend Lady Diana, but I cannot spend another moment in your company."

"Would you like to go outside for some fresh air?" he asked quietly. She nodded miserably and he swiftly guided her between the other dancers and out of the open French windows.

CHAPTER SIXTEEN

PRESENT

Long shadows were falling across the garden, but Joanne and Libby barely noticed. Both were now entirely wrapped up in the story of Decima Watkins and Libby's fight to prove her innocence.

She had just begun to tell the journalist how she had started to believe the house was haunted by the young girl's distraught ghost when a voice behind them made them both jump, "Libby, what the hell are you thinking?"

Libby gave a nervous giggle, "For goodness sake, David! I almost had kittens. What do you mean by creeping up on us like that?"

David ignored her and looked directly at Joanne, "Didn't I tell you this morning at the garden centre that we had no comment and no wish to be interviewed?"

Joanne looked coolly at him, "You told me you didn't wish to say anything, but your wife, I presume, is her own person and free to make her own decisions?" She raised a quizzical brow at Libby, who found herself torn. She had no wish to cause further discord between herself and her husband – on the other hand, she was irked by his high-handed assumption that he spoke for both of them when he had not even consulted her.

"Of course my wife agrees that we have nothing to say to the papers, don't you, Libby?" he asked calmly.

"Well…" she began, but her hesitation was enough for David to realize that she had no intention of backing him.

"I think I'd like you to leave," said David brusquely. Libby was astounded. She had never known him to be so rude to anyone – except perhaps Brendan, but that was understandable. She glanced at Joanne and noticed the girl had blushed and was hastily gathering up her coat and bag. It seemed she was not quite the hard-faced, thick-skinned hack that David obviously believed her to be. The hint of a tear in her eye roused all Libby's sympathies and she suddenly found herself furious with David. This was her house and she had invited Joanne in. It really was beyond a joke that David was now throwing her out, resembling just the sort of Victorian tyrant head of the household that she had been writing about with no fondness whatsoever.

"Stay exactly where you are, Joanne," she said between clenched teeth, "This is my house and you are my guest."

David went white with suppressed fury. She could have said nothing more calculated to provoke him than to remind him that he lived under her roof. It had been an early problem in their marriage, with him feeling they should either move to a house which belonged to them both, or that she should allow him to give her half the value of the house and have his name on the deeds. She thought he was being ridiculously macho, wanting to be the 'master of the house' and the main breadwinner and had refused to contemplate either option. Seeing his livid face and the tensing of his muscles as he strove not to say something he would regret, she understood why it had been a problem for him. She wanted to take the words back, but it was already too late.

David turned abruptly away, "Please yourself, but take my word for it, you'll regret talking to the woman. All journalists are poison."

He walked out of the house and slammed the door behind him.

Joanne gave a grimace, half sympathy, half annoyance at the insult, "I'm really sorry, Libby, I didn't mean to cause a domestic."

"You didn't, he did. But you should have told me you'd already seen my husband."

"I honestly didn't think it would be an issue. You would either agree with him and I'd never have managed to cross the threshold, or you would disagree and be happy to talk to me."

Libby had to admit she had a point. David's attitude did seem a trifle over the top. What possible harm could it do? Did he think she was some sort of a half-wit who would tell their most intimate secrets? He was obviously over-reacting and it was up to her to show him that they really weren't so interesting that their privacy was going to be invaded on a regular basis. This was a one-off chat that would possibly give her a chance to mention her book to the public and perhaps get some publishers interested, other than that, it meant nothing at all.

Joanne offered a tentative hand, "I really am sorry. Am I forgiven?"

Libby forced a smile, "Of course. He'll calm down when he's been for a walk. I really don't know why he has such a downer on the media. You'd think he'd be glad to have his business mentioned."

"Hey, maybe that's the way to repair this," suggested Joanne, "Do you want me to give the garden centre a plug when I write my piece?"

Something made Libby wary. A little voice in the back of her mind was telling her that if David hadn't wanted to be interviewed, then there was a good chance he wouldn't want publicity either. A glance at Joanne's hopeful expression, obviously so eager to make up for her previous error, made her ignore the warning, "Yeah, why not? I can't think of any business that doesn't need a bit of help from time to time."

The younger woman looked relieved that she had found a way to make amends, "Great, I'll make sure I praise him to the heavens. Now I'd better get on my way."

"Okay. It's been nice talking to you."

"And you," said the journalist warmly, "What do you say to us meeting up again soon, for a coffee or something?"

The one thing Libby had missed since moving to the Peak District had been her female friends. She only had one or two – Brendan had seen to it that she had been more and more estranged from the rest when they were dating, and the move from London had finally severed a lot of ties. The thought of having girly chats and shopping trips was too tempting to be resisted.

"I'd love that, thanks," she agreed warmly.

They exchanged numbers and email addresses, then Joanne took her leave.

The fact that David came back into the house within five minutes of her departure told Libby that he had simply walked up the hill behind the house and had been watching for the all clear.

"That was very nice behaviour, I must say," she snapped at him before he had even closed the door behind him, "What a way to speak to a guest."

"She was no guest of mine," he said bitterly.

"Oh, very mature!" she scoffed, getting more and more annoyed with him. She couldn't believe this was the man she had married. He was usually so laid back as to be almost horizontal. This was a side to his character she had never seen before – and she was finding it hugely unattractive.

He was furious that she couldn't see how foolish she was being, "For crying out loud, Libby! Have you completely lost what bit of sense you were born with?"

"I beg your pardon?" she said icily, "Are you listening to yourself? You've just thrown a perfectly nice young woman out of our house …"

"Oh, so it's 'our house' now is it? It was just yours five minutes ago."

"Don't be ridiculous, we're married for God's sake."

"You've decided to remember that little fact too, have you?"

She was having difficulty keeping her hands to herself. She just wanted to slap some sense into his thick skull, "What's that supposed to mean?"

"Some support wouldn't have gone amiss back there," he said coldly, "I don't expect my wife to make a fool of me in front of a stranger."

"Oh, I think you managed that all by yourself," she told him viciously, "throwing your orders around and expecting me to jump to attention. Just who the hell do you think you are?"

"I thought I was your equal, not some hen-pecked little yes man."

"Suddenly you're hen-pecked just because I don't happen to agree with you?" She was incredulous.

Suddenly David realized the futility of the argument. His usual placidity had been ruffled, but he refused to let the ripples continue to spread, "Look, Libby, this is ludicrous. I suggest we agree to differ and leave this alone. I don't trust reporters, but you evidently think you've found your new best friend. Let's just wait and see who turns out to be right, shall we?"

"Absolutely," she snapped back, "I look forward to hearing your abject apology."

"If that woman doesn't stab you in the back, you'll get your apology, don't worry."

He went to the fridge, "Do you want a glass of wine?"

"No thank you, I'll have tea." He glanced at her, then realized that she hadn't moved towards the kettle.

"I'm making it, am I?"

"That would be nice – unless of course it would unman you to lift a teapot."

He gave a wry grin, "Alright, madam, I take the 'hen-pecked' back."

"I should think you do," she said emphatically, "that was low, even for you, Mr Wright. You know how I feel about my mother and father's relationship before their divorce. I would never boss you around – but I don't expect you to do so either."

"Okay, okay, I went too far. Can we forget it now?"

"Nothing would give me greater pleasure."

He made the tea and poured himself a glass of wine, then they sat on the sofa together with the television on, but neither watched it and they both knew that the ceasefire was merely temporary. They were finding cracks in their marriage and neither quite knew how to repair them.

* * *

Having neglected her PC for a couple of days, Libby found several emails waiting for her when she finally switched on the following day. As she deleted the scams and adverts, she found one containing a name from the recent past. An old friend she had known since school had traced her through a website. Without hesitation she sent an acceptance and within half an hour she had another message.

It made her smile and recall the heady days of youth when she and Ilsa had nothing more to worry about than sneaking make-up on in the loos at school and if the boys they fancied would ever ask them to the youth club disco. They had only really lost full contact when she had moved to London, then distance and Brendan had made sure that any tenuous links had been finally severed. After the exchange of several ever more gossipy emails, she found herself swept away on a wave of nostalgia and before she knew it, she was inviting Ilsa over for the weekend. She didn't admit to herself that it might just be a desire not to be alone with David that was feeding the eagerness to recapture her youth.

When Ilsa immediately accepted, she knew a moment of panic, but quickly suppressed it. David spent most of the weekend at work anyway, and took days off in the week to compensate – at least he was supposed to, but actually rarely did so. She understood that he was still building his business, so she never objected, but she was beginning to realize that she was lonely and that her husband was doing very little to address the fact, so wrapped up was he in his own concerns. Marriage wasn't supposed to be like this, she was sure – certainly not after less than a year – but the mystery of why a wonderful guy like David had already had one failed marriage behind him was starting to become glaringly obvious.

She determinedly sent another email, confirming the details and sending directions to the house, then turned back to her book. It had, by now, become her escape and her passion. When real life went wildly out of control, she knew she could enter a world that was totally hers. Her characters would behave the way she wanted them to, the weather was how she wished it, she had the power of life and death – and it calmed her in a way that nothing else ever could.

Even though Lazarus and the others had been real people, the information she had was sketchy and it meant that she was free to put meat on the bones of the story. Meg had evidently been Lazarus' confidante but even he kept certain things to himself and Libby had to guess at an awful lot. She wished she had his private diary instead of his work notes, but she would make the best of what she had – and who could gainsay her?

She wondered if she could track down any other research material.

Lady Stafford-Naylor seemed like the sort that would have either written her own story or had someone else do it for her. Who was it had said that a woman should keep a diary because in her old age it would keep her? Someone famous at any rate and Lady Diana had been fairly notorious in her day.

Without further ado she rang Dan at the museum and asked him if he knew of any books about the Stafford-Naylors.

"How the heck should I know?" he complained, "I'm not the oracle. Go to the library or check the internet."

"Don't be so grumpy," she said, not in the least put out be his attitude, "I know I'll have to go to the library, but I thought you might have a contact who could be persuaded to give me a bit of one to one advice – it would save me a lot of wasted time."

"You are becoming a bloody liability," he said tersely, "What on earth makes you think I know everyone in the town who might help you with your research?"

"You do know someone, don't you?" she grinned happily.

"Go to Braxton Library and ask for Bill in the archives. Tell him I sent you – the rest is up to you. See if you can charm him the way you have me – but he'll probably tell you to buzz off!"

"Thanks Dan, you're a pal."

His response was a grunt, but she knew he was acting the part. Secretly he was delighted she was finding his antecedents so very entrancing.

Bill was easy enough to find. She was directed to the basement when she explained who she was and that Dan at the museum had sent her.

"Not another history buff," Bill groaned, when she explained what she wanted.

"Do you get a lot of us?" she asked curiously.

"Not particularly," he answered shortly. Libby thought there was something more than he was telling her, but it wasn't really her business, so she moved swiftly on.

"So, do you think you can help?"

"I expect so. Give me the names and let's see what we can find."

He held out his hand and she gave him her cast of characters with a real sense of excitement mixed with trepidation. What if she found nothing? Worse still, what if she found information that made a non-sense of everything she had written so far? She was a third of the way through her book – and she was now faced with the very real possibility that she might have to scrap it all and begin again.

She could hardly bear the suspense.

CHAPTER SEVENTEEN

LAZARUS 1862

The evening air was still warm from the heat of the day and redolent with the scents of the garden. Constance was relieved to find that no one else was on the terrace just at that moment. Obviously most people wanted to either dance, watch the dancers or eat. She noticed that Lazarus had held her arm to lead her outdoors, but the instant they were alone he released her. He reached into his pocket, "Do you mind if I smoke a cigar now that we're out here?"

"Not at all," she answered testily. Was there no end to the man's insensitivity? He'd brought her out because she was upset and now he was using it as an excuse to light up.

Lazarus was feeling so tense that nothing but a soothing smoke would help him now. He had never known how to deal with women's tears. He had been useless when his late wife cried and he felt even more discomfited now. This young woman was a virtual stranger to him, she belonged to a clan for whom he had nothing but contempt and for some bizarre reason his every action was either offending or upsetting her and he had no idea why.

Drawing the cloud of cigar smoke into his mouth gave him a brief respite as well as immense satisfaction. He savoured his peace for a little longer then exhaled and spoke to her as gently as he was able, "I don't pretend to know what is troubling you, Miss Allingham, but evidently something is. Do you feel you might like to confide in me?"

"Do you really want me to, or are you just being polite?" she asked, leaning against the cool stone balustrade for support, her knees suddenly weak.

"Well, it can't be the latter – you've already told me that I'm a boor of the worst sort."

In spite of her upset, she gave a small gurgle of laughter, "That was rude of me, but you deserved every word."

"I usually do," he admitted ruefully, "I fear my years in the police force have knocked every refinement of character right out of me. I'm more used to dealing with the criminal element in society than the gentry – though I have to admit the terms are not always exclusive."

"Sergeant Stonier manages to be a gentleman," she chided him.

He tipped his head back and blew smoke into the air. "Sergeant Stonier is a grumbling old humbug who has been showing you his best face."

"That's a terrible thing to say about your friend," she tried to sound suitably appalled, but the laughter still hovered in her voice.

"Ask his wife if you don't believe me," he said, delighted that he seemed to have distracted her from the personal conversation she had seemed determined to have a few minutes before. He had no wish to become emotionally entangled with an Allingham, no matter how personable she appeared to be.

"I will – when she has had the dance she has been allowed to enjoy!"

"Good God, are you still harping on the blasted dancing?" he muttered, finally allowing his exasperation to get the better of him, "I don't dance – never have, never will."

"Fine!" she snapped back, "I only accepted your invitation because Lady Stafford-Naylor ordered me to – you need not blame me because you were forced onto the dance floor."

He closed his lips against further snipes. It was painfully clear that he was never going to win this argument.

"I'm going back inside," she remarked, when she realized he wasn't going to respond.

He threw his butt into the bushes below them, "Just a moment, if you please, there is something I need to discuss with you."

"What?" she asked rudely.

"I've spoken to young Crabtree. I think I may have a notion where Soper has taken Arabella."

Her attitude underwent a miraculous softening. She smiled and reached out an impulsive hand and gripped his sleeve, "Really? Where are they? Oh, pray, don't keep me in suspense. Tell me everything he said."

He was surprised she seemed so passionate, "You seem uncommonly fond of your cousin," he said, not bothering to try and hide his own feelings of contempt for the idea of the spoiled Allingham daughter, though he could hardly claim to dislike a girl he had never met.

"Is there any reason why I shouldn't be?" she asked testily, horrified that he should have suggested she would be so undutiful as to display the slightest ambivalence towards her young relative.

"Every reason in the world, I would have thought. The girl has left you in the most trying of circumstances. You are being forced to lie on her behalf, be denied the freedom that is your right and worst of all you are having to spend time in my company when it is painfully evident that neither of us desires the association."

She looked aghast, the tears welling once again, "I'm sorry you are finding my presence so very irksome, Inspector. I can assure you I feel no such abhorrence but I can do little about it. I have promised my Uncle I will endeavour to find Arabella and to do so I must inflict myself upon you."

"That wasn't quite what I meant," he said hastily, eager to fend off more tears, "But even you must see that this is hardly a satisfactory situation."

"I can only suggest you find my cousin, and then you will be free of the nightmare I obviously represent for you." She took out a tiny scrap of lace-edged muslin and attempted to wipe her eyes. It was very clear to Lazarus that the handkerchief was in no way large enough to mop up the tears that were now falling in good earnest. He took his own from his pocket and offered it to her. She turned her back on him and sobbed quietly, "Please just go away," she managed to whisper, "I will have to stay out here until I have composed myself."

"Don't be ridiculous," he said briskly, "I can't possibly leave you here in this state." He took her arm and forced her to turn back towards him, "Here, dry your eyes and let us agree to call a truce. I apologise for offending you. I truly never meant to speak so bluntly."

She took the proffered handkerchief and blew her nose, "What is the point in pretending? You hate me because I am an Allingham. It makes no difference to you that I never knew about that girl who was hanged and that I have to live on my Uncle's bounty because my parents died and left me penniless."

For a moment he was too shocked to reply and she threw a side-long glance at him suddenly aware that she might have said too much. He caught her eye and they looked at each other for a long time. The tears dried on her cheeks and her breath came fast and light. Feelings stirred in him that he had not experienced for many months and he knew suddenly that he was in the direst peril. He tried to frame a calm and non-committal answer but he found himself saying gruffly, "Don't be so melodramatic, of course I don't hate you."

"You certainly appear to do so," she said quietly, "But you know I cannot help who my family are."

"I'm aware of that, but you must understand that I am required to keep a professional manner with you at all times. Your uncle has entrusted you to my care and for that reason if no other I must keep a suitable distance between us."

"Is that really the reason you have been so horrible to me?"

"I don't think I've been horrible, have I?" he countered with a small smile.

"Yes, you have. Utterly beastly."

"Then for that too I apologise."

"I forgive you – on one condition," she said moving a little closer to him.

"And that is?"

"That we shall be friends from now on."

Friends! Dear God, could anything be worse than to count an Allingham as a friend?

"That's hardly possible, is it? Your own sense must tell you that our social status prevents any such thing, quite apart from the fact that our genders would generate the most appalling scandal."

"Not if we don't tell anyone," she pointed out ingenuously.

He lifted a despairing hand to his overheated brow, "My dear girl," he began, but she refused to allow him to finish the sentence.

"That is all I ask, to be a 'dear girl' to someone. Since my darling mama and papa died I have had no one who cherishes me. My uncle calls me his 'dun heifer', do you know that? He pretends it is affectionate, but in reality, that is exactly how he sees me. I'm merely livestock which he'll sell to the highest bidder when the time comes."

Lazarus knew Allingham to be callous in the extreme, but this he found profoundly shocking, "I think you exaggerate."

"Do I? I think you know I do not. You say he has entrusted me to your care, but you know that the truth is that he didn't give my welfare a second thought when he cast me in the role of go-between. He has no desire to sully his reputation by associating with the Police. I've been thrown to the wolves and he doesn't care what happens to me. In fact, it would suit his purposes admirably should I fall into mire, for then he could, with a clear conscience, cast me into the street and give me no further succour. I am the child of his youngest brother and a wife of whom no one in the family approved."

He could not deny she probably told nothing but the unvarnished truth, but still he resisted her,

"Miss Allingham, I sympathise, but I fail to see why this outpouring of emotion should be directed at me. We are virtual strangers, I have given you no encouragement – on the contrary ..."

"It's very simple, Mr Lazarus. I like you. I have liked you since the first moment we met. You told me the truth and so very few people ever do that. Despite your irascibility I can see that you are an honourable man. I felt a connection with you – I feel it still. And I believe you feel it too."

"You are mistaken, Miss Allingham. And I should caution you that it is dangerous in the extreme for you to bestow your affections upon persons who have done nothing to merit your trust."

She stepped away from him with a gasp of shock, "Is that what you think of me? That I am so flighty and foolish that I speak this way to any man who crosses my path? Inspector Lazarus, I have just confided my deepest and most personal feelings to you and I assure you it is the first time in my life I have ever done such a thing. I can only regret that I was mistaken in my estimation of your character. I will speak to my uncle in the morning and tell him that I feel unable to continue to act on his behalf in this matter – will that satisfy you?"

Every instinct he possessed told him to accept her offer. Nothing but heartache on both sides could result from this odd relationship. Before he could frame a suitable response Meg came flying out of the doors, breathless and laughing, "Good gracious, I feel twenty again! I had quite forgotten how if felt to be swept around a dance floor in the arms of a strong man."

Constance hastily wiped away the remains of her tears and by the time a puffing Sergeant Stonier joined them, her face was adorned by a bright smile and the only evidence of her recent outburst were slightly wet and spiky lashes. She took a step forward, "Oh, Sergeant Stonier, take pity on me. I long to dance but Inspector Lazarus refuses to oblige me. Would you be so kind?"

Stonier felt exhausted and utterly bored with spinning around past the same four walls and crowd of faces, but he gallantly bowed over her hand and led her back indoors. Meg leaned back against the stonework and fanned herself vigorously, "Danby, you ought to be ashamed of yourself. How could you let the poor lass sit out the dances like a wallflower?"

"Dammit, she's not my responsibility!" he protested.

Meg stared at him, surprised by his vehemence, "No one said she was, my dear. What brought that on? It's merely a dance not a walk down the aisle."

"Try telling her that!"

Meg laughed, "Oh, dear, what ever has happened between you two? You'd better tell me everything."

Lazarus was reluctant to discuss the highly embarrassing events of the past few moments, but Meg was the one person in the world whom he knew would listen without prejudice. He gave her a short rundown of the words he had exchanged with Miss Allingham and ended his rendition with the despairing words, "Dear God, Meg. It is the most dreadful mess. How can I continue to see her when she is expecting a romance from me – and how do I avoid her without letting people know the reason why?"

To his astonishment Meg merely laughed at his dilemma, "You silly fool," she said fondly, "From what you've told me, the poor child is not looking for a lover but a father figure. You are years older than her, a widower with a child, living on a policeman's wage – not exactly any young girl's dream match."

"What?" he said huffily, much affronted, "I'm not that old."

"You are to her. How old is she? Twenty?"

"A little older, I think. I really have no idea."

"She's still at least ten years your junior. Stop worrying, Lazarus. You can be sure she merely sees you as solid, reliable and unthreatening. She's lost her real father and her uncle is a monster – she sees safety written all over you."

"Are you sure?" he asked doubtfully. Had his own confusion really coloured his thinking so oddly that he had mistaken the frisson of emotion that had passed between them when their eyes met?

"Take my word for it, Danby. Miss Allingham just wants a trusted repository for her secrets. She'll meet a young man presently and you'll be a thing of the past."

"Thank the lord for that. I have enough to contend with."

Was it Meg's imagination or did her companion sound ever so slightly wistful?

When they returned to the ballroom, they found quite a gathering in their little alcove. Lady Stafford-Naylor had brought the curate to join them, having taken pity on his drifting aimlessly about the place, feeling he could neither dance, nor drink, nor even occupy himself with cards or billiards. The vicar was here too, but he felt no compunction at indulging in a few hands of whist with the elderly ladies who stood as chaperones.

Lazarus felt compelled to speak quietly to Miss Allingham, having had his fears put at rest by Meg, "There's really no need for you speak to your uncle on my account. Your help with your young cousin will be invaluable when the time comes."

She rewarded him with the saddest little smile he had ever seen and he could not have felt more of a cad if she had slapped his face, "Very well. Shall I see you at the police station on Monday morning?"

"I'm at your disposal, madam," he answered formally. She bowed her head in acknowledgement, then turned back to Lady Stafford-Naylor who had been talking to the group, telling them who various people were in the room. Of course her purpose was to find out who was interested in whom, but she was destined to be disappointed. They were all fully aware of her machinations and had no intention of letting slip any of their secret desires. Vanquished, she turned to swapping gossip and as one young woman swept past them in the arms of a particularly saturnine young fellow, she nudged Constance and said, in a whisper that penetrated, "Now there's a young lady who should be in the card room watching her husband play – or perhaps on second thoughts, he should be here, watching her play!"

"Whatever do you mean?" asked Constance quietly, "Surely you don't mean the girl in the white dress with the pink ribbons? She cannot be more than sixteen or seventeen. She's never married already?"

"God bless her, Josette Bennett is seventeen and been married for a twelve-month to a man old enough to be her grandfather. The young man is her lover. I know I should discourage her, but my heart bleeds for her. She was in love with the young Denham boy until her father intervened and married her off to his business partner. She is utterly miserable for her husband shows no interest in her. He has never been married, never had children and been entirely wrapped up in his business since his youth. The poor child is simply expected to sit at home with a mother-in-law who resents her presence in the house and despises her for taking her precious son away. They are simply waiting for her to produce an heir, then her usefulness will be at an end."

Constance glanced at Lazarus with deeply expressive eyes and he knew that she was telling him that such a fate awaited her, if her uncle had his way. He had no idea how to react and was relieved when she dropped her gaze.

"Does her husband know about her lover?" asked Meg, at once appalled and fascinated by the goings on in the upper classes.

"Good God, no! If he suspected for a single moment that any child might not be his, he would divorce her and cut her off without a penny."

"It might perhaps be wise, then," said Stonier grimly, "to desist from discussing the matter. Who knows who might be listening."

"Nonsense," said Lady Stafford-Naylor, "We're all friends here," but she looked uncomfortable and hastily changed the subject.

Lazarus took the opportunity to speak to his sergeant, "We can leave as soon as you're ready, Tom. I've spoken to Crabtree and I think we may have a lead on the whereabouts of our missing heiress. I've also warned him that he had better visit us in Braxton and explain his relationship with Mollie Waters or we'll be slapping the cuffs on him."

"Do you think he'll turn up?"

"If he doesn't, then he'll probably report us to his father who'll make another complaint. We may both be out of work by next week."

"We'd better hope you scared him, then. I'll be damned if I want to explain to Meg that you lost my job for me."

"If it comes to that, I'll take full responsibility."

"Indeed you will, my friend. In the meantime, I'd better keep her sweet by giving her one more turn about the floor. God bless her, she's having the time of her life."

"I'm glad one of us is."

"Why don't you have a spin yourself, Danby? Miss Allingham keeps looking longingly at the dancers. You would make her day if you asked her – properly this time!"

Lazarus knew he was right and when Stonier took Meg off once again, he did start towards the younger woman, but he was thwarted at the last moment when the tall, gangling fellow who was friends with Crabtree approached her and bowed over her hand. She smiled up at him and graciously accepted his invitation. Lazarus was uaccountably annoyed and very shortly after that he insisted that the party take their leave.

He noticed the curate still hovering, looking more at a loss than ever. He wondered what on earth Lady Diana had been about, inviting the young fellow. It was hardly ideal for the man, to have to watch other young people enjoying themselves, whilst he had to merely observe and perhaps imagine a different life for himself. He took pity on him and asked kindly, "Mr Holbrook can we offer you a lift back to Braxton?"

"That would be most generous Mr Lazarus. I own I've grown a little weary and Mr Bembridge looks set to be playing cards until midnight and beyond. I'll just let him know I'm leaving, if I may?"

"Of course. We'll wait in the carriage for you."

He found he couldn't bid farewell to Miss Allingham as she was still dancing. This lack left him feeling curiously frustrated and he assured himself that it was merely because he felt unmannerly not taking formal leave of her.

As the carriage drew further away from the house and the music grew fainter, he allowed himself a backward glance at the twinkling lights. That, he told himself, was one of the oddest evenings he had ever experienced.

"What a perfect night it has been," sighed Meg happily, "I do hope Lady Diana asks us again, Tom. I have never enjoyed myself so much before."

Tom Stonier could have been offended to hear that in twenty odd years of marriage to him, his wife had never been happier than at a party held by an ex-concubine and peopled by those of a supposedly superior class who had shown themselves to be anything but superior, morally at least – but he merely smiled and patted his wife's hand affectionately, "I'm glad you had a good time, my love."

CHAPTER EIGHTEEN

He had been hoping that the weather might break, but Lazarus woke on Monday morning to sunshine pouring through his bedroom window once more. He covered his head with the blankets for a few more precious moments, but the 'knocker-up' was continuing down the street with his long pole, tapping on the windows and the noise couldn't be ignored.

That was, Lazarus reflected, another job that was in danger of disappearing over the next few months if the war in America didn't end soon. The man bearing the pole needed the few pennies from each family he earned in exchange for waking the mill workers for their shift, as more and more were laid off due to the shortage of cotton, then he was needed less and less. He was already hearing stories of girls turning to prostitution to keep bread in their bellies and men thieving and sheep stealing up on the moors to feed their families and he dreaded the time when he was going to be sent to make arrests. How could he in all conscience uphold a law that was forcing these poor wretches into crime in the first place? The mill-owners swore they had no choice but to close their mills as they could no longer afford to pay workers standing over idle machinery, but he noticed none of them were losing their fancy houses, or watching their children run starving in the streets with no shoes to their feet. One thing could be said for the good weather and that was hunger gnawed less viciously at a warm stomach than a cold one.

He heaved himself out of bed, recalling as he did so that he had an appointment to see Lord Allingham, as well as the much anticipated visit by young Lawrence Crabtree. He also remembered, with a slight wince of embarrassment, that he would also have to face Constance Allingham. After his conversation with Meg, he could scarcely believe he had been foolish and vain enough to think the young woman was interested in him as anything other than a father-like figure of stability and good advice. Dear God, what on earth was he thinking, that a beauty of Constance Allingham's status would be attracted to a cynical policeman who was nearing middle-age and had left all his best years behind him?

Will Carter was in his usual spot on the corner of the street, outside the Police Station, but the cap pulled down over his left eye did nothing to hide the fact that he was sporting a bruise that seemed to get blacker even as Lazarus looked at him.

"Been in the wars young Will?" he asked jovially, to hide the very real concern he felt.

"Fell over, Mr Lazarus," muttered the boy, turning his face away and pretending to be looking for potential customers. The street was empty so there was no escape from the policeman's solicitude.

"Nasty fall – and a strange place to fall onto, your eye," commented Lazarus, who knew the evidence of a fist when he saw it and who had heard all the excuses under the sun to explain such injuries, "You'd better step inside for a few minutes and we'll see if we can take a bit of the swelling down."

"I can't do that, sir, thank you all the same. I've got my papers to sell."

"There's a distinct lack of buyers at the moment, son, so do as you're told and step inside."

Will preceded Lazarus up the steps with a reluctance that merely amused the policeman. Once inside Lazarus had the foresight not to take the boy into his office, though doubtless he would have preferred the privacy. One could not be too careful and being alone with a child sporting an unpleasant injury would not have been the best idea in the world. Instead he sent one of the constables for a pitcher of cold water and prepared to make a cool compress in the hope of bringing down the swelling.

He was dabbing the bruise with a damp cloth and trying to silence Will's protests as his inept ministering made the injury smart when a voice behind him enquired briskly, "What on earth are you doing to the poor boy, Mr Lazarus?"

He turned and found Miss Allingham watching him, a quizzical look upon her face. He wondered how long she had been there as a few of Will's epithets had been choice to say the least.

"Miss Allingham, is it time for our appointment already?"

"No, I'm a little early. My uncle wished to change the venue and there was not time to send you a note."

"Very well, let me finish here and I'll be with you directly."

"I hope the young man isn't a victim of over zealous policing," she said with a laugh in her voice. Will Carter frowned blackly at her, "Course not!" he retorted, "I fell."

"Onto whose fist?" she asked tartly, taking the cloth from Lazarus and setting about the child herself, "tell the truth and shame the devil," she added, lifting his chin with a gentle forefinger, "Have you been fighting?"

He looked at her for several tense seconds before he sighed and admitted ruefully, "My pa did it – he didn't mean to," he added hastily, "I got between him and my ma. It was accidental, like."

"So he didn't mean to hit you, but he did intend to hit your mother?" asked Constance softly.

"It's not how it sounds," muttered the boy, leaving neither listener in any doubt that it was exactly how it sounded – and very possibly worse.

"He's out of work and he gets mad about it. Ma says things that get to him. She gets angry too, when there's no food on the table and he spends the money from the pawn shop on beer. He just needs a drink to get him through the worse days and she doesn't understand." The explanation petered out and Will's head sank as he avoided their gaze.

The two adults exchanged a meaningful glance, then Lazarus said bluntly, "If you wanted me to, Will, I could call on your pa and have a quiet word with him."

The boy leapt to his feet and shook his head vigorously, pushing Constance's hands away as he did so, "No, no! Don't even think about it. You'll just make things worse. Just keep out of my business, why don't you?"

Lazarus reached out a calming hand, "Alright, boy, no need for this. I know it's your family and your affair. We'll say no more about it. Here's a penny for my paper, now cut along and watch your step in the future. Stay out of grown-up quarrels and you'll not go far wrong."

Will took the coin and ran, seeming not to notice that he had failed to hand over a newspaper in exchange. Constance stared after him, a worried frown creasing her brow, "Will he be alright?" she asked Lazarus as the door slammed shut behind the fleeing boy.

"He'll be fine." Lazarus spoke the words, but there was no conviction in his tone.

"Is there nothing you can do?"

"Not without good reason. A man is entitled to discipline his wife and children in any way he sees fit. They would have to sustain a serious injury before it became a police matter."

"I suppose a black eye isn't classed as serious then?" she asked coldly, not angry with him, but the law.

"Sadly not. Now, what were you saying about your uncle?" He pushed the thought of Will Carter's domestic trouble firmly out of his mind and turned his attention to the matter in hand. If there was one thing police work had taught him, it was that ruminating on things he couldn't change was the way to madness. He saw children and women beaten, starved and neglected every day of his life – as well as other things that he was not prepared to acknowledge. Miss Allingham could afford to fret and weep over Will Carter – he could not.

"I wish you would do something," she murmured and he found himself sharing the thought. He wanted her to believe that he was not powerless and feeble, but the truth was that Carter senior could hand out as many black eyes as he liked and Lazarus would have to stand by and do nothing.

"Next time I'm in the neighbourhood I'll visit the family," he assured her, feeling a fraud, but impelled to say something in his own defence.

She smiled in pure relief, "If only you would, I should be so grateful."

He gestured that she should go ahead of him into his office, then regretted the action. He shouldn't be alone with an unaccompanied female any more than a child. Where the devil was Stonier when he was needed? It was too late, however, she had already swept past him, her dress shushing with every business-like step.

He carefully left the door open and beckoned the young constable to stand in the corridor with a crook of his finger.

"Now, Miss Allingham, you were saying something about your uncle?"

"Oh, yes. I had almost forgotten. Is every day so full of incident, Inspector?"

"Most of them," he answered shortly, "The message from your uncle?"

"He decided that he doesn't want you to come to the house. He thinks it would cause comment. He has asked me to take you in the carriage to his club. He says they are discreet there and no-one will ask who you are. They will assume you are a business associate."

"Very well. What time?"

"Eleven thirty."

"Very well. I presume you have the address?"

"No need. I shall fetch you there."

"Very well, but I have work to do in the meantime."

"Of course. I shall take myself off shopping and return for you at eleven."

Not five minutes after she left Crabtree arrived, looking sulkier and more rebellious than ever.

"I don't know what the hell you want with me. I had nothing to do with Mollie's death."

"Well, that's a step in the right direction," said Lazarus grimly, "at least you are admitting to knowing her now. The last time we spoke you denied even being aware of her existence."

"Alright, damn you, I knew her. We had a bit of fun together then went our own ways. It's not a crime, is it?"

"No, sir, it isn't a crime. Morally reprehensible, but not a crime."

Crabtree had slouched in the chair opposite Lazarus, but now he leapt to his feet, his face suffused with blood, "I swear to God I'm going to dust your jacket for you if you don't stop presuming to stand in judgement on me! I know my rights. You have nothing on me. I haven't done anything wrong and you can't pin a murder on me just because you don't approve of my morals."

Lazarus subdued him with a glare, "Do you really want to take this outside with me, boy? Because I'm happy to forget I'm a police officer if you are."

Crabtree might have been young and hot-headed, but he knew danger when he saw it. He slumped back in his chair, "No," he muttered, "But, dammit, stop provoking me. I've come here of my own free will to assist with your enquiries."

That phrase smacked of a lawyer and Lazarus realized that he was going to have to tread carefully or the boy would bring in his legal advisor and then they could forget any hope of getting information. He clenched his hands under the desk, but forced a less forbidding expression onto his face, "You're right, Mr Crabtree and I apologise. I'm forgetting what it's like to be young. But you have to understand that poor Mollie ended up dead. I'm sure that you are as eager as I to find out who put an end to a young and pretty girl. The baby she was carrying might even have been your son or daughter – that must mean something to you."

To his astonishment, tears started into the boy's eyes, "I never meant it to end like this, I swear it."

"What do you mean, son," asked the Inspector gently, realising that finally he was getting somewhere and that he needed to handle the boy with kid gloves if he wasn't to find everything slipping away from him.

"I … I sent her to see a woman. She told me she was having a baby and I was terrified of what my father would say. I asked around my friends and they said they knew a woman who could give Mollie a potion. She'd have a bit of belly-ache, maybe a few nights of fever, then it would all be over. The problem would be solved. I gave her the money and sent her on her way. That was the last I heard, I promise you. Mollie never came near me again and the next I heard, she was dead."

"Do you remember the woman's name and where she lives?"

"Her name is Mrs Riley and she lives out beyond Braxton in a hamlet called Little Lowton."

"Thank you, Mr Crabtree. You've been most helpful."

The young man looked up at his interrogator, "Is that it? Can I go now?"

"You can. I know where you are if I need to speak to you again, but I suspect that this is the end of the matter for you."

Crabtree looked as though he could barely believe in his good fortune, "Thank you, Inspector," he muttered gruffly, wiping his nose on his sleeve.

As he reached the door Lazarus couldn't resist one last comment, "Mr Crabtree, all I ask is that you remember that all your actions have consequences – sometimes tragic ones."

The boy nodded and staggered out into the corridor.

* * *

As Stonier reached for his overcoat, Constance sent a desperate look in Lazarus' direction and gave the slightest shake of her head. He understood at once what she was trying to communicate to him and he clapped his companion on the back and said heartily, "No need for you to come, Tom, I'd rather you pursued this woman Riley. See if you can find out where she lives and we'll go together to see her when I get back. This interview with Allingham shouldn't take above a few minutes."

Stonier looked dubious, "I'm not sure that's a good idea, sir."

"What do you mean?" asked Lazarus, inclined to be offended by the implication that he couldn't handle Allingham, or anyone of his ilk.

"Well," muttered Stonier, glancing at Constance, obviously reluctant to speak freely in front of her, "will you keep your temper? You know Lord Allingham is a red rag to a bull where you're concerned."

"Normally you'd be right, old friend," admitted Lazarus, unblushingly frank, "but on this occasion, I'm the one dispensing the favours. He'd be very unwise to provoke me."

"Unwise, maybe, but will that curb his tongue?"

Constance cut in before Lazarus could reply, "I'll look after the Inspector, sergeant, don't you worry."

Lazarus didn't like the conspiratorial grin they exchanged and lifted a sardonic brow, "Shall we go, Miss Allingham?" he said sternly.

In the carriage, Constance attempted to be conciliatory, "I'm sorry about all the secrecy, Inspector Lazarus, but my uncle is determined to keep this matter as quiet as possible. He was adamant that you came alone. He thinks the less people in on it, the better."

"Much good may it do him," grunted Lazarus, "He can keep Stonier out of out meeting, but he will be fully informed when I return to the station."

"That, of course, is entirely up to you, but for my sake, at least give my uncle the illusion that his shame is still well hidden."

He wanted to ask why it was for her sake, but was afraid he would hear something unpalatable if her questioned her further, so he held his peace.

Allingham had covered his tracks well. They were ushered into the club via a back door and crept past kitchens that were alive with the rattle of pans and the shouts of orders to waiters and cooks alike. They were shown into a private room on the first floor and found Lord Allingham waiting there for them, staring out of the window, his visage grim – and suddenly old. For the first time Lazarus felt a faint stirring of pity for the man. He was obviously as fond of Arabella as it was within his power to be, though that wasn't saying much, considering the flint-hearted old sinner loved money and power above everything, even his own flesh and blood.

"About time you got here," he said gruffly to Constance, who almost physically cowered at the sound of his voice, "We're not late, are we, uncle?" she faltered.

"No, we are not," said Lazarus briskly, "What did you wish to see me about, sir. I'm a busy man and can spare you only a few minutes."

Allingham turned to stare at the policeman, but if he hoped to intimidate Lazarus with one of his devastatingly quelling glances, he was sadly disappointed. Lazarus met his eye coolly and almost dared him to say anything derogatory.

"Busy, are you? Then I'll not bother to offer you refreshment."

"It would have been refused. I'm particular who I take hospitality from."

Constance gasped audibly and Allingham clenched his fists briefly before he forced a laugh,

"At least you have pluck, Inspector, if no manners. You are right, however, we are not engaging in social niceties and it is pointless to pretend we are. The heifer here tells me you have tracked down my daughter."

It was not his money, his power or his title that saved him from a blow, but only his age. Lazarus felt his own hands ball into fists before he realized he could not strike an old man – nor engage in fisticuffs in the presence of a woman. He gritted his teeth and ground the words out as though they could cause damage if they were allowed to fly free, "Miss Allingham rather overstated the case. I have an idea where Soper may have taken the young lady, but as yet no proof."

"They may be in Stockport, I understand?"

"Possibly."

"Then you will go to Stockport at my expense and bring her back, if you find them."

Lazarus was left breathless by the sheer arrogance of the man, "I'm not your man to command, Allingham," he sneered, "Send your own agents."

"No one I can send will know how to handle Arabella. She is headstrong and all too easily batters her inferiors into submission."

"A family trait, perhaps? It may very well be so, but I cannot run about the country doing your bidding. I have my duties to perform."

"Your Superintendent assured me that you would do this one thing."

Lazarus couldn't have felt more winded if the man had actually delivered a kidney punch. Of course he had Superintendent Gregson in his pocket! He knew when he was beaten, but still he struggled against the tide, "Even supposing I find the girl, how do you suppose I can get her back to Hanbury, unseen and unremarked by the gossip-mongerers? Do you suggest I go in your carriage, with your crest emblazoned on the doors, and drag her screaming out of whichever house she presently occupies?"

Lazarus had the satisfaction of seeing the older man for once lost for words. He paced the room, obviously thinking of a way around this dilemma.

"I could hire a carriage, but you are right, it would still cause a stir. She is bound to be living in some hovel where a cart would cause comment, let alone any decent vehicle."

"I would say so."

"Then you must take the train," said Allingham, as though he had thought of something particularly clever. Lazarus was scathing in return, "Of course, the train. And Miss Allingham will climb aboard like the sweet little lamb that she is. I'll get two yards before I'm arrested for abduction, with your daughter screaming murder and blood to anyone who'll listen! Far from concluding this farrago in secret, you'll have half the population of Stockport wondering why a gently-reared young lady is alone in the company of a man who is not a relative of hers, or even of the same class."

Allingham looked around and pointed at Constance, "Not if you have her loving cousin with you. If anyone can persuade Arabella to come home, it is she."

"But you will allow me to take Sally with me?" asked the young woman breathlessly, painfully aware of the eyes of both men upon her.

"Absolutely not – we cannot have the servants privy to our affairs!" said her uncle, brutal in his dismissal of her fears and sensitivities.

Constance grew pale then red by turns, "Oh, no, uncle," she whispered, "You cannot expect me to travel alone with the Inspector!"

CHAPTER NINETEEN

PRESENT

While Bill searched the archives for her, Libby decided to go and do a little shopping ready for her weekend visitor. She was beginning to get quite excited by the idea of having an old friend around. She bought plenty of wine, lots of calorific goodies and even went to buy a couple of DVDs of films that were favourites when they were teenagers. It briefly crossed her mind that she was doing everything she could not to include her husband in the girly events, but she dismissed any guilt she might have felt by assuring herself that he wouldn't want to be around two reminiscing women anyway.

She took her purchases to the car and went back to the library to find that Bill had come up with some interesting stuff. Lady Stafford-Naylor had indeed left diaries which Libby took very gratefully from a long-suffering Bill. He had also kindly made copies of the newspaper stories of each of the murders Inspector Lazarus had investigated in his career. He had also found information on Superintendent Gregson, who in his later years had found himself in some considerable trouble when his Mason membership had caused a conflict with his ideas of the pursuit of justice. Crabtree the elder also featured in a scandal sheet from around the same period and Libby smiled at him with a heartfelt gratitude.

She had offered to buy Bill a drink or a meal to express her thanks, but he had been decidedly surly, "No thanks," he said tersely, "I got involved with a writer before and I've learned my lesson."

"Oh dear, that sounds very ominous, Bill. What on earth happened?" she tried to sound sympathetic, but in reality she just wanted to be allowed to go home and examine her treasures.

"Let's just say you are all a bit too single-minded for me," he returned shortly. Libby, who single-mindedly wanted to get home to continue her research, merely shrugged, "Okay. I'll return this stuff when I've finished with it. Thanks again – and let me know if you change your mind about that drink."

"Bloody writers," muttered Bill as she almost danced away and up the stairs.

* * *

It was beginning to be utterly predictable that when Libby had something exciting to do, the phone would ring and drag her bodily back into the twenty-first century. This time it was Matt Piper.

"Would it be convenient for me to call round now, Libby? I'd really like to get this matter sorted sooner rather than later."

She repressed a frustrated sigh, "I suppose so. What time will you be here?"

"Say half an hour? Will your husband be with you?"

"He's not due home just yet. Do you really need him here?"

"I'd prefer it, if it's not too much trouble."

"Alright, I'll ring him and ask him to come home early. I'll see you in a little while."

Libby really had no desire to bring David home early, but she didn't feel she had much choice – and if she was honest, she could do with a bit of support. If Brendan was twisting his story as much as Matt had hinted, she could be facing a pretty grim few weeks ahead.

Fortunately David had evidently decided not to be awkward and simply agreed to come straight home when she rang him, much to her relief. She really didn't need another row with all that was hanging over her head.

Matt arrived first and was comfortably ensconced and drinking coffee by the time David walked into the house. He did a small second take when he heard the two of them chatting quite happily as he came in. Part of him thought it was rather odd that a policeman and prospective victim of crime should be quite so pally, but he told himself he was being unreasonable. Libby was a friendly person. He had once told her that she seemed to have a personal relationship with everyone she met. DI Piper was probably trying to set her at her ease before he broke the bad news to her – because David was quite sure it was going to be bad news. Policemen didn't ask for interviewees to be accompanied by a third party when everything was going smoothly.

Matt rose to his feet and offered a handshake when he saw David, which David duly returned before coming straight to the point, "So, what is this all about? Libby tells me that Brendan has decided to change his story, and your lot are taking him seriously."

Libby was again shocked by her husband's change of attitude. The old David would never have spoken so aggressively and she wondered anew what exactly was bothering him. There was definitely something going on with him and when Matt left she fully intended to find out what was eating away at his usual good humour. It was getting beyond a joke. She was beginning to dread inviting people to the house in case they had their heads bitten off – and now she had a weekend guest coming too!

It was Matt's turn to be the conciliatory one and he did so beautifully, thought Libby, with an inward smile, "I do understand your frustration Mr Wright, but everyone is entitled to a fair trial and we have to take account of everyone's opinion. It may seem to you that the case is clear cut, but we have to explore every claim. You would want that it if was you who were in court, wouldn't you?"

David grunted and sat down – not in his favourite chair, as Matt had already, unknowingly, claimed it, "I suppose so. Tell us the worst then."

Matt retook his seat and began, "As you know Maddie claimed that she came into the house after worrying about Libby and found Brendan apparently trying to lift a drugged and semi-conscious Libby into a noose, presumably with the intention of killing her. Maddie says she knew that their Great Aunt Lil kept her late husband's old rifle under the bed in the master bedroom. She threatened to shoot Brendan if he didn't release Libby and when he refused, she shot pellets into his knees to make him let go."

"That's exactly what happened," said Libby with as much emphasis as she could muster.

"Not according to what Brendan is saying now. He maintains he was actually lifting you down, having found you trying to commit suicide, and that Maddie got entirely the wrong idea and refused to listen when he begged her for help."

"How does he account for the drug in my bloodstream that he'd forced me to drink?" asked Libby, not unreasonably feeling that this fact alone would refute everything Brendan was claiming.

Matt looked uncomfortable for the first time, he looked down at his hands and refused to meet her intent gaze, "That's a bit of a problem for us, Libby. By the time you had a blood test, there was nothing to prove you'd been drugged. That's the trouble with rohypnol – it dissipates in the body really quickly, within hours, and by your own admission, he only managed to get a few sips down your throat. It was just bad luck that you were particularly susceptible to it."

"So, there's no proof that he was trying to kill me?" she asked, aghast.

"Only your word and your sister's," said Matt, "And frankly he has some disturbing things to say about your state of mind at the time."

"The bastard," snapped David, suddenly, "I know what I'd like to do to him right now!"

DI Piper looked at him grimly, "I'm sure you do, Mr Wright, but quite honestly that's not really going to help your wife's case."

"And how can we help it, DI Piper?" asked David with deep sarcasm, "Because it sounds to me like you've come here with the express purpose of trying to persuade us to drop our accusation."

Matt had the grace to look uncomfortable, "That's not quite true, sir, but I do need you to think very seriously about how this is going to affect you. Brendan is adamant he has no wish to damage Libby any further. His solicitor is making it clear that there is an offer on the table and he suggests you consider it."

"No," said Libby emphatically, but in the same breath David asked, "What is the offer?"

Libby had thought she couldn't be any more shocked than she already was, but David's question made her gasp, "David, what the hell are you doing?"

"Let's just hear what the man has to say," said her husband, but he never looked at her and kept his eyes firmly on the policeman's face. Libby subsided into a horrified silence, unable to quite comprehend that he was even prepared to listen to any of this rubbish from her ex-boyfriend.

Matt was speaking again, but Libby barely registered what he was saying. It seemed as though he was talking from a long, long way away. His voice sounded dull and reverberated as though she was at the bottom of a well and he was calling down to her, "Look Libby, I don't like this any more than you do, but Brendan reckons he has witnesses who will testify that you were on the verge of a nervous breakdown when you were caring for your dying aunt. Amongst them is your own mother. You must see how this is going to sound to a jury when they hear it in court, spoken on oath."

Her mother – the woman who had given birth to her, but had done very little for her since. The woman who had taken Brendan as a lover when Libby dumped him. As if that had not been enough of a betrayal, she was now prepared to lie in court just to please her ex-lover.

"What's the offer?" repeated David, unable, for the moment, to look at his wife's ravaged face.

"Drop the attempted murder accusation and Brendan will promise not to pursue the malicious wounding case against your sister. He'll accept an out-of-court settlement for his injuries and you all walk away from this with no further repercussions."

"Mighty big of him," Libby managed to whisper.

"We'll think about it," David said shortly, "I'll ring you when we come to a decision."

Matt realized that he had said enough. He reached out and patted Libby's hand in a comforting gesture that was not lost on David, then took his leave without another word.

Libby found she could not look at or speak to her husband. She sat staring at nothing until he went away. Tears began to roll slowly down her cheeks, but she refused to let him see them and when he came back a few minutes later and handed her a glass of wine, she turned her face quickly away. He put the glass on the table.

"I know how that looked to you, Libby, but I promise you, I did it for you."

"That was for me? You practically admitted to a policeman that everything I said was a lie and that I'm so sick in the head that I tried to hang myself," she said dully.

He took hold of her and pulled her around to face him, "That's not what happened and you know it. Brendan is going to drag you through the mud and in the great scheme of things is it really worth all the heartache it's going to cause? For God's sake, your sister shot him! Isn't that punishment enough? Give him a couple of grand and get him off our backs once and for all."

So many words flooded into her head that she didn't know which to give voice to. Instead she simply looked into his eyes, "Have you ever loved me, David?"

"Of course I love you, that's why I'm even considering this," he told her, giving her a slight shake, as though to knock some sense into her, "Do you think I want to watch you, day after day, in a hostile courtroom, having your character ripped to shreds, your confidence destroyed and your family torn apart forever?"

"You would rather I let Brendan get away with trying to drive me insane, then kill me when he didn't succeed?"

"I think that's a small price to pay," he admitted.

She pulled herself out of his arms, "But I'll be paying it, not you."

"Do you really believe I won't be paying too?" he asked softly, "But at least think about it. Brendan has done enough damage, please don't let him do any more."

She knew she could never back down, but she was weary now and wanted the conversation to end, so she simply said, "I'll think about it."

"That's all I ask."

He went into the kitchen to find them something to eat, but Libby knew he was wasting the effort for her. She couldn't eat. She wouldn't be able to sleep. Not now.

When he was safely out of earshot and clattering pots and pans, she picked up the telephone and dialled.

"Hello Mother, it's Libby here."

"Oh. Elizabeth, dear, how are you? I haven't heard from you for a while."

"No, I didn't have anything to say to you."

Her mother laughed nervously, "What an odd thing to say. I presume you mean that you do have something to say now?"

"Oh yes, I have plenty to say now, but I'll keep it brief. Why have you offered to testify against me for Brendan Tulliver?"

There was a stark silence, then she heard her mother clear her throat and take a sip from what Libby assumed was her nightly G and T, "It's really not as simple and straightforward as all that, my dear. When Brendan told me what he planned, I realized that all round it was the best solution."

"For who? You?"

"No, my darling girl, for you! And for your sister if you must know. Maddie had this crazy idea of taking the Allinghams to court over this Decima Watkins affair. How much ammunition do you think it will hand to that family if they can prove you are a complete psychopath or hysteric?"

"What has anything to do with me? I'm not the one who is claiming the Allingham Estate, Maddie is. I don't even come into it."

"You are being very naïve if you believe that, dear. They are going to rake up every bit of dirt they can find to throw at us and you are simply handing them a wheelbarrow full."

Libby cut the connection.

CHAPTER TWENTY

Lazarus 1862

It was obvious to Lazarus that Constance was extremely nervous and he hoped it was the idea of being on a train and not that she was mortified by the very notion of bearing him company. They could very well have to spend a couple of days together and her mousy attitude would hardly make it a comfortable journey.

"Never been on a train, Miss Allingham?" he asked kindly.

"No, and I'm terrified," she admitted, then gave a little scream of shock when the great steaming machine gave a shrill whistle.

"Time to climb aboard," he told her, taking her elbow and guiding her towards the door. She allowed him to hand her up, but he could feel her trembling.

He travelled by train every month, but he had never yet entered a first class carriage, so it was with some trepidation that he followed her. They had agonised long over their arrangements, debating whether to stick to their separate classes or defy convention and sit together. In the end Constance's nerves won the day and he found himself agreeing, reluctantly, to take Allingham's offer of first class. It was not a place he felt at home and for once Constance held the whip hand – not that she was in any fit state to savour the experience.

They took their seats and he tried to engage her in conversation to keep her mind off the fact that the clouds of steam and another whistle presaged a gathering speed. For anyone used to only horse-power, the locomotive was very fast indeed.

She bravely tried to reply, but he could see she was still shaking.

"It's really quite safe you know," he said softly.

"I know, and I shall grow used to it presently," she assured him, trying to be bravely stoic and failing miserably, "I'm so sorry, what was it you just asked me?"

"I wanted to know how your uncle has explained away your absence? There must surely be some puzzlement in his household by now. First his daughter takes to her bed and is allowed no visitors, now his niece has taken herself off on a jaunt with a policeman."

"Oh, good heavens! No one knows I'm with you, Inspector!" she exclaimed in horror.

He smiled, "I didn't think so for a moment. I was joking."

She managed a small smile in return, "Of course you were – though how I was supposed to recognize the fact, I have no idea. You've never done it before."

"I'm sure I must have done."

"Well, if you have, it entirely escaped my notice," she said frankly.

He shrugged, "Perhaps you are singularly unobservant," he said, "Now, am I going to have to ask for a third time, or are you going to make me privy to your uncle's machinations?"

She gave a tiny laugh, "My uncle never feels it necessary to explain himself and it would have looked odd had he done so on this occasion. Of course it was left to me to make up the lies and tell them to the servants!"

"And what did you tell them?" he asked, pleased that she sounded irritated. Feeling annoyed with her guardian would distract her for long enough to allow her to grow accustomed to the movement of the train.

"I have had a message from a distant relative on my mother's side. An elderly cousin, who has fallen ill and has made a last request to see me before the end. She is very poorly and I may be gone for a few days."

"And your uncle has no objection to your fraternizing with the poor relations?"

"This one is not particularly impoverished and I hinted that there might be a mention in a will. Of course not one of them blamed me for making the journey."

"What a pity you'll not inherit a penny," he sympathised.

"Ah, but I shall have the satisfaction of knowing that I did my duty," she returned wryly.

"Cold, hard cash would be better," he said with a grin.

"You are heartless, Inspector," she chided him, "When I think of that sick old lady …"

"You are quite an actress, Miss," he told her, not without some admiration in his voice.

"I know. I shall perhaps run away from home and tread the boards. It could not be a worse life than that which my uncle has in mind for me."

"Take my advice, my dear, and don't even consider it. You would have a harder time of it than you imagine," he told her solemnly.

"You sound as though you are well acquainted with actresses," she ventured, looking at him from beneath lowered lids. She was surprised to find herself suffering a pang of jealousy at the very notion, and dared not let him see the evidence of it in her eyes.

"I've pulled one or two lifeless from the river. Believe me, they didn't end up in the drink by accident."

That silenced her and he regretted being quite so blunt.

Another topic was required swiftly.

"Do you actually have any long lost relations, Miss Allingham? Perhaps it might be in your interests to find out, if living under Allingham's roof really is so abhorrent to you."

"I don't think so. I know so very little about my mother. I was quite young when she and my father died and I was not encouraged to speak of them."

"I find it ironic that a man such as your uncle would be quite readily referred to as a 'gentleman' and yet there is not a gentle thought in his head, nor a sensitive bone in his body."

"When put like that, I suppose you have a point," conceded Constance, "And yet I must be eternally grateful that he took me in, destitute as I was, and raised me in his household, alongside his own child."

Lazarus knew that the main reason Allingham had done so was merely for show. It would have damaged his precious reputation had his peers known he had thrown his own flesh and blood onto the street. And how much had it really cost him? The young Constance would have eaten very little, her clothes and shoes would have been hand-me-downs and her education taken care of by a governess who was already paid to teach his own daughter. When viewed cynically Allingham would be more than repaid for his 'generosity' by the devotion his niece showed him. Of course Lazarus could say nothing of this to his companion. She believed her uncle had cared for her out of kindness and perhaps a certain degree of duty. What would be the point of disabusing her?

By now the locomotive had gathered speed and a glance through the window made Constance draw in a shocked breath, "It's very fast, isn't it?" she whispered. Lazarus grinned, "Fairly fast," he agreed, "though I've known them go faster."

They were silent for a while, watching the countryside rushing past. They had descended from the peaks and left the moors behind. The view was of a much gentler land, with trees, streams and wide sunlit meadows. Constance was entranced, "You know I rarely travel and I have lived in the hills for so long, I had almost forgotten that England was not entirely made up of the harsh, rocky outcrops of the Pennines."

"Yet you were not, I think, living with your uncle when I first made his acquaintance three years ago?"

"No, not then. I had been sent as companion to my uncle's mother-in-law. She was ill for a long time and I nurse-maided her."

"You really have been used as an unpaid servant, haven't you?" he asked, trying very hard to keep his voice calm and without a hint of the disdain he felt towards her relative.

"Hardly that," she countered, "no servant is treated half so well as I. At least I have been educated, and given the best of everything, even if some of it came to me as 'second hand'."

He wanted to point out that even the meanest household would grant their maids a new piece of cloth to make their yearly uniform, but once again he was forced to bite his tongue.

Just at that moment they were plunged into darkness and Constance gave a hearty scream. Lazarus laughed aloud, "There is no cause for concern, Miss Allingham, we are merely entering a tunnel."

"A tunnel? Why would we go underground? I don't understand."

"Sometimes it is less trouble to cut through a hill that to try and climb over it."

"You mean there is a hill over our heads right now?"

"Indeed there is, thousands of tons of rock and soil, all held up by millions of carefully laid bricks."

"Oh dear," she murmured, rendered almost speechless by the very notion. Lazarus realized that he could actually see her in the half light and he glanced about to find the source. An oil lamp was attached to the wall above their heads, turned as low as possible, but still alight. He stood and turned up the wick, flooding the carriage with its golden glow.

"That's better," he commented, "In third class one has to travel in darkness and like it."

"I don't like it," she said decidedly, apparently much comforted by the light.

"Tell me more about yourself, Miss Allingham," he said, determined this time to turn her thoughts away from the terror of railway travel. He was beginning to find her anxiety a little wearisome, forgetting how terrified he had been himself on his first train journey.

"I can't think what else to tell you, inspector. I have led a very dull existence."

"Where were you born? Do you recall anything at all about your parents?"

"I was born in Manchester. As I told you, my father was Lord Allingham's youngest brother. He had been intended for the army or the clergy, but neither life appealed to him. He was sent to Manchester to study law, but he had no taste for that either. Then he met my mother and they had a runaway marriage in Gretna Green, much to the disgust of his family."

"Who was your mother? How did they meet?"

"Mama was a governess. She was from a good family herself, but they had fallen on hard times and she found herself at the age of twenty with a widowed mother to support. Her only recourse was to use the education she had been given before her father lost the family money and died in debtor's prison."

"Her name?"

"Towey."

An uncommon enough name, thought Lazarus. He wondered vaguely if it would not be possible to trace some of Constance's maternal relations. They might perhaps be in a better position to care for her than she supposed. He stored the name in his memory for future reference.

Unaware of his plans, Miss Allingham was continuing with her story, "She met my father in the drollest way possible. They were ice-skating on a pond and she fell over. My papa helped her to her feet and she slipped and fell again right into his arms. Of course he always teased her after that she had fallen the second time on purpose so that he might fall for her."

Lazarus smiled dutifully, "And did she?"

"Very probably. She was a most determined woman, and full of life. If she had decided that he was the man for her, she would have no difficulty in bringing the union about."

"You see, you do remember them quite well," he said encouragingly.

She gave a sad smile, "It is talking about them that is bringing things back. It has been so long since I've been allowed to do so, it almost felt as though that part of my life was some dimly recalled dream. Until this moment I had forgotten even what they looked like."

"And what did they look like?"

"My father was taller than my mother by a head and shoulders. I suppose she must have been quite tiny. She was very pretty, with dark hair and eyes, a heart-shaped face and a beautiful complexion. I don't think I take after her in the slightest. Sadly I resemble the Allinghams more."

The inspector didn't agree. He thought there was no trace of Allingham in her face or figure. He also thought she was pretty, but he could hardly say so, given the circumstances.

"The accident that ended their lives must have been horrifying for you."

She nodded thoughtfully, as though debating whether to tell him more. There was a short silence, then she evidently decided to continue, "I was four or five years old – I surmise that was why I was not with them in the carriage. They were hurrying to get home. I suppose the carriage was being driven too fast for the driver to see the danger ahead. It was during a most terrible storm and the bridge ahead of them was about to be swept away by the strength of the flood waters. In the dark and rain they saw nothing was amiss until it was too late. They were all plunged into the water and all drowned. The horses couldn't even escape because they were fastened to the carriage as it sank beneath the current. It seemed my father had tried to save my mother. He had let down the carriage window and had tried to drag her out, but the flood had been too strong for them and they were found clasped in each other's arms a few days later."

Neither had noticed that the tunnel was a thing of the past and they were once more travelling through sunlit countryside, where haymaking was going on. One or two of the gleaners stopped to watch the train go by, but most of the farm workers were now used to the modern age and went on with their scything with never a glance.

A sudden shrilling of the whistle caused Lazarus to look anxiously out of the window. As he suspected they were nowhere near a station or even a halt and still moving at full speed. That could only mean something or someone was on the line and the train driver was trying to warn them off. When it blew again with much more emphasis and a longer louder blast he realized that the incident might well be serious. His suspicions were confirmed when the screech of the brakes began to rend the air and he instinctively threw his arm across Constance saying at the same time, "Hold on, Miss Allingham, I think there's something amiss."

The application of the brakes at the speed they had been travelling could only be a bad thing and sure enough they both found themselves being flung forwards by the cessation of momentum. His quick thinking saved his companion, but unfortunately left him wide open to injury. As they lurched across the carriage, Constance found herself falling hard against his protecting body, but Lazarus' head hit the opposite wall with a resounding crack and for a few minutes he knew only darkness then pain.

When he opened his eyes he saw only an indistinct female figure looming over him and in his dazed state he said the only name he could think of, "Rosamund …"

"No, it's me, Constance. Are you alright, Inspector? For one horrible moment I thought you were dead."

For one horrible moment he had thought the same thing, but he managed not to voice it, "I'm still alive, never fear. But what about you? Have you hurt yourself at all?"

"I feel as though I have strained every muscle in my body in trying not to fall against you, but other than that I'm fine. What on earth happened?"

Lazarus gave himself a couple of moments to recover his equilibrium, then he staggered to his feet and threw open the door to try and see what had befallen them.

It was obvious at first glance that the engine and two of the carriages were derailed. Fortunately none had rolled over but the damage was considerable just the same. The engine lay askew and was hissing gently like a winded horse fallen badly at a jump and like a horse with broken limbs it was quite useless and unable to travel an inch further. The engineer and his companion both stood looking helplessly at the carnage without appearing to have much of an idea how to repair it. They seemed relieved to see Lazarus walking towards them, though he was a sobering sight, with a trickle of blood running down his face.

"What goes on?" he asked as he approached. The engineer pointed towards the front of the engine,

"Some bloody fool laid a tree trunk across the line. We had to brake to avoid a crash, but it might almost have been better if we'd risked hitting it, judging from the result."

"You mean it was deliberate? Are you sure it wasn't just blown over by the wind?"

"The wind doesn't wield an axe," said the other fellow sourly, "And to be truthful, it's not that unusual an occurrence. There are plenty who haven't welcomed the railway."

"You've had incidents such as this before then?" asked Lazarus in surprise.

"More often than I care to recall."

"What happens now then?"

"There's a village just over the hill. We'll send a message to the Company and they'll arrange for horses and machinery to help us clear the line. But there will be no more travel today. I suggest you head for the nearest inn and see if you can hire a vehicle or failing that, get yourself a bed for the night. I'd call a doctor, too, if I were you."

He indicated Lazarus' wound with a pointed finger and the inspector lifted a hand to his scalp, unaware until that moment that he was covered in gore. He examined his fingers, "Good Lord, you're right. I knew I'd hit my head, but I hadn't realized I was bleeding – it's nothing, I'm sure – looks much worse than it feels."

"I hope you're right."

"Is anyone else injured?"

"Not as far as we know. The conductor is checking now. There's not that many passengers on board at this time of the day – but the post won't get through until tomorrow at the earliest."

Lazarus bade them farewell and went back to appraise his companion of the situation. It looked very much as though either fate – or a human agent – was determined to prevent them from reaching Stockport for at least another twenty-four hours.

Constance was at the door of the carriage waiting anxiously for him, "What have we to do, Mr Lazarus?" she called as he drew near.

"Climb down. We have a walk ahead of us. Are you sure you're not hurt in any way?"

"My back and my neck ache a little, but I'm quite able to walk," she assured him, "But where are we going?"

"To the nearest village. It will take hours for them to right the train. We need to find food and shelter."

"Oh," she obediently stepped out of the doorway then realized just how big a drop it was to the floor. Of course the carriage was designed to stop at a raised platform at the station and it was quite a step down without it. Lazarus saw her hesitate and hurried to offer her his hand. She took it and jumped, her voluminous skirts billowing out and revealing a glimpse of shapely ankle clad in neat little leather boots with tiny jet buttons. She landed awkwardly and he was forced to catch her under the arms to stop her from falling face down on the grass verge that edged the track. She blushed hotly as she glanced up at him and realized he was altogether too near to her, but he simply set her briskly on her feet and released her.

"Let us see if we can find your luggage. You'll need your night clothes and fripperies if we have to spend the night at a lodging house."

Fortunately, since they were two of only about fifteen other passengers, they found both their bags without much difficulty. Lazarus recognized his own Gladstone bag from the ground and hoisted himself to the roof of the carriage to release it and Miss Allingham's, which was directly behind it. By this time several other gentlemen had arrived on the scene and Lazarus found himself throwing various bags and valises to their owners – at least he hoped they were the owners! He had no way of checking, but he did announce his police credentials before handing them over, hoping that would be enough to discourage theft.

This of course resulted in them being the last to arrive in Drakemoor village. They found the inn, but every available vehicle had been commandeered and were already trotting out of the yard and heading towards all points of the compass.

It seemed a waste of time trying to hitch a lift into Stockport, which was, anyway, still a considerable distance, so Lazarus and Constance simply went into the Navigation Hotel and requested two rooms for the night. It was named a hotel, but was really nothing more than a large public house, but they did offer rooms to travellers and at that moment that was all that concerned either of them. Constance had certainly never stayed anywhere quite so basic, but she was far too exhausted to notice her surroundings.

They were soon accommodated and Lazarus was about to take Constance to her room and settle her when he glanced at her face. She was chalk white and looked not only weary but appeared to be in pain. He turned back to the landlord and asked quietly, "Is there a local doctor available? My companion needs someone to look over her and ensure she wasn't injured in the train accident."

"You look as though you could do with the once over yourself, my friend," said the landlord, reminding Lazarus once again that he must look thoroughly disreputable with his tousled hair and blood-stained face and shirt, "I'll send the boy to fetch him for you directly. Can I get you something in the meantime? A couple of brandies perhaps?"

"Brandy for me, tea for the lady," said Lazarus firmly. Constance had not heard the beginning of this conversation, but she heard this and immediately took umbrage at his high-handed attitude, "If I need anything, I can ask for myself," she said briskly.

"Do you want something other than tea?" he asked, with studied patience.

"No, tea would be perfect," she admitted, "But I have a tongue in my head!"

"Oh, I'm very well aware of that," muttered Lazarus and threw a wink towards the landlord, who laughed and went off to get their drinks.

"You are insufferable," said Constance crossly, well aware that she was being designated 'a little woman' who would do as she was told, and deeply resenting it.

"I'm aware of that too," said Lazarus, "Shall we sit down?"

He led her into the coffee room, which was away from the public bars and would afford them a little privacy.

"What were you asking the landlord?" she asked curiously, sinking gratefully onto a well-padded and be-cushioned settle in front of a empty fireplace.

"He's sending for a doctor for you," he said, in a tone which would brook no argument – but Constance argued anyway, "There's no need, I told you I'm perfectly well."

"You said your back and neck were hurting – and you look like a ghost. A little laudanum will help you sleep."

"You look more in need of a doctor than I," she said archly.

"And I shall consult him also," said Lazarus calmly, "I have a devil of a headache now and I'm not too proud to take help when I need it."

Both his points silenced her more effectively than any threat would have done.

CHAPTER TWENTY-ONE

When the landlady arrived with a pot of tea, she also bore a bowl of hot water and some clean rags, "The doctor is on his way, but in the meantime, I suggest you clean that blood up – you'll be frightening my other customers. They'll wonder what sort of a rough-house I'm running here."

Lazarus looked startled; he had forgotten again that he had hit his head and had been bleeding. Seeing his shocked face, Constance started to get a little frightened that he was far more badly hurt than had first appeared. She rose to her feet and took the tray with a smile of thanks, "I'll take care of him, don't worry. Do you think the doctor will be long?"

"Not at all. He was getting the boy to put his horse to the carriage before my lad left."

"Thank you," she said fervently, "I think we might have need of him." Constance cast a worried glance towards the policeman and the landlady understood at once and gave her a sympathetic nod, "Try not to fret, love, I'm sure everything will be fine."

She went away and Constance put the tray on a side table and doused a cloth in the hot water.

"Are we having tea?" asked Lazarus.

"Let me tidy you up first."

"I can do that myself," he said fending her off as she moved toward him.

"No, you can't. There isn't a mirror in here and you can't see the blood. I can. Now sit down and behave yourself."

With bad grace he allowed her to begin her ministrations. She took the opportunity to look closely at him and was relieved to see that though he was pale and perhaps a little distant, he looked very much his usual self.

"How do you feel?" she enquired as she endeavoured to remove the streaks of rapidly drying gore.

"I have a devil of a headache, but other than that I'm well enough," he replied tersely, "Too well, at any rate, to have you nurse-maiding me. Don't you ever get tired of a life subjugated to others' welfare?"

"That's a long word for a man with a headache," she said lightly.

She was glad to hear him laugh, but concerned when it obviously pained him and he winced.

"By God, I'm suddenly tired. I could just fall asleep."

That made her even more afraid, but she managed to keep her voice steady when she replied, "Well, I fear you'll have to wait a little while for that. You insisted on sending for a doctor and he's on his way here."

"The doctor was for you," he pointed out, "I have no need to see him."

"We'll let him be the judge of that when he gets here. There, you look a little less disreputable. Drink your tea."

She laid the bowl and cloth aside, trying not to notice the amount of blood which now coloured the water and stained his shirt and coat. She handed him a cup which he drank thirstily and she was grateful he said no more about sleeping, although he looked heavy-eyed and still frowned a little against the pain in his head.

With admirable discretion the landlady came to the door of the sitting room and called Constance out into the hallway, "Dr Bell is here, Miss, but I thought you would want a word with him first without the gentleman overhearing. I know how gentlemen hate a fuss made by us women-folk."

Constance smiled, "I strongly suspect that you are a treasure, Mrs … I'm sorry, I don't know your name."

"It's Locke, Miss, Florence Locke. Just call me Flo."

"Thank you, Flo. Now where is Dr Bell?"

"In the front room. Come and have a word with him."

Dr Bell proved to be much younger than Constance had anticipated, probably only thirty or so, and very good-looking. She wondered at his being a country doctor, then realized it was more than likely a stepping stone to bigger and better things. Buying a practice in a large town or city was expensive and he would need to build a reputation and find a rich patron to get himself started. If she was any judge, there would be a couple of large estates in the vicinity to whom he could show himself to be equally adept with the lady of the manor and the poor of the district.

They went into the coffee room together where the beginnings of an unseemly quarrel threatened between Lazarus and Constance when the doctor asked who needed to be seen first.

As he watched the words fly between the pair, who seemed quite at ease in each other's company despite their very obvious differences in class, the doctor wondered what on earth was going on to bring them together alone on a train to Manchester.

Constance had the final word when she pointed out that though she had complained of some pain, she was not, like Lazarus, actually bleeding – for his wound had indeed begun to seep again.

"For goodness sake, woman, I'm well enough but for this damned headache," was the growled response from the irascible policeman. That was enough to convince Dr Bell that he required immediate attention. No gentleman would swear before a lady unless he was far from being his usual self.

He took the decision upon himself, "You, Miss, can go and find Mrs Locke and ask her to accompany you upstairs as a chaperone. There you will ready yourself for an examination of your neck and back. By the time you have done so, I will have seen to this gentleman and all will be settled."

Constance blushed hotly at the thought of even semi-nudity in his presence and hurried off lest he see her embarrassment. At least she would not be alone with him, but bearing the comforting company of Flo Locke.

Once they were alone Dr Bell approached the still seated Lazarus and with gentle fingers probed his scalp and moved aside the dark hair, dyed still darker with dried blood, "For how long were you unconscious?"

"A few minutes, I believe."

"No more than that?"

"Not as far as I'm aware."

"Any trouble with your memory? You do recall everything about the accident?"

"I was a little confused when I first came around, but it lasted only seconds." He winced as the doctor pressed a little too hard on the bruise that lay under the cut.

"Do you still have a headache?"

"Your prodding has done nothing to improve it," he replied tersely.

"Are you normally prone to such ailments?"

"Never. I usually enjoy rude health, I'm grateful to say."

"Umm," mused the doctor, "It's a nasty injury, but there's not much I can do for you. Unless you want me to, there's not even much point in bandaging your head, the bleeding is stopped now. I can give you some laudanum for the pain if you want it, but frankly I would rather you had a good night's sleep and let nature cure you in her own good time."

Lazarus shrugged off the suggestion, "I could not take laudanum anyway. I'm responsible for the young lady and I have to have my wits about me. She's not accustomed to travelling without a maid or the niceties to which she was born."

Dr Bell was more convinced than ever that they were a odd pairing. This comment merely made him think that they were a run-away couple, fleeing parental disapproval. However, it was no concern of his, he only wanted to know who would pay his fee, which he duly intended to mention, though not before he had seen the young lady.

He grunted noncommittally, "That's neither here nor there to me. I'm merely treating your injuries. If you don't want pain relief, I'll not force it upon you. If the pain does not subside overnight, send for me again in the morning."

He took himself off to ask where he would find Constance, and Lazarus closed his eyes against the ache that the evening sunlight through window was exacerbating.

Dr Bell found Constance's room with no trouble. It wasn't the first time he had been called to the inn for ailing patrons, though, to be fair, they were much more likely to be suffering from the after affects of overindulgence than a train crash.

She had removed as little of her clothing as she could, thanking heaven that she had worn sensible travelling garments and not one of her pretty silk dresses. She need only take off her tightly fitted jacket, with it's many tiny buttons, and a fine lawn chemise beneath, leaving her bell-shaped skirt with it's crinoline, and her stays firmly in place. This way she need only bare her shoulders and the top of her back – which now ached more than ever, though she was sure this was due to the strain of keeping herself calm and unruffled by all the trials she had endured on this very adventurous day.

The doctor was kindness itself and kept up a continuous friendly chatter whilst he felt her neck with warm and gentle hands.

"It would be very hard to tell, but I seriously doubt you have broken any bones," he said, much to her relief. Suddenly his hands became still and he leaned forward to better see something that had caught his attention, "What are these bruises on your back?" he asked softly. He felt her stiffen and pull away from his touch, "They must be from the accident," she said hastily, but he heard the tremble in her voice. There was something here that he needed to investigate, but he sensed she would never speak with another person present. Accordingly he turned to Flo, who had sat quietly through the examination, "Mrs Locke, we're done here. Could you possibly get me a cup of tea? I'll be downstairs in two minutes."

"Certainly, doctor. You'll be alright, Miss?" she asked, as she passed the white-faced Constance.

"Yes, yes, quite alright. I can button myself back into my pelisse. Thank you for your help."

When the door closed upon her, Dr Bell said firmly, "I'm going to undo the top few laces of your stays. These bruises look serious and I don't think they are new. I want you to tell me truthfully how you came by them."

She made no protest and he loosened the laces, exposing enough of her back to see more of the livid slashes, which were in places fading to yellows, greens and mauves.

"How did it happen?" he asked.

She drew in a deep breath, "I was pushed against a stable wall by a horse last week. I had no idea the bruises were so bad, otherwise I should have done something about them, of course."

"Very well. There's nothing more to be done. I deduce the pain you have in your neck and shoulders is muscular and will fade with time. Try not to do anything strenuous. I would suggest you avoid horses for a few weeks. I'll send Mrs Locke up to help you dress."

"Thank you, Dr Bell." She avoided meeting his eye and he left the room looking grimly thoughtful.

Conveniently Mrs Locke had left a fresh tray of tea for him with Lazarus, who had perked up enough to have a cup himself. He glanced up when the doctor entered the room and was concerned by the frown adorning the younger man's face, "Is there something amiss with Miss Allingham?" he asked, starting to his feet.

The doctor, who had been inclined to jump to the conclusion that Lazarus might be responsible for the injuries he had just witnessed, was relieved to see the very real solicitude in the policeman's whole demeanour.

"There's no cause for worry, sir. The young lady is not badly injured, however …"

Lazarus frowned, "However, what?" he demanded belligerently, irritated beyond measure by the air of mystery.

The doctor sat and poured himself some tea, "I'm not sure I ought to tell you this, but since you say yourself that you are presently responsible for the lady, I will confide that she has some bruises for which she gave me a very unlikely explanation."

Still on his feet, Lazarus looked down at his companion and spoke in a deceptively calm voice, "Would you care to expand upon that, Doctor?"

"She says she was knocked against a wall by a horse, but what I saw were the marks of a whipping – possibly by something similar to a riding crop."

"Dear God," whispered Lazarus, then aloud he added, "Pray excuse me, Doctor Bell, I have something pressing to attend to."

Dr Bell drank his tea and decided that tomorrow was soon

enough to send in his bill. He rather thought the two lovers had a considerable amount to discuss.

Lazarus in the meantime demanded directions of Mrs Locke then took the stairs two at a time. He knocked on Constance's door, but he needn't have bothered because he didn't wait for her to give him permission to enter and simply burst in upon her. She turned at first startled, then horrified when she realized whom she faced across the expanse of the bedroom. Hastily she grabbed her coat off the bed and held it to her bosom, "Inspector Lazarus, what are you thinking of?"

He flicked the door shut behind him and said grimly, "Show me your back."

She looked as though she might faint and sinking into a chair she managed to stutter, "I will not!"

He walked across the room, determination writ on his face and she quailed from him, "It is nothing to concern you – only an accident…"

"Accident by God! I think not." He took hold of her arm and left her desperately clasping her jacket one-handed to cover her modesty, "turn around or you'll force me to …"

"To what?" she gasped, tears starting to fill her eyes, "force you to beat me into submission?"

That stopped him in his tracks and he stared down into her eyes for several long, painful seconds before he released her and regained mastery over his anger.

"I would never do any such thing, Constance, but I know someone else has."

She looked up at him pleadingly, "It is not your affair, there is nothing you can do."

"Of course there is," he blustered, still furiously angry.

"No, there is not. You told me that young Will's father could take a stick to him whenever he chose. My uncle can do the same."

"So it was Lord Allingham? Is this a regular occurrence, your being used as his whipping boy?"

"No. It hasn't happened for years, not since I was a little girl …" she realized that in trying to placate him, she was making things worse. She took a deep breath and tried again, "Please, please listen to me. It was not his fault. Not really. I was the one who brought him the news of Arabella's flight. He was furiously angry and he blamed me for not keeping a better guard on her. He was right. She was my charge and I allowed her to charm me as she did with everyone else. I should have known she was planning mischief."

His expression grew increasingly bleak and she knew he was now beginning to plot a revenge which would only cause heartache for everyone. She wondered what else she could say that would make him understand that he had to forget he had ever been told about her uncle's abhorrent behaviour.

She reached out and took his hand, "Danby, I will not be responsible for your destruction. I have forgiven my uncle and that must be enough for you."

He gripped her hand tightly for a fleeting moment before he released her and said as gently as he was able, "If you do not allow me to see what he inflicted upon you, my imagination will paint a picture more horrific with each passing day. In those circumstances I can never leave this alone."

She realized he spoke nothing but the truth and she had no choice but to accede to his request, reluctantly she nodded and slowly turned to expose her back to his gaze. His indrawn breath told her that he was shocked and appalled and she wanted to die of the humiliation she felt. When she felt his fingers brushing against her skin she shuddered and began to sob bitterly and he drew her into his arms, "I am so very sorry, my dear. If I had known what you were enduring …"

She felt his arms loosen and before she could understand what had happened, he crumpled in a heap at her feet. Horror struck as she stared down at his recumbent form. Fool that she was, she had allowed him to argue with her when he was still unwell and this was the result.

In utter panic she threw on her jacket and ran for the doctor, whom she hoped was still downstairs, her trembling fingers struggling to fasten the stupid little buttons, which slipped from her suddenly damp hands. Dear God, she prayed, don't let him be dead. Don't let him die now, just when they had found each other.

CHAPTER TWENTY-TWO

PRESENT

The hair was still bottle blond, the nails still beautifully manicured, but Ilsa looked older than her thirty-three years. She had always, Libby recalled, had a weakness for 'bad boys' and it seemed the strain of keeping them was finally showing on her friend's face.

She glanced at the clock. It was past six, so the offer of a glass of wine was not inappropriate, not that Ilsa had even been known to worry about yardarms and suns in the past.

"Come on in, and I'll show you to your room. Once you've dumped your bags, we'll crack open the vino. I've bought a bottle of your favourite Shiraz."

Ilsa looked as though Libby had offered her a glass of hemlock, "Unless it's non-alcoholic, I won't bother, thanks."

Libby tried but couldn't hide her shock, "Whoever heard of non-alcoholic Shiraz?" she snorted, sure that this must be one of her friend's jokes.

"It's very nice," said Ilsa calmly.

With a laugh Libby managed to say, "You really had me going for a minute there, Ilsa. I should have known you were pulling my leg. The day you don't drink will be a cold one in hell!"

Ilsa managed to look both disdainful and supercilious at the same time, "I don't drink, actually," she said, "Do you have any idea what booze does to the human body?"

"No, and I don't want to know," said Libby frankly, "Since when has all this happened?"

"It must be a couple of years now."

Libby did a quick mental review of Ilsa's past boyfriends, "Oh, I get it. This is all since Loony Luke, isn't it?"

Ilsa had been living with Luke for two years before she finally got sick of being his punch-bag when he'd had a few too many lagers. That had been partly why she and Libby had grown apart. She didn't much appreciate being told what an idiot she was for putting up with the abuse. The cry of "you don't understand, I love him" had not cut much ice with Libby or any of the other girls they were pally with at the time. By the time she had finally seen sense, Luke had succeeded in driving most of her friends away. Of course Libby had then become involved with the similarly controlling Brendan, so she had cause to regret being quite so vociferous in her condemnation of Ilsa's weakness in forgiving Luke his many and varied trespasses – but at least Brendan had never hit her until they had parted company.

Thankfully Ilsa was honest enough to admit the truth, "I did join Al-Anon to try and understand why Luke was the way he was and they made me see that in drinking too, I was enabling him."

"There were times when you kept pace with him, drink for drink," agreed Libby reasonably.

"I wasn't an alcoholic!" snapped Ilsa, obviously highly offended that Libby should have suggested any such thing.

"Of course not," said Libby hastily. Oops, that was evidently a sore point, she thought, better not mention drinking again.

She picked up Ilsa's bag, "We'll have a coffee in a few minutes, but let's get you settled before we do anything else."

She led the way up the stairs and Ilsa looked around her, "Funny, I imagined this place was going to be much classier," she said musingly.

It was Libby's turn to be offended, "What do you mean?" she asked, with a slight edge to her voice, "What's wrong with it?"

Ilsa smiled condescendingly, "Nothing at all, if you like old-lady décor," she said with a shrug.

Truth to tell Libby had loved the house so much and had been so delighted to find herself the owner when her Aunt died, that it had never occurred to her to change anything. It wasn't a house which lent itself to excessive modernisation, being an old farmhouse which had been in her family for at least five generations. She intended to have a new bathroom and kitchen at some point, but the present ones were serviceable, so why be in any hurry?

"I've had one of the bedrooms made over into a study for my writing," she said defensively, "Look I'll show you. I think it's lovely."

She opened the door to the one room in the house she felt was truly her own with a flourish, "Isn't it lovely? I have a fabulous view when I'm writing."

"Whoopee doo!" said Ilsa with biting sarcasm, "You've inherited a house and a couple of million quid and what do you do with it? You line a room with a few bookshelves and buy a desk and a computer."

Seeing the room suddenly through her friend's eyes made Libby realize just how shabby and old the place must seem to other people. For the first time she felt a sense of disappointment in her surroundings. How easily she had been satisfied. That was her trouble. She had no discernment, no taste. She settled for less than nothing and didn't even have the gumption to notice that she was being short-changed.

David was as bad as her, not even appearing to notice the squalor in which they were living. Why on earth had he not said something sooner and helped her to alter the house to fit in with their new lifestyle?

"Of course we have lots of plans," she faltered, painfully aware of the scorn Ilsa was feeling towards her, "These things take time. And I've had other things to think about."

"Like what?" said Ilsa, following her out of the study and into the guest bedroom.

"The book I'm writing, for a start."

"That doesn't take all day, every day. And with your money, you should be employing someone else to do it for you."

"I don't know where you get the idea that I inherited a fortune. It wasn't anything like that much and having a court case hanging over me isn't helping," floundered Libby, desperately trying to win back a little pride from her crushingly exacting friend.

Ilsa finally looked impressed, but Libby would have preferred not to talk about the anguish Brendan was causing her.

"Oh, do tell," said the visitor, throwing her real leather weekend bag onto the bed and unzipping it, preparing to unpack. She had not changed that much, thought Libby, eying the expensive bag and catching a glimpse of some of the designer contents. Nothing but the best for Ilsa, even if she had to go into debt to get it.

"We'll talk later. Let's go down and get a drink and something to eat," she said hastily.

They were drinking coffee and chatting happily when David finally came in. He lifted a questioning brow at Libby and she suddenly realized that she hadn't actually had the chance to explain about her old friend coming to stay. A tiny pang of guilt about springing a guest on him without consultation made her tone slightly defiant when she introduced the two of them to each other.

"Ilsa's staying for a few days, David, she was dying to see the house."

"Absolutely," purred Ilsa, flashing her eyes at the obviously startled David. He had had his fair share of women in the past, but since being married, he had rather fallen out of the habit of dealing with flirtatious blonds. Libby could see that he was uncomfortable, and also annoyed at having the unexpected visitor. She found herself making excuses to herself for him when he was less than the perfect host and practically grunted at Ilsa, "Hi there, Ilsa. I hope you have a good time, but if you'll forgive me, I could do with a shower, I've been at work all day."

He left the room with unflattering haste and Ilsa laughed, "Good job he's good looking, Libby, because he has no finesse whatsoever! I suppose you just suit him up and tell him to stay quiet when you take him into mixed company."

"He's tired, he works very hard."

"Yes, but it's from choice, my dear," said Ilsa smoothly, "You have money enough for the pair of you. If he wants to labour like a navvy, that's entirely his own choice, isn't it?"

Libby had to agree that it was, but she had never seen that as a bad thing in her husband. Why should he want to live off her aunt's money? She tried to say something along those lines to Ilsa, but she was having none of it, "Oh, don't give me that old-fashioned, sexist stuff! Since when is it a threat to manhood to be rich? You wouldn't think twice about living off him if things were reversed, would you?"

"Actually I think I would," ventured Libby, reluctant to argue with her friend, but forced by her natural truthfulness to be accurate if not forceful.

"Then you're an idiot too," said Ilsa decisively.

Libby suddenly remembered that there was no compromise with Ilsa. She was always right and she would quarrel quite happily for hours until you were worn down enough to agree with her just for the sake of some peace. She had driven away most of her other friends by being so obnoxiously self-righteous, but Libby, being fairly easy-going, had usually managed to avoid contentious subjects and they had rarely fallen out – until the fatal day she had finally had the guts to stand up to Ilsa and tell her straight that she was a fool for putting up with the odious Luke. That had earned her twelve months of frosty silence, until Libby had remembered that she had lent Ilsa a favourite handbag, which she desperately needed as the only thing to go with her lucky shoes for an important job interview. She had debated for days over what to do, even contemplating buying a new bag, but the one in question had cost her a small fortune and she was suddenly determined to get it back. She had written Ilsa a pleasant but neutral note, simply asking for the item to be returned. To her amazement, Ilsa had taken this as an olive branch and had turned up on her doorstep, toting the bag, a bottle of wine and a gracious acceptance of Libby's apology. Of course Libby had done no such thing, but it had seemed easier at the time to pretend she had sent the note with the express purpose of making up.

Now that didn't seem such a good idea.

She decided a change of subject was necessary and asked brightly, "So, what would you like to do tomorrow? I have several ideas, but I didn't make any firm plans until I heard from you what you would like to do."

Successfully side-tracked, Ilsa immediately began making her list of demands,

"I suppose it's too much to ask for there to be any decent shopping in this God-forsaken corner of the country? Where's the nearest Harvey-Nicks?"

"Manchester," said Libby, "We can go in on the train if you like."

"Are you telling me there isn't a road between here and the big city?" asked Ilsa with deep sarcasm.

"Of course there is, but it's a bit of a trek and I just thought the train would be easier."

"No thanks, If it's that much trouble to you, don't bother."

This comment was designed to make Libby immediately take back the suggestion and offer to drive, but a tiny growth of rebellion was beginning to sprout within her and she chose to ignore the challenge, "Oh, okay, well, we could look at some of the lovely old houses around here, or walk in the hills …"

She trailed off at the expression of total disdain on Ilsa's face.

"Obviously you've never met me," said the guest from hell, "If you had, you'd know that I don't possess the sort of garments or shoes that look good covered in mud."

Libby drew in a silent breath and counted to ten in her head, "Sorry, I just thought that you knew you were coming to the countryside for the weekend."

"And I thought you had inherited the family pile in the country – that's an entirely different thing!"

"We're obviously at cross purposes then," snapped Libby, finally reaching the end of a very long tether, "What would her Ladyship like to do? There are shops in Braxton, but I don't know if they reach your exacting standards. The only other thing I can think of that won't offend your sensibilities is the spa at Hanbury."

Ilsa's eyes lit up, "A spa? Why didn't you say so? Now, I could go for a day at a spa. What's it like?"

"I've never been in, but I believe it's very nice," answered Libby, torn between relief that she had finally found something to please her friend and dismay that she might have to spend a day in a sauna. She could think of so many other ways to spend her time – and none of them included getting naked and hot – well, not with Ilsa anyway, she thought with a wicked urge to giggle out loud, which she managed to quash.

"It's not just one of those council-run swimming pools, now is it?" the interrogation continued, "It is a proper spa?"

"As far as I know, it is privately owned and is very posh. Do you want me to ring and make an appointment for us or not?"

The very fact that they would have to make appointments was enough to satisfy Ilsa that it was indeed 'posh' enough for her and she graciously allowed Libby to get on the telephone and find the number.

"Do you want any treatments?" asked Libby, her hand over the receiver, as she made arrangements with the receptionist.

"I assume this is your treat?" answered Ilsa, with studied non-chalance.

"Absolutely," said Libby, aware that it was now going to cost her a small fortune, but thinking that it was going to be worth every penny just to shut her friend up.

"Great. What do they do?"

"Swedish massage, hot stones, aromatherapy, reflexology – you name it, they do it."

"Then I'll have a couple – but I'll decided tomorrow when I've seen the place. Tell her to provisionally book us a couple of slots and we'll tell her when we get there, and we'll want to use the sauna and the steam rooms."

Libby obediently relayed the instructions and was gratified to realize that she was obviously classed as a superior sort of client because she was being so annoyingly vague. The tone of voice was infinitely more reverential than it had been at the beginning of the conversation. She wondered if she could get used to throwing money around and taking the obsequiousness which seemed to go with the action of spending. Somehow she doubted it.

She rejoined Ilsa on the sofa and switched on the television, "Shall we watch a film or something?"

"If you like," shrugged Ilsa, "but I thought you wanted to chat."

Libby had come to the painful conclusion that chatting to Ilsa was the last thing she wanted, but she was now far too committed to back out. She conceded by turning the sound down a little.

"We can watch and chat," she said brightly, thinking that she could always pretend to be fascinated or distracted if Ilsa came out with one of her stinging comments.

"Fair enough."

They had been silent for only a few minutes when something occurred to Libby and she turned to her companion, "Ilsa, we haven't been in touch for ages now, but you seem to know all about my inheriting this house and the money. How did you find out?"

For the first time since her arrival, Ilsa lost her air of self-assurance. She looked decidedly flustered, "What on earth are you talking about? You told me yourself."

"I don't think I did," said Libby quietly, "I'm pretty sure I would have remembered having a conversation with you about all this."

Ilsa was nothing if not coolly calculating. She had quickly regained her *sang-froid* and said dismissively, "Good heavens, it must have been you. If it wasn't I really can't recall where I heard it. It was in all the papers, wasn't it? What with the court case and everything."

"I suppose it was," admitted Libby slowly.

"Now, hush, I want to watch this," ordered Ilsa and Libby was only too happy to hush.

But the question remained.

CHAPTER TWENTY-THREE

LAZARUS

The only light in the room was a single flickering candle, but Lazarus blinked and winced against even this. It took him a few seconds to realize where he was and to remember what had happened. He had been undressed, put into his night shirt and placed in his bed in the inn. When those facts were established he looked around.

Constance was sitting in a chair beside his bed and had fallen asleep. She was still in the same clothes that she had travelled in, thank God. This told him that it must still be the same day and he had not been unconscious for any length of time. For one dreadful second he had been forced to wonder if something untoward had occurred of which he had no memory, but her serene face and the fact that she was fully dressed reassured him that although someone had undoubtedly disrobed him, it certainly had not been her.

He looked at her for several seconds, aware that she must be utterly exhausted to be able to sleep in a chair which looked far from comfortable. She looked very young and vulnerable in the dim light, her lashes casting long, curling shadows against her smooth, pale cheek. He had a sudden vision of the creamy expanse of skin on her back, marred by the vivid red slashes of the whip marks and he felt the impotent fury against Allingham rise again like bile in his throat. He would see the man paid back for his savagery if it was the last thing he did.

Almost as though she felt his gaze upon her, Constance stirred, yawned and opened her eyes. She smiled softly when she saw that he was finally awake, "Good evening, Inspector," she said.

"Good evening, Miss Allingham," he responded formally, "How

late is it, exactly?"

She looked at the small, jewelled watch that hung on a chain around her neck,

"It's after midnight."

"Then you should be tucked up in your own bed, shouldn't you?"

She blushed at the mention of the word 'bed', but attempted to keep the conversation light-hearted, "I shall retire presently, but I couldn't have left you, not knowing if you were going to …" she trailed off, suddenly aware she had been about to say the thing that one must never say to a patient.

He laughed a little unkindly, "Were you about to say 'die'? Good heavens, miss, there was never any chance of that, I can assure you. I have a harder head than you give me credit for."

"Oh, I think I'm well aware of how hard-headed you are," she retorted tartly, "But the doctor was worried about you."

"And you were not one whit worried?" he asked teasingly.

She gave a wry, half smile, "Well, perhaps just a little."

"As you can see, there was no need. I'm fully recovered and in the morning we will resume our journey and forget this ever happened."

She shook her head, "Dr Bell says you must rest for at least another day. He says it was not a good sign that you passed out so long after the knock on the head. He thinks you might have fractured your skull. He says you are a lucky man."

Lazarus grimaced and misquoted a little rhyme, "'I do not like thee, Dr Bell, the reason why I cannot tell, but this I know and know full well, I do not like thee, Dr Bell.'"

"Like him or no, he'll be back in the morning," she said firmly, "And you'll not get out of bed until he says you may."

"I might have to get out at least once," he told her and delighted in her deeper blush when she realized what he was hinting at.

"You are incorrigible," she told him severely, "Now, do you want anything before I leave you?"

"A pint of ale," he answered promptly.

"No alcohol," she said, "But I am allowed to bring you a cup of tea – or beef tea if you prefer it."

He gave a theatrical shudder of distaste, "I do not prefer it. Tea will suffice – and some bread and cheese, I'm starving." He had suddenly recalled that he hadn't eaten anything since early that morning and his stomach was beginning to protest.

"I'll see what I can persuade Mrs Locke to bring for you, but I'm not sure cheese is a good idea at this time of the night. It will give you nightmares." She rose to her feet and busied herself in pulling his covers straight, unable to cure herself of the motherliness she had always been expected to show to the sick or young.

He took hold of her hand and stilled her, forcing her to look into his eyes, "Do you think the memory of your injuries won't do that?" he said seriously.

Her breath became short and agitated, "Please don't," she whispered, "Please, please don't talk about it. I want to forget it."

"I want to forget it too, but I don't think I can. You must let me help you, Constance. I cannot send you back into that house unless I know you will always be safe from such treatment."

"There is nothing you can do – you told me so yourself, when young Will Carter sustained his beating from his father. A man can do as he pleases under his own roof, to his own family. It is the law of the land."

In his determination to convince her, he sat up and leaned forward, talking earnestly to her, "That was entirely different. Will is a minor, you are a full grown woman, Carter is the father, Allingham only your uncle. He had no right to belabour you and I feel sure you could bring a charge of assault against him."

"How can I do so?" she asked, growing increasingly distressed, "He is my guardian. I am penniless. Without his support I am homeless."

Lazarus had to accept that she had a point, but he also needed to save her. For his own peace of mind he could not fail again. Decima Watkins still haunted his dreams and he didn't intend to have Constance join her.

"Listen to me, Constance, I know this is difficult for you, but I think I have a solution."

Constance felt her breath stop for a few painful seconds. This is it, she told herself incredulously, this is the moment when he will ask me to marry him. He will offer for my hand to take me away from the torment of my present life. She forced herself to draw in a deep breath for she was growing light-headed with the suspense.

"Yes?" she whispered.

"The mere threat of legal action will force Allingham to promise no further violence will be visited upon you. He thinks too much of his reputation to allow it to be broadcast that he laid a riding crop across a young woman's back. When we return to Braxton, I will come with you and speak to him myself. Believe me, when he hears what I have to say, he will never dare lay another finger on you!"

She felt as though she had been slapped in the face and it was all she could do not to recoil physically from him and run from the room. She gently withdrew her hand from his fervent grasp, "You would face my uncle for me?" she asked, amazed at her own coolness, that her voice emerged without a quiver to betray her churning emotions.

"Of course I will do so, gladly."

"Thank you. I will consider what you have said. If I can find the courage, I will do as you suggest. Now, I must fetch Mrs Locke. She will bring you a drink and something to eat."

"That's right. You take yourself off to bed. We'll talk more in the morning. I admit I'm devilish tired now."

"Has the pain gone, or do you want a dose of laudanum?" Even as she spoke to him, on the surface so very placid and businesslike, she wondered if laudanum would take away the pain of a broken heart. If so, perhaps he could spare a dose for her.

"There's still a dull ache, but nothing like it was before. Stop worrying about me and try to get some sleep."

She had very little choice but to obey him.

* * *

When they met at breakfast, Lazarus looked more like his old self. He was evidently well rested and ebullient, which irritated her beyond measure and she was inclined to wish him back to his usual surliness. She had slept very badly, if at all, and had wept silent, bitter tears, which had left her with a head-ache, heavy, gritty eyes and a very pink nose. He seemed not to notice and made a good meal of cold meat and bread and butter, whilst she picked daintily at a little toast and drank copious amounts of tea, to ease her sore throat, made raw by stifled sobs.

"If Dr Bell insists upon our staying another day, I must telegraph to Stonier and let him know what has happened. If we are not home today, they will all wonder what has become of us."

Constance had very little idea what a 'telegraph' was and under normal circumstances would have been fascinated to find out, but she found she could rouse no interest whatsoever that morning. She merely shrugged her assent and for the first time, Lazarus seemed to notice that something was amiss.

"Does anything ail you, Miss Allingham?" he asked solicitously.

She wanted to answer, yes, Inspector Lazarus, I have fallen deeply, painfully and stupidly in love with you, but sadly you don't even know I exist except as a charity case whom you must protect as a matter of duty. Of course she said nothing of the kind only waved a dismissive hand as if to show how small her troubles were and told him briskly, "I never sleep well in strange places. I'm just a little tired and still rather overwhelmed by out adventures of yesterday. What a tale I shall have to regale when I go home. A train crash and a night in a public house! Imagine it."

Her flippancy convinced him and he grinned, "And all with a man in tow. You could create quite a scandal if you wanted to, miss."

"I could indeed. Well, what shall we do with our illicit day? I feel I should make the best of my rare day of freedom. It happens so infrequently I think I have forgotten how to enjoy myself."

He glanced out of the window, "It is another lovely day. What do you say to a walk and perhaps a picnic?"

She looked at him with her head slightly to one side, weighing the possibility of a relapse, "Are you well enough to walk?"

"I think so. We needn't go far and I do need to get outside. If I have to sit or lie for much longer, I swear my bones will fuse together."

The decision made, Constance went off to beg a basket of food from Mrs Locke and Lazarus waited on the arrival of the doctor, who, fortunately, was concerned enough about his patient to make his call early.

Satisfied that Lazarus was on the mend, Dr Bell felt no compunction at presenting his bill and assuring Lazarus that if he continued to improve at his present rate, there was nothing to prevent their departure on the first train the next morning. Lazarus had been amply provided with cash by Lord Allingham for the journey and he paid the doctor with grim satisfaction.

Constance met them in the lobby as the doctor was taking his leave and she was glad of the opportunity to thank him for his services.

"The pleasure was entirely mine, Miss Allingham," he replied, bowing slightly over her hand, "And please be aware that I am available at any time should you need me." He presented her with his card and she put it quickly into her reticule, sensing Lazarus' amused gaze upon both she and her new friend.

Once out in the lane, Lazarus took the basket out of her hand and they strolled in the sunshine, relishing the warmth of the day and the sound of birdsong and the lazy buzz of foraging bees in the hedgerow.

They headed first towards the railway station so that Lazarus could arrange for the telegraph message to be sent to Braxton, then they walked on in the direction Flo Locke had told them would eventually bring them to the river and a 'lovely place' to eat their cold pie and salad.

They spoke very little except to draw each other's attention to various things of interest or to remark upon the weather or the loveliness of the countryside. Lazarus had been particularly enamoured of the pretty little village church, with it's crennelated tower and carved wooden lych gate. For her part Constance was enchanted by a tiny, thatched cottage, with the obligatory roses around the door. She allowed herself to indulge in a little daydream which saw Lazarus in his shirtsleeves digging in the garden and herself in a crisp white apron bringing him a glass of foaming beer from her well-stocked, cool, clean kitchen.

He caught sight of her dreamy expression and asked, with barely concealed amusement, "What on earth are you thinking about? You look as though you were gazing upon paradise."

She blushed to think how heartily he would laugh if he had known that he was featuring very heavily in her idea of 'paradise'.

"Don't be silly. I was just admiring the pretty cottage. Don't you think it would be quite wonderful to live somewhere like that?"

"Hardly," he grunted, bringing her back down to earth with a bump, "It's poky and small, probably two rooms, if that, and dark, cold and damp to boot."

From a purely practical point of view he was quite correct and now she looked again with new eyes, she realized he was right. The windows were tiny and set deep under the over-hanging eaves. Moss grew on the thatch and the walls were so thick that the sun never penetrated.

But she still wanted to live there with a husband and children.

He found them a spot by the river where the grass had been nibbled by sheep to a length that would cause no dampness to penetrate the rug Mrs Locke had had the foresight to provide. They were shaded by a gnarled old oak and the sound of the rushing water was the perfect accompaniment to their meal.

While Constance busied herself serving the food, Lazarus lay with his head cushioned on his interlocked fingers and looked up between the branches at the sky.

"I've changed my mind," he said presently, "You are quite right about the cottage. On a day like this, it would be idyllic to live here, away from the bustle of town."

"You would soon be bored," she said with great practicality. A day in his company had very nearly knocked every scrap of romance out of her and she was back to being reliable, comfortable Constance, whose only use and purpose in life was the service of others.

"I would find plenty to occupy me," he countered, lifting himself onto one elbow and accepting a plate of food from her, "I've always fancied myself as a stone-mason or a carpenter."

"Do you have any talent in either of those professions?"

"Not a scrap, in fact I would probably lose my fingers the first time I picked up a chisel."

They both laughed and she said bitingly, "I thought as much. You would be lost without a murder to solve."

"What about you?" he asked with equal scepticism, "You would be a milkmaid who was afraid of cows, and who was too much of a weakling to churn butter."

"I am not afraid of cows," she retorted, "I just don't like them very much. Anyway, I wouldn't be a milkmaid."

"What then?"

"I would be a writer, or an artist. I would paint glorious sunsets and be invited to show them at the Royal Academy. I would rival the Misses Brönte in my passionate rendering of gothic novels."

"And can you paint and write?" he asked.

"I have no idea, I have never tried."

They laughed again, "I think you could do anything you set your mind to, Miss Allingham." he admitted.

Suddenly she was sad again. There was one thing she could not do, no matter how much she set her mind upon it.

"I'll never get the chance," she said bitterly, "Once back under my uncle's roof, my life will be over."

CHAPTER TWENTY-FOUR

Of course the birds had flown, as Lazarus had known they would. Constance seemed shocked that Arabella was not there waiting for her, all eagerness to be taken home.

"But how did they know we were on our way here?" she asked, utterly confounded by the empty room they were shown into by the landlady.

"A man on foot could have reached them in half the time it has taken us," said the stoic policeman, a huge part of him glad that Allingham had been outwitted by his daughter and her lover.

"You mean someone warned them? I don't see how. No one was supposed to know Uncle had involved the police."

"There is no such thing as a secret when one has servants in the house. Of course someone warned them. A man on a swift horse could have been here within a few hours. It took your uncle at least two days to arrange train travel for us, not to mention the accident that has so disastrously delayed us."

"But Marcus and Arabella couldn't have known about that," countered Constance reasonably.

"Couldn't they? Don't you think it was rather a convenient derailment? Marcus Soper must know a dozen ruffians who would drag a tree onto a railway line for a few shillings, no questions asked. He has too much to lose to let Arabella simply walk away. She is worth a fortune to him. If she marries him, he allies himself to one of the most powerful families in the country. If Allingham finally realizes that the only way to get her back is to pay – then pay he will."

"I suppose so, but who would have warned him? I didn't think he had many friends in Braxton other than young Crabtree."

"I suspect Crabtree is not so much a friend as in the man's debt.

Soper holds something over that boy – and I think that may very well be the death of Mollie Waters."

She looked even more shocked, "You can't really believe that Lawrie had anything to do with that unfortunate girl's death?"

"Can't I?"

As they had been speaking, Lazarus had taken the opportunity to look around the room, lifting cushions and opening drawers – there was little enough furniture so it didn't take him long to make a thorough search. He found nothing to give him any indication of where the lovers had fled, but having expected Soper to play the game with caution, he was hardly surprised.

"There's nothing more to be done here, so unless you have some other errand, I suggest we take the next train home."

Constance shrugged resignedly, "I hardly have the heart for shopping now," she said mournfully, "We may as well go to the station." She looked around and saw a shawl cast over one of the mismatched chairs, "Oh, my poor Arabella, where on earth can that cad have taken her now?"

"I dare swear there's one man who has a good idea," said Lazarus grimly, "And when we get back, I intend to make him speak, whether he tries to hide behind his pa's tailcoat or not."

It occurred to Constance that she had been too easily charmed by both Crabtree and Soper and she vowed that she would not be taken in again by a smooth-talking rogue.

Lazarus had one more thing to do before they left. He knocked on a couple of doors and asked the neighbours if they knew anything. It was unlikely, but there was always the slightest chance that Arabella might have been lonely enough to confide over tea and sympathy.

Sadly the three women they spoke to had only had the shortest of conversations with the young lovers. Marcus had made sure that Arabella would have to rely on him for everything, including company. One fact did interest him, however. The aunt to whom Soper had fled had not survived long once he and Arabella had arrived. According to the gossip he gleaned, Lazarus learned that the elderly lady had been persuaded to sign an insurance policy and tragically within days she had expired of suspected typhus. The doctor who signed the death certificate was puzzled that there had been no other cases in the district, but what else could have caused the violent vomiting and fever that had afflicted the lady?

Lazarus had a very good idea what might have caused it, and it most certainly wasn't typhus. His final visit was to the local police station, where he showed his warrant then advised the detective in charge that he might do well to exhume the late aunt of Marcus Soper and look for evidence of poison in the corpse.

The journey back to Braxton was uneventful and Constance spent most of it staring out of the window, lost in thought. The two days she had been away now felt like an eternity. She could scarcely believe so much had happened. She felt as though she was going back quite a different person than the one who had set forth so timidly, so very afraid of travelling by train, frightened of defying her uncle and refusing his quest and even more afraid of what people would say had they known she was without a chaperone and in the company of a man. None of that seemed at all important now.

The fear reasserted itself when they alighted from the train and Lazarus climbed into a carriage beside her and gave the driver the direction.

She looked at him, horrified, "You cannot possibly come home with me. I will drop you at the police station. My uncle will be so angry if you come back to the house."

"Be damned to that! Your uncle set me a task, I failed. I owe it to him to deliver the news in person."

"But, what will people think?"

"What people? Your uncle's house is not overlooked by any neighbours. The only people who will witness my arrival will be servants, and both you and your uncle are vastly mistaken if you imagine for a single moment that every member of the household is not fully aware of this whole sorry mess."

She opened her lips to protest further, but he lifted a hand to halt her.

"Nothing you can say will change my mind, so you can save your breath, Miss Allingham."

Wisely she decided that he was right. Let him provoke my uncle into anger, then, she thought, but I hope to God it won't rebound upon him.

At the front door Lazarus refused to allow the butler to intimidate him. He simply walked in, gently moving the man aside as though to allow Constance free entry. The man could hardly bar the path of a member of the family and so he let them both pass into the hall.

"Where will I find your master?" asked Lazarus in clipped tones which brooked no denial. The butler looked helplessly at Constance, but she merely nodded her head to give him leave to answer the question.

"Lord Allingham is in the library, sir. If you'll wait here, I'll acquaint him of your arrival."

"No need. If you'll show me the way, Miss Allingham?"

What choice did she have? She could have refused, whereupon several menservants would be summoned and Lazarus would be physically ejected from the property. Fully resigned to her fate she dismissed the butler and led Lazarus off down the hall.

At the door Lazarus didn't hesitate, he walked straight in without knocking to find Allingham seated at his desk, smoking a cigar and reading the newspaper. He leapt to his feet at the sight of Constance and the policeman, but so eager was he to hear their news that he didn't even bother to chastise them for their unmannerly arrival.

"Where is she? Where is my Arabella?"

"Soper took her away before we could reach her, uncle, I'm so sorry," said Constance hastily, tripping over her words with anxiety and haste. She was terrified by what Lazarus intended to say and could only hope to speak first and deflect her aged relative's anger.

"You lost her? Idiots!"

"That is hardly fair …" whispered Constance, trying not to show fear, but hardly succeeding.

"Get out, heifer! I can't bear to look at you. I have no further use for you. And take the policeman with you."

She gasped at the insult, utterly humiliated to be spoken to in such a way before anyone, but most especially Lazarus, and with tears starting blindingly into her eyes, she made her unsteady way across the room. She felt rather than saw Lazarus accompany her to the door and she was overwhelmingly relieved that he was going to leave without causing a scene.

She should have known better. He merely held the door open for her, and when she had gone through it, he closed it quietly behind her – with him still in the room with her uncle. She was tempted to go back in to drag him out and away, but her courage failed her and she simply walked down the long corridor, weeping silently, and sank into a chair in the hallway and waited for whatever might come next.

Until that very moment Lazarus had no clear idea what he intended to do. A myriad of possibilities had occurred to him on the journey home. He had considered, and then rejected, at least half a dozen courses of action, ranging from simply punching the aged bully on the nose, to telling him a few choice facts about himself and his behaviour. He had even thought about leaving the house in dignified silence, having merely thrown Allingham a contemptuous glance. He now saw that none of these things would give him any satisfaction. Allingham needed a fright and Lazarus needed to be the man who gave it to him.

Thinking he was alone, Allingham had turned back to the window and Lazarus was quietly pleased when the sound of his voice caused the older man to start violently.

"Now that Miss Allingham has left us, I can say what I came here to say," he said, his voice soft, yet strangely menacing.

"I thought I told you to get out of my house," snarled Allingham, quickly recovering himself.

"I'm afraid things aren't quite that simple, sir," answered the policeman, "I require you to come along with me to the police station. I am arresting you on suspicion of a serious assault."

He had the supreme satisfaction of seeing the older man for once completely bereft of words. The blood drained from his face and Lazarus could see him desperately trying to think what he could possibly have done to provoke this astounding accusation.

"What the devil are you talking about?" he managed to ask, but his usual arrogance was missing.

"Because of the train accident, Miss Allingham required medical attention. The doctor who examined her reported to me that the young lady had been badly beaten. When questioned, she admitted that it was you who had administered the whipping and I have prevailed upon her to press charges against you." Lazarus was careful not to disclose the fact that he had seen Constance's bruises for himself – too much could have been made of that little nugget of information.

Allingham's relief was palpable, "Good God man, for a moment I thought you were serious! The girl is in my charge, I am perfectly at liberty to chastise her if I think fit."

"No, Lord Allingham, I'm afraid you are not. I have been at pains to consult the law on this matter and you are not Miss Allingham's legal guardian. You brought her to live here with you when her parents died, but never at any time did you bother to make the arrangement legal. You were not named by your brother as his child's guardian, and you never adopted her. You are not her father and therefore have no rights over her. You assaulted her and I am arresting you for that offence."

The older man sank into his chair and though Lazarus could see that all the fight had been thoroughly knocked out of him, still his expression was one of calculation as he struggled to find a way out of the dilemma, but no ideas were occurring to him and he looked very much like a cornered rat.

"Alright, Lazarus, you win. What do you want?"

"Want? I have no idea what you mean to imply by that. I am merely doing my duty. I'm sure that with a good lawyer and a magistrate who is known to you, you will escape with nothing more than a fine."

"Don't be ridiculous. I cannot possibly damage my reputation by appearing in court on a charge of assaulting a woman."

"You should have thought of that before you raised your hand to her," hissed Lazarus, showing his temper for the first time. It was a mistake. Allingham immediately saw a weakness and attacked it.

"Ah, all becomes clear. You have dared to raise your eyes well above your station, Inspector, realized that it can never be, and this is to be your revenge."

"My duty ..."

"Duty, be damned! You have taken a fancy to my niece and you think I would not countenance the match."

Lazarus felt the colour rush into his cheeks and he silently cursed himself for allowing the old fox to get under his skin, "You could not be more wrong," he said, but he convinced neither himself nor Allingham, who laughed cruelly.

"By God, who would have thought it? The great Inspector Lazarus has a weakness after all. I'll make a bargain with you, my friend. Make this nonsense go away and she's yours."

The policeman couldn't quite believe what he was hearing, "I beg your pardon?" he asked incredulously.

"I mean it. Persuade the girl to drop the charges and she's yours. Marry her, or not, the choice is yours. I'll settle a small sum on her and she's yours for the taking."

Even though Constance had assured him that her uncle cared nothing for her, that he saw her merely as a chattel, Lazarus still could not comprehend the callous disregard Allingham showed for her welfare. He could see that the man was perfectly serious; that he fully expected the policeman to walk out of the house with his prize on his arm, in exchange for a few pounds and immunity from prosecution.

"You utterly appal me," he told Allingham, his voice low, but filled with vicious bitterness, "We will pretend this conversation never took place. You will undertake here and now to find Miss Allingham a comfortable house in the best part of town. You will find her a respectable woman to chaperone her and you will leave her alone to live the rest of her life in peace. If she ever wishes to marry, you will pay for her wedding and give her a generous dowry. And if I ever hear of you laying another finger on her, you will answer for it to me."

Allingham grinned, "Very convenient for you, Lazarus, a grateful young thing, in a house of her own, waiting with bated breath for your weekly visits."

"That may be the way you conduct yourself, Allingham, but I

most certainly do not. Miss Allingham will be free of you. That is all I require to find satisfaction in this situation. Your have exactly one week. Then I will be coming to arrest you."

"You wouldn't dare. I can break you, Lazarus."

"You are right, you can. But I can tell the world that your precious daughter is nothing but a little hussy, living in sin with a man who will hang for murder as soon as I catch up with him."

For one dreadful moment Lazarus thought he had given the old man a heart attack, but even though his face was whiter than the blotter that lay on the desk, Allingham managed to nod, "Very well. You shall have your way. Now get out."

Lazarus had never been more delighted to obey an order.

CHAPTER TWENTY-FIVE

Present

Hanbury Spa attained approval from even Ilsa's impossibly high standards. By the end of the day, Libby wished she could say the same.

As the town had essentially been a country village until the Regency period, whereupon it became a fashionable watering place, the renovations on the old bath house, assembly rooms and other associated buildings, followed the same themes prevalent at the time. Because of Nelson's victory at the Battle of the Nile, all things Egyptian had dominated the early part of the 1800's, with the passion for the Grand Tour close on its heels, encompassing Greek and Roman culture.

The modern spa was accordingly divided into rooms with different treatments and décor depending upon one's desires. One could indulge in a volcanic mineral mud body wrap in a Pompeii inspired room, relax in baths refreshed with rose petals and milky waters in a setting which rivalled Hollywood's version of Cleopatra's Palace. The moist air in the Athenian steam room was redolent with Mediterranean herbs and draped with gauzy hangings and flowers of every hue. Statues of diaphanously-garbed nymphs poured water into crystal clear pools.

Libby knew it was going to cost her a packet as soon as she walked into the marble-floored foyer and was handed a fluffy and eye-wateringly white towel, robe and slippers.

Ilsa was in her element, Libby could not have felt more out of place. She had not had sufficient time to get used to having unlimited funds and she felt quite sick at the money she was wasting, and had to tell herself severely that she was being miserly in resenting spending a little bit of her inheritance on one of her oldest friends.

Her next nightmare occurred when they reached the dressing rooms. These were the height of mock-Regency elegance, panelled with dark-wood wainscotting, ceilings of moulded plaster and mahogany-fronted lockers and polished brass fittings.

As she self-consciously undressed, more than acutely aware that her underwear was serviceable rather than glamorous, Ilsa suddenly shrieked, "Oh my God, Libby!"

Startled Libby answered, "What? What's wrong?"

"When was the last time you shaved your legs?" was the horrified rejoinder, "Or bought new lingerie?"

Libby now realized that she couldn't open her bag and display her over-stretched lycra gym-wear, or scuffed trainers.

She looked shame-facedly down, desperately trying to recall the last time she had done any serious person grooming. The truth was that she had begun writing her book, she had been tending to jump in and out of the shower without much thought other than to be clean and inoffensive to eye or nose. A winter spent in slacks meant that her legs had not been on display since the previous autumn, so why would she worry about a little thing like shaving? She didn't think David was very bothered – he had certainly never said anything either derogatory or complimentary about her appearance. She rather suspected he liked his women as he liked his garden, wild and untrimmed.

"It's only been a couple of weeks," she said defensively.

"The shaving maybe, but that bra has certainly seen better days," sneered Ilsa, "No wonder your marriage is in trouble."

If she had just thrown herself into the freezing plunge pool Libby could not have been rendered more breathless, "What?" she managed to splutter, "What do you mean? My marriage is perfectly fine, thank you!"

Ilsa gave her a pitying look, "If you say so. Now, let's see what we can do about you. You can forget any treatments until you've been exfoliated and depilated. I'll go and find someone to take you to the beautician."

She was gone before Libby could argue – and indeed she didn't have the heart to do so. She had denied the charge vigorously, but once left alone, she could not help but reflect on what Ilsa had said. Was her marriage really in trouble? She knew, of course, that she and David were having a little tiff just now, but that was a passing thing, surely, and nothing more sinister?

But if it had been obvious to Ilsa, in the house for so few hours, then perhaps it was something to worry about?

She wanted to cry, but pride stopped her from breaking down in front of Ilsa, so sure of herself and so judgemental of everyone else. She submitted herself to the ministrations of the beautician while Ilsa went off to have an aromatherapy massage and whatever else she desired.

For the first five minutes she tormented herself with whirling thoughts of her husband and his dissatisfaction with their life together, but eventually she realized that the fretting was simply futile. She needed to distract herself until she could speak to David herself and find out exactly what was going on. Until that moment arrived she might just as well forget her troubles and relax. It was costing her enough, after all!

A couple of hours later the pampering had done its job. She was pink and glowing, smooth and hairless in all the right places, chilled and warm all at the same time in the best possible way.

She met up with Ilsa and they found their way into the conservatory to eat lunch. The spring sun shone through the glass domed roof into a sort of mini Crystal Palace, full of wicker furniture and potted palms, and if one tried really hard, one could imagine oneself in a much more exotic location than Hanbury in the County of Derbyshire. Not that Libby wanted to be anywhere else, though she was pretty sure Ilsa felt she really belonged in the South of France.

Most of the other ladies in the restaurant were obediently sipping water after their treatments, but Libby rashly asked for a latte to go with her salad, and Ilsa nearly caused her to choke on suppressed laughter when she gave her order.

"I'll have a decaffeinated macchiato, with lightly steamed skimmed milk on the side," she said loftily. Of course such fussiness only gave her an even greater aura of respect from the waitress, but Libby could hardly believe what she was hearing. No doubt it was a coffee which was made every five minutes in London, but it seemed hopelessly pretentious here in the wilds of the Pennines. Apparently it presented no difficulty in this oasis of refinement, but Libby cringed inwardly to think what sort of a reaction Ilsa would get if she tried to make such a request in one of the charming little coffee shops or tea rooms she frequented when she was out and about.

When they had eaten – Ilsa had a rocket salad with the dressing on the side, plenty of olives and capers, a smidge of anchovy and feta only if is was genuine imported Greek – Libby made what she thought was a kind suggestion, "I suppose you'll be wanting a cigarette now? I think they have a spot in the garden where you can go."

"God no! An appalling habit. Utter filth in the lungs, and a stench on the breath."

Libby had every reason to look confused. Ilsa had been a thirty a day woman, and was never happier than with a glass of red in one hand and a fag in the other.

"I gather you've given up, then?" she ventured.

"I prefer to forget I ever smoked, actually," answered Ilsa, "I barely did really. I only ever smoked a couple, just to be sociable."

This brazen alteration of the fact deprived Libby of the power of speech for several seconds, which gave Ilsa the chance to hastily change the subject.

"Never mind about me, we need to discuss you, Libby." she said smoothly, "We really need to sort out this silliness between you and Dave."

"It's David," said Libby automatically, "I prefer David."

"Whatever," dismissed Ilsa impatiently, "The fact remains that you two are in deep trouble and I can't possibly leave you like this. The man is obviously a boor of the worst sort, but I suppose he's your choice, so we'll have to do our best to make a silk purse out of the sow's ear."

This was just about the limit of what Libby was going to take from her friend. David might be behaving badly, but he didn't deserve this, “Now just a minute, Ilsa, I think you need to back off. David is my husband and if he needs sorting, I’ll do it myself.”

“You really think you can handle if all by yourself?”

Libby could feel the heat rising in her cheeks, and she knew that if Ilsa said one more thing in that condescending tone, she was going to smack her right in the mouth, “David and I will be just fine, thank you. Now can we change the subject? I’d hate us to fall out after all these years.”

Ilsa shrugged, infuriatingly calm, “Whatever you say, sweetie, but I can’t help it if I think you could do so much better.”

“There is no one better than David,” said Libby firmly and then looked at her friend, silently daring her to say one more thing.

Even Ilsa’s thick skin had some sensitive spots and she recognized the danger signals. She laughed lightly, “The day we fall out over a man is the day Hell freezes over,” she said, but Libby knew that there was a barb at the back of even that pronouncement, for, of course, they had fallen out over a man – but it had been Ilsa’s rotten choices that had caused that rift. Was the intimation here that it would be Libby’s bad taste that caused the parting this time? Libby chose to ignore the comment.

“Shall we get dressed? – I’m all spa’ed out. There’s only so much pampering I can take in one day.”

Ilsa agreed rather sulkily – she had been planning a couple more treats. Never mind. There was always the next time she visited.

It was rather cold when they went out into the fresh air. They had been in the steamy heat for so long, they had almost forgotten that it was still early in the year and the wind was biting up in the hills.

Even so Libby was determined not to go home. She was slowly realising that it wasn’t a particularly good idea to be alone with Ilsa. The other woman was taking full advantage of her easy going nature and innate good manners to hone her waspish tongue and Libby was not too sure how much longer she was going to be able to take the constant criticism. Ilsa had changed and Libby did not like the result. She seemed suddenly more bitter and bitchy and Libby could not help but think that she might very well have completely altered her lifestyle but it really had not made her a happy person.

She deftly suggested they look around the shops, which luckily were literally a stone's throw away from the Spa. Hanbury was, after all, a very small town, and really only existed because of the pure, rock-filtered waters that bubbled up from the depths of the earth, bringing a residue of heat from below.

For once Ilsa didn't protest. She saw this as the ideal opportunity to force her hostess to buy some items which would be chosen with her impeccable taste. Of course the shops were too, too provincial for her, but for Libby they would do – anything was better than the dross she already owned.

Even Libby had to admit that she needed some new undergarments. The shame of exposure at the spa had convinced her of that much. They spent a very companionable couple of hours renewing Libby's wardrobe and Ilsa was pleasantly surprised to find a few select bargains which passed the acid test of her discerning eye.

They were so busy chatting and comparing purchases that Libby had her named called twice before she heard and recognized the fact that she was being hailed. She looked up to find Matt Piper grinning at her, and she wondered vaguely what was amusing him. Had she but known it, he thought her girlishness was rather funny. He had only ever seen her in serious situations and to see her behaving so naturally, and simply enjoying life instead of being worn down by tragedy, was something of a relief to him. The truth was he liked her – not in any romantic way, he was in love with Tess – but he thought her a feisty little thing and he admired her spirit. He really felt she had been dealt a rough blow in getting involved with a snake like Brendan Tulliver and he wanted to see her triumph.

"Oh, hello, Matt. Fancy seeing you here."

"It's hardly that much of a surprise, the Police Station is only over there," he countered, pointing behind him to the building from whence he had recently emerged.

"So it is," she laughed, a little flustered. She realized that she was going to have to introduce him to Ilsa and she didn't particularly want to inflict her upon him – nor explain him to her!

It seemed to her that they both looked expectantly at her, so she suppressed her natural reluctance and did what courtesy forced her to do, "Ilsa, this is DCI Piper, he's in charge of my case against Brendan. Matt, my friend Ilsa, down for a girly weekend."

They shook hands and Libby winced inwardly when she realized that Ilsa had turned on her well-practiced flair for flirting with new men. The blond hair was tossed over the shoulder and the eyelids fluttered, "So Libby has her very own DCI, how very Midsomer Murder-ish."

He laughed politely, "I do have other clients," he assured her, "I don't spend all my time following Libby around."

"I'll bet she wishes you would – I know I do," she flashed her most brilliant smile and Matt simply looked uncomfortable and turned his attention back to the now furiously blushing Libby.

"I'm glad I've seen you. It's saved me a phone call."

"Not more developments on the Brendan front," said Libby, on the verge of despair, but he hastily reassured her.

"No, nothing to do with that. I promised you I would have a word with Tess on your behalf and she was really interested in what you are writing about. She says she would love to meet up sometime."

Libby was transformed in an instant from careworn to glowing, "Matt! That's wonderful. How can I thank you enough?"

"Actually, you'll be doing me a bit of a favour if you visit. Tess has been really low since all that business last year. She's barely written a word since her accident and if you can get her interested again, I'll be forever grateful."

"I don't know if I can promise that, but I'll do my best," she said earnestly, "When can we get together?"

"I'm off on Monday next week. How about coming to the house for lunch, then I'll buzz off and leave the two of you to talk books?"

"Perfect, I'll see you about twelve?"

"Fine." He quickly wrote the address on a sheet from his official notebook and handed it to her, "See you then. Bye, Ilsa. It was nice to have met you."

"The pleasure was all mine," she purred in return, then barely waited for him to cross the road before she turned on Libby, "What was all that about?"

Libby was reluctant to tell her, but how could she refuse?

"His girlfriend is Tess Brookes. He's arranged for her to have a look at my novel and give me a bit of advice."

For the first time since her arrival, Ilsa was robbed of the power of speech. She opened and closed her mouth a couple of times before she managed to splutter,

"You don't mean the Tess Brookes?"

"The historical novelist, yes."

Ilsa suddenly grinned and gave her friend a playful slap on the shoulder,

"Wow, Libby, I think this is the only time you've ever impressed me!"

"Thanks," answered Libby, with deep irony.

CHAPTER TWENTY-SIX

Lazarus

Life had to go on in the absence of Inspector Lazarus, so accordingly Stonier took himself off to find the mysterious Mrs Riley.

Lawrence Crabtree had told them nothing more than the village where she lived and Stonier feared he would be wandering aimlessly around for hours, but he had underestimated just how small a place Little Lowton was – the clue was in the name, he realized, but who knew it was a hamlet of perhaps half a dozen cottages, without a church or even a hostelry?

He knocked on the first door he saw and was instantly directed to the far end of the lane, where he found the abode of Mrs Riley. It was evidently an old, but still sturdily standing, squatter's cottage from the previous century. The rule of law was that if you could raise four walls and roof it, in the hours between dusk and sunrise, you could live there. Some relative of the lady had probably done just that, and though it had been added to with a couple of tacked on rooms and a rough wooden lean to, it was still a very basic one room building, with thick walls of uncut stone and a thatch that had seen better days.

The door stood open and the aroma of a good country stew wafted out and Stonier felt his stomach rumble appreciatively. He stuck his head inside and called,

"Hello there, anyone home?"

He had to be honest, he had been expecting a bent old crone, toothless and white-haired – the very essence of the sort of witch who sold potions to gullible young girls trying to get rid of an unwanted baby. He couldn't have been more mistaken.

The woman who stepped out of the shadowy interior of the cottage was tall and slender, her long, almost black hair was neatly plaited and pinned up in a demure bun, but a few tendrils had escaped and clung to her damp forehead, she had obviously been getting very over-heated stirring the pan which hung from an iron hook above the open fire.

She smiled, "Good afternoon," she said softly, "Can I help?"

"Mrs Riley?" asked Stonier, making no attempt to disguise the surprise in his tone.

"That's me. What can I do for you?"

"I'm from the police, madam," he answered, "I'm afraid I have to ask you some questions."

"Well, I've nothing to hide, so you'd better step inside. Would you like a cup of tea?"

Stonier did as he was asked, taking his hat off as he entered, "That would be kind, ma'am," he said gratefully, "It's a fair walk from Braxton and the day is hot enough to cook an egg on a stone."

"Can't say I've ever tried to do that," she laughed, standing aside for him to pass.

He looked around while she busied herself swapping the pot over the fire for a kettle and set the tea things out on the table.

It was a larger room that he had been imagining from looking at the outside, and the ceiling was surprisingly high, with thick, rough-hewn oak beams exposing the underside of the thatch above. All sorts of herbs and plants hung drying from hooks adding to the delightful smells and he tried to identify a few of them, being a keen gardener. He could barely recognize half a dozen of them.

Much of the furniture looked home-made, including a dresser which filled one wall, and was over-burdened with row upon row of bottles and earthenware pots, but it was well done and he guessed that most of it was of a similar age to the house itself. Whoever had been enterprising enough to erect it had also been a true artisan.

"Have you lived here long?"

"All my life," she told him and added proudly, "My grandfather built it. He was a Romany but his wife, my grandmother, was a diddikai and wanted a house. He and his brothers laboured all night and hoisted the last bundle of straw on the roof as the sun rose. There have been Southworths here ever since."

"So Riley is your married name?"

"That's right, my dear, but he's away at sea, has been for a long time. He was always worried about my calling."

"Calling?"

"Because I'm what they call a wise woman. I know the ways of the countryside, all the cures and medicines, he was frightened to death of being married to the 'witch in the wood.' He comes home every couple of years or so, but he really can't cope with any of it, poor lamb."

"I see. Well, it's about your potions I've come to see you."

"It usually is," she responded calmly, apparently not in the least worried by his suddenly grim visage, "Ask away, I've done nothing against the law."

"We'll see about that when I've done with my questions," he said sternly.

She sat opposite him, the wooden table between them and poured him a cup of tea, which she slid over to him, "I'm ready," she said.

"Have you ever had a visit from a young lady called Mollie Waters?"

"I can't answer that, I'm afraid."

Stonier grew belligerent, "Are you obstructing an officer of the law in pursuit of information?" he blustered.

"Not at all. I really mean I can't answer you. The people who come to see me don't give me their real names – or usually any name at all. Why would they? I don't keep records, or even accept money for my services. That's how I avoid breaking the law. I'm not selling anything because no money changes hands."

"How do you live, then? You must get money from somewhere," said Stonier, forgetting to be severe in his genuine shock at her come-day-go-day attitude.

"I barter. People bring me food stuffs or do little jobs for me. If I ever do need money, I take in washing or mind children or old folks while their families work in the fields."

"And you manage to live like that?"

"My needs are very small," she assured him, "I can live off what I grow or what I find in the fields and hedgerows."

"Which brings me neatly to my next question," said Stonier triumphantly, sure that he now had a subject which would break through her calm demeanour, "Do you ever pick mushrooms in the fields and woods around here?"

"Of course,"

"And you know the difference between the various fungi? You'd know, for example, which ones are poisonous?"

"I'd be in a bad way if I didn't," she said with a grin.

"Mrs Riley, I have to tell you that I am investigating the case of a young woman who is in a bad way – in fact she's dead and buried – and she died from eating poisonous toadstools."

"I'm sorry to hear that – it can happen of course, if you don't know what you're looking for."

"I have it on good authority that the young lady in question was a customer of yours. You are in very deep trouble, madam, and I suggest you think very carefully about what medicines you have handed out in the past few months."

"I can tell you I've never handed out any mushrooms or toadstools."

"You seem very sure of that."

"I am. Most of my remedies are plant based, but none include fungus."

"You know that, even before I tell you what the lady came to see you about?"

"I do. But just out of interest, what did she want with me?"

Stonier took a long draught of his tea, thinking furiously whether he should tell her any more. He knew that Lazarus would tell her in no uncertain terms that he was asking questions, not answering them. However, if he was to jog her memory sufficiently to recall the unfortunate Mollie, he would have to at least confide the reason for her visit.

"She was sent by her lover, to try and get rid of an unwanted baby."

"Then I would have given her tansy and not mushrooms," said Mrs Riley in a matter of fact tone that stunned the policeman.

"You're admitting that? You do know that it is an offence to procure an abortion?"

She shrugged, "I did not say that it would do any such thing. Tansy is a perfectly legal plant, not included on any poison register. If the truth be told, it would only cause a miscarriage if the young lady was already inclined that way. They take the tansy and if nothing happens, then they've usually had the time to grow accustomed to the idea that the baby was meant to be. Sometimes it only needs the first panic to fade away for girls to realize that having a baby isn't the worst thing that can happen to them. I give girls a bit of comfort when they feel abandoned by all and how can I be blamed for that? You asked me if I had given this woman toadstools and I have truthfully told you that I did not. I think it is more than likely that she ate them by mistake, thinking that she was eating harmless mushrooms. I can't tell you any more than that."

The sergeant realized that he couldn't go any further. She had been surprisingly honest with him – and oddly enough, he believed her. Mollie might have eaten poison, but she wasn't fed it here.

"Did you give her tansy?"

"If she came for the reason you say, then yes, I would have advised her to take tansy – I would have also counselled most strongly that she face up to her situation, try her utmost to get the father to marry her, and to live to a ripe old age with her grandchildren gathered around her."

She looked into Stonier's eyes with steady blue orbs, as dark blue as the seas her husband was currently sailing, "I don't kill for fun, sir," she said softly, "Everything I do, I do to help. These girls are young and foolish, they are not wicked – I wish I could say the same for some of the men who get them into trouble."

Stonier had seen enough of that to half agree with her, though he could never condone what she was doing. However, as she pointed out, she wasn't breaking any laws and so he was powerless. He could not leave her without a timely warning, which he delivered in his most lugubrious voice, "Be that as it may, you are playing a dangerous game. One girl has ended up in her grave, and there will be others. If you take my advice, you'll cease your helping and send these girls about their business when they come to you with their sob stories. The way you are going, Mrs Riley, you'll end your life on the gallows."

"I'll help as long as I'm needed, sir, but thank you for the warning. I'll bear it in mind."

There didn't seem to be anything more to be said, so Stonier left her and went back to the police station to write his report and await the return of his superior.

* * *

As he came out of the study and walked down the long passageway to where she was sitting, Constance raised tear-drenched eyes to Lazarus' face and he felt a clutch of pity in his belly for her. How would she feel if she knew her uncle had just tried to give her away in exchange for his own reputation? He was still so furious that he scarcely heeded his own words when he spoke to her, not caring how they might sound to her, "Pack your bags, Miss Allingham, you will be leaving here within a few days," he said gruffly.

If it had been possible for her to go any paler, she would surely have done so, the shock of his pronouncement was so great, she stood up and clutched at his lapel,

"You mean my uncle is throwing me out on the street? Oh, God, where will I go?"

He realized he had spoken too hastily and raised a hand to ease her gently back onto her seat, "Calm yourself. He has dared to do no such thing. I have told him that you no longer wish to live under his roof and he has agreed to find you a small house of your own."

To her ears this sounded very little better than the street. She had never lived without other people, had never been free to please herself, to take care of herself. The prospect of this sudden liberation was terrifying.

"Why have you done that? What right had you to tell him any such thing?" she stuttered, in a blind panic.

He was livid at her ingratitude. He had placed himself in an invidious position merely to protect her and now it seemed all she cared about was living in luxury.

“Forgive my presumption,” he said coldly, “I had naturally assumed that you would wish to escape from physical harm, but evidently I was wrong. Stay under this roof and be that man’s whipping boy, if that’s your preference.”

He began to walk away and she realized how deeply concerned he had been for her wellbeing, “I do wish to escape, Mr Lazarus, of course I do. You merely shocked me. I had not thought my uncle would agree to release me quite so easily.”

He glanced back, tempted to tell her with what alacrity her relative had agreed to her removal, but an essentially kind heart prevented him. Instead he created a kind lie, “I left him no choice, Miss Allingham. If he should ask, you must allow him to believe that you were prepared to take him to court for assaulting you. I had to convince him of that in order to gain your freedom.”

For the first time she saw a glimmer of humour in the situation, “Oh, my goodness, Inspector, he really thought you were going to arrest him on my behalf, didn’t he?”

“I’m a very accomplished actor, Miss. Of course he believed it. I was about to handcuff him when he conceded.”

“I wish I had seen that,” she said wistfully. She would have paid good money to witness the sight of the bully finally cowed by the policeman.

He couldn’t help but smile himself at her very obvious joy, “It was immensely satisfying,” he admitted, “But now I must go. I have to see Stonier and find out if he has made any progress with the case in my absence.”

“Very well. And thank you, Mr Lazarus. I know this cannot have been easy for you. Of all people I have reason to know how formidable my uncle can be.”

“Think nothing of it. I hope you’ll be happy in your new home.”

“I’m sure I shall be.” As he turned to go she delayed him once more, “Might I ask you a question, Inspector, before you leave?”

“Of course. What is it?”

“Who is Rosamund?”

Her heart sank when she saw how startled this question made him.

"Where did you hear that name?" he asked in clipped tones.

"From you. When you regained consciousness you seemed to think I was Rosamund and I wondered who she might be."

"I said her name?" he asked in surprise.

"You did. Is she perhaps your sister?"

"No. My wife." he said curtly and he walked swiftly away.

Constance sank back onto the chair and stared after him, her mouth falling open, her eyes wide, "Wife?" she whispered in horror. Why had it not occurred to him that he might be a married man? How much of a fool had she made of herself these past few days? And how could she ever face him again, after this?

CHAPTER TWENTY-SEVEN

When he reached it Braxton Police Station seemed to hold every constable except the one Lazarus most wanted to see. Stonier, he was informed, had returned to the hat shop to see if he could any more witnesses to Mollie Waters' last movements. Everyone was now painfully aware that time was rapidly running out. Sir Alan Corfield had given Lazarus and Stonier the chance to prove foul play in the case, despite vigorous opposition from their Superintendent and he now needed desperately to produce some usable evidence or the inquest would re-open and return a verdict of accidental or death by misadventure and any slight hope they had of finding her killer would be gone.

With so few other options open to him, the Inspector decided it was time to return to the scene of the crime – or at least the scene of the death – for they could not be sure where the crime took place and that was the main stumbling block. If they could only discover where the food had been prepared, then they might be able to find who had prepared it. He needed to speak again to Mollie's landlady. Perhaps she had been mistaken about Mollie cooking – or lying about it. Of course it was always possible the old woman had used the toadstools herself, panicked when she realized she had killed her lodger, and was now lying to cover the fatal error. She wouldn't be the first who had ventured into the woods to try and find a free meal and chosen the wrong fungus.

It was time to ask a few more weighted questions.

Mrs Brown looked even older and much more frail than she had on the day Mollie died and Lazarus felt the first stirrings of pity for her. He had to steel himself to see her as a potential suspect, especially when her face lit at the sight of him and she ushered him into her kitchen and put the kettle on without even being cajoled into doing so.

"I admit I thought Mollie was a bit of a pest at times," she confided as she brewed the tea, "But it's lonely here without her. She brought a bit of life into the place."

"I can imagine," Lazarus sympathised. He wondered if his own landlady had taken him in just to hold loneliness at bay. If she had, she would be sadly disappointed in him for company. He was hardly ever at home these days, except to eat a late meal and sleep. He spent more time with Stonier than anyone else of his acquaintance. Doubtless he and Rosamund would have been having quarrels by now at his constant absence from home, if she had still been around to be annoyed by it. Or maybe they would be existing in perfect harmony and the reason he stayed out such long hours at work was that his little family had been torn asunder and his house was empty and cold. This thought led to another, that it was his weekend to travel to his mother-in-law's home in Sheffield to see his little daughter. Once a month was not often enough, but what choice did he have? She was too young to be farmed out to strangers, so he couldn't have her living with him. No, she was better off where she was, for the present anyway. If he ever remarried, she could come and live with him in Braxton again.

For some reason the notion of being married made him wonder about Constance Allingham and whether her uncle had yet found her a place to live. He banished that thought too. It was none of his business and, after his behaviour, it was extremely unlikely that he would ever see her again. If Lord Allingham needed the help of the police, it was doubtful he would be asking for the assistance of Inspector Danby Lazarus.

The old woman presented him with his tea in a chipped china cup and a saucer that did not match, but he took it from her as though he were taking tea with a duchess. She giggled delightedly at his formal manners and watched him as he drank the brew, which was far too weak and was obviously at least a second outing for the tealeaves, but he gave every indication of enjoyment. Times were hard, especially for the elderly and the infirm. In good times their families and neighbours made sure they didn't go without, but when everyone in the community was feeling the pinch, there was no room for sentimentality or generosity.

Lazarus took his leisure over his drink, to compose himself before beginning to question her. She had given the impression of being a wily old thing and he needed to be on his guard lest she outflank him.

As it happened she began the interrogation for him, which was inclined to irk him until he realized that she had probably not exchanged a word with another soul for several days and sheer isolation was making her verbose. That fact alone was enough to make it more likely that she would trip herself up and tell him more than she ever intended.

"So, what brings you back here, Inspector? I thought we had seen the last of the poliss."

"You won't be seeing the back of us, Mrs B. until we found out who killed Mollie," he answered grimly, "We're like a dog with a bone."

She gave a cackle of laughter, "If you say so, but I reckon you'll have forgotten all about her in another week or so."

He looked even more severe, "Don't rely on it."

"I'm glad to hear it. Seems to me that young lasses from poor families are ten a penny. The whole lot of you would be out on the streets looking for the killer if it were a child of the gentry who died."

The comment was uncomfortably near the truth when he considered the lengths he had been forced to go to in order to try and track down Arabella Allingham.

"Maybe with some, but not me. A life is a life, rich or poor, and I'll do my best to find Mollie's killer."

She threw him a sceptical glance, "If you say so. But that's not telling me why you are back here with me. You've not called on an old woman just to cadge a brew, I know that much."

"No, you're right, I haven't. I want to go back over that last night when Mollie died. We're missing something and it could hold the key."

She heaved herself out of her chair with a visible effort, "You did miss something – I found it after you left. I wasn't sure it was important, but I kept it anyway."

She crossed to the battered old dresser and pulled open a drawer by its base, since it had long since lost its handle. She took out a small, crumpled scrap of paper and handed it to him, "It had rolled under the bed and it hadn't been there the last time I cleaned her room, so it hadn't been there long. It's not her handwriting, that's why I thought I had better keep it, just in case."

He unravelled it and read the words it contained, written in capitals, in slightly smudged ink, as though from the heat from Mollie's hand when she screwed it into a ball.

"AS YE SOW, SO SHALL YE REAP"

He frowned at the message, wondering exactly how long it had lain on the floor. The old woman might feel she was a thorough cleaner, but it could have been there for months. It was really only relevant if it had anything to do with Mollie's demise, but knowing the girl's mother, that little billet-doux could have come into her possession at any time in the past year or more, as a stark warning about the dangerous and unholy path she was treading.

"Is it important?" asked Mrs Brown, bringing his attention back to the present.

"I don't know yet, but you did right to hand it over."

"I hope it helps."

He put the paper in his pocket, "Now tell me again about that last evening. What time did Mollie go out and are you sure she didn't tell you where she was going or who with?"

"She told me nowt. She was all excited and girlish, as though she were going to meet her chap, but I knew he had finished with her a couple of months before – as I now know, when she told him she was in the family way."

"You think they might have been meeting anyway? Perhaps he had told her he wanted to see her again, and she was hoping he was going to come good for her?"

"Could be, but I couldn't swear that was it. She said nothing about him. All I can tell you is that she did seem happier than she had for a while. More hopeful like."

"So, someone had convinced her there was going to be a happy ending for her – but who?"

"As to that, I can't tell you."

"What about when she came home. You said it was late?"

"Late enough. I was already in bed and drifting off to sleep."

"And you are quite sure she didn't go into the kitchen and cook herself something to eat?"

"It's possible – but not very likely. Let me tell you, Inspector, when you go to bed with an empty belly, then the smell of food would wake you, no matter how deep asleep you were."

It was true enough. He couldn't argue with her. That was evidently the end of the matter. She seemed fond of the girl and was obviously missing her, for all she appeared uncaring when they first visited. He suspected the reality of the girl's death had not sunk in that first morning and now it most assuredly had. Mrs Brown was grieving and Lazarus was glad that at least someone was missing the poor lass.

He finished his tea and rose to his feet, "Thank you Mrs B, and you can be sure I'll be in touch if I find anything."

She laid a light, but restraining hand on his arm, "You won't give up on her, will you, Inspector? You won't let poor Mollie down?"

"I'll do my best," he promised, but he pondered on the likelihood of being able to honour that oath. He found himself no further forward no matter how many questions he asked.

On the doorstep he hesitated, realizing suddenly that he would never have a better opportunity to call on Will Carter's mother with the boy absent and without making his presence too obvious. He tried not to admit to himself that it was the image of Constance's wheals rather than Will's black eye that prompted him to cross the dusty roadway and knock on the door of number 12.

It seemed Mrs Carter was alone with the younger children. Lazarus didn't inquire as to the whereabouts of Mr Carter. He knew the answer – and it wasn't work!

She ran a self-conscious hand over her untidy hair and glanced down at her grubby apron, "Mr Lazarus, you've caught me at my housework. I'm not fit to be seen."

"Not at all," he assured her smoothly, "Do you have a moment to spare to talk to me?"

"There's nothing wrong, is there? Our Will's alright, isn't he?" she was suddenly anxious and he held up at calming hand.

"Nothing is amiss. I just wanted a quiet word."

"Then you'd better come in," she was obviously reluctant to let him over the threshold and when he entered he understood why. He had rarely witnessed worse poverty than he beheld in that house. Every stick of furniture was gone – probably to the pawn-shop – and not one of the children had a pair of shoes to their feet. The kitchen table was a plank of battered wood suspended on a pile of bricks. The fire was unlit and not a scrap of food was to be seen on the empty shelves.

He resolutely tried not to look around, nor show on his face how appalled he was, simply saying, "I'm sorry to trouble you, but I was a little concerned the other day when Will came into the station with a couple of bruises."

She gave a nervous laugh, "Well, Inspector, boys will be boys. He'll have been getting too rough playing with his friends, I expect."

"Could be ..." Lazarus glanced down at the youngsters, who were gathered around their mother, staring at him, open-mouthed. She realized that he was reluctant to speak in front of the little ones, so she spoke to the oldest, who couldn't have been more than five, "Bridget, take the little ones upstairs to play, there's a good girl."

Bridget obeyed without demur, evidently quite used to being in charge of the younger three, including the one that could not yet walk and had been shuffling along on his bottom, keeping up quite well with his elders.

Lazarus waited until they were gone before turning back to the woman. He looked at her face. She looked fifty, but he suspected she was still in her twenties. She bore the yellowed ghosts of old bruises on her cheeks, and her eyes looked dead and defeated.

He decided he had nothing to lose by being candid with her.

"Mrs Carter, Will told us how he got the black eye – coming between you and your husband, when you were fighting."

She was already pale – the sickly pale of a woman who was malnourished and worried to death, but when he said this, she went whiter than he could ever have believed was possible, "I … I don't know what you're talking about."

"Yes, you do. And you know that you should gather up your children and walk out of that door right now."

"And go where?" she asked bitterly, "The workhouse?"

He couldn't believe he was even contemplating what he was saying to her, but the words were out of his mouth before he could prevent their escape, "At least you'll get fed there – and no man will lay a finger on you."

"Maybe not. But my children will be taken from me. You don't know what you are asking me to do. You know nothing about it. You come here in your fancy clothes, not a care in the world, never short of money, and think you can order me about just because you've given my boy a few errands to run."

"I'm not trying to order you about," he protested, "I'm merely trying to help."

"Well, I don't want your help. Get out of my house."

"I'm sorry. I've offended you and that was never my intention. Is there anything at all I can do to help?"

"No."

"Perhaps I could have a word with your husband. Point out to him that if he was a little less handy with his fists …"

She flew at him, spitting like a cat, "Don't you dare go near him! Are you bloody insane? He'll kill me if he finds out the peelers are on his back because of me."

He staggered backwards, astounded by the violence of her attack, "All right, calm down. Forget I spoke. I was never here. But that boy had better not be beaten again or that husband of yours is going to find himself behind bars, whether you like it or not."

"Get out and mind you own bloody business or you'll find yourself in trouble. You won't be the first policeman found down some dark alley with his head bashed in."

In the silence that followed this pronouncement he looked down at her for a long time his face expressionless and initially she stared back, but she wavered and lowered her eyes, "I'm sorry. I shouldn't have said that, but you don't know how dangerous my man is. If I could leave him, I would, but I daren't. He'll hunt me down and I'll pay, believe me."

"Oh, I believe you. But believe this, I can take care of myself and your husband will live to regret it if he takes me on."

He left, but outside the door he was astonished to find himself shaking not only with shock, but with fury. How a lad like Will had come from parents such as those, he could not imagine. He wished fervently there was some hope of getting him away from their malign influence before he began to tread the same path.

Sadly he could think of no way to do so.

CHAPTER TWENTY-EIGHT

PRESENT

There was still no sign of David when they reached the house and for the first time Libby really started to worry. This was not how things were supposed to be. It was all very well having disagreements and minor fall-outs, but this was getting beyond a joke. How could they even begin to repair the cracks if they never saw each other from one week's end to the next?

She said nothing but put on a brave face when Ilsa asked where "The Scarlet Pimpernel" had got to this time. She merely laughed and told her friend that this was the busiest time of the year for the garden centre and that she and her husband more than made up during the slack season of winter, but inside she had never felt more like simply retiring to bed and crying her heart out.

She thought things couldn't be worse until she walked into the sitting room and found that the furniture had been moved around. For some reason it distressed her to a level quite out of proportion to the situation. The very thought that David had been having a reshuffle without including her was enough to make her want to sob out loud. She had never been called upon to act so hard in all her life. So determined was she that Ilsa would never know how upset she was, she pinned a smile on her face and played the gracious hostess to the hilt.

By the time her friend was packed and ready to leave, she felt as though her whole face was stiff and aching with the false smile with which it had been adorned.

She didn't even have the energy to make excuses as to why Ilsa couldn't visit again soon and found herself getting the calendar off the kitchen wall and booking another girly weekend only a month hence. She had the oddest sensation of being someone else and being outside her own body and watching herself grin like a maniac and plan yet another sauna session and shopping expedition. She wanted to slap her own face and scream at herself, "Tell the bitch you never want to see her again!" but she just wrote the dates in and gave Ilsa a warm hug goodbye.

Then suddenly she was in an empty house – and the tears she had been damming up burst forth and she threw herself onto the sofa, and cried and cried for what seemed like hours, but in reality was about five minutes before she heard the door open and she shot upright and tried to wipe her face with trembling fingers, horrified in case Ilsa had forgotten something and had come back to catch her at her weakest.

She looked up to meet the startled eyes of her husband, "Bloody hell, Libby! What on earth is wrong? I thought you'd been having a whale of a time with your mate."

Taken by surprise she had no time to marshal her thoughts or plan what she wanted to say, instead she found herself wailing like a five year old, "You've had a move around without me!"

He seemed stunned and glanced around the room, "What?"

"You've moved the furniture," she snivelled.

"No, I haven't. Why the heck would I do that? I've been out all day, you know I have."

She took a moment to process what he was telling her. She gulped back further tears and stared at him, utterly baffled, "I've been out all day too. You're really being serious? You haven't moved anything?"

"Of course I haven't. I can assure you, I have better things to do with my time – anyway, what was wrong with it the way it was?"

"Nothing. That's the whole point."

He joined her on the settee, taking her hand, "What's going on, Libby?"

"How should I know? I came home and everything had been moved around. I thought it must be you."

"I've not touched a thing. It doesn't look that different to me. Are you sure your friend didn't do it while she was waiting for you this morning? Perhaps she thought she was being helpful."

Libby wrinkled her nose in deep distaste, "It's exactly the sort of thing she would do, actually, because her way of doing things is so superior to mine – but she can't have done it. I never left her alone for long enough."

He examined her face and Libby had the oddest sensation that he was trying to read her expression, to see if she was really telling the truth. The idea made her furious. In all their time together he had never before doubted her word.

"You think I'm losing it, don't you?" she asked aggressively.

He shook his head, "No way. But there must be some sort of an explanation. Stuff doesn't move itself. Who has a key to the house besides the two of us?"

"Only Maddie, in case of emergency. We don't live near enough to any of the neighbours to ask them to be key-holders." That was true enough. Hill Farm was isolated, situated at the end of a long, rutted lane, at least a mile from the nearest public road.

"Didn't Brendan have a key? I seem to recall him pinching a set and letting himself in. Damn it, we should have changed the locks. I'm an idiot for not thinking of it!"

She interrupted before he could berate himself into a frenzy of self-reproach,

"But even if he still has the key, Brendan is in prison. They locked him up on remand after he came out of hospital."

"So they did. Well, it must have been Maddie then. One of her more bizarre ideas, no doubt."

"But why would she? It doesn't make any sense."

"Nothing your sister does surprises me. She could quite easily have thought it was funny to spook us both. She might even have thought she was being helpful. She's weird."

Libby wasn't quite sure whether she ought to defend her sister from this smear, or simply admit the truth of it and leave well alone. After a moment she decided on the latter. David had a point.

"Well, it's too late to ring her now. I'll call her tomorrow and find out what the hell she thinks she's playing at."

"You do that. In the meantime, don't you think it's about time you and I had some make-up sex in the peace and quiet of our own home?"

Part of her wanted to discuss the source of the arguments before going straight to the forgiveness, but one look into his smiling eyes and she found herself grinning in return, "On the strict understanding that you are not off the hook," she said primly.

"Good God, no! I wouldn't have it any other way."

The way to the bedroom was littered with discarded clothes, the furniture removal forgotten.

* * *

Her husband was long gone, leaving her sleeping as he usually did, when Libby finally woke. She smiled to herself as she stretched and recalled last night. She and David might not always see eye to eye on every little thing, but all differences were forgotten in the big brass bed.

She took her time having a shower and cleaning her teeth, luxuriating in the knowledge that she had nowhere to go to, nothing to do and no-one to answer to – freedom felt good. She hadn't realized how much of a strain the weekend had been until it was over. She wondered vaguely what the hell Ilsa's problem was. She had always been a bit of a pain, with a superiority complex and a snobbish streak a mile wide, but she had tempered that with a sense of humour. Now she seemed to have lost all her good points and retained and magnified her flaws. Perhaps she was unhappy and this was her way of hiding it. She certainly didn't appear to be at all happy for Libby now that she was married and had found something she felt passionate about in her writing. Libby liked to think she would have wished her friend well if their situations had been reversed, but maybe it wasn't that easy to be magnanimous when you were miserable yourself.

When she finally went downstairs, ravenous and dying for a coffee, she was touched to see that David had re-arranged the sitting room furniture back to it's old way. One or two things were misplaced, but on the whole he had done a reasonable job of putting everything back. She had been about to ring Maddie to ask her if she had been responsible for the odd reshuffle, but seeing how hard her husband must have worked, being quiet enough not to wake her, she decided to ring him at work first and thank him for the effort.

He wasn't in his office, so she had a longish wait whilst his assistant went to find him. Her stomach gave a little excited flip when she heard his deep voice down the telephone line, "Hi, sleeping beauty, you've finally dragged yourself out of your pit," he said, but she could hear the laughter in his voice and smiled warmly, "Finally," she agreed, "and I just wanted to ring and thank you,"

He gave his reverberating, sexy laugh, "For last night? There's really no need, the pleasure was all mine," he said.

It was silly, but she felt herself blushing at the memory this evoked, "No, don't be daft," she told him, trying to be severe, "I meant thank you for putting the furniture back where it belongs."

There was a blank silence, then he said carefully, "But I didn't touch a thing. I went straight out, didn't even stop for coffee, because I'd overslept. In fact, if I'm honest, it never looked that different to me, and I'm not sure I could have recalled where everything went in the first place."

Libby couldn't have been more shocked if he had thrown her into an icy pond. She had a similar sensation of breathlessness. It felt as though shock had made her windpipe snap shut. For one horrible moment she couldn't get her breath and silver dots danced before her eyes. She knew that if she didn't sit down she was going to pass out. She managed to gasp, "Don't mess about David. This isn't funny."

"Believe me, love, it's not something I would joke about. Are you sure things have been altered?"

"Positive. So unless one of us did it in our sleep ..."

"Do you want me to come home?"

It was a testament to how scared she was that she hesitated for several long seconds before she decided that she couldn't possibly drag him home from work for something that probably had a perfectly logical explanation, though she couldn't at that precise moment think of one.

"No, it's fine. Someone is playing silly buggers at our expense and I intend to find out who it is. I'll be fine. I'll see you later."

"If you are sure," he said doubtfully.

"I'm sure."

"Well, if you change your mind, ring and I'll be home in twenty minutes."

"Okay, thanks."

"See you later – and don't bother cooking any tea, I'll take you out."

"That would be nice," she answered dutifully, but her mind wasn't on the prospective treat, she was looking around the room, trying to work out exactly what had been happening.

David rang off and she sat looking around for a long time, all sorts of possibilities presenting themselves in her churning brain and each one being dismissed for various reasons.

The only theory which she refused to acknowledge was the one that she feared the most.

She couldn't help recalling the odd happenings in this house when her Aunt Lil was dying. She had even gone so far as having a sèance to try and get to the bottom of the mystery and it had frightened the life out of her. So much so that she had been afraid she wouldn't be able to live in the house when Lil was gone and she was alone.

Things had settled down when she found the marriage licence that proved Decima Watkins had not had her baby out of wedlock, but what if current events had reawakened whatever it was that had been disturbed before?

Libby didn't even want to entertain the possibility.

A knock at the door almost gave her a heart attack. She jumped violently, then managed to force a nervous laugh at herself, "Pull yourself together, Elizabeth," she said aloud, before drawing in a deep breath to slow her hammering heart and going to answer the door.

It was Joanne Pooley, the journalist, who was smiling warmly as the door opened, but swiftly her expression changed to one of deep concern, "Good God, Libby, are you okay? You look like you've seen a ghost."

"Funny you should say that," said Libby ironically, before she could stop herself. Joanne was not a newspaper woman for nothing. She scented a story with the unerring instinct of a hunting predator. She hid her interest well, wrapping her intrigue in a cloak of solicitude, "Let me make you a drink of something hot. You look as though you could do with it."

Libby allowed her to precede her through the kitchen door, "I must admit I've had a bit of a turn, but don't worry about me. I'll be fine. What can I do for you? You didn't call because you were passing. We're miles from anywhere out here."

Joanne waved a dismissive hand, "Don't you worry about that. I just had a couple more questions for you so I can put the finishing touches to my piece on you, but it can wait. You are the important thing at the moment. You really are dreadfully white. Are you sure you don't need a doctor or something?"

"No, honestly I'll be fine. But I would be grateful if you would make a drink. I must admit I do feel a bit wobbly."

She hoisted herself onto a high stool and leant on the breakfast counter while she allowed Joanne free range of the kitchen as she watched. Joanne knew better than to bombard her with questions, so she simply made the tea, all thc while keeping up a light-hearted conversation about how astounded she was to find her subject in such a state when she had always given the impression of being so calm and level-headed. She knew that Libby was going to find herself having to justify her over the top reaction and before she knew it, she was going to be giving the journalist chapter and verse as to what had upset her.

Sure enough, once Libby had a strong coffee in her hands, she began to talk. Joanne wished she had her tape recorder running, but she was just going to have to try and remember everything that was said.

And boy was it worth hearing. She was stunned by the revelations that came pouring out of the still shocked Libby.

She found herself listening to a better story than she could ever have imagined and she realized that she had two choices. She could either try and persuade Libby to let her write this story – which was likely to be refused outright. Or she could write it anyway and take the flak afterwards.

And she didn't much care which option she ended up with, so long as she got her story.

CHAPTER TWENTY-NINE

Lazarus

On Friday morning the weather finally broke and Lazarus found himself being grateful for the rain. He never thought he would ever see the day when he was sick of sunshine, but it had been unrelenting for weeks now and he felt the heat was making everyone around him irritable and unreasonable.

Apart from all the other problems which beset him, he was heartily sick of Stonier complaining about the effect the lack of water was having on his garden. He feared that if heard about just one more wilted lettuce he was going to take the said vegetable and ram it down his sergeant's throat.

It had not helped his equanimity when he had found his office crowded with people on his return from his miserable failure with Mrs Carter, with Stonier nowhere to be seen.

The constable on the desk tried to warn him with a lifted brow and a swift jerk of the head, but he had misunderstood the tacit message and had frowned at him and walked straight into the lion's den.

He was faced with an irate Mrs Waters, accompanied as usual by the vicar, but also there was Sir Alan Corfield the Coroner and another unknown man who he presently learned was a lawyer sent by Sir Walter Crabtree in defence of his son Lawrence.

As soon as he entered they all began to talk and it was with the greatest difficulty that he forced his way between them and took his place at his side of the desk. Once ensconced, though not seated, in deference to the lack of chairs for the others, he felt much more in control and called everyone to order with a loud, "I beg your pardon, one and all, but if we are to make any progress at all, I shall need to hear you one at a time." Accordingly they all fell silent and Lazarus removed his overcoat and hung it over the back of his chair, "Perhaps you could tell me what this is all about, Sir Alan, as the most senior person here?"

Sir Alan nodded, held the one chair in the room for Mrs Waters, as the only woman present, then began, "Mr Lazarus, I'm here at the behest of Mrs Waters. She is terribly concerned that this unfortunate matter is dragging on and I must say, I am inclined to agree with her. I feel you have now had sufficient time to find some evidence of foul play in the death of Miss Waters."

"You did allow me some time to investigate, Sir Alan," said Lazarus with quiet reason, admirably hiding his annoyance at the very obvious interference in his case. The smug look on the face of Mr Bembridge told him all he needed to know about whom he had to thank for this invasion.

"I realize that, and I do understand the problems you face, but Mrs Waters feels that whilst this is unresolved, it is a continuing slur on her daughter's memory."

"I do see that, sir, and I assure you that I am making enquiries. Sergeant Stonier is due to report back to me any moment."

"Concerning what?" asked the coroner.

"That is hardly something I can discuss here and now."

It was the lawyer's turn to speak. He scented blood and was quick to strike,

"If this line of enquiry is aimed at criminalising my client, then I demand to know what it is," he said loudly.

Lazarus turned a piercing eye upon him, "And you are?"

"Timothy Sawyer, representing Lawrence Crabtree – whom, I might say, you have been pursuing with unwarranted vigour."

Lazarus' first thought was of the aptness of the name. He was sorely tempted to say aloud, "Really? Sawyer the Lawyer?" but he managed to restrain both the comment and the grin, "I dispute the 'unwarranted' Mr Sawyer. Lawrence Crabtree was the father of Mollie Waters' unborn baby."

There was a collective gasp that Lazarus had dared to voice the accusation, but Sawyer remained coolly sceptical, "So said she! But what proof was there? She was a woman of few morals who managed to get her claws into an impressionable young man ..."

"Now, just one moment," interrupted Mollie's irate mother, "I'm not having my daughter's name dragged though any more mud! Mollie was a good girl until she was seduced by that bounder ..."

Mr Bembridge held out a placating hand and tried to calm his housekeeper down, but Mrs Waters was having none of it. She had spent years being a dutiful woman. She had been a reluctant wife and mother, an even more reluctant widow. She had worked her fingers to the bone in the service of others – most of whom didn't deserve their position in life. Now she found herself the possessor of a dead daughter and grandchild on whom everyone was pouring scorn and threats of eternal retribution. She found deep within herself a level of affection and loyalty to Mollie she had never felt during her lifetime. Suddenly clearing Mollie's name had become the one thing that gave her existence any meaning and she fired at it every weapon in her armoury.

Hearing the wild accusations the woman was throwing about, Mr Sawyer realized that it was imperative that he try and silence her. If the observing policeman gave credence to even half of her ramblings, Lawrence Crabtree was going to find himself in very serious trouble, possibly even facing the hangman's noose.

Consequently the level of sound rose rapidly and Lazarus found himself helpless – and indeed without the desire – to silence the combatants. He took his seat, leaned back nonchalantly and watched the battle with a small smile and a large sense of satisfaction. Sir Alan and the vicar had now joined in the skirmish, each trying to sue for peace and failing miserably.

It was into this melee that Stonier walked and said, loudly and with a singular lack of originality, "What's going on here, then?"

"Ah, Sergeant Stonier, the very man," said Sir Alan with great relief, "Perhaps you would like to explain where you have been and what you have found out for the benefit of Mrs Waters and Mr Sawyer?"

Stonier had no idea who Sawyer was, but he knew Mollie's mother, the vicar and most significantly he knew Sir Alan Corfield, so it was without hesitation that he confided, "Certainly, Sir. I have been to see Mrs Riley of Little Lowton, a woman who dispenses herbal remedies. She freely admitted that she gives assistance to young ladies who find themselves in 'trouble'."

"That's enough, Sergeant," said Lazarus hastily as he realized that given free rein, Stonier was likely to give chapter and verse on their investigations – which he felt should be kept confidential, and which actually were so lacking in real evidence that Sawyer could very well insist that they cease immediately.

"I hope you arrested her," said Mr Bembridge, obviously appalled.

"I will certainly do so when I have enough evidence, but her story is that her potions are harmless and only act as a comfort to the women. By the time they realize it hasn't worked, they seem to come to terms with their dilemma."

"A likely story!" he snorted with open contempt, "The woman is quite obviously a menace and it is more than probable that her noxious potions are what killed Mollie!"

"That is something we are endeavouring to discover, sir." said Stonier stolidly.

"What has this woman to do with the matter?" intercepted Sawyer, "I fail to see how this could possibly involve my client."

"Your client, Mr Sawyer," said Lazarus coldly, "was the man who suggested to Mollie that she might like to visit Mrs Riley and put an end to both their 'troubles'."

That successfully foreshortened any comment from the lawyer, but he wasn't silenced for long, "Allegedly," he said succinctly. Lazarus raised a quizzical brow at him, but didn't contest the word or the sentiment behind it.

Sir Alan withdrew his fob watch from his waistcoat pocket and flipped open the case with a practiced thumb, "Good Heavens, look at the time. Well, I think we've wasted enough of the Inspector's valuable time. It is obvious to me that he has certainly found some discrepancies with the case which warrants further investigation, so I suggest we leave him to get on with it. Thank you for your time, Mr Lazarus. I'll expect your full report in due course."

Lazarus acknowledged this speech with an inclination of his head and without further ado, the coroner ushered the party out of the office. Stonier watched them leave with something approaching incredulity. He had very little idea what had been going on in his absence, but he had more sense than to ask until he and Lazarus were alone.

"What the devil was that all about?"

Lazarus wiped his forehead with his handkerchief, "Thank goodness you arrived when you did, old friend, I was in danger of having the case taken out of our hands. Certain interested parties feel we don't have enough evidence to pursue this any further – and I fear they are sadly right."

"Not necessarily. I think if we take a picture of Mollie to Mrs Riley, she may well be able to tell us if she visited her for the purposes of procuring an abortion."

"Do we have a picture of Mollie?"

Stonier grinned, "As a matter of fact, we do. Dr Scattergood is a man of many talents and hobbies. One of the things he is interested in is daguerreotypes. He took the liberty of arranging for a likeness of Mollie to be taken just before her interment."

"Dr Scattergood is a useful man to know."

"Indeed he is. I'll go and see if I can get hold of the picture and we will take ourselves off to see Mrs Riley."

"Excellent. But let's have a cup of tea first, shall we? I need to recover from the invasion."

Stonier needed no second bidding.

* * *

It was rather later than they had intended when they finally set forth for Little Lowton. The tea had taken time to consume, since it was accompanied by a rendition of Lazarus' adventures in Stockport. These had to be carefully edited to remove all mention of Miss Allingham's personal problems. Stonier guessed more than he was told, but he kept his own counsel. Meg would have useful insight to offer when he talked to her that evening over supper. Lazarus also mentioned in passing the set-to he had had with Mrs Carter. Stonier shook his head sorrowfully, "You just can't help some folk, can you?" he asked lugubriously, "God knows how that boy will turn out in the end. He'll start by being appalled by his father's behaviour and end by doing the same to some poor girl who has the misfortune to fall for his charms."

"Good God, I hope not!" muttered Lazarus, truly horrified by this prediction, "Surely he would want to break away from his father, not ape him?"

"That's not what experience tells me," said Stonier, "But who knows, maybe he'll be the exception that proves the rule."

As they left the livery stable in the hired trap, they almost ran into the reverend Bembridge in a very similar vehicle, going in the opposite direction but on the wrong side of the road. At first Lazarus, who was driving, assumed the gentleman of the cloth had merely strayed off the straight and narrow by accident, but as he hailed them, a bad-tempered expression on his face, it became obvious he had swung in front of them deliberately, "Hey there, Lazarus, I was just coming in search of you. They told me at the Police Station that you were here hiring a trap."

"You have just caught me, Bembridge," responded Lazarus, using just the surname on purpose, to show the vicar that he was in no way superior to the policeman and liberties could be taken on both sides.

"I trust you are on your way to arrest that woman."

"What woman would that be?" asked the Inspector, fully aware of whom Bembridge meant, but determined to make the fellow spell it out. However, he was wasting his breath, for the clergyman was now too fired up to be distracted.

"It is scandalous that she has been so brazen about it. No wonder young girls are so free with their favours, when they know someone like her will simply make the problem 'go away'. It is nothing short of witchcraft – what a pity that the old methods of dealing with her sort don't still exist!"

"I think the ducking-stool and burning at the stake are a little out-dated," said Lazarus, hiding his amusement at the red-faced, apoplectic old hypocrite. It seemed to entirely escape his notice that none of these young women were alone in their 'sin', but the male of the species were never singled out for criticism. He evidently took the Bible literally and felt it was always 'Eve' who led poor, simple, gullible 'Adam' into wrong-doing.

"More's the pity. Still, at least you are going to arrest her now. She'll have to face the law as it stands."

"You have misunderstood me, sir. I have no intention of making any arrests just yet. As far as I am aware, Mrs Riley has broken no laws. She offers herbal remedies and makes no charge for them, therefore she is not setting herself up as a pharmacist and therefore not subject to the rules and regulations they follow."

Mr Bembridge's mouth dropped open, then closed again with a snap as he tried to find words to adequately convey his sense of horror at this pronouncement. Lazarus took the opportunity to escape before the diatribe could resume, "Good day to you, sir," he said and swung the pony's head sharply to the side so that he could manoeuvre his trap around the vicar's vehicle. He slapped the reins to encourage the animal to sharpen its pace so they could be away before Bembridge recovered his power of speech.

"You've made yourself an enemy there," murmured Stonier, glancing back to see Bembridge still in the middle of the road, staring after them with a face of thunder.

"Good," answered Lazarus.

They found Mrs Riley at home and as welcoming as ever. Stonier was astounded that Lazarus seemed inclined to be rather more friendly than was his wont,

"So you're the witch in the woods?" he joked and she grinned in response.

"That's me – but you can call me Janet. Come inside, I've just made a spiced honey cake, it will go well with a cup of tea."

They tasted the cake and declared it to be delicious. The tea was strong and hearty. Oddly enough they both felt better when they had finished their repast and Stonier did wonder vaguely if there might be something more than 'spices' in the cake, but he said nothing. These days, anything that put Lazarus in a good mood was to be thanked and never questioned.

As they ate, Janet looked them both over, then addressed herself to the Inspector, "That's a nasty bruise on your forehead. Been in the wars?"

He lifted a self-conscious hand to the still-tender spot, "Believe it or not, I was in a train crash," he admitted ruefully.

"That doesn't happen every day," she told him, rising to her feet, "you need Arnica and Comfrey. I have a pot of balm here somewhere." She searched the over-laden shelves until she found what she was looking for, "Here, put that on, morning and night, you'll soon take the swelling down."

"Thank you. How much do I owe you?"

She waved away his offer of payment, "Not a thing. I grew the arnica, and the comfrey grows on its own. Mother Nature always provides." With that she took off the lid and with a firm hand under his chin, she turned his face to the light and smeared some of the concoction carefully over his injury before he could even think to protest.

Stonier was astounded that he submitted to these ministrations, but had the sense to say nothing.

"It feels better already," said Lazarus with a smile, Janet grinned and tapped his cheek gently, "Even the witches' brew doesn't work that fast!" she chided him.

Stonier thought it was time to bring Lazarus back to the matter in hand and he cleared his throat loudly, "If Mrs Riley could look at the picture, now, sir," he said gruffly.

They showed 'the witch' the picture they had of Mollie, taken in her coffin and looking as though she was peacefully asleep after all the trials and tribulations she had gone through.

"Yes, that's one of my girls," said Mrs Riley, sadly touching the glass on which the daguerreotype was captured, "But she had left it too late when she came, so I refused to give her anything at all. If she was poisoned, I swear to God, she never had it from me."

"Did she strike you as the sort who might have known which poisonous toadstools to look for, if she had decided to do away with herself?"

She shook her head, "No, she wasn't a country girl. And I don't think she was suicidal anyway. She had reached that stage when acceptance takes over. She simply smiled a little and said, 'Well, that's that. Lawrie will have to keep his promises and put a ring on my finger, won't he?'"

"Those were her exact words? She used the name Lawrie?"

"She did. How else would I have known it?"

"True enough. Thank you for your help, madam."

"My pleasure, Inspector."

"Since you wouldn't take payment, take a word of advice and keep your head down for a few weeks. There are one or two people who would like to cause trouble for you, now that your name is known."

"I'll do my best. But my name has never been a secret, you know."

"Maybe so, but it was only privy to those who might need your help, not to those who wish you harm."

She didn't seem to be very concerned, merely shrugging her shoulders, "I'll be careful," she promised.

CHAPTER THIRTY

It being mid-afternoon by the time Lazarus and Stonier arrived back in Braxton after interviewing Janet Riley, they decided to take a detour and find out if Meg had been doing any of her own baking. The spice cake, far from filling them up, had given them a definite appetite – they were both in a curiously good mood too, and tended to find everything very amusing for some strange reason.

As it happened Meg had spent the best part of the day bottling, pickling and brining various products from Tom's garden, so they were treated to cheese and homemade pickle sandwiches and fresh jam on newly baked scones.

With his mouth full Lazarus answered Meg's endless questions about what had happened whilst he had been in Stockport – and indeed before and after his arrival in the town. As Tom had suspected, she winkled far more out of his friend that he could ever have hoped to discover.

She also knew Lazarus' business better than he knew it himself, "Last weekend of the month tomorrow, Danby," she reminded him, "You'll be on the train again in the morning, off to see young Lucinda in Sheffield."

Whilst Lazarus had not forgotten that he saw his daughter every month, he had failed to recall that it was indeed the last weekend of July and the reminder startled him into ceasing to eat for a few seconds, "Good God, has it really come round again so quickly?" He smiled delightedly, "Being busy has its compensations, it makes the time fly by."

They quickly finished their repast, then headed back to return the pony and trap to the ostler and make a final note of their day, ready for further work on Monday morning. Stonier would take his ease that weekend, since his superior was on leave, and already had plans of what needed doing in his sadly neglected plot of land. He hated it when Meg took it upon herself to harvest his precious vegetables, knowing that she would take all the youngest, sweetest produce and leave him with the woody old stuff that would never grow into prize winning specimens.

Back at his lodgings Lazarus packed his small carpet bag with essentials, and faced with a unappetising looking stew, filled with greasy lumps of gristle which passed for mutton, he decided to take the evening train and spend an extra night with his daughter.

Lucy was already in bed when he arrived, but his mother-in-law was delighted to see him and greeted him with a warmth which he always found surprising. He felt that she would have blamed him for Rosamund's death, since it had happened whilst giving birth to his child, but Dorothy Mason was a woman of the world who knew that the most dangerous moments in life were those which gave the most fulfilment. She knew Rosamund would not have chosen to avoid childbirth, even had she known it could kill her. Little Lucy was all the more precious for her mother's loss, and Lazarus had behaved well throughout. He had asked his wife's family to care for his daughter, was meticulous in matters both financial and in visiting regularly. He had shown proper respect for his late wife in being in no hurry to replace her – all in all, Dorothy was well pleased with her daughter's choice of husband, though she had been understandably reluctant at the beginning of the romance, when she had found that Rosamund's suitor was a policeman. It seemed to her a profession which made no friends on either side of the law. It was obvious why criminals should hate the police force, but tax-payers could be equally disdainful since they felt that the majority of the constabulary were 'poachers turned gamekeepers' and could be bought by whomsoever paid the highest price. This had been sadly true at the inception of Sir Robert Peel's force, but was hardly the case now, since all policemen were required to uphold the highest standards of behaviour, whether on duty or off, but old prejudices still remained.

However, Dorothy had no such concerns about Lazarus, who had always behaved impeccably and treated his wife and her family with the greatest affection and respect.

He declined to eat when he arrived in Sheffield, but gladly accepted a glass of ale and settled with a sigh into a comfortable chair by the fire. Dorothy looked him over with a motherly eye, "Been in the wars, Danby?" she asked, nodding towards his now rapidly fading to green and yellow bruise.

"You're not the first person to ask me that," he answered with a smile, "and I'd like to be able to report that I received it in the course of my duty, whilst apprehending a vicious criminal, however, I was simply on a train that braked too hard and threw me against the far side of the carriage."

Dorothy obliged him by laughing at his self-deprecating version of events, but she sensed he was hiding something from her and went on a little fishing expedition,

"Well, it's an old injury, so it didn't happen on the way here, so what were you doing on a train if it wasn't coming to Sheffield?"

"It could have been going home," he pointed out, observing her over the rim of his glass.

"That's never a month old," she told him decidedly, "But you don't have to tell me if you don't want to. I know it's none of my affair what you get up to in the course of your duties, as you call them."

"You should have been a detective," he said with a grin, "As a matter of fact, I was injured whilst gallantly protecting a young lady from serious injury."

"How very intriguing," she responded, "tell me more."

He decided that no harm could come from telling her the full story, without revealing any names, since she lived so very far from the scene of the case, and who knew, she was a wise old thing, and might just have a few ideas as to where a wilful girl like Arabella would go to hide from her dearest papa.

Dorothy listened, but as the story unfolded, she found herself much more interested in the lady in the train than the young wanton who had run off with her lover. There was an air about Lazarus, a wistfulness in his expression when he mentioned her that alerted

Dorothy to something more than mere business in the way he dealt with her. When he described the visit from the doctor and the evidence of physical abuse, his anger seemed to be tinged not only with pity, but a desire for personal revenge on the man who had inflicted the beating. She realized that the moment she had been dreading might very well be upon them and it was up to her to deal with it in the best possible way. She had always known that Lazarus might re-marry and that when he did, he would want his child living back with him and his new family. Dorothy adored Lucy, but she was well aware that the child's place was with her father. It was her Christian duty to make it easy for him to move on with his life, no matter how hard that might be for her. Lucy was all she had since her widowhood and the death of her only child, but she had been lent to her, not given, and this could be the time to give her back.

"You know Danby, how very fond I am of you, and that if you feel it is time to find a new life, you would do so with my blessing."

Danby looked utterly startled, "Good grief, Dorothy, what on earth brought that on? My life is going on the way it always has, nothing has changed."

"Hasn't it?" she asked.

"No. What makes you think anything else?"

"I thought perhaps ..." she trailed off, but he was hardly going to allow her to leave him in suspense.

"What? What did you think?"

"The young lady you mentioned. She seems to have caught your attention."

Now he was thoroughly confused, "Arabella? Good God, no. I've never even met her. I've simply been asked to find her and her lover. Except for her youth, I would have told her father to go to the devil before I would have put myself out for her."

"Not Arabella," said Dorothy patiently, "The other – the lady you saved on the train."

Lazarus opened his mouth to deny this too, but found himself unable to frame the words for a telling few seconds.

"Constance? No, not really. I feel the utmost pity for her situation, nothing more."

"Yet you use her first name. That is rather more intimate than I would have expected for someone who is merely involved in a case."

Again he was lost for words and Dorothy decided the moment had come to release him from his embarrassment. She patted him affectionately on the hand, then rose to her feet, "Well, I'm off to my bed. But just so you know, when the time comes that you feel you have found a renewed interest in life, I shall be prepared."

He wanted to deny the possibility, but in the face of her complete acceptance, and her kindness, he knew he couldn't even think about lying to her. He too retired to bed, but he lay awake for a long time before sleep overtook him.

* * *

Early mornings were usually set aside for Meg's shopping expeditions, but on this particular day she felt no desire to traipse about looking at what was on offer at the market. Tom was about to set off to the station and was having one last regretful look at his depleted plantings, so she decided to take herself off on a little treat. She would go to the smart end of town and look at the expensive shops. Of course she wouldn't buy anything above a yard of ribbon or a small piece of lace for some pretty cuffs on her best Sunday dress, but she would enjoy pretending that she could afford to shop there, just this once. Ever since being invited to the ball at Lady Stafford-Naylor's she had longed to live the high life again, and this was her chance. What Tom didn't know wouldn't hurt him. She dressed carefully in her second best dress, including the crinoline she kept for special occasions – it simply wasn't practical to wear it about the house for doing housework, but she wore it whenever she went into town.

She called goodbye to Stonier from the doorstep, not daring to wander down the garden and let him see her in all her finery, for then he would surely guess she was up to mischief – but if a woman of her years couldn't get into a little mischief now and then, what was the point in being alive?

She was near enough to walk into town, though it would have taken her over twenty minutes, but in her best leather boots, she had no intention of walking any further than she had to, so she took the omnibus, which fortunately passed the end of their road once an hour. A few months before it would have been crowded with eager shoppers, but now there was short time and unemployment at all the mills, most other industries were suffering too. It was amazing how misfortune impacted on everyone eventually – and all because of a war in far away America.

She had no trouble accommodating her bulky skirts on the wooden seat, with only one elderly gentleman as the other passenger. He raised his hat politely and she nodded in acknowledgement.

Once she reached her destination, Meg strolled and gazed longingly into shop windows, wondering if the day would ever dawn that she could afford such expensive trinkets, when she heard her name called and she turned to find herself facing Constance Allingham, her maid three steps behind her, as befitted her place in life.

Constance smiled and held out her hands in delight, "Mrs Stonier, I thought it was you! How wonderful to see you. I was just thinking that I needed a cup of tea and was loath to go into the teashop all by myself. Would you do me the kindness to join me?"

Evidently the maid didn't count, thought Meg, but without rancour. It was not Constance's fault that she came from a class who knew no better.

"I should enjoy that very much," she assured the younger woman, who consequently turned to the maid and said, "Sally, you may have a hour or two to yourself, now that I have Mrs Stonier with me. I will see you back at the house later."

"Very good, Miss." Sally sketched a curtsey and withdrew with obvious relief.

Meg and Constance crossed the road and went into the tiny teashop which Meg had been gazing longingly at only minutes before, but which she had lacked the courage to enter.

With the discerning eye of good business woman, the owner at once realized that Constance at least was from the upper echelons of society and was immediately all attention, fluttering around the pair, showing them to the best table and taking gloves and bonnets so that they might eat and drink unencumbered. Constance was accustomed to such treatment, but Meg was half enchanted, half embarrassed by the fuss. She told herself crossly to enjoy it while it lasted, but she found it hard to relax, feeling clumsy and out of place. When presented with the tiny china cup and saucer she shook so much with nerves that it rattled alarmingly and she set it hastily in the table and could barely drink the scalding liquid.

Constance became aware that her companion was unsettled and quickly guessed the reason. She attempted to keep up a steady chatter to try and calm her new friend.

"I can't tell you how happy I was to see you, Mrs Stonier. I was feeling a little lost and lonely, I have to admit."

"You were?" asked Meg in surprise, "But how can that be? You must shop here all the time?"

"Not at all. In fact I rarely shop at all. My uncle has kept a tight rein upon me all these years and if I have ever needed anything, it was bought for me – or shop-keepers have brought things to the house, and I was allowed to choose from the array of goods."

Meg was stunned, she could hardly imagine a life with so little freedom. She knew it would drive her insane not to be able to make the occasional escape from the house, even for the drudgery of grocery shopping.

Constance observed her expression of horror mingled with pity and smiled sadly, "It is going to take some effort to grow accustomed to my liberation. I hope I can rely on your assistance."

"Of course," Meg assured her warmly, reaching out an impulsive hand and patting Constance's long, pale fingers, "But what has brought about this change in your uncle? Why has he suddenly allowed you to wander when he has always been so protective?"

"Ah, I have your friend Inspector Lazarus to thank for that," answered the younger woman, "He has been my knight in shining armour."

Something in her tone aroused a curious sense of jealousy in Meg's breast and she found herself saying tersely, "The armour is perhaps a little tarnished, Miss Allingham."

Constance took this as a joke and laughed merrily, "Perhaps you are right. But nevertheless he has helped me escape from my ivory tower, for which I will be forever grateful."

"I'm sure he was delighted to be of assistance."

"Perhaps he was – but I rather think his motive was more to annoy my uncle than to aid me, however the result is the same, so I shall not complain."

Meg could only hope that was true. She had a true affection for Lazarus and felt a proprietary annoyance that he might be showing an interest in another woman, though she told herself firmly that it was only because Miss Allingham was so very wrong for him and that it was her Christian duty to discourage any hint of a romance between the two of them. It was be nothing short of disastrous for Lazarus to fall in love with someone of a different class and could only end in his utter desolation. After his distress at the loss of his wife, Meg was determined never to see him go through such agony again.

"You can do me a small service, Mrs Stonier, and tell the Inspector that should he need to contact me, I no longer live at Allingham Hall." She took a small notepad from her reticule and wrote her new address in neat script, tearing off the sheet and handing it to Meg.

"I'll see he gets it when he gets back from visiting his girl in Sheffield," said Meg.

Constance blushed, "Of course," she stuttered. She had been so excited about her new house that she had almost allowed herself to forget the complications which attended her friendship with the Inspector, "It might be better if you kept the address. I should be so pleased if you would call on me. I shall feel a little apprehensive until I am used to living alone. It would be delightful to have some-one whom I could call a friend."

Meg smiled, "I would enjoy that very much," she said, pleased with the outcome of their little chat, "After all, Danby's business was with your uncle, wasn't it?"

Constance could only nod miserably.

CHAPTER THIRTY-ONE

PRESENT

The intention was to give Joanne a quick resume of the events of the previous year, with no detail and no emotion, but as she began to tell her tale, Libby found herself recalling the horror she had felt then, and she said far more than she ought to have done.

She was fully aware that belief in ghosts was a contentious subject and the truth was that she had been the world's biggest sceptic herself when she first arrived at Hill Farm to help her Aunt Lil, but things had happened she couldn't explain then and still had no explanation for now. And that was what came across most strongly when she began to tell Joanne the story.

"It started with a penny," she said and Joanne frowned in genuine puzzlement, obviously trying to keep an open mind, but struggling to do so.

"A penny? What do you mean, a penny?"

Libby sighed heavily and realized she was going to have to start right at the beginning, "What you have to understand is that I hadn't been to this house, other than for quick visits for an hour or so, for years and years. My mother never really liked Aunt Lil. She felt that my father should have inherited the house, because he was descended from the oldest member of the original family, the Watkins clan. However that was four or five generations back and there had been lots of in-fighting, feuds and fall-outs in the intervening years."

"So this Decima you were telling me about? She was the eldest of the Watkins'?"

"No, the youngest. It's complicated, but I'll try to simplify it for you. Decima was near enough deaf, so her father had decided she would never marry, but would stay at home and care for her parents as they aged. She had other ideas and managed to fall in love with the son of the local bigwig, Lord Allingham."

"I'm with you so far – this is where the Court case comes in?"

"Sort of. It was far from straightforward. Both sets of parents objected to the match, each for their own reasons, so Decima and Richard Allingham sneaked off and married in secret. The trouble was, it was so secret that no-one knew about the wedding, so when Decima fell pregnant, everyone assumed the baby was illegitimate and she was forced to hand her son over to her oldest, childless, sister. My father was always thought to have descended from her."

"But really it was from Decima?"

"Exactly – so according to my mother's ideas of justice, we have no right to this house, but we do have a claim on the Allingham Estate."

"Whew! I can see why the Allinghams are upset with your sister. But why didn't Richard Allingham just tell everyone that he and Decima were legally married – and why didn't Decima object to having her baby taken away?"

"That's where the tragedy lies. Richard was sent back to the army by his father, which he probably thought was temporary – unfortunately for him, the Crimean War broke out and he was sent to fight. He was killed, never knowing that Decima was expecting his child."

"That doesn't explain why Decima kept quiet. Why didn't she just tell everyone that she and Richard were a legal couple, and that his baby was the true heir?"

Libby paused to take a sip of her drink, "I wondered about that too. She seemed to have a death wish, to be honest, and I thought she was just being a total wuss and letting everyone walk over her. Then I realized her difficulty. Richard had taken the wedding licence and hidden it – so well that it wasn't found for over a hundred and fifty years! She had no proof and she was only too conscious of the power that William Allingham wielded. She was afraid for her child. She was terribly afraid that Lord Allingham would have no compunction about ridding himself of any inconvenient relations. And it turned out she wasn't wrong. He managed to turn her family tragedy of losing three of her sisters into a murder charge against her."

"You really believe she didn't poison her sisters?"

"I know she didn't. And in the end she allowed herself to give up without a fight and let them hang her. She knew it was the only way to protect her son. Allingham wouldn't bother harming him, once the threat of him inheriting the estate was gone."

Joanne reached for the coffee pot and poured herself and Libby a top-up, "Okay, so I now see the connection with the past, but how has that come to affect you so profoundly?"

Accepting the refilled cup from the journalist, Libby drank deeply before embarking on a potted version of the circumstances that surrounded her arrival at the house and her great aunt's insistence that they try and clear Decima's name before Lil's terminal illness beat her.

The truth was that Lil had been so adamant that Decima was framed that it had quickly convinced Libby and perhaps that had coloured her reaction to some of the subsequent incidents.

At first she had been able to convince herself that there were perfectly logical explanations for the odd events.

When the Victorian penny, as bright and shiny as new, but minted in 1859 – the year of Decima's hanging – had appeared in the sitting room, it had been easy to think that it might have fallen between the bedroom floorboards long years before and had, by some quirk of nature, just worked it's way through a crack in the ceiling plaster. The sound of footsteps in an empty house could have simply been the ancient beams expanding and contracting with changes in temperature. Pictures were bound to fall from walls from time to time. Smells of decay, the stench of rotting flesh – well, perhaps that was down to old pipes and an archaic sewerage system.

But what she had never been able to satisfactorily explain was the night she dreamt of Decima's hanging and woke in the morning to find vivid and painful rope burns around her neck. Perhaps she had caught herself in the bedcovers – but how then could those marks disappear as quickly as they occurred?

Her state of mind at that time had given Brendan every opportunity to exploit the situation and convince her mother and sister that she was having a mental breakdown with the strain of looking after the dying Lilian.

It was the marks on her neck that had given him the sick idea of stringing her up in the attic and making it look like the suicide of a severely disturbed girl and for that he deserved to go to jail for a very long time. Something which he was now showing every sign of managing to wriggle out of, the slimy, sneaking bastard!

Joanna listened with barely an interruption, merely asking for clarification if Libby's story grew too entangled for her to follow clearly, giving every appearance of interest and credence. Libby found herself relaxing her guard and telling everything she could remember. Joanna was a good listener and Libby had been forced to bottle up quite a lot of the tale since Lil's death. David hadn't wanted her to relive unpleasant and frankly horrifying memories – after all, they now had to live in the same house that had almost seen Libby's murder, and which had almost driven her out of her mind with terror.

Libby failed to notice how Joanna's expression altered when she admitted that she had also had a sèance in the house, to try and contact Decima.

"You are pulling my leg," she breathed. This was priceless copy and the journalist in her could not believe her luck. What a story! This was going to go down a storm with the Sunday rags.

"I wish I was," said Libby dryly, "I knew it was a mistake, but I was so desperate by that point that I would have pretty well tried anything to try and placate what I thought was Decima haunting me. I couldn't shut my eyes without seeing her last moments on earth, feeling the rope biting into her neck, but into mine too. It was truly grotesque and I just wanted it to stop."

"What were you thinking at the time? Why did you think she was, to use your word, haunting you?"

"She said she wanted her son back."

Joanna was astounded, "What the hell does that mean? Surely he's long dead, as well as her?"

"Of course. But she just kept saying it. In the end we realized that she wanted the record set straight. She wanted the world to know that she was his mother and not her sister Adelaide. Well, of course at first we thought he was born out of wedlock, but that just made her madder and the spooky incidents in the house got worse and worse."

Joanna gave a theatrical shudder, "What? You mean like blood oozing out of the walls and unearthly shrieks keeping you awake all night?"

"You've watched too many horror films," admonished Libby casting a disgruntled look in the direction of her guest, "No, just more noises, smells, and things like the electricity going off and the fires refusing to light. It sounds quite mild now, but believe me, when you've lived through it, it's no joke."

"I can imagine. So how did you resolve it in the end? I mean, I assume you did, since you are still living here, apparently quite happily."

"I was – until last night."

Libby then explained about the furniture being moved around and Joanna looked thoughtful, "You really believe she's back?" she asked, trying not to sound as sceptical as she felt.

"God knows," said Libby frankly, "I sincerely hope not. I'm sure there's a logical explanation, but the only person I can think of who would find it amusing to break into my house and do a re-arrange would be Brendan Tulliver – and he's in jail on remand."

"But even supposing the dead can come back and wreak havoc, why should she do it now? What would it achieve?"

"I don't know why you think I have all the answers," said Libby irritably, "I'm not an expert on the Occult. I suppose it's because of the Court case against the Allinghams. I can see why she would want her revenge on that family – they killed her and were responsible for the death of her husband and for cheating her son out of his birth-right."

"I suppose so, but it seems a bit unreasonable to target you – after all, you are on her side, if anyone is."

"Try telling Decima that, will you?"

"What about having another sèance?"

Libby shuddered at the memory, "God, no! I'm never playing

with any of that stuff again. I'll just have to hope that she – if it is she – realizes that I'm not the enemy and takes herself off into the light – or wherever spirits go."

"I suppose so. It all seems a bit tenuous though. If I had to live here, I'd want a bit more of a guarantee that I was going to be left in peace."

"I couldn't agree more, but I fail to see what I can go about it."

"What did you do last time? You never told me how you calmed the undead down before."

"We found the Wedding Licence. It proved she hadn't been a fallen woman. That seemed to do the trick."

"You found it? After a century and a half? Where the heck had it been for that length of time without discovery?"

Libby laughed, "Irony of ironies, the Allinghams had it the whole time and never knew it! Richard had put it in a secret drawer in his campaign chest. The present Richard Allingham had felt so guilty about the ill-feeling that still exists between our families that he made me a gift of the chest. My sister Maddie was fiddling about and out sprung the hidden drawer with the licence in it."

"Hence the court case?" asked Joanna.

"Hence the court case," confirmed Libby with a grin, "Poetic justice to be hopefully followed by real justice."

"Ironic indeed," smiled Joanna, "Well, your family history is nothing if not colourful. I'm not surprised you've turned to writing."

"That's the only thing keeping me sane at the moment," said Libby with feeling, "I'm trying to leave the Allinghams to Maddie, but she insists on involving me and I feel I have no choice but to support her, but I could do without the stress. I'm already facing another court when Brendan tries to convince a jury that I'm a loony and he was trying to save me from myself."

"You seem pretty normal to me," said Joanna, in a tone she hoped was both comforting and friendly.

"Thanks. Perhaps I'll call you as a character witness," Libby was only half-joking and the journalist took her seriously.

"Hey, anything I can do to help," she said, reaching out and briefly squeezing Libby's arm.

"I'll need all the help I can get, I'll hold you to that."

Joanna looked at her wristwatch, "Crumbs, look at the time, I've got to make tracks. Thanks for the coffee – and the tale. It was fascinating. I promise I'll do what I can to help your case."

There was nothing Libby could imagine Joanna could do, so she simply shrugged and took these words as a polite nothing. She could not know that Joanna was already hatching a plot which she felt would be foolproof. She had a story that would not only make her name, but would, she was sure, also help Libby to convince people that she had really experienced something inexplicable and other-worldly. How could that be anything other than helpful and altruistic?

CHAPTER THIRTY-TWO

LAZARUS

Lulled almost into sleep by the steady rattle of the train on the track, Lazarus closed his eyes and reviewed the case so far. He was as sure as he could be that Mollie Waters had been murdered. The usual reasons for a murder to be committed were a heat of the moment blow, money or self-preservation. There was nothing 'heat of the moment' about a poisoning – that was as premeditated as it could be. Mollie was virtually penniless and there was no evidence she had possessed life insurance which would make her death profitable. That left only self-preservation. Her pregnancy pointed to the Crabtree boy, but what if there were something else? Could she have known something damaging about anyone else? It was not beyond the bounds of possibility that she had met someone, probably through the shop where she worked, who might have something to lose if she had a wagging tongue.

Lazarus decided that Eliza Dunne could hold some information that she might not even be aware of herself. First thing Monday morning he and Stonier would interview the shop-girl once more. She had been so intent on blaming Crabtree, and convincing them of his guilt that she could very well have overlooked something else of importance.

That decision made, he allowed himself to drift off to sleep until the piercing whistle of the engine woke him just as they were pulling into Braxton Station. The rain had stopped, but the streets were still glistening and wet under the gas lamps on the high street. It was the only place in Braxton that boasted lighting, the side alleys and narrow roads off the main street were as dark and mysterious as ever. Here and there undrawn curtains showed a glimmer of the warmth and cosiness that dwelt within. Lazarus caught a glance of a family just sitting down to tea, the mother toasting crumpets on the fire, the father reading aloud to the bright-faced youngsters gathered at his knee. Obviously a middle-class family with little of the financial worry that dogged the likes of Will Carter's clan.

For a moment he saw himself sitting with Lucy on his knee and Constance facing him across the firelit room, but he quickly dismissed the image. Lord Allingham might pretend to offer the girl in exchange for his reputation, but the truth was very different. If he took one step in that direction, Lazarus knew he was more likely to find himself at the foot of a cliff with a broken neck than walking up the aisle with Constance on his arm. If he ever allowed himself to flirt with the idea of trusting Allingham and his ilk, the vision of the broken and terrified Decima Watkins stumbling her way to the gallows was always there to remind him of the folly of doing any such thing.

* * *

He would have preferred to keep his visit to Eliza Dunne quiet, but fate was against him from the start. As he and Stonier prepared to leave the station, the Superintendent was just walking in and irascibly demanded to know where the devil he thought he was going. His irritation was such that he answered fully and refused to be intimidated into staying and pandering to his superior, simply saying, "Constable Fletcher will make tea for you, sir. Stonier and I have a pressing appointment after we have seen Miss Dunne."

"With whom?" asked Gregson with deep suspicion.

"Lord Allingham," invented Lazarus and had the satisfaction of seeing the words of protest die on the other man's lips. He was fully aware that Lazarus had been engaged in some mysterious errand or other for Lord Allingham, and he itched to know that nature of it, but both the Inspector and the aristocrat had been close-mouthed about the affair.

"Very well," he said gruffly, "Get yourselves off then, but don't be all day about it. This matter has taken up quite enough of our time and I want an end to it."

As they walked onto the street Stonier ventured to remark, "I didn't know we had a meeting with Lord Allingham."

"We haven't," said Lazarus tersely, "but there's no need for Gregson to know it, is there?"

"Absolutely not," agreed Tom with a grin.

They had barely walked five yards when a pony and trap drew to a halt by the side of them and they heard themselves haled with a mock heartiness which spoke of strong dislike being overcome with determination, "Inspector Lazarus and Sergeant Stonier, I thought it was you. Good morning to you both."

The two men turned and greeted the vicar and his silently engrossed curate, who was reading and seemed not to notice either their presence or the halting of the vehicle. Both their voices betrayed a distinct lack of enthusiasm and Lazarus reflected on how ironic it was that they were all forced by convention to pretend civility. How much better would it be if they could simply agree to ignore one another instead of indulging in this false bonhomie.

"Where are you two off to? Can I offer you a lift? It's not exactly pleasant weather for walking."

He wasn't wrong about that. The rain of the past few days had stopped, but a low grey cloud held the heat and smoke from the many fires and factories in close to the earth and the result was an unhealthy fug which made breathing hard and depressed the spirit as mere rain could never do.

Before Lazarus could stop him, Stonier was accepting the offer. He was not built to withstand such oppressive heat and already his face was sweaty and his breathing laboured.

"Very kind of you, sir. We're off to the hat shop where Mollie used to work."

Bembridge lifted a quizzical brow, but made no comment, merely digging his young companion in the ribs with his elbow so that the curate would get down and open the door at the back of the dog cart for the two policemen. He looked startled, as though woken from a reverie and hastily apologised and leapt to the ground. He offered Lazarus his seat at the front with the vicar, but the Inspector shook his head and climbed into the back with Stonier. It was bad enough to be accepting the lift – he certainly drew the line at actually sitting with the odious old humbug and making polite conversation.

Of course this in no way stopped Bembridge from questioning them most rudely about their intentions regarding Miss Dunne. He wanted to know what on earth they thought she would be able to tell them that she had not already disclosed. Lazarus kept his lips firmly shut and Stonier was forced from sheer embarrassment to answer, though he was careful to give nothing of any importance away. He knew Lazarus would never forgive him if he pandered to the vicar's frankly salacious interest in Mollie and her "downfall".

Their arrival at the shop ought to have been the end of the association between the policemen and the men of the cloth, but Bembridge had no intention of missing out on what he hoped would be a fascinating conversation. He climbed down and said to Lazarus, with an approximation of charitable concern, "I don't suppose you will be long, I'll wait for you, if you like. Sergeant Stonier looks as though he could do with a lift back to the police station."

"I wouldn't dream of troubling you," answered Lazarus evenly, but the vicar waved a dismissive hand, "No trouble at all, my dear sir."

Realising that he was never going to discourage the fellow without deliberate rudeness, Lazarus gave in and they all entered the shop. Once again fate was determined to make difficulties for him, for Constance and Meg were both at the counter, admiring a pretty straw bonnet and discussing its many merits with Miss Soffley, who was displaying a stomach-turning obsequiousness in the face of possibly paying customers that was almost worse than her petty bullying of the staff in the back room.

Constance was evidently unaware of their entrance but Meg glanced up and had the grace to blush deeply at being caught out in such an expensive shop by her unsuspecting husband. Stonier stared, open-mouthed, unable to quite believe the evidence of his own eyes. He had left his wife at home that morning, a huge apron covering her oldest dress, a scarf tied around her head, to keep her hair out of her eyes whilst she set about her housework. Now he found her neat as a new pin, not a hair out of place, shopping in a prestigious emporium as though she was born a duchess and had money to spare for such fripperies as were displayed so prominently about the counter.

"Oh, hello Tom," she said defiantly cheerful, "I was just helping Constance choose a bonnet."

"So I see," he replied grimly and she realized that she was going to have some explaining to do once they were alone.

Constance glanced up from her perusal of the hat, "Good afternoon, all, what brings you here? I can't imagine all you gentlemen are here to purchase bonnets."

"Hardly," growled the vicar, casting a disparaging eye over the fripperies laid out on the shining mahogany counter, "The inspector is here to see Eliza Dunne, though, if you ask me, he's wasting his time. The girl is simply a trouble-maker and will tell him whatever she thinks he wants to hear."

"I can speak for myself, thank you," intercepted Lazarus tetchily. This was not how he had imagined this conversation progressing. The woman Soffley was drinking in the comments with the eagerness of a drunk quaffing blue ruin, "If you want to see Dunne, you'll have to come back when she finishes work. I know my rights and I'm not having you disrupting my business any further," she sniped with a triumphant sneer.

"Very well," answered Lazarus, not unhappy with this turn of events. He had been envisioning interviewing Liza with an audience, so coming back later, with only Stonier for company, was not such a bad idea."

"She works until seven."

Be damned to that, thought the inspector, adding, aloud, "I'll be back for her at five. Make sure she is ready to speak to me." Such was the grim determination in his tone that the woman didn't even bother to argue. Even one as densely arrogant as she could recognize the fact that she would be courting trouble if she persisted.

Constance looked down at the watch she had strung about her neck on a long chain, "It is only half past three – you must all come to my house and take tea. I've been longing to show off my new abode and this is the perfect opportunity! It will save you a journey all the way back to the police station, Mr Lazarus and Sergeant Stonier."

The response to this offer was divided. Stonier and Bembridge were delighted with the notion of tea and an escape from duty. Lazarus and Meg were more reluctant. The Inspector was all too aware of the time ticking away and him no nearer to solving Molly's murder. Meg had no wish to demonstrate to her oblivious husband just how close she and Constance had grown and exactly how often she was deserting her household duties to play the lady with her new friend.

Only the curate seemed unconcerned. He looked from one face to another, trying to follow the conversation and indeed to read the undercurrents that swirled about them all. There was more going on that he knew and he looked as though he was wondering vaguely if he ought to be more interested.

In the end good manners won the day and they all filed out of the shop and followed Constance and Meg down the street. As she had promised, Miss Allingham's new house was but a stone's throw away and they all politely complimented the outside as she opened the gate with a flourish.

Lazarus had to admit that Allingham had kept his word. He had half expected the old sinner to dump the poor lass in some hovel in the hope that she would beg to come back to him, but as usual pride had prevented him from showing anything but lavish generosity. He might be parsimonious in private, but when there was any chance at all he might be judged by his peers, nothing was too much trouble. He had provided Constance with a solid little detached house, surrounded on all sides by pretty, well-stocked gardens, and situated in the very best part of town, near to the shops on one side, and facing the park, with a view of the river. It was plainly Georgian, but well maintained and large enough to impress without being a mausoleum for a single woman.

"It's truly lovely," he told Constance warmly and she smiled shyly at him.

"I have you to thank for it, Mr Lazarus."

"Not at all," he said swiftly, all too aware of the flapping ears of the vicar. The last thing Constance needed now was a scandal to arise about her, "Your uncle has been most wise to provide you with your own home. We all need some measure of independence to grow and prosper."

She took them indoors and fluttered about, happy and excited, showing them around then ensconcing them in the drawing room, with many apologies for the lack of home comforts, "I'm only just moved in, you see," she explained diffidently, ringing the bell for Sally and when the older woman appeared, gave orders for tea to be brought.

Meg, well aware that she stood in danger of being button-holed by her increasingly irate husband, immediately offered to go to the kitchen and help with the preparations. She needed to show him that she wasn't getting ideas above her station in life and allying herself with the servant and not the mistress was the only way she could do so just at that moment.

Tea was a jolly affair and Lazarus surprised himself by enjoying it – though he would have sworn that taking tea in an elegant drawing room was his idea of hell on earth. Constance was on sparkling form, so happy to be, at long last, mistress of her own domain. She had spent her whole life as the poor relation, always over-looked and despised, alert to ways in which she could be useful, to be at pains to show that she was worth her keep. She had grown in confidence so much that she was like a different person, witty and flirtatious. Bembridge was captivated, Stonier amused and Lazarus felt the stirrings of jealousy when she turned her charms upon the other men.

Before they knew it every cake and muffin had been consumed, and the teapot had long since run dry. Bembridge took his watch from his waistcoat pocket and popped open the front, "Good grief, gentlemen, it's half past four. Time for us to be getting back to work I think. Thank you for a most entertaining afternoon, Miss Allingham. I've rarely enjoyed tea more. You are now, of course, a member of my congregation, so I will look forward to seeing you in church on Sunday and perhaps you would be interested in joining my other ladies on the Charity Committee? So much work to be done in these sad times."

Evidently Constance had not been expecting this and she blushed rosily as she said, "Why, yes, of course." Lazarus grinned wickedly at her behind the vicar's back and she raised a rueful eyebrow at him in return.

With the vicar and the curate gone, the atmosphere became much less formal. With a grim determination, Stonier asked Meg to be kind enough to show him around the garden, "Since you are so well acquainted with Miss Allingham's house," he added pointedly. Meg resigned herself to her fate, "Come on then," she said with a sigh, and took him out through the French window.

They had barely left the house before the raised voices began and Constance looked startled, "Are they quarrelling?" she asked Lazarus.

"I rather think they are," he replied, settling himself back in his chair and grinning unkindly, "Do you mind if I smoke?"

"Not at all – but that means we shall have to leave the door open and wouldn't that rather cause us to eavesdrop on the sergeant?"

"I live to eavesdrop on the sergeant," he said amusedly, "And in particular on this conversation."

"Is there something going on that I don't know about?"

"Oh, you know about it – you just don't comprehend the consequences."

"Please stop talking in riddles and tell me what I am missing here," she said, showing a flash of temper. Delighted to have gained a rise out of her, he lit a cigarillo and deigned to explain.

"Meg has been less than honest with her husband about her whereabouts during the day. He thought she was scrubbing the steps and cooking his meals, now he finds she has been living a double life, and flitting about like a lady of leisure, frequenting expensive shops and taking tea with you."

She raised a hand to her mouth in mortification, "Dear me, I had no idea I was the cause of dissention between a man and his wife. I will go at once and explain to the sergeant that the fault is entirely mine. Meg merely took pity on me in my loneliness."

She rose to her feet and made to walk past him and out of the doors, but he caught her hand, "Leave them be. Meg can handle Tom with no trouble at all. He'll come back in penitent and ready to hand over a week's wages to buy her the bonnet she craves."

She glanced down at his hand holding her wrist and then raised her eyes to his. They looked deeply at each other for a few tense seconds, then he released her and drew deeply on his cigarillo.

"Are you lonely?" he asked suddenly.

"Sometimes," she admitted, "But it's a nice kind of loneliness, if you understand me. I'm not used to being left to my own devices. It's a luxury that I have not quite learned yet to appreciate."

"You will," he assured her, "Being alone is often the greatest gift – almost as great as having company."

"You are talking in riddles again," she complained.

He smiled and flicked the butt of his smoke out of the door, "You'll understand one day."

"Do you really think I'll ever understand you, Inspector?"

"Dear God, I sincerely hope not!"

CHAPTER THIRTY-THREE

Whatever it was that Meg had told Tom by way of explanation, it was evidently satisfactory, for the sergeant was looking mollified when the couple came back into the house. Constance drew a silent sigh of relief. The last thing she would ever want would be to cause trouble between her new friend and the amiable policeman.

They had another cup of tea to celebrate, then Lazarus indicated to Stonier with a jerk of his head that it was time for them to be leaving.

"You'll be safe going home on your own?" Stonier asked his wife, suddenly solicitous. Lazarus wondered if it had been a promise of a good meal or some other more personal gesture that had restored his colleague's good humour with his erring spouse.

Meg laughed, but gazed fondly at her man, "I always have been up to now," she assured him, "but if you are really concerned, I could always come with you to the hat shop. You'll not be talking to 'Liza for very long and then you'll be heading home, won't you?"

Stonier threw a quizzical glance at his superior officer, who nodded briefly,

"Aye, you've done enough for one day, old friend. We'll have a quick word with Miss Dunne, see if she really has anything useful to tell us, then you can go home. If I think we need to speak to her any further, I'll ask her to come to the station tomorrow for a more formal interview."

With that they took their leave of Miss Allingham, failing to notice how wistfully she watched them all walk away, envying the ease with which they bantered with each other – the product of many years familiarity. Would she ever feel so comfortable with people that she would be able to laugh and joke with them? Or would the hide-bound way she was raised forever prevent her from letting go of the steely control she had to keep over her emotions? On reflection she had to admit that the only person who had ever made her lose her grip on her temper had been Lazarus himself, the very first moment they met. What did that say about either of them? She went sadly back indoors, wondering how she was going to kill the next few hours before bedtime.

Miss Soffley was as sour-faced as ever and showed them into her office with very bad grace, "I'll send Miss Dunne in to see you, but I'll thank you to be quick about it, I have a business to run and I don't appreciate the disruption."

"It will take as long as it takes," said Lazarus, flicking open his notebook by way of dismissal. To give her credit, she took the hint and bustled off, every stiff line of her retreating figure showing disapproval and annoyance.

"I'm afraid you'll have to stay in the shop, Meg," said Lazarus with genuine regret. He was pretty sure Meg would be an invaluable help in getting every last ounce of gossip out of Eliza Dunne, but he dreaded to think what the Superintendent would say if he ever found out that he had allowed a member of the public to attend an official interview.

"That will be no chore," said the lady happily, "I could look at these bonnets all day! They are so lovely."

Eliza had entered the shop just as Meg spoke these words and was rewarded with a smile of genuine pride, "We do a fair job on them, don't we?" she asked and Meg enthused for a further few minutes until Lazarus interrupted and withdrew into the office. He thought it amazing that Eliza could take such pleasure in her work, bearing in mind that the chances of her ever being able to afford even the simplest of the hats were slim to non-existent.

"Take a seat Miss Dunne," he invited and Eliza grinned at him.

"It was 'Liza the other day in the pub," she reminded him impertinently.

"So it was," he was unperturbed by the memory. If she thought she could wrong-foot him with that, she was very much mistaken, "in that case I can take it we're still classing each other as friends, so we can dispense with formality and get down to the matter in hand."

"Nothing would please me more," she assured him, "I want to know when I can expect to attend the hanging of Lawrence Crabtree, the murdering bastard!"

"I wish I had better news for you on that front, 'Liza, but I'll be straight with you. Crabtree is surrounded by people determined to protect him and I've got nothing to break through that fencing. You are going to have to come up with more than you have before I can make an arrest."

For the first time she looked aghast, "You are jesting! Crabtree gave my friend a bellyful of arms and legs then killed her and you can't arrest him?"

"There's no proof of any of this, 'Liza," protested Lazarus, "Believe me, I've done my best, but I'm being warned off by his lawyers and I could only speak to the boy by subterfuge. My boss is breathing down my neck for embarrassing him and Stonier and I are on a last warning to prove Molly's death was murder before we either give up or lose our jobs."

She stared at him for a long time, searching his face as though to find some hint that he was lying to her, trying to put her off so that he could happily close the case and save himself any more effort, "My God, you are telling the truth, aren't you?"

"Of course I am. Unless you can give me something solid, something I can bring up in a court of law, then Molly is going to lie in the ground unavenged."

A look of sheer determination came over her face, "What do you need?"

"Everything you can remember. I want to know who she knew, where she went, what she did. I need you to tell me about every minute of her last day. We have got to run this killer to earth. But you also have to face the fact that it might not have been Lawrence Crabtree. I've met the boy and I have to tell you, 'Liza, he didn't seem like a murderer to me. He was a frightened boy who dreaded his dear papa finding out what he had been up to, but he didn't seem to hate Molly and he was genuinely upset about her death – that's why he showed up at her funeral."

This did not make sense to Eliza and she said so, "Who else could it have been? Who else would want her dead?"

"Well, not to be throwing unfounded accusations around, but let's just say that her mother was none too pleased to be presented with a bastard grandchild."

This was apparently something that Eliza had not considered and she took a few minutes to digest the possibility, "Would a mother do that to her own child?"

Lazarus gave a short, grim huh of laughter, "If you did my job, sweetheart, you would know how stupid that question was! Besides, who said the woman meant to kill Molly? Has it ever occurred to you that she might just have been trying to get rid of the problem, not her daughter?"

"Trying to see the baby off, you mean?"

"That's exactly what I mean. Stonier here went to question the so-called witch in the woods, Mrs Riley. She made no secret of helping young women out in similar circumstances to Molly's. It could have been a tragic accident that Molly died."

This view of the events made up Eliza's mind for her, "Right, let's start at the beginning. What do you want to ask me?"

"Was Molly seeing anyone else besides Crabtree? Did she have followers?"

"No, I swear to God, she didn't – well, none she told me about anyway – and I think she would have done. Crabtree was a secret, but she told me about him."

"What about before Crabtree? Is there anyone in her past who might have come back and perhaps been jealous of her new situation?"

"Some fellow who might have wanted to kill her when he found out she was carrying another man's child, you mean?"

"Exactly."

"I don't think so. Not really. You see Molly was always ambitious. She was going places and wasn't going to be stuck here forever. That was why she grabbed the chance to work in the shop with that owd bitch Soffley, even though she hated her guts. She knew it was better than being stuck in the back with us lot."

"Did you resent that about her? Didn't you think it was disloyal of her to better herself and leave you behind?"

Eliza gave a great shout of laughter, "Bugger me, Lazarus! You trying to pin Molly's murder on me, now, are you? You saying I was jealous and poisoned her out of spite?"

He smiled, a pale reflection of her amusement, "Can't blame a man for trying," he said, "Did you?"

"No, I bloody didn't – and I'll thank you to remember that it was me who told you that Molly was murdered and didn't die of natural causes!"

"Actually, it wasn't you, but I take your point. However, that could merely have been a clever way of shifting my suspicions in a different direction."

"True enough – but knowing me as you do, don't you think I'd simply give her a slap for being uppity, then never speak to her again? I'd hardly kill her for the sin of spending every day with that bitter-faced old harridan."

"True enough. I'll cross you off the list then. Now, who else was she seeing beside you and the other girls?"

Eliza frowned as she tried to remember, "You know, now you come to mention it, in the past few weeks, she'd taken to going to the church quite a lot. I don't know what was behind it, whether she was going to show her mother that she was penitent, hoping the old misery would change her mind and take her and the baby in, or if she was hoping perhaps the vicar would intercede for her, I don't know."

"You mean Reverend Bembridge's church?" asked Lazarus, throwing a speaking look at the busily note-taking Stonier.

"Yes – and she seemed to get some comfort from it. In fact that last day, she was all smiles, telling me that she thought everything was going to be alright. I just assumed that she had convinced herself that Crabtree was about to come good and make an honest woman of her. I thought she was a fool, but when I told her that, she sulked and said I didn't understand. I asked her to explain, but she said she couldn't, she had been sworn to secrecy, but there was someone who was going to see her right."

"You've no idea who?" asked Lazarus, his frustration writ

plainly on his face. This was the nearest he had come to finding out exactly what had happened to the girl, and it looked as though he had come up against yet another dead end.

"No, but it was in the same conversation she mentioned the church, so I think it may have been connected with that."

Lazarus could see he was going to get no further – Eliza wasn't being obstructive, she simply didn't know. Molly had kept her secret well. But he was going to uncover it if it took him a lifetime.

"I think we need to go to the station and get you to make a statement about all this, 'Liza." He turned to his sergeant, "You and Meg can get off now, Tom. I'll take Miss Dunne to the station, then see her home."

"If you're sure, sir," said Stonier gratefully. He had plans for that evening, which he was eager to get to.

They left the office and collected Meg on the way to the door, only to be halted in their tracks by Miss Soffley, who had been hovering by the counter, waiting for them to vacate her office, "Where do you think you are going, Miss Dunne?" she snapped, "You are contracted to work until seven."

"Miss Dunne is required at the police station," intercepted Lazarus, but if he thought that would stop the manageress, he was sadly mistaken, she followed them out of the door and into the street still ranting, "Oh no, you don't! You go to the police station in your own time, Miss, not mine."

"Miss Soffley, I've had a long day and I'm not in the mood for this," Lazarus turned back, his tone clipped.

"Who do you think you are?" she screeched, "You have no right!" With that she stepped directly in front of Eliza, obviously intending to stop her from taking another step away from the shop.

What happened next stunned them all. The woman stopped her gabbing and gave a curious gurgling sound before dropping at their feet like a stone. A pool of blood began to creep towards them and they all stepped back in unison to avoid it. Slowly it dawned on them all that of all things an arrow was sticking out of the back of the woman's neck as she lay face down on the pavement.

"See to her, Stonier," yelled Lazarus, as he scanned the street, desperately trying to see from which direction the missile had flown.

Stonier was on his knees, lifting and turning Miss Soffley, holding her in such a way as to not force the arrow any further into her flesh, but he might as well not have bothered. It had gone right through and the head had pierced her throat causing blood to pump from the wound with every weakening beat of her heart. Even as he held her, she tried once more to speak, her hands clawing desperately at her throat, then she died in his arms.

Lazarus began to run in the direction he thought was the most likely had been the position of her assailant, but streets spread in all directions, all of them full of houses, shops, warehouses, tree-lined gardens and public houses. Anyone could have fired the shot then disappeared into an alleyway or even jumped onto an omnibus or hailed a cab. He had no doubt he would find the bow abandoned somewhere nearby, and the killer would have walked or run away, without so much as a spot of blood upon his person to prove his guilt.

The Inspector walked back to Stonier, a question on his lips, to which Stonier's reply was a swift shake of the head. Miss Soffley was dead – but why and by whose hand, he was none the wiser.

Eliza and Meg were standing a little way away, their arms around each other's waists, their faces pale and etched with horror.

"Go back indoors and make yourselves some tea – you need it for the shock." he told them quietly, "Tom and I will take care of her."

They obeyed him without a word of protest. Lazarus spoke to his sergeant, "Where is your whistle, Tom? I don't carry mine about with me."

Stonier gently laid the body on the ground and reached into his breast pocket,

"Let's hope there's someone around to hear it," he said, as he began to blow several piercing blasts on the shiny police whistle.

"Let's hope he doesn't come back with another arrow," added Lazarus, "We are sitting ducks at the moment."

"What the devil is this for?" asked Stonier, when he felt he had made enough noise to wake the dead, "Why would anyone kill the manageress of a hat shop?"

"I suspect she wasn't the target," answered Lazarus grimly, "Didn't you notice that she had stepped in front of 'Liza as the arrow flew."

Tom lifted a brow and blew softly between pursed lips, "You think someone was trying to stop Eliza telling us what she knew?"

"I do – and who knew we were about to question her?"

"Miss Allingham, the curate and …"

"And Reverend Bembridge." supplied Lazarus, looking down at the dead woman,

"Old holier than thou Bembridge! Whose name is beginning to appear more frequently in this tale than is good for him."

CHAPTER THIRTY-FOUR

PRESENT

It was rather a sad reflection on modern life that Libby was surprised when someone kept a promise. Surprised? She was stunned! Matt Piper rang her to tell her that he had – as promised – arranged for her to meet her writing heroine, Tess Brookes. He would pick her up at two and take her to Tess' house himself. When Libby politely protested and assured him that he had no need to go to all that trouble and she could make her own way there – or meet Tess in a café or somewhere similarly anonymous, he quickly demurred. Tess had been pretty unwell after her experiences the previous year and was more or less a recluse. She didn't go out much and she rarely received visitors. Libby was highly honoured to be allowed into the house and if she had any sense at all, she would take what was offered without causing any ripples. Put like that, Libby simply agreed to whatever Miss Brookes decreed.

She left a note for her husband explaining her absence should he return before she did and happily climbed into the car with the off-duty policeman.

"How's the writing going?" he asked politely as he put the car into gear and pulled easily away.

"Really well, thanks for asking. I'm pleased with it. Do you think Ms Brookes will have a little look at it for me, tell me what she thinks?"

"I expect so," he answered distractedly, leaning far forward so that he could try and see around a particularly sharp corner before nosing his way out. The country roads were narrow, high-hedged and dangerous and he had no intention of becoming a rural road statistic.

"I'd be grateful for her input. I've never written anything like this before and I'm hoping I'm doing it right."

"She was interested when I told her what you were writing about. Historical romance is her genre but since we met, she's been toying with the idea of doing a crime novel."

"Well, they do tell you to write what you know, so having a policeman on tap it would seem to make sense," mused Libby, catching her file and notebooks as they threatened to slide off her knee as Matt braked rather hard on another of the hairpin bends.

"Didn't you say you were writing a murder mystery yourself?"

"Yes, but you wouldn't be much use to me as a research tool," she informed him with a smile, "It's set in Victorian times – so no forensics, DNA or finger-prints to help my policeman."

"There are times when all those things don't help us much either!" he said, turning, with relief, onto a B road.

"Tell me about it," she retorted, "I wouldn't be up in court against bloody Brendan if you could just prove I was telling the truth and he's a filthy liar!"

Matt felt that he was safer not responding to that bitter little speech and put his foot down as a small celebration for having attained a decent road.

It wasn't far to Tess Brookes' house and Libby was relieved to see that it was a fairly ordinary stone-built detached house. She had been a bit concerned that it might be a mansion with an indoor pool and ponies in the paddock. That would have completely undermined her already delicate ego. She knew Tess was a successful writer, but if she had been ostentatiously rich and famous, Libby would never have dared enter the house, let alone show her anything she had written.

Oddly, once outside the house, Matt picked up his mobile phone and rang someone. Libby sat and waited as he spoke, "We're here, darling, I'm just bringing Libby in now, is that okay?"

Evidently permission was given and Matt climbed out of the car then with old-fashioned civility hurried around to help Libby out. Of course she dropped half her papers on the floor as she struggled to get out of the seat, whilst trying to be equally polite and accept his hand, which she didn't really need, but felt she couldn't ignore.

They almost banged heads as they both bent to retrieve the notes, then laughed companionably when they came up nose to nose.

"Sorry," said Matt, "go on up the steps, I'll get your handbag."

"Thanks."

The front door opened as she approached it and she was confronted by the woman she recognized as Tess Brookes, but thinner and older looking than the pictures on her dust jackets.

She held out her hand, forcing the file clutched to her chest up under her chin,

"Hi, I'm Libby, and I'm so pleased to meet you."

Tess Brookes gave the most glorious smile, so that Libby suddenly understood completely why a younger man like Matt was in love with her, "Welcome Libby, come inside and we'll relieve you of your burden."

She was led through the house – beautifully decorated and tastefully furnished – to a conservatory at the back, where she was pressed into a plumply-cushioned sofa, had her notebooks taken out of her hands and was offered a drink.

"Tea, coffee? Or shall we be naughty and crack open a bottle of wine? Matt's driving, so you can indulge yourself."

"Wine would be tremendous," quavered Libby, thinking that a bit of alcohol might just sooth her jangling nerve-endings. This was far worse than she had ever imagined. It had been great in theory imagining the great Tess Brookes reading her book, but now she was actually there, in the house, sitting on the famous author's sofa, she realized that she was going to shrivel up and die of embarrassment if Tess so much as glanced over her manuscript.

While Tess was getting the wine, Matt came in with her handbag and one or two more sheets of paper that they had both missed when they were scrabbling under the car.

"I'll leave you to it, then."

Libby threw him a look of pure panic, "Please don't go," she whispered, "I'm terrified – she's going to think I'm a complete moron."

He laughed, "Tess said the same thing about you! She took some persuading to agree to this meeting – she thinks she's yesterday's news and you are the up and coming young pretender to her throne."

"Oh, no!" gasped Libby in horror, "I could never imagine reaching her heights. She's a genius!"

"I wish you'd tell her that. She hasn't written a word for about twelve months. Luckily past royalties are keeping her going, but if she doesn't begin writing again soon, she's in danger of never writing again. And I know what that would do to her."

"What would do what to whom?" asked Tess as she came back, bearing a tray of glasses and a bottle.

"Here, let me help you," said Matt, ignoring the question and deftly setting the tray down and pouring the wine, "Do you mind if I don't join you ladies? I can't think of anything worse than watching you two guzzle wine when I have to run Libby back home later."

"Oh, please do have a glass, Matt. I can easily get a taxi home."

"I wouldn't hear of it. Anyway, you two have much to discuss and I'll only be in the way. I'll be mowing the lawn if you want me."

With that he left them alone and Libby gratefully took a large sip of wine.

"Was he talking about me just then?" asked Tess matter-of-factly, sitting down opposite Libby in an equally puffy chair.

Libby nearly choked on her wine. What was she supposed to say now? She decided that honesty was the best policy and nodded, "He's worried because he says you've stopped writing and he thinks it's bad for you."

"He's right – but I don't know how to get past it. Something bad happened to me just over a year ago and I haven't been able to write since."

"Instead of writing fiction, have you tried writing about the thing that happened?" asked Libby, sipping and observing her hostess over the rim of her glass. It seemed an obvious thing to do, but evidently it hadn't crossed the writer's mind, because her whole expression changed to one of thoughtful wonderment, "No, I hadn't! I've been so busy trying to forget it and finding it constantly intruding on my thoughts, that I finally gave up."

"I find if I write things down, even if I destroy it later, I feel much better. You should try it."

"I will – thanks Libby. Now, enough about me. Tell me about what you've been writing."

Libby gave her a quick outline of her book, mentioning Lazarus, Stonier, Meg and the Allinghams. She told her about the diaries and how she was reading and writing at the same time, so that even she didn't know the outcome of the story. Tess laughed, but it was friendly and not critical, "That's brave – though I can see what you are driving at. It is going to give your work an immediacy, an edge of danger. But what on earth are you going to do if it turns out Lazarus never solved his case?"

Libby joined in her laughter, "Disappoint my readers, I suppose," she admitted ruefully, "Let's hope he was as clever as I think he was."

Tess looked thoughtful, "Did you say the Allinghams were connected with this story?"

"Indirectly, yes."

"Didn't Matt tell me you have some other dealings with the Allinghams?"

She had no choice but to give her companion a quick run down of that tale too and Tess was obviously intrigued, "You are not going to believe this, Libby, but I'm another link in the chain."

"You? What do you mean?"

"Cast your mind back. Do you recall the name of the lawyer who was set to defend Decima Watkins?"

For a few seconds Libby's mind was blank. Who was Tess talking about?

"You must have heard of Sir Horton "Babbling" Brookes?" said Tess with a smile at the gossiping old barrister's nickname.

"Sir Horton," breathed Libby, "The man who failed to save Decima and was accused of being in love with her."

"I think he was, a little. Apparently she was bewitching."

"And he's an ancestor of yours?" Of course, her name was Brookes too, wasn't it?

"I'm a direct descendent. He was my great, great, don't know how many greats grandfather. Decima is notorious in our family history. She's the woman who ruined Sir Horton without ever having his hand laid upon her!"

"Oh dear," said Libby weakly.

"Oh dear, indeed!" responded Tess, "Poor old Horton never recovered from the scandal. Either way he couldn't win. Perhaps poor Decima had been innocent and he had tragically failed her, or she was a scheming floozy who entranced the great man into defending her, even after her death. He never wavered, you know, from believing in her innocence. It destroyed him, completely took away any credibility he had. It was always understood that he was headed for London and a glittering career at the bar until the fateful day he met Decima Watkins."

For a moment Libby contemplated the sad fate of the unfortunate Sir Horton, but then she was reminded of her own situation and she realized that this information might very well be turned to her advantage.

"Forgive me for asking, but I don't suppose you have any papers belonging to him, do you? Something in writing pertaining to Decima's innocence might prove very useful."

Tess gave a slow smile, "I like your thinking," she said, "and, yes, I do. My father gave me all Horton's archive when I began writing. He always hoped I would write a biography that would vindicate the old man."

"Perhaps the time has come to do just that," suggested Libby slyly.

"I'm beginning to think that you might just be my saviour, Libby Wright." said Tess, "Now, show me what you've been writing."

They spent a happy couple of hours going over what Libby had so far, Tess giving her some very good tips on researching historical detail and making sure the language she used was current at the time. The author had some superb reference books with many of the more obscure facts that Libby had struggled to confirm or reject. Libby made copious notes and made sure she would remember to tell Dan all about the meeting. Anything that might make the book more commercially viable was all to the good, after all, she had him to thank for the diaries in the first place and the least she could do was to try and make him a few pounds.

Tess then went to dig out some of Sir Horton Brookes journals and together they looked for any reference to Decima Watkins, of which they found plenty. Sir Horton really had been quite keen on the girl and seemed genuinely devastated when she died. Tess photocopied the relevant pages, with a promise to lodge the originals with the courts should they be required in the future.

It surprised them both when Matt popped his head around the door and offered to send for a takeaway for supper.

"Why, what time is it?" asked Libby, startled by his sudden re-appearance.

"Gone six o'clock."

"Good heavens! My husband will wonder where on earth I've got to."

"Ring him and tell him you're staying for something to eat," urged Tess, "He won't mind, will he?"

"I shouldn't think so," replied Libby, completely forgetting they had agreed to go out to dinner, and far too wrapped up in her conversation with Tess to want to prematurely end it.

In the end she sent David a text, suddenly reluctant to try and explain what a fantastic time she was having discussing writing with a real author. Much as David loved her, he didn't really understand her desire to spend all her time with her books and papers. He was an outdoorsman through and through and barely read anything that wasn't connected with work or sport.

She barely even noticed that the reply text was curt to the point of rudeness, preferring to see his "do wot you like, I'll c u when I c u" as approval of her new friendship rather than annoyance at being stood up.

Matt went off to collect the pre-ordered Chinese meal and she and Tess opened another bottle of wine.

"I can't tell you how much I've enjoyed today, Libby," said Tess warmly, as they abandoned the now chilly conservatory and migrated to the warmth of the newly lit fire in the sitting room.

"Me too," answered Libby, "You've been great Tess, you really have. I feel so much more confident now that what I'm writing makes sense and is interesting. I'm not much of a judge of my own work."

"None of us are. The stuff I thought was rubbish always had the best reviews and my favourite characters get cut in the first edit when they go to the publisher!"

"That's not very reassuring," protested Libby and for some bizarre reason they both started to giggle helplessly.

Matt came in and took one look at the two of them, "Time to eat, I surmise ladies," he said, "And lay off the booze!"

Tess and Libby fell against each other on the sofa roaring with laughter and Matt shrugged resignedly and went to make coffee.

CHAPTER THIRTY-FIVE

Lazarus

A good hour passed before Lazarus and Stonier were able to leave the shop and head back to the police station. There was no question now of Stonier going home – nor, indeed Meg or Eliza. A carriage was summoned and they all went back together to the station. Lazarus had no intention of losing Eliza to an assassin, if, indeed, she had been the target. She obviously held some vital information – vital enough to his case for the perpetrator to want her dead. Lazarus didn't know what it was, but he had every intention of finding out. In the meantime poor Eliza would have to spend her time in protective custody. She was not best pleased about it, but had taken the news stoically, the sight of the late Miss Soffley clearly illustrating the need for extreme care.

He had been expecting the station to be buzzing with activity when he entered, for it was not often that a murder was committed within full sight of the constabulary, but an odd silence fell and he felt an undercurrent of apprehension. At first he thought it must be because the superintendent was on the rampage since he had so signally failed to protect a member of the public – though how he could have been expected to do so in the circumstances, he could not comprehend. However Benson never appeared and the silence grew heavier.

"What the devil is going on?" he asked with undisguised irritation.

There were several exchanged glances before a young constable was thrust forward and stood, tongue-tied, shuffling his booted feet, "Well, sir, it's like this ..." he stopped again and Lazarus lost his temper.

"Like what?" he roared, "If someone doesn't speak up, I'm going to take one of you outside and dust your jacket for you!"

The threat was enough to make Higgins gulp audibly and gasp, "It's young Will Carter, sir."

Lazarus felt his stomach lurch. Dear God, not the boy too! This was too much to take, "What's the matter with him?" he asked, the fury evaporating as swiftly as it had erupted, "Is he ill?"

"Not ill, sir, about to be arrested."

For a moment he was bereft of speech, then burst forth with a scornful riposte,

"Don't be ridiculous man, Will Carter can't have done anything to warrant arrest. The boy is as honest as the day is long." Unless it was for sticking a knife between his father's ribs, he added silently, suddenly fearful that was precisely what the boy had done. He was horrified that he could even think such a thing, but he was all too aware that it wasn't beyond the bounds of possibility. He wouldn't be the first, nor sadly the last, to raise his hand to a bully when driven to extremes.

"I'm sorry, sir, but it's true," chimed in one of the others, finally taking pity on the unfortunate Higgins, "The fellow who owns the newspaper stand came in not half an hour ago. He went round to Will's this morning to collect the monthly takings and when the boy went to fetch it out of the sideboard drawer, every penny was gone."

"But that doesn't mean the boy stole it," protested Lazarus, "It could have been anyone."

"But the boy is responsible for it, sir, that much was made clear to him from the start – and he has no explanation as to where it has gone. Unless he points the finger, he'll be going down for it."

Of course Lazarus knew who had taken the money – and he was damned sure Will knew it too, which was why he was keeping quiet.

"All right, Higgins, stand aside. As soon as I have seen to Miss Dunne, I'll go and see Carter myself. If anyone is going to arrest the boy, it will be me."

Higgins was horrified that his superior was even thinking of lowering himself to so minor a task, "You can't be bothering yourself with that young scoundrel," he gasped, "You've a murder to solve."

Are you telling me my job?" asked Lazarus, dangerously quiet. Higgins stepped back, shaking his head, suddenly aware that he had gone too far.

Lazarus turned on his heel and headed for his office, indicating with a jerk of his head, that Stonier, Liza and Meg should follow him. Once ensconced he had to put Will out of his mind for a while as he set his mind to the puzzle of the sudden demise of Miss Soffley.

"Eliza, I'm aware you don't know Miss Soffley well, but can you think of anyone who might harbour feelings of malice toward her? Had she any enemies? Was she involved in anything nefarious?"

"What's nefarious mean?" asked Eliza, frowning suspiciously. She didn't trust policemen any farther than she could throw a wet one and she wasn't about to let Lazarus put words in her mouth, for all he seemed more decent than most of the breed.

"Illegal – were there ever any shady characters hanging around her? Did she seem to have more money than the shop could make for her?"

'Liza snorted contemptuously, "Miss Goody-Two-Shoes? You have to be joking. She wouldn't so much as knock a ha'penny off the price of a bonnet for any of us in the back room for our own wedding! You could search her books with a fine tooth comb and you'd not find a farthing missing. The only enemies she had were us girls, who were sick to death of her carping and complaining – and I can tell you for nothing, there's not one of us who is handy with a bow and arrow. It's not your usual murder weapon, now is it?"

The inspector shook his head, "I'll grant you that, Miss Dunne, who the devil is an expert archer these days? If I find him or her I'll find my killer."

"Shouldn't be too hard, should it?"

"I hope not. Now, is there anything you need besides something to eat?"

"Only to know where you are planning I should sleep – because I can tell you for nowt, I'm not bedding down in one of your cells and you're not letting me go home, are you?"

"I can't risk it, I'm sorry."

"Not even if you send a policeman home with me?" she asked

hopefully, having set eyes on the handsome young Higgins and decided that not all the constabulary could be tarred with the same brush."

"I can't spare a man to be with you constantly, 'Liza, and that is what it would take to keep you safe."

"Perhaps she could come home with Tom and me," suggested Meg, "Just for tonight, and see what the morning brings. You may have your man and all will be well again by then."

Lazarus threw her a grateful glance, "If it's all right with Tom, that would solve a problem for me."

"Aye, it's fine by me. Let's go, then, ladies. You both need to get away from here and recover. You've had quite a day of it, haven't you?"

When they had gone, Lazarus leaned back in his chair and closed his eyes for a few precious seconds. Now he had another task to perform and he was dreading it. But better him than some clod-hopping constable with duty on his mind and no room for compassion or patience.

It was dusk when he reached the Will's, but the dingy street was over-crowded with too-close set houses and the last streaks of evening sun didn't permeate so that it might just as well have been midnight. The house was in darkness and seemingly uninhabited, but he hammered on the door anyway, and called through the paint-blistered panels, "Open up, Will, it's Inspector Lazarus. I've come to sort this thing out for you, so let me in."

For an eternity of seconds, there was no response, then the door opened just enough to allow the policeman to sidle through. In the murky light of the un-curtained front room he could just make out the frightened, tear-stained face of young Will, staring up at him as though he were the saviour reborn.

"Chin up, lad," he said softly, "I'm here now and you can tell me the truth. You didn't take the money, did you?"

"'Course I didn't. I swore to you that I'd behave and I have."

"I know that, son, but you're going to have to tell the truth, even if that means getting someone else into trouble."

"I can't," gasped the boy, and a slow tear formed and rolled slowly down his cheek.

"Come on, Will. Let's go into the other room. Is your mother in there?"

Will nodded, "And my pa. The little ones have been sent to bed."

The back room was lit with one candle and Will's mother and father were sat on either side of the small range, though it contained no fire, nor any evidence of one having been lit for months. Lazarus thought he saw a cobweb strung across the grate, though he couldn't be sure in the dim light.

Mrs Carter looked up as he entered, but her husband continued to snore, his head thrown back, his mouth hanging open.

In that moment Lazarus realized he had the situation gauged all wrong. He had been assuming that Will's takings had been taken by Mrs Carter in her desperation to feed her family, but one look at the slumbering man of the house and it became obvious that the money had gone to the pub with Carter senior. Lazarus wished it was within his remit to drag the man out of his chair and toss him into the street, but he could only thrust his bunched fists into his pockets, to stop himself doing the drunken sot a serious injury.

"Good evening, Mrs Carter," he said formally, "You know why I'm here?"

She looked terrified and simply nodded, evidently unable to frame a reply.

"I'm not going to lie to you, Will is in deep trouble. There is only one solution and that is for the one who stole the money to admit it."

If he had been in any doubt as to the true culprit, then the way her eyes flicked across to her husband's face then back to his confirmed it. It was an involuntary gesture, but it was enough to convince him.

"Wake him up," he ordered her, losing all desire to treat the woman gently. How she could allow her son – the one good thing in her life – to suffer, whilst the idiot she married left him to be torn apart, he could not understand.

She shook her head, barely able to control her own body, so fierce was the trembling which his tone had engendered, "I dare not," she whispered.

"Then I will." Lazarus suited words for action by kicking the feet of the comatose Carter, which, he noted with disdain, were warmly booted, whereas his wife and children were shod in burst and broken clogs, when they were shod at all.

The man gave a pig-snort and blearily opened his eyes, "What the bloody hell …" he was about to say more and had even lifted his hand in an automatic reaction, obviously intending to strike whoever had disturbed his sleep, but he spluttered into silence when he realized he was in the presence of the police.

"'Evening Mr Carter," said Lazarus evenly, "I'd like a few words, if that's all right with you?"

"No, it's bloody not. Get out of my house," he answered, his words slurred and his attempts to get out of the chair frustrated by the effects of alcohol on his body and mind.

Lazarus regarded him with a calculating eye for a good long moment, so that even Carter stood in no doubt of his contempt, despite the drunken haze.

"Please tell me that there's at least some of it left, you spineless, useless lump of manure," he hissed viciously.

Carter realized that he had hit a sore spot and grinned maliciously, "Not a fuckin' penny," he replied with evident satisfaction.

The inspector was across the room and gripping him by his shirt front before he could say another word.

"Is that a confession, scum?" spat Lazarus, his face so close to Carter's that he could smell the beer on his breath.

"Not a bleedin' chance, mate." answered Carter, "The kid will only get sent to the House of Correction for a couple of months. I don't know what all the fuss is about."

The breath was knocked out of him as Lazarus threw him bodily back into his chair, which tipped precariously then fell back onto all four feet with a clatter.

"You are actually going to let the boy take the blame for this, aren't you?" he was incredulous, unable to understand how a parent could be quite so unfeeling, so callous. He could only imagine himself in the same situation with Lucy and he knew beyond any shadow of doubt that he would gladly die to protect her.

"If it means that much to you, friend, why don't you put your hand in that deep pocket of yours and give the boy the money yourself. What's a couple of guineas to you?"

If only it were that easy. Lazarus was only too aware that he would do exactly that, except for the fact that he simply didn't have it. It would have stuck in his craw to indirectly pay for Carter's binge, but he would have done it. Unfortunately it took every penny he earned to keep himself and send enough to Dorothy Mason for Lucy's needs.

He glanced to one side and was faced with Mrs Carter, her arm around Will's shoulders, both of them silently begging him for help, their eyes pits of pain mixed with hope. It was like a physical blow to have to shake his head, "I can't do that. There is only one thing you can do to save your son and that is to admit what you've done."

"I'll see you in hell first. Now take the boy and get out of here."

Mrs Carter stepped forward, "No, it wasn't either of them. It was me ..."

"No!" wailed Will, "It was me. You're not taking my ma."

"Shut up, the pair of you," roared Carter, "She's not going anywhere. Her place is here, looking after me and the other kids. If you think I'm wiping snotty noses and listening to their whining, you're wrong woman. One more word and you'll get what is coming to you."

She shrank away from her husband and bit her lip as if to prevent any more words spilling forth.

Will looked at her, waited for her to stand up to the bully, to tell him that he had to take responsibility for his actions or she would leave him, but she just sank back onto her chair.

"Mother," pleaded Will softly, "don't let them arrest me, please don't let them take me." The child he still was cried out to her, but she turned her face away. Given the choice of helping her child or defying her husband, she chose the wrong one.

"You'll never see me again, mother. I'll run away and I swear I'll never come back."

She didn't even look at him.

"Come on, son," said Lazarus gently, "I'll put in a good word for you. We'll try and see you don't get too harsh a sentence."

"No, I'm going. I'm not going to prison for him!" The vitriol with which he said the word, and the look he cast at his father made Lazarus shiver. He had not been far wrong. In that brief moment, Will looked more than capable of sticking a knife into his father.

"I can't just let you walk away, boy. Don't be foolish. Just come along with me. I promise I'll look after you."

Will looked up at him, wiped away his tears and squared his shoulders, "I've just learnt that I can't depend on anyone but myself. I'll not trust you any more than I would him or her! You'll have to kill me before I'll let you take me in."

Their eyes met and clashed and oddly it was the grown man who looked away first, "All right, son. You weren't here when I came for you, and I won't report it until tomorrow. You've got the night to get as far away as you can. But promise me you'll stay in touch, that you'll write and let me know where you are and how you are doing."

"I've told her and I'm telling you, when I walk out of that door, you'll none of you ever see me again."

Lazarus knew he had lost. He pulled all the money he had in his pockets out and handed it to the boy. It amounted to a few florins and some copper, but it meant he would be without funds for a week, "Take this and look after yourself. Stay out of trouble and if you need me, I want you to call on me."

Will took the money, grabbed a threadbare jacket from the back of the door and within seconds he had gone out of the back door and disappeared into the dark alley behind the houses.

Mrs Carter gave a huge sob and went to follow him, but was knocked off her feet by a back-hander from her husband.

Ignoring the instinct to bend and help her, Lazarus simply turned and walked towards the front door, "That boy could be dead in a ditch by tomorrow – or worse – and you'll never know what became of him – let that be your punishment – and may God forgive you," he said, to the snivelling woman and the rapidly sobering man.

"And as for you, Carter, watch your back, because the minute I have anything on you, I'll have you behind bars and I'll make sure you don't see freedom for a very long time."

For once Carter didn't have a response.

CHAPTER THIRTY-SIX

As he walked into the street, Lazarus cast a glance into every alley and darkened doorway, hoping against hope that he would see the boy and persuade him to abandon his madcap scheme of running away. There was nothing. Not even a stray cat crossed his path and in despair he wandered on and on, heedless of time or direction. He felt sick to his stomach, all the old guilt and horror resurrected from the death of his wife, and the hanging of Decima Watkins. He had felt this complete helplessness and impotent anger then, and it surged back now in increasing waves of misery and hopeless fury.

He must have walked for an hour or more before he glanced up and found himself looking at the house he had left only a few hours before. Had he cared to analyse the situation he would have thought it profoundly telling that he was standing outside the house which Lord Allingham had rented for his niece, but he merely noted the unlighted windows and wondered if he dare knock at the door and ask for a cup of tea and a warm by the fire, for he was chilled to the bone and exhausted.

He hesitated for a few minutes, debating the wisdom of risking waking the neighbours with the clatter of the knocker, when he realized that there was indeed a light showing, but it was at the side of the house, not the front. Servants were late abed and early risers and it looked as if Sally might be burning the midnight oil (though it was actually only a little after ten o'clock).

He opened the gate and cautiously made his way to the back door, past a window through which he saw the redoubtable Sal, busily ironing and singing to herself. She started violently when he tapped on the glass, but seemed to recognize his face and hastily ran to let him in.

"I'm sorry to call so late," he said, "I was passing and I could do with a cup of tea, if you'll take pity on a poor, overworked policeman."

"Bloody hell, Inspector, you nearly gave me heart failure! What on earth are you doing wandering about at this time of the night?"

"It's a long story."

"Well, come in, then," she admonished impatiently, "Don't be letting the night air in. I'll catch my death of dampness!"

He obeyed her, shedding his coat at her gesture and taking the seat she indicated to him.

He spread his fingers gratefully to the warmth of the fire as she rattled a poker between the bars of the grate to coax a flame to boil the kettle.

"Miss Constance is in bed, but I can go and tell her you are here if you like," she told him as she busied herself making the tea.

"Good God, no!" he answered swiftly, "Don't wake her on my account. This isn't really a social call. It's just as I said, that I was out on a job and realized I was nearby and hoped to beg a brew."

As he finished speaking, they heard Constance's voice calling from the hall,

"Sally, are you all right? I thought I heard voices ..." she opened the baize-covered door which protected the rest of the house from the noises and smells of the kitchen and stood shocked as she realized just who her maid's visitor was.

He had never seen her with her hair loose before and he was struck by how pretty she looked with the chestnut locks tumbling over her shoulders.

For her part, she thought she had never seen him look quite so tired and sad. It made her want to rush to him and put her arms around him, to make whatever was troubling him go away, but she was painfully aware of the existence of a wife and the presence of her own servant.

"Oh, Mr Lazarus, I wasn't expecting it to be you. I came down here armed with a poker in case Sally was being attacked by intruders." She showed him that she was indeed carrying a cast iron poker hidden in the folds of her dressing gown and he managed a smile, "I must say I'm glad you checked first, before bursting through the door wielding that thing!"

Sally tutted crossly, "A fat lot of use that would be against burglars and the like," she said gruffly, "You should know better than to put yourself in danger, Miss. I can take care of myself."

Lazarus nodded, "She's right," he said ruefully, "I'd back Sal against a ne'er do well any day of the week."

Constance laughed, but pretended to be offended, "Charming! I rush to the rescue, risking life and limb and this is the thanks I get."

"It was very nice of you, Miss Constance," conceded Sally, "Now, are you back off to bed, or do you want tea or hot milk?"

"Not when I have a visitor, I'll have some tea, please," said her mistress promptly, laying aside her weapon and joining them beside the fire, but Sally was having none of it.

"You can't sit in the kitchen," she exclaimed, clearly horrified, "What would your uncle say? Into the parlour, the pair of you, and I'll bring in the tea tray."

Lazarus thought ruefully that he would have been expected to sit in the kitchen with the servant classes if the lady of the house hadn't arrived on the scene, but Miss Allingham was barely allowed to set foot over the threshold. Servant snobbery was almost worse than the gentry's condescension.

When they were both served with tea, Constance took the opportunity to observe Lazarus covertly over the rim of her cup. She thought he looked tired – no more than tired, he looked drained and melancholy. She debated whether to ask him what ailed him, or if she should simply hold her tongue and mind her own business. Curiosity won the day and she eventually gathered all her courage and asked softly,

"Is there something troubling you, Mr Lazarus?"

He could not meet her eyes for several long seconds then he conceded with a deep sigh, "I would protect you from all this, Miss Allingham, if I could, but the truth is that it will be common knowledge by the morning and I would rather you heard it from me."

"What is it?" she was assailed by a sudden feeling of dread, an oppression so real and deep that she felt physically sick.

"Miss Soffley, from the hat shop, has been murdered, and young Will Carter has run away from home."

"Dear God," she breathed, "Surely the two are not connected? You are never telling me that Will did murder?"

He smiled sadly as he realized how misleading his statement had been, "No, no connection between the two events – except perhaps that I feel responsible for both of them!"

"Oh no, how can that be? Tell me everything," she demanded, loath to believe that he could in any way be at fault.

He gave her a potted version of each incident and not surprisingly she was rather more distressed by Will Carter's tragedy than the death of a woman whom she scarcely knew and had not particularly liked.

As he related how Carter senior had watched his boy walk out into the night, alone and almost penniless, with a callous disregard that had shaken even the hardened policeman, she began to weep bitter, silent tears.

"Is there nothing we can do, Danby?" she whispered, "Can't you go after him and fetch him back?"

"How can I fetch him back to face a spell in the House of Correction or prison? Kinder to let him wander into obscurity."

"But he's only a boy."

"Do you think I don't know it? I would have paid the money myself, had I had it, and brought him to live with me, but the truth is I don't have it to spare. I have a family to keep on a policeman's wages."

"I don't have any money either," she admitted, "My uncle pays all my expenses and holds accounts with all the shops I use so he sees no reason to give me anything more than a few shillings for fripperies. Perhaps I could ask him for more?"

He reached out and clasped her hand in a gesture meant to give her comfort,

"It is a sweet thought, my dear, but the boy will be miles away by morning and he refused to even tell me where he intended to make for. He could be on the way to London, Scotland or the Continent for all I know."

Much as she longed to accept his touch, the memory of the family he possessed was enough to bring her to her senses with an icy coldness which struck into her heart like a knife. She withdrew her hand from his and rose to her feet, proceeding to pace in her agitation, "You are a detective, it cannot be beyond your capabilities to find him."

In his own frustration at his helplessness he saw both her withdrawal from him and her words as an accusation and a criticism and he could not bite back his angry response, "Dammit, Constance, I cannot work miracles, nor see into the boy's mind! I would find him if I could. God knows I've had enough failures in my life. I do not need another to haunt my waking hours and rob me of sleep."

She knew he was referring to Decima Watkins – the one thing that stood between them and true friendship. He could never forget that she was an Allingham, nor forgive her for it.

"Decima, Decima, always Decima! Am I to be punished always for Decima Watkins!" she burst out with sudden passion. He was shocked that she should have guessed to whom he referred, thinking that he had kept his secret misery well hidden, but more than that, he was astounded that she should care so much for his good opinion.

"I never mentioned Decima Watkins," he said quietly.

"You have no need to speak her name for me to know that she will forever taint any hope of friendship between us. Decima died because of an Allingham, and I am an Allingham so that is the end of it, as far as you are concerned. It does not matter that I feel as horrified as you that my uncle was capable of such cruelty and deception. You don't care that every mouthful of food that I eat, every favour I am forced to take from him, makes me burn with shame and humiliation. Would you have me starve on the street to prove myself to you?"

"Of course not, you are being ridiculous," he said tersely, fully aware that she was right and that he had been entirely wrong to hold her family against her, to make her suffer for the sins of others.

"Am I? Am I really? Or is it you who has blown this whole matter so far out of proportion that there is no reasoning with you? I do not understand you, Danby Lazarus. I simply cannot comprehend how that young woman can have taken over your thoughts so completely that you see no one's point of view but hers. Were you in love with her? Is that why she has become this obsession?"

For some reason that accusation merely made him angry, "Of course I wasn't in love with her. I was a married man and I met her only two or three times."

"Then why? What was it about her that has left such an indelible mark upon you. Please tell me. If only I could understand, then perhaps I could learn to accept that she will always come between us."

He looked at her for a long time before he sighed and gestured that she sit down once more, "Above all else, Constance, I love justice. It may seem quaint and possibly even pretension on my part, but that is why I became a policeman. I saw it, I still see it, as a sacred duty. I have no religion, no belief in God, but I do believe that we are put upon this earth to do right by each other. Decima Watkins had done nothing wrong. She had not killed anyone, she had not stolen, nor defrauded anyone. She had simply fallen in love with a young man, and he with her. For that she paid with her life. Your uncle had no possible reason to hate her. She was not so much lower in class than his son as would be an embarrassment to him, she was from a family who had money so she couldn't be said to be a fortune-hunter. He has simply taken against her because his son had the temerity to make his own choice and not bow to his father's wishes. For that Decima was vilified, debased, slandered and dragged to a humiliating and agonising death at the end of a rope, having lost her child to her sister and her lover to the blast of a cannon in the Crimea. And I failed to save her. When I was threatened with losing my job I took the easy way and left her to her fate, when I should have fought and won for her, even at the cost of my career. Is it any wonder I can neither forgive myself nor your uncle? There he sits in his mansion, cushioned against life's trials by his money and his servants. He will never pay for killing Decima. He is guilty of murder, albeit second hand, but he will live and die a rich man."

Constance had no more affection for her uncle than Lazarus, but her own innate sense of fair play forced her to play the devil's advocate, "You seem very sure that Decima was innocent, but you must realize that though my uncle could undoubtedly cause her to be arrested and tried, he could not possibly force a jury to find her guilty unless there was some evidence …"

"You were not there, you have no idea what went on in that court. To a man they believed every word the prosecutor said – and in whose pay was he? Allingham's of course. No one thought anything of it at the time, because her liaison with Richard Allingham was kept very quiet. It was not central to the trial, because she was accused of poisoning her sisters – and what had that to do with her lover? Nothing. They made sure they told the world that she had borne an illegitimate baby though – just to prove how very wicked and immoral she really was. A woman who could bear a child out of wedlock was equally capable of dosing her sisters with arsenic."

She shook her head, "That doesn't make any sense at all. Surely people are not swayed by such nonsensical arguments?"

"You would be astounded to know what might push a jury in the direction a clever counsel wants them to go. All those upright citizens, manipulated and driven by their own self-importance. Find this girl guilty, let her be a lesson to your own daughters. Free her and you will find yourself in possession of a brace of bastard grandchildren. And those with sons, horrified that a clever woman might entice those darling boys into temptation, a sin that will cost papa very dear when it comes to paying off the girl, sending her away to avert scandal, or worse still, a hasty marriage and a son who will repent at leisure when he finds himself tied for life to a termagant."

He sounded so bitter, so very angry, that Constance almost wished she had never raised the subject – but how could she regret it? This would ever fester between them unless it was broached.

"Forgive me, but how can you be so sure that my uncle did all those things you say he did? Surely even he deserves justice, the right to defend himself?"

"You think I have acted as judge and jury in his case, don't you? You couldn't be more wrong. I know he did it all because he told me he had done so. When he had me removed from the case, I went to see him, to ask him why. He told me that he feared my interference because he wanted Decima out of the way. He laughed in my face and told me that he would have his way and her bastard would never inherit his estate. I knew then that I should have pursued him to the bitter end, but I was helpless. He made his admission when we were alone and I would have been thrown out of the police force had I tried to prove him a liar and a perjurer."

"I'm sorry," she said simply.

He had almost forgotten she was there, he had merely been speaking his thoughts aloud, swept away on a wave of memory that was painful, yet oddly cathartic. He realized now that he had not only been blaming himself for Decima's death, but for Rosamund's too. She had died so soon after Decima's hanging that it had seemed as though he was being punished for his cowardice and failure.

"No," he replied, "No, I'm sorry. You have nothing to apologise for, I however, have much. I had no right to hold you in any way responsible for the actions of your uncle. I have been grossly unfair – unforgivable in a man who holds justice in such high esteem."

She gave a sad little smile which made him feel even more of a bounder than he already did, "I understand," she whispered, "and I wish it were in my power to change things, but sadly there is nothing I can do to alleviate your pain."

"I don't deserve your sympathy, my dear girl, but thank you. Now, may we leave this painful subject behind us and start afresh?"

"I'd like that," she said shyly.

He looked at his watch and made an exaggerated face of horror, "Good grief, look at the time! I should be on my way. I have a murderer to catch. Not that it should be too difficult – how many people in the district are proficient enough with a bow and arrow to kill a woman?"

Constance looked shocked, "Did you say bow and arrow?" she asked incredulously.

"I did. Not a usual weapon these days, so I surmise we will soon have a suspect."

"I wouldn't be too sure of that, if I were you," she told him bluntly.

"Why? What makes you say that?"

"Because it has become traditional that my uncle holds a large garden party every summer, which is attended by every half decent family in the county. The highlight of the event is an archery competition. Over the years it has grown beyond all expectation and now there are upwards of thirty or forty young people who all spend their spare time in practise with a bow and arrow to win the fifty guineas he gives as first prize. I enter it myself, so does Arabella, then there is Lawrie Crabtree, and all his friends whom you met at Lady Stafford-Naylor's party, the Dickson twins, the Westerdale girls …"

Lazarus stared at her in disbelief then gave an audible and rather theatrical groan, "Oh dear God, why does it always have to happen to me?"

CHAPTER THIRTY-SEVEN

PRESENT

Her fingers suddenly stopped flying over the keys. Libby was astounded by what she had just written. Was it in her own imagination that Lazarus had known Decima was innocent, or had it actually been said in something she had read and she had failed to analyse it until it had flashed up on the computer screen?

As she shuffled her papers, searching for the elusive note somewhere amongst the scattered journals and diaries, her hands trembled. This was probably the most important thing she had come across in all her research and she had no idea if it was true or her own wishful thinking.

When she finally found the quote, she could only curse softly under her breath. Yes, there it was in black and white, but it was contained in Meg's diary, reported to Meg, from Constance who in turn said she had heard it from Lazarus. Hearsay. No use to anyone really. But worth making a note of it and keeping the reference. If Lazarus had said it, perhaps he had also written it somewhere – and it could be vital in Maddie's fight with the Allinghams.

As she stretched her aching back, she glanced at the clock and realized that it was past six. David ought to be home any moment, so she saved her work and went downstairs to greet him and find out what he wanted for his evening meal.

In her amiable mood she was not prepared for the frown which adorned her husband's face when he walked though the door.

"Had a bad day?" she asked and was stunned to have a newspaper flung at her across the room, which she caught automatically, but didn't bother to glance at.

"Bloody awful, thanks to you," was the growled reply.

"What have I done?" she responded mildly, determined not to let him provoke her. There had been enough cross words thrown about in the house in the last few days and she didn't intend to hear or dispense any more.

"Look on page five and you'll see," he said, heading straight for the sideboard and pouring himself a large whisky. That alone was enough to concern her. David very rarely drank in the house unless they had guests. With some trepidation she did as he suggested and opened the paper to page five.

It was bad enough to see a not particularly flattering picture of herself, but the headline made her want to curl up with embarrassment. "LIBBY WRIGHT AND THINGS THAT GO BUMP IN THE NIGHT!"

To be fair to Joanne the rest of the article was measured and analytical, she hadn't mocked or even been sceptical, but to see her own words in print, describing Decima and her possible haunting was cringe-worthy and Libby could understand why David was furious.

She looked up at him, trying to smile apologetically whilst looking as though it really wasn't such a big deal. David was very evidently not in the least impressed. He drank the spirit in one gulp and poured another, "I specifically asked you not to speak to that journalist and especially not to let her print anything."

"I couldn't stop her," protested Libby, "it's a free country! And from what I've read, she's only told the truth."

"Huh! The truth? Whose truth exactly, Libby? Your's? the truth about your obsession with a dead woman? You and your crazy sister dragging up the past and trying to prove something that no-one gives a damn about any more? Don't you realize that you are making a laughing stock of yourselves and in the process me!"

She couldn't believe what she was hearing from the man who was supposed to love her. He knew how much Decima meant to her, how horrified she had been when she learned of what the poor girl had gone through at the hands of the Allinghams. Now he was throwing it all in her face, treating her like a basket case. So many bitter words came to mind that she had trouble deciding which to throw at him first. Perhaps that was fortunate because the momentary hesitation made her realize that she had no desire to say anything to him. Silence on this occasion would be far more eloquent. She simply looked at him then turned away and went to the kitchen to cook. She maintained the non-speaking all through dinner, simply serving him, then taking away the empty dishes. He fulminated, but also refused to be the first to capitulate, eating everything she gave him, even though she piled his plate with the broccoli he hated so much. He made the coffee after the meal and washed up, as was their usual habit, while she went into the sitting room and turned on the television. They sat and watched some rubbish that neither wanted to see, then retired upstairs in silence, the gap between them in the bed a chasm of just a few inches.

He was gone in the morning when she woke up, but within an hour of her going downstairs and making herself a strong coffee – she didn't feel she could face any breakfast, since there was a little knot of nausea in her stomach which she didn't seem to be able to shake off – the telephone rang and she rushed to it with all the eagerness of a teenager waiting for her first call from the school heartthrob.

She had never been more relieved to hear her husband's voice and she put every ounce of warmth into her own tone that she could manage, willing him to be ready to apologise and make up.

"Hi, I'm glad you called," she said softly.

"You won't be when you hear why I'm calling," he said curtly.

The little knot turned into a huge wave of sickness, followed swiftly by burning anger. What a complete knob he was being!

"Well," she snapped back, "What is it then?"

"We've been summoned to Allingham Hall by Rick's mother. The dowager has the reputation of being the most obnoxious old dragon ever to walk the earth. Rick is terrified of her."

"Oh, Rick's terrified of everyone," said Libby dismissively, but she was worried just the same. Things were getting serious if old Lady Allingham was acknowledging their existence. She had never felt the need to do so before.

"That's as may be, but it's not a meeting I'm looking forward to."

David sounded almost normal, almost friendly and she took hope from that and responded equally amiably, "Well, there's nothing to say we have to go. Who the hell does she think she is, anyway, sending out her directives? Tell her if she wants to see us, she can come here."

She heard David laugh, though she wasn't quite sure if it was her response, or simply the notion of telling Lady Allingham where she could go, "Good idea. Let the old trout take a hike. I'll see you later."

"Bye," she said and placed the phone back in its cradle, feeling happier than she had for some days – even with the threat of a visit from Rick Allingham's redoubtable mother on the horizon.

When the phone rang again she almost jumped out of her skin and her heart was still thumping painfully when she answered.

"Hi, Libby, it's Tess. I've just been reading your piece in the paper and thought I give you a call. I guessed you might feel the need for a bit of moral support."

Libby managed to laugh, though she was still feeling jittery, "Hi Tess, thanks for calling. It has been a trying time, I admit."

"I'll bet. Are you okay with what Joanne Pooley has written? She didn't exactly pull any punches, did she?"

Libby was surprised. Was it just her who didn't think the article was all that bad? David had been infuriated by it and now Tess was hinting that she'd found it less than salubrious too.

"She only wrote what I told her," she said, a little defensively, "What's wrong with it?"

Tess back-tracked hastily, "Nothing at all, if you are happy with it. Anyway, enough of that, I really rang to say I've been reading all you left with me the other day and now I'm hungry for more. Any chance of you coming over for lunch and bringing me a few more chapters?"

"Sure, why not. I'm flattered that you're enjoying it."

"It's good, Libby. Really good. I'm impressed, especially if it really is your first attempt at writing a novel."

Libby grinned to herself. This was high praise indeed from one of her favourite authors, "Thanks Tess, that really means a lot. I'd love to come over."

"Great. We can discuss the few little errors and other stuff that needs putting right when you get here. There's too much to address over the phone."

As high as she had just flown, this comment brought Libby plunging back to earth, "Oh, okay," she said quietly. Tess was more intuitive than she had given her credit for because she laughed, but in a light, friendly way, "Don't sound so gutted, it's nothing serious. You've just made a few beginner's bloomers that I want to help you iron out. Nothing major, I promise."

They made the arrangements for the visit and Libby once more set the phone down.

Unbelievably it immediately rang again, once more startling her. Normally if the phone rang once a day that was a lot, now it was beginning to resemble a call-centre switchboard.

"Yes?" she said impatiently, losing the will to put on her posh telephone voice and pretend to be interested in the caller.

"Mrs Wright?"

"Yes. Who's that?"

"Justine Allingham."

"Oh," she was glad that Rick's mother couldn't see her grimace of dislike and irritation, "What can I do for you, Lady Allingham?"

"I have just spoken to your husband and he seems to think, ridiculously in my opinion, that you have refused an invitation to Allingham Hall."

"Why is that ridiculous?" said Libby with a very distinct edge of annoyance to her voice. She was glad this conversation was taking place over the telephone, because she knew if she wasn't safely ensconced in her own front room, with at least six miles between herself and the dragon, she would not be half so brave.

This apparently stumped the woman, because there was a distinctly icy silence before she spoke again, having decided not to rise to the provocation, "We need to meet, Mrs Wright. This whole sorry mess is getting out of hand."

"What has any of it to do with me? My sister Maddie is the person you need to deal with not me."

There was an impatient sigh, as though she were dealing with a particularly recalcitrant child, "Oh, if only it were that simple. Seriously, is there something wrong with your sister?"

Libby was well aware that Maddie could be infuriating when she had a goal in sight and refused to be turned, so she could almost sympathise with her caller, but she reminded herself of the sheer arrogance being displayed and it hardened her resolve quite nicely.

"No, I believe she's in perfect health, thank you," she answered, deliberately obtuse.

"I didn't mean physically," said Lady Allingham testily, "She seems rather unbalanced to me. She threatened my solicitor with the Law Society, and now she utterly refuses to speak to me."

"Can you blame her? He tried to shred a vital piece of evidence!"

"I only have her word for that,"

"No, you have mine, too. I was there. The way he behaved – on your instructions – was scandalous. Is it any wonder she doesn't trust you?"

This time the silence stretched for so long that Libby was beginning to think the woman had hung up on her. She held her nerve and refused to speak and eventually there was another impatient sigh, "I apologise for that. He took too much upon himself. I would never have approved of his actions. Now, will you be reasonable and meet to discuss what we do next?"

"You can certainly come here and I'll gladly pass on your comments to Maddie, anything more than that, I cannot promise."

"I'll be there in an hour," said Lady Allingham and this time Libby heard the click of the disconnected line.

"Shit!" she said succinctly, and started dialling David at work. There was no way she was dealing with the old bag alone.

CHAPTER THIRTY-EIGHT

A cry of triumph went up when one of the constables found the bow discarded in the backyard of an empty house not far from the hat shop.

Lazarus felt a certain satisfaction that they had found the murder weapon, but it moved the investigation no further forward. It was the sort of bow which any one of the guests in Lord Allingham's archery competition could buy – and probably already possessed. If only there were some way, he thought, of testing the thing to find out to whom it belonged. They might leave some invisible trace upon it, but it was beyond him to discover the owner.

The yard was searched and searched again in case the culprit had left some tiny fragment of cloth or paper which might lead them to him, but there was nothing. The only recourse left to him was to try and persuade the names of every archer out of Lord Allingham and see which of them had an alibi for the time of the killing, or a motive to wish either Miss Soffley or Eliza Dunne dead. It would take every policeman under his command a week or more to do so, and even then, it would mean nothing without firm evidence.

Reluctantly he had to admit to Superintendent Gregson that the chances of finding the murderer were remote to say the least.

"All the more reason, I think, to take Mollie Waters off our books and call it suicide," said his superior grimly, "It's over, Lazarus. The investigation is finished. Now, what's this I hear about you interfering with a case of theft?"

"If you mean young Will Carter, I thought it my duty to go and arrest the boy myself, since I had recommended him for the job in the first place."

"Odd then, that you didn't manage to arrest him," said Gregson cynically.

"Not so very surprising, sir, is it? The boy knew he was in trouble and he took to his heels. Wouldn't you have done the same thing?"

The superintendent grunted, "I suppose so. But in future, keep to your own cases and let the uniformed division deal with theirs. They weren't very happy to be berated by the shop owner at the loss of both his money and the chance of revenge!"

Lazarus endured a few more pithy comments on his handling of all his most recent cases and some searching questions on the nature of his relationship with Lord Allingham, but he managed to keep both his temper and his secrets, much to his superior's chagrin.

Stonier was waiting for him in their office, with a cup of tea and a sympathetic expression, "Did he give you a hard time, old fellow?"

"Not as hard as he would have liked," answered Lazarus, accepting the tea and enduring the sympathy, "We're off the Mollie Waters case. This murder has given him the opportunity he was looking for to put her death down to suicide. He quite rightly says that we can't have an ever-growing pile of corpses and no arrests without the public beginning to panic."

Stonier cocked a brow at him, "And are we really off the case?"

"Are we bloody hell!" responded Lazarus tersely, "That girl was murdered and I'm going to find out who did it if it sends me into an early grave."

"What about Miss Soffley?"

"It's the same man, Tom. I know it is. He was trying to silence Liza and hit the wretched woman by mistake."

"What's the likelihood of a killer using two different modus operandi? Doesn't a knife man always use a blade, and a thug a blunt instrument?"

Lazarus looked thoughtful, "Normally I would agree with you, my friend, but this fellow is cleverer than that. He doesn't kill on the spur of the moment, everything is planned to the last degree."

"Are we even sure it's a man?"

"Good point. They say poison is a woman's weapon – and the archery at the Allingham summer party is open to both sexes. Ladies can become quite as proficient as men – but why would a woman want these two young lasses dead? It doesn't make any sense."

"Does murder ever make any sense? One usually leads to another, to cover the first. It has to be a very sick mind to think that killing will ever solve a problem."

"I can think of a few that it has solved, even right here in Braxton. Lord Allingham is living very well on the bones of his victims."

Stonier could have made a comment about the illusion that Allingham was a happy man, for all his wealth and power, but he realized that Lazarus would simply see it as him defending the enemy, so he kept his mouth shut on the subject.

"What next, then? We still have the problem of Liza Dunne. If she was the intended victim, then the minute we take our eyes off her, she is likely to end up dead."

"Can't she stay with you for a few days longer, old friend?" asked the inspector, a note of pleading in his tone. He liked Liza and had no intention of attending her funeral.

"She gets on well with Meg and has made herself useful, but it can only ever be for a short while. We can't spend the rest of our lives following her around."

Lazarus gave an impatient sigh, "Yes, yes, I know that. Give me a couple more days, Tom. I can break this, I know I can. Our killer is going to make an error and then we'll have him. He's been fortunate so far that no one has seen or heard anything, but his luck must run out sooner or later."

"I'm not sure we can rely on that," muttered Stonier, as far as he was concerned, the mystery was deeper than ever. Two completely unrelated killings, with only the most tenuous of connections, he really couldn't see how Lazarus was ever going to draw the events together into a cohesive tale which would stand up in court.

"It's all I've got, Tom." said Lazarus and for the first time, he sounded utterly weary and defeated.

Suddenly the door flew open, so violently that it bounced off the wall and sprang back nearly knocking Constance off her feet, for it was she who had burst into the room, her face white and tear-stained, her hair coming loose from its pins, giving her the appearance of a mad woman.

"Oh, Danby!" she could say nothing more but began to sob wildly. The inspector was on his feet and around the desk in a flash, grasping her arms and shaking her slightly to ward off the threatening hysteria, "Calm down, Constance and tell me what is wrong,"

Stonier stood back, too astounded by the unusual entrance and unconscious exchange of first names to say a word.

She gulped back her tears and tried to speak, "You must come at once. The most dreadful thing has happened … my uncle …"

"What? Don't tell me the old devil has dropped dead!"

She gasped with shock, "Don't, pray don't! I can't bear it …"

"Tell me!" he snapped, finally losing all patience. In his eyes the untimely death of Allingham could be nothing but a good thing."

"No," she whispered, "not dead – not yet, but who knows that the shock will not kill him!"

"He's had a shock? Evidently so have you. Please just tell me what it is," pleaded Lazarus, as the gravity of the situation was bourn upon him. A deceased Allingham merely filled him with grim glee, but a distressed Constance was an entirely different matter.

"In the post, this morning …" she suddenly sank into a chair and shuddered, "It is too horrible to contemplate. In a box, sent in the post … oh, dear God, Danby. That animal has sent Arabella's finger …"

It took a moment for Lazarus to fully understand exactly what it was that she was saying. He looked down at her for a few seconds, then his face took on an expression of deep distaste, "You are absolutely sure of this?"

"Of course my uncle did not show it to me – he merely told me to fetch you with as much haste as I could."

He needed no further encouragement, he grabbed his hat and coat and headed for the door, "Come, Stonier. Miss Allingham, I suggest you go home. There is nothing more you can do."

"But my uncle is at my house. He came to ask me to find you. He could not have you coming to the Hall."

"I rather think the time has passed for hiding Arabella's flight. The loss of a finger may be the very least injury she has suffered at the hands of a man capable and probably culpable of murder."

Constance looked as though she might faint and Stonier could gladly have strangled his companion for his lack of sensitivity. Lazarus, of course, was oblivious to the effect his words had on the young woman, so intent was he on getting on to the scent of a new case.

She bravely pulled herself together and followed Lazarus out of the police station and into the waiting carriage, aided by the solicitous Stonier.

Under instructions to get the police to his master in the shortest possible time, the groom whipped up the horses and reached the house in a remarkably prompt manner.

They found Lord Allingham pacing the floor like a caged animal, looking older and more ill than Lazarus had ever seen anyone who was not confined to bed. He knew pity should move him, but Lazarus felt nothing for the old man but a trace of satisfaction that he was finally feeling just a tiny portion of the despair he had spent his life inflicting upon others.

Without a word Lazarus held out his hand and Allingham placed the small, brown-wrapped package into his possession. The Inspector took a magnifying glass from his pocket and began his observation of the gruesome contents.

One glance and Lazarus drew in deep breath of relief, "Calm yourself, sir. It is not your daughter's digit."

Allingham seemed not to comprehend what the other man was saying to him and for a moment Lazarus thought that the shock had unhinged the old fellow's mind.

"What? What did you say, Lazarus?" His voice had a distinct quaver to it and it occurred to them all that he was an older man than any of them ever realized.

"I said it does not belong to Arabella. Take a deep breath and sit down. Allow me to explain."

He turned to Constance, "Tell Sally to bring tea – hot and sweet. Your uncle needs to take a few minutes to gather his thoughts."

"But how do you know?"

"Tea first, then I'll expound."

When Lazarus felt they were all sufficiently composed he began to speak, keeping his tone even and unruffled, "I can understand how the error was made – in fact I would go so far as to suggest that it was just such a reaction that Soper was relying upon to cover his subterfuge – but had you looked carefully at the article, you would see that it could not possibly belong to a gently raised young lady such as Arabella."

"How can you possibly know that?" barked Allingham, by now well on his way to recovery and back to his usual irascible self.

"Because it is the finger of an older woman who has endured a life of hardship and physical labour. There are calluses and scars, the nail is thickened and broken. Furthermore the severance was not done neatly with a knife, but is torn and bruised. I would venture to guess that it has been wrenched off in an industrial accident of some kind, because of the traces of black grease. In fact I would say it was caught in the machinery found in a cotton mill."

"How the devil can you possibly know that?" asked Allingham, impressed in spite of himself and trying his best not to show it.

"Because there are tiny shreds of cotton caught in the rough edge of the torn nail. I'd stake my life that Soper heard of an accident in a local cotton mill and hit upon the idea of frightening you into paying the money he has so far failed to wrench from you."

Finally the old man looked as though he was daring to hope that the inspector was right and that he need have no fear that his precious daughter had been mutilated by the cad who had abducted her.

"Lazarus, if you are right and you can find her and bring her back, you will have my eternal gratitude."

"I think that can be accomplished, though I will need a free hand with your money and your agents."

"Anything, my dear fellow, ask for anything and it is yours."

"Very well, then I shall leave for Stockport on the next train."

"How do you know they are in Stockport?"

"Soper has friends there. He slipped away last time, but in order to do so, he must have had somewhere to hide. They may not still be there, but I suspect the boy thinks he is clever enough to fox me.

Where is the last place you look for something? The place you have already searched, of course! Besides, Stockport is famous for cotton production and if there is anywhere that still has a working mill in these hard times, it will be there."

"Stockport is a big place. How will you flush him out?"

"Simple. All legal industry must keep careful records of accidents on the premises. I shall ask until I find someone who has lost a finger in a mill in the past …" he glanced again into the box and considered the digit for a few seconds, "the past week, I would estimate, judging by the state of decomposition."

Constance paled at the word, but Allingham was unmoved now that he knew the relic did not belong to his darling child.

"Very well, my bank shall be told to grant you whatever monies you require."

"I'll also need access to your lawyers, sir."

Stonier glanced at him in puzzlement, wondering what was behind that particular request, but Allingham had no such quandary, he merely nodded his assent.

"Ask them what you will. I'll give instructions that you are to be aided in any way you request."

"Thank you. Now, Sergeant Stonier and I will go and prepare for our journey. I suggest you both attain some measure of serenity before you attempt to face others if you wish to continue with the illusion that all is well with Arabella."

Allingham rose and shook Lazarus warmly by the hand, "I won't forget this, Lazarus, that I can promise you."

"And I can assure you, Lord Allingham, that my only concern is Arabella's safety. If this was your pain alone, I would leave you to suffer the pangs of hell."

CHAPTER THIRTY-NINE

A more unhappy man than Sawyer the Lawyer Lazarus had rarely seen. It obviously sat ill with him that he had been instructed to give the Inspector a free hand with his major client's private dealings. He blanched at the amount of money Lazarus asked for, 'just in case', but he became almost apoplectic when Lazarus requested information about Constance.

"What the devil has Miss Constance to do with this matter? I fail to see how knowing about her maternal relations has anything to do with the issue of Miss Arabella."

"I'm sure you don't," answered the policeman smoothly, "but fortunately your understanding of the situation is not really necessary, is it?"

"But I'm sure Lord Allingham didn't mean you to have access to his private family affairs."

"Sure enough to deny me, then approach his Lordship with a complaint?" asked Lazarus, "If you must know, I have a suspicion that Marcus Soper has had help from someone who is privy to Lord Allingham's affairs. I'm merely being thorough in checking Miss Constance Allingham's long-lost relatives are not out to cause mischief, but if you really think you should delay my rescue of young Arabella, then by all means write your missive to Lord Allingham. I'll happily sit here for a couple of days whilst the two of you debate the matter. We cannot, of course, discount the possibility that Soper will be driven to actually mutilating the young lady in his desperation for money."

Sawyer handed over the information without another word.

On the way to the station, Stonier asked diffidently, "All that about Constance's kin was so much stuff and nonsense, wasn't it?"

"Absolutely," responded Lazarus with a grin, "I have my own reasons for wanting the information."

"And what might they be?"

Stonier thought that he might never get an answer to this question, for they had reached the ticket office and Lazarus was busily purchasing their first class tickets.

"First class?" he queried with a raised eyebrow.

"The old skinflint can afford it."

The inspector's timing was impeccable and the train was already gently hissing and steaming, ready to go, when they emerged onto the platform. Within minutes they were aboard and once settled into their very comfortable seats, Lazarus rather more at home in the opulent surrounds than his stoic sergeant, he continued the conversation as though there had been no break in his thoughts, "Constance confided in me the other evening that she finds life in her new house rather lonely, hence her spending rather more time with your wife than is strictly wise."

Stonier shot him a sharp look, "What the devil do you mean by that, Danby? What's wrong with Meg befriending the girl?"

"Nothing at all if she were a free woman of similar class and income, but seriously, old man, are you happy that Meg is getting into the habit of shopping in expensive shops and neglecting her duties towards you and your house?"

Stonier had to admit that Lazarus had a point. He and Meg had had words several times over the past few weeks, something which would have been unheard of in the normal course of their lives.

"Huh," he muttered grumpily, then added, "So what do you intend to do about it?"

"I am hopeful of finding some young female relative of Miss Allingham who would be willing to come and bear her company."

The sergeant acknowledged the sense of this, but could not help but remind Lazarus of his own part in this unhappy situation, "I grant it's a good idea, but of course, if you had left Miss Allingham well alone and not interfered between she and her uncle, she would still be safely living under his roof with as much company as she could ever want or need."

"I had my reasons for getting her out from under Lord Allingham's roof," he admonished his companion, "take my word on that!"

The reminder that Danby was Tom's superior was enough to silence them both for a good few minutes and when they resumed their conversation, the subject had turned to the most important matter of how they intended to find and arrest Marcus Soper without causing injury to Arabella, or drawing undue attention. Allingham was still adamant that the girl's reputation must be protected. He was still hopeful that society was unaware of her fall from grace and that an advantageous marriage could occur within the next few years. It did not seem to occur to him that her experiences over the past weeks might very well have had an effect upon Arabella which could make all his ambitious plans come to nought.

Without the delay Lazarus had last experienced upon this same journey, it was accomplished in what seemed to him a remarkably short time.

As they alighted, Stonier asked, "Where to first, sir?"

"The Town Hall. They should know which mills – if any – are still working. Taxes must be collected, even in times of hardship."

"Especially in times of hardship," amended Stonier.

They were lucky that times were so hard. Currently only three mills were working and all those on short time. Lazarus didn't want to imagine how many they would have had to search in better times. Hundreds just within Stockport's town boundaries, many more just outside. Cotton and hat-making were the town's principal industries and at one time they had supplied the world with both.

With the directions to all three mills in his notebook, Lazarus next led the way to the police station where they were welcomed warmly. Lazarus had not been forgotten. As he had suggested on his last visit, Soper's aunt had been exhumed and evidence of foul play had been discovered at her post mortem. Stockport police were equally as eager to find Soper as were Lazarus and Stonier.

Inspector Tiplady was impressed with Lazarus' plan of action and happy to supply a number of men to go with the visiting constabulary and surround the house when Soper was tracked down.

The three senior officers went first to the mills to demand a view of the accident books. These were kept meticulously on account of the lack of work all around the district. The few manufacturers still producing were only too aware of the huge numbers of factory inspectors who were vying for something to do in case it should be decided that they were no longer needed. The last thing any of them needed in such a harsh economic climate was to be caught out by an over-zealous factory inspector and closed down.

The third mill had a note of a woman called Edna Watling who had trapped her little finger in the machinery of a cotton spinner. The digit had not been quite severed, but very nearly. The mill had offered a doctor and when he was called he recommended amputation, which she had refused and had gone home, bandaged and in shock.

They took her address and went in search of Edna, something which didn't take long as most mill workers lived in the streets surrounding the mill in which they laboured, day after day, rarely seeing the light other than that which forced its way through the myriad tall windows, and fought its way past the dancing cotton motes which forever filled the air.

The door was answered by a meek little woman in her late forties, though she looked older, her hair prematurely grey and new lines of pain etched on her face. She tried to look calm, but Lazarus could see the terror in her eyes and knew they had found what they were looking for. She had no choice but to let them in and once in the back room, Tiplady headed straight for the range and made a great show of warming his hands, "By gum, Edna, you've a goodly lot of coal. Compensation must be grand at your mill."

"It's all right," she admitted grudgingly.

Lazarus nodded towards her bandaged hand, "that looks as if its still causing you some pain, Mrs Watling. Tell me, did the doctor manage to save the finger?"

She looked startled that he should know so much about her injury, "Er, er, yes, I was lucky there. I'll be back at work in a couple of weeks."

"Very lucky. We heard the doctor wanted to cut it off – bit of a miraculous recovery, that, wasn't it?"

"Well, a different doctor had a different opinion – what do I know? I just took the advice I was given."

"Of course. So you won't mind us fetching that doctor here and asking him to explain how he managed to save your finger, then he can change the dressing and we can all have a look."

She looked like a hunted animal, casting her glance from one to the other of the three men, hoping for some sign that they didn't mean what they were saying.

"I can't … I can't recall his name. He was sent by a friend."

"A friend called Marcus Soper by any chance?"

The colour drained from her face and her mouth dropped open. She valiantly tried to pull herself together and fight back, but they all knew it was useless. She garbled a few denials, tried to plead with them that she was a poor widow and in terrible pain from her injury, but to no avail. After a few moments she merely sank into a chair and said wearily, "All right, what do you want?"

"Where's Soper and is the young lady still with him?"

"He'll kill me if I give him away – you don't know what he's capable of," she pleaded with them, genuinely afraid and, thought Lazarus, with good reason.

"He won't get the chance, love," he said kindly, "We're on the way to arrest him for murder and he'll be swinging on the gallows before the year is out."

Perhaps she simply knew the game was up, but Lazarus liked to think he had reassured her with this calm statement. She told them where to find Soper and within seconds they were on their way, leaving a constable to keep an eye on her. Both Tiplady and Lazarus had no intention of letting anyone have the chance to run and warn the felon before they could get to him.

As they approached the street, it was growing dark and Lazarus drew Tiplady to a halt with a restraining hand on his arm, "One moment, sir, before we go in. You know that Soper has a girl with him, what you don't know is that she is very young and was abducted by him, charmed away from her family by his promises. I need to be allowed to take her away, quietly, with no fuss. She has nothing to do with all this and her father is frantic to have her returned unscathed in both body and reputation."

For the first time Tiplady frowned and pulled at the ends of his long moustaches, "If she's with him, Lazarus, then she's an accessory. I can't allow her to just walk away from all this. I have to arrest them both. She can explain her behaviour to the magistrate."

Lazarus shook his head but it was merely to give him time to marshal his thoughts. This was his last chance to save Arabella and he needed to make sure he didn't fail her by speaking too hastily or provoking the other man into an action which would condemn them all.

"I'm asking this as a personal favour, Tiplady. Think about this. I have done right by you all the way. I tipped you off when I suspected Soper had killed his aunt. I came to you now and I'm giving you the arrest. My name need never come into it, you can have all the glory. All I'm asking in return is that Stonier and I leave now, with the girl and you never see any of us again."

He could see that the Inspector was wavering, but he hadn't quite convinced him, "What about the court case, Lazarus? How do I explain all that has happened? What reason can I give for having the old woman exhumed?"

"It can't be beyond your ingenuity to think of something, my friend. An anonymous tip off, perhaps?"

"I suppose so. But why are you so eager to protect this girl? How can you be sure that she's not with him, hand in glove, murder, fraud and all?"

"She's barely seventeen," protested Lazarus, "And she means a great deal to someone who is special to me." Tiplady raised a quizzical eyebrow and Lazarus was surprised himself by this last. He had convinced himself that Constance meant nothing to him, but somehow, at the back of everything he had done for Arabella. The memory of her anguished face at Arabella's loss had spurred him on when his instincts had been to let the girl go to the devil in her own way.

Suddenly Tiplady grinned, "We men are fools, are we not? There's nothing we won't do, when there's a woman to impress. All right, Lazarus, you shall have your way. But you must waste no time. The less of my men who notice the girl in the house, the better. One or two I can silence, but not half a dozen!"

"Thank you, sir. I'm forever in your debt." Lazarus thrust out his hand and Tiplady shook it.

"Now, my good knight in shining armour, let us save your damsel!"

One good kick and the door flew open. As Lazarus had expected, Soper gave them one startled glance, recognized him and Stonier and knew his little game was over. As the frightened and emaciated Arabella gave a tiny scream, he leapt to his feet from the wooden settle where they had been contemplating the fire, and headed for the back door. Tiplady had expected just such an action and they heard a roar of anger and frustration as the man ran straight into the arms of a waiting policeman outside the yard gate.

Arabella cowered in her seat, looking utterly bewildered. Lazarus and Stonier exchanged a glance. She would have no difficulty, once back at home, in convincing everyone who saw her that she had indeed been sick unto death and had spent the last month recuperating by the seaside. She was pathetically frail and thin. Either Soper had been starving her, probably to ensure he kept control over the fiery young miss, or she had begun to fret and pine for her family. Either way, she needed fresh air and good food immediately.

Lazarus offered her his hand, "Come Arabella, we're here to take you home."

"Home?" she whispered, as though he was talking of some mythical place, a haven that only existed in her dreams, "You mean really home? To my papa?"

"As fast as the next train can get you there," Stonier assured her kindly.

She smiled, "Oh, thank you!" she said and Lazarus thought he had never heard such heartfelt gratitude in his life before. So much for his fear that she would kick up such a tantrum that they would have to throw a blanket over her head and drag her screaming from the house. Whatever Soper had done to her, he had ensured she would never run away again.

They could only hope now that the one thing he hadn't done was to leave her with a baby on the way.

That, however, was Lord Allingham's concern and not his. He took the confiding little hand in his own and led her quickly out of the house, ignoring the melee which was now going on in the back alley, as neighbours of Soper came out to his aid, automatically on the side of one of their own against the police.

CHAPTER FORTY

PRESENT

She was the living image of Maggie Thatcher, which didn't endear her to Libby right from the start, down to the bouffant blond hair and the supercilious sneer.

The sneer only deepened when she walked into the house, "I understood you had inherited quite a considerable sum of money from your Great Aunt," she said as she looked around.

Libby frowned, sure she was being insulted, but not able to pin down exactly how, "That's a strange greeting," she said, trying hard to keep her temper, "What exactly does that have to do with anything?"

"Just an observation," said Lady Allingham pleasantly, "though one would perhaps have expected your home to be …" she trailed off with one last glance around the hall, "Through here?" she asked, gesturing towards the sitting room.

Rick had followed his mother into the house, both of them using the front door, which no-one else ever did, and he shrugged both helplessly and apologetically as he passed Libby. She glared at him but flung her arm wide, allowing him to go before her into the room.

It stuck in her craw to say it, but Libby was determined not to be wrong-footed by the dragon, so she asked politely if anyone would like a drink.

"It's a little early in the day for me, dear," said her ladyship, "but please go ahead if it is your habit."

"I meant tea or coffee," said Libby through gritted teeth.

"Well, this is hardly a social call, is it?" was the ungracious reply. Libby silently counted to ten and wished David would hurry up.

There was an uncomfortable silence, then she heard, with huge relief, his footsteps down the hall and she excused herself and went out to warn him that their visitors were already ensconced.

"I swear to God, David," she hissed, "If that old bag insults me once more, I'm going to bloody swing for her."

"Hello to you, too, love," he said with a grin, "Now stop letting her wind you up. That's exactly the result she wants. We can get through this if we keep calm."

There was a tiny little bit of Libby that was delighted when David walked into the room and Lady Allingham immediately turned on him. She felt it served him right for being so bloody laid back.

"David, I can't imagine why you have come dashing over here. We really don't need you. This is a private family matter."

For once Libby witnessed her husband with nothing to say, so she stepped swiftly in, "As my husband, David is family," she said curtly.

"Not for the purposes of this conversation," said the older woman nastily, "however, we can kill two birds with one stone now that you are here. Richard has something to say, don't you Richard?"

Rick's mouth opened and closed like a landed fish, his face puce. His eyes sent messages of regret and apology to his old friend, but the words wouldn't come. His mother threw him a look of utter disdain, "Very well, I shall say it for you. Richard feels that it is no longer appropriate that your little garden centre provides for the needs of the Allingham Estate. We didn't appreciate that dreadful newspaper article using us for cheap publicity and we'll get a much better deal from one of the larger companies. I'm sorry a long association has to come to an end, but that's business I'm afraid."

David was very still, very quiet and Libby recognized the danger signals. Her husband lost his temper probably only twice a year, if that, but when he lost it by God, he really lost it. She saw now that if David spoke it would kill forever any chance that he and Richard would ever regain their long friendship. They not only did business together, but spent every summer playing cricket together. If David was forced out of his cricket team by this fallout, she knew he would lose a huge part of his social life and the pure love of the sport he had played for so long.

She laid a comforting and restraining hand on his arm, "Not to worry David," she said softly, but with underlying malice, "when Maddie is running the estate she wouldn't dream of dealing with anyone but you."

That was a dart that hit home. Colour rose in Lady Allingham's cheeks and she glared at Libby, no longer ever pretending to be civil.

"You ridiculous creature! Do you really imagine this fantasy created by your strange sister has the least chance of coming to fruition?"

"Well, you obviously do, or you wouldn't be here!"

The older woman rose to her feet, "Come along, Richard, I'm obviously wasting my time trying to be reasonable with these people," she spat the final word as though it were the worst insult she could offer, "If this is what you want, young woman," she hissed at Libby, "Then we shall indeed see you in court!"

"I'll look forward to it," said Libby coolly.

"You'll regret it," said Lady Allingham and swept out. Libby had a sudden vision of her ancestress being bullied by the antecedents of this same woman and she felt a sudden surge of violence rising in her breast. It was rare for Libby to want to hit another human being – so rare as to be non-existent, except perhaps, she thought wryly, where Brendan was concerned – but she could gladly have tripped the old trout up and pummelled her into the ground. She drew in deep breath and focused on her husband. He looked stunned and could barely bring himself to speak to Rick, who waited for his mother to flounce out of earshot before he tried to apologise and explain to his friend.

"I'm so sorry, Dave, I really am. This has nothing to do with me. She came up with this petty revenge all on her own."

"Why don't you have the guts to stand up to her, then?" asked Libby bitterly, aching with sympathy for her man. She had never seen him so gutted and it gave her a physical pain to witness his distress.

Rick turned pained eyes upon her, "You don't understand, Libby. Every day of my life I'm a disappointment to her. Do you understand how it feels to know your own mother wishes you had never been born – or at least born differently? She's terrified that I'll never marry, that the Allinghams will end with me. How can I ever go against her when that's the burden I bear?"

Libby was not in the mood to be sympathetic, "Oh, don't be so pathetic, Rick," she said harshly, "You could enter into a civil partnership with your boyfriend and adopt or have a child by a surrogate – your mother is living in the dark ages!"

"No, I couldn't! Not the way the entail is tied up – don't you think I've tried to have it altered? If I don't marry and have a son, everything goes to a distant cousin."

"Well, why the hell does she care? She won't be around to see it."

"It's all principles with her. You've no idea how strongly all that Queen and Country stuff runs through her veins. She and my father are second cousins and only married for the sake of the estate. She thinks if she didn't marry for love, but duty, then I should do the same."

"Perhaps you should, and stop being so selfish," said Libby, "Anyway, I wouldn't worry about it, because there's a good chance Maddie is going to win this court case and it will be her son who inherits, not yours!"

Libby didn't notice, but this final remark seemed to have a surprising effect on Rick. The anguish faded from his face and he looked merely thoughtful. He bade them farewell and shook the still silent David's hand, then followed his mother down the hall, only to return a few seconds later with a large brown envelope in his hands,

"This postman just handed this to me at the door," he said, thrusting the package at David and making good his escape.

The young couple looked at each other when the sound of the slammed front door faded away.

"Well, that's that," said David, after a painful silence, "The Allinghams are my biggest client. Without the year round plantings and estate maintenance, I doubt I can keep the business running. That's five people out of work."

Libby moved across to him and tried to put her arms around him, "Don't say that, David. Don't just give in. We can get through this. The money Aunt Lil ..."

"Don't say it! Don't you dare to offer to bail me out with your money, Libby." he cut across her pleadings and shrugged himself out of her embrace, "I swear I won't be responsible for my actions if you say one more word about it."

"But," she spluttered, hardly able to speak so stunned and angry was she. Why had this suddenly become such an issue? He had always known she had enough money to keep them both quite comfortably, "David, it isn't my money. We are married, it belongs to us both. What is wrong with that?"

"I don't want to discuss it," he said coldly, "but it will be a freezing day in hell when I allow myself to be kept by a woman."

She staggered away from him, horrified that she was suddenly seeing a side to his nature that she had no idea existed. She knew he was quaintly old-fashioned at times, always wanting to pay the bill when they ate out, walking on the outside of the pavement when they were near a road to protect her from traffic, not liking her to go to the bar when they went to the pub, but she had no idea that his medieval streak went quite as deep as this. A dozen protestations and arguments sprang to her mind, but she rejected them all. To say anything now would simply cause another huge row. He was shocked and upset by Rick's betrayal and he needed time to get over it. Best to leave him to cool down.

"I'll make a cup of tea," she said softly.

"Yeah, why not? That'll solve everything, won't it? I could kill your bloody sister with her stupid ideas!"

She wanted to tell him to go and do something obscene, but she kept telling herself that it wasn't real, none of this was the real David and when he had a moment to think about it, he would realize that he was blaming her for something that wasn't her fault.

She had thought things couldn't get any worse, but while she was in the kitchen making the tea, he opened the envelope. She came back bearing two mugs to find him staring at what looked like a bundle of photographs.

"What have you got there?" she asked, wondering why he looked so livid. Her heart sank as she wondered what the hell Maddie had done now – she couldn't imagine anything else could make him look so furious.

He held the pictures out to her, "You tell me," he said.

She put the cups down and took the photos. It took her a moment to analyse what she was seeing. That was Matt Piper kissing some girl. Why had these been sent here? The next picture was a girl hugging Dan from the library – no, not a girl, not just any woman, it was her. These were grainy, indistinct pictures of her with Matt and Dan. But she had never kissed either of them, she was sure … or was she? Hadn't she hugged Matt once when he told her he would arrange for her to meet Tess Brookes?

Her husband was looking at her, searching her face for what? Some sign of guilt or innocence? How dare he? How dare he, even for a single second, believe that she might be guilty of having an affair?

"These have been photo-shopped," she said curtly, "But I'm appalled to see that you have taken them to be genuine. What do you really think of me, David, if you can believe I would ever sneak around behind your back for a cheap thrill with other men?"

"I never thought you could speak to a journalist when I specifically asked you not to nor allow your sister to wreck my business, but you've done that, why not this?"

"I'm telling you that I haven't had an affair, that there is nothing between me and these men but friendship. As far as I'm concerned that should be enough."

He rose wearily to his feet, "You're probably right, Libby. I should know whether you are capable of lying and cheating – but the truth is, I don't. We've never discussed my first marriage much, but I can tell you now that she was unfaithful to me. She had an affair and I didn't know a thing about it until she told me and left me. I had no bloody idea, because that's the kind of trusting idiot I am. So you'll forgive me if I say that I need a bit of time and space to process all this."

She swallowed deeply, trying to keep control, but all the while feeling as though the walls of the room were falling in on her and that she was floating up and out of her body.

"Are you saying you are leaving me?" she managed to croak

through dry lips.

"I'm saying that I think we could benefit from a few days away from each other. I'll camp out in the office for a while. You can get hold of me if you need me."

She wanted to stop him, to bar his way, but instead she just stood there like a shop-window manikin and let him brush past her. It wasn't until she heard the door close behind him that she pulled herself out of her reverie and ran after him. He was already half way down to the road when she caught up with him.

"David, please …"

He wasn't looking at her, his eyes were on the path ahead and he suddenly gave a humourless grunt of laughter, "You didn't waste any time," he said bitterly and speeded up, desperate now to get away from her.

"What ..?" she had been concentrating on his face, trying to get him to look at her and read the truth in her eyes, but now she hesitated, confused by the comment and transferred her gaze to her surroundings.

Striding up the path, his face set and grim, was Matt Piper. Her heart sank. How much more bad luck was she going to endure today? Of all the moments the policeman could have chosen to visit, this had to be the very worst.

"Don't be stupid, David, I had no idea he was coming," she called after her husband's retreating back. He ignored her and carried on walking. Matt glanced at him as they passed, but he said nothing and made no attempt to make any sort of greeting, not even a polite smile.

"Can we talk, Libby?" asked Matt, barely able to control his anger.

"Not really," she answered, "my husband has just left me and I've got more important things on my mind just now."

"So, he's had the photos too?" asked Matt severely, "Well that makes two of us with our relationships in shreds. I think we really do need to talk."

Libby felt nausea sweep over her as the import of his words hit home. Tess had seen those pictures too. What the hell must she be thinking of her? Someone she had trusted, after months of isolation and depression, and it now appeared that person had been betraying her in the worst possible way.

"Come inside," she said curtly, "You are right. We need to get to the bottom of this."

She was confident that David would come to his senses after a day or two apart, but she had no such faith that she could convince someone as emotionally damaged as Tess Brookes that she and Matt were nothing but good friends – and judging by the policeman's expression of mixed fury and despair, he feared the same.

CHAPTER FORTY-ONE

Darkness made it easier for Lazarus and Stonier to bundle Arabella into a carriage outside the railway station without being observed. One look at her white face, and heavy-lidded eyes convinced the policemen that far from trying to get her back to Havering Hall that night, it would be much more sensible to take her to her cousin Constance.

Though the journey was one of mere minutes, the girl was swooning by the time they reached their destination and Stonier hurried to hammer on the door, while Lazarus lifted her and carried her up the path, having thrown a substantially larger fee than was strictly necessary to the delighted cab driver. What did he care? It wasn't his money.

Once again the mistress of the house had been abed, though reading and not asleep, when Sally ran to answer their imperious knocking, and she came hurrying downstairs, agog for news of her young relative.

The relief and delight on her face when she saw Lazarus carrying his precious load made all that he had been through worthwhile and he grinned at her with genuine pleasure, "We have had quite an adventure, Miss Allingham," he assured her jovially.

"I'm sure you have," she answered, but the expression in her eyes said much more.

Arabella was carried up to the pretty spare bedroom at the back of the house and Sally busied herself making beef-tea and bread sops to tempt the appetite of the young prodigal, whilst Constance, in the inept way of those not used to domestication, made tea and sandwiches for the ravenous policemen. Her bread was cut far too thick, and the tea was too weak because she had failed to wait for the kettle to boil before pouring the water on the leaves, but neither man was in any mood to be critical.

They gave her a rousing and occasionally embroidered account of their rescue mission, but all the while Lazarus watched her face, enjoying the change of emotion flitting across her features as they recounted their adventures, like the shadows of scudding clouds racing over the high hillsides of the moors.

When the story was concluded and they told how they had secreted Arabella away and ensured she would not be required to appear in court at the trial of the odious Soper, Constance clapped her hands in delight, "My uncle will be so relieved that all is still unknown. You deserve a reward and I shall ask that he is generous."

Both men protested at this, and Lazarus became their spokesman, "I must ask you not to do any such thing, Miss Allingham. What Stonier and I have done, we have done for Arabella's sake and nothing more need be said on the matter. It is over and forgotten. To reward us for doing the right thing, would be an insult. In fact, you can perform a small commission for me. I have here the money your uncle gave us to use should we need it. We have spent some, obviously, but the majority is there for you to return to him. The sooner the better."

He handed her the roll of notes and a few coins and she gasped when she realized how much she held, "There is a great deal here," she said softly.

"There is. I needed a large sum in case Soper evaded justice and I needed to bribe him to part with Arabella, luckily that didn't happen."

She gazed at the cash for a few seconds, then raised her eyes to his face, "Do you think it would be very bad of me to take a little of this and pay Will Carter's debt to the newspaper vendor? At least that way if he ever comes home, he will not be at risk of arrest."

Stonier looked shocked that a gently raised lady should even suggest such a thing, but Lazarus was much more hard-headed. He too wanted Will Carter cleared and he knew the piffling sum owed by the boy would scarcely be noticed by a man as rich as Allingham.

"As to that, Miss, I leave it to your conscience. I suppose if you were to deprive yourself of several shopping trips for which your uncle would expect to pay, then you could be said to have paid him back. And in truth, he did get his daughter back with far less outlay than he was expecting."

"I will make it right, I promise," she said firmly, "But I must also make sure that no blame can be laid at your door. Do you have a list of what you spent?"

"Stonier does," said Lazarus with some amusement. His instinct had been to spend Allingham's money lavishly, give him what was left and leave it at that – let the old miser dare to ask for an account, when they had saved him a fortune, rescued his daughter and protected her reputation! But Stonier had been adamant that they make a note of every penny.

"Give me your notes, Mr Stonier. I will present it to my uncle and make sure I admit that the extra money was taken by me. He shall not be told what I wanted it for, and I doubt he will pursue the matter when he finds Arabella here, safe and sound, but if he does, I shall think of something, never fear."

By this juncture, Stonier was ready for his bed and tired of the whole enterprise, so he capitulated, albeit reluctantly, and handed over the pages torn from his notebook.

Presently Sally came down and announced that Arabella had eaten every scrap of food put before her and was now drifting off to sleep.

Lazarus and Stonier rose at once, aware that it was far too late for them to be in the house with two lone young women and a single servant. They thanked their hostess and bade her good night and she politely followed them down the hall to see them off at the door. Stonier was eager to be off home and was half way down the path before Lazarus had even moved off the door step. He held out his hand and when Constance took it in her own, he bowed over and kissed her lightly on her knuckles.

"Inspector Lazarus," she said formally, "I cannot begin to thank you for all you have done."

"Think nothing of it, Miss Allingham," he responded, "Merely doing my duty, nothing more."

"Oh, I think you have done a great deal more than your duty, sir."

He straightened up and smiled at her, "Good night, Constance. May I take the liberty of calling on you and Miss Allingham tomorrow to see that she is recovering from her ordeal?"

"We would be disappointed not to see you. Good night."

He half turned away, then recalled something and came back to her, his hand withdrawing something from his pocket.

"Constance, I give this to you now on the strict understanding that it stays between us two. I acquired the information in a somewhat nefarious manner and I prefer not to have to explain myself to my superior."

"Oh? How exciting. What is it?"

He gave her the notes he had made – was it only that morning? It seemed eons ago since the meeting with Allingham's lawyer.

"These are addresses of several of your maternal relatives. I understand that there have been several attempts by them to gain access to you, but it has always been blocked by your uncle and his representatives. I believe an approach by you would be welcomed most warmly, but I leave it to you to decide whether to contact them."

She looked at him in amazement, clasping the paper to her breast as if it were a most precious child, "Truly, Danby? You have found my mother's family for me?"

"I have. You perhaps need never be lonely again."

With that he walked away into the darkness and she stayed on the step and listened until the last echo of his footfalls were lost to her in the night.

* * *

Everything, it seemed, had returned to normal. Arabella was whisked back to Havering Hall in the middle of the following night and once safely ensconced there occurred a similar subterfuge to her departure some weeks before whereby a bundled and veiled figure was brought back in a carriage from the seaside.

The girl was pale and thin enough to convince all who saw her that she had indeed been dreadfully poorly, but was now at home and on the mend. The vague rumours that had begun to circulate about the disappearance of she and Marcus Soper at the same time were swiftly eclipsed when Josette Bennett and her young lover also absconded.

Lazarus took little notice of the gossip. From what he recalled of the wanton behaviour of the flighty Mrs Bennett at Lady Stafford-Naylor's ball, it had only been a matter of time before she grew tired of kowtowing to her elderly husband and his bullying mother and took to her heels with her lover in tow.

All this changed, however, when the two were found down a country lane, a dry-stone wall collapsed upon them, he quite dead, she unconscious and barely alive.

This might, perhaps, have been dismissed as a dreadful accident but for two things. The first was that a scrap of paper was found clasped in the dead man's hand.

"As ye sow, so shall ye reap" was the legend written upon it. Lazarus knew without doubt that he was now faced with yet another murder – two, if Josette should succumb to her injuries.

The second occurred when Dr Scattergood was sent for and asked to perform a post mortem on the young man. After the operation, Lazarus, Stonier and the doctor all met in Lazarus' office and discussed the result of the investigation. To their surprise he was found to have eaten a meal of roast quail just prior to his demise.

"No poisonous toadstools, doctor?" asked Lazarus, "Then how the devil did the killer manage to subdue two healthy young people? They were not tied up, and one was hardly like to stand meekly by while he killed the other, then lie down to die!"

"I agree. But quail is a very telling clue."

"It is?"

"It is. Quails can eat hemlock seed with no ill effect – however, it renders the flesh of the bird poisonous."

"I see. Are we to assume the young lady also ate the quail, Doctor?" asked Lazarus.

"I suspect so."

"Then why is she still alive? Surely they were poisoned, then crushed?"

"Sadly not," said Scattergood grimly, "This was a very specific toxin which rendered the victims paralysed, but still very much alive and *compos mentis* when the wall was pushed onto them."

There was a horrified silence, then Lazarus ventured to clarify, "You mean they could see the stones falling onto them, but could not move to protect themselves, not even raise a hand?"

"Exactly so. The action of a truly diabolical mind. Whoever we are looking for, Lazarus, needs to be caught, and quickly. God knows what other horrors he has planned."

"But why?" asked Stonier, intrigued despite his repugnance, "What is behind it all? Most murders, I know, are committed for money or in a passion of anger or jealousy. These seem to have no rhyme nor reason to them that I can fathom."

"I think your clue lies in the notes left by the bodies. A quotation from the Bible, coupled with two young people known to be committing adultery. If effect, they were stoned to death for their sin. Mollie was killed for conceiving a child out of wedlock. This is someone who has a deeply religious belief that prompts them to mete out their own form of rough justice."

"But why only Mollie and not young Crabtree?" asked Lazarus.

"The killer may not have known the identity of the father at the time he poisoned Mollie, he had, after all, done all he could to hide from the responsibility of fatherhood. Crabtree may be in danger if his name has become common knowledge."

"What about Josette? She still lives."

"She may also be in jeopardy if she ever wakes. For the moment she hovers between life and death and the murderer may feel that the rest can safely be left in God's hands for the moment at least."

"So we cannot even use her as bait to draw him out?"

"Too dangerous. He may outwit us and succeed in killing her – how would that look on your record?" protested Stonier.

"Very well," said Lazarus testily, aware that Stonier disapproved of any such tricks. He was a man who believed in straight dealing. He would feel he had cheated should he ever resort to lies and subterfuge, whereas Lazarus felt that anything which brought about a good result was permissible.

"What else do you suggest?"

Scattergood frowned. "We still come up against the same problem. Yet again this killer has managed to cook and serve a meal without being obvious about it. That points to someone who lives alone."

"Or two killers working together?" suggested Stonier diffidently. He always felt a little intimidated by the doctor, who seemed to have a wealth of knowledge that went well beyond medicine. That about the quail, for instance. Who the devil knew about stuff like that?

Scattergood seemed to take the suggestion seriously and mulled over it for a moment or two, "Umm, possible, but I would say unlikely. It would require the other partner to have a similar religious mania or to be so in thrall to the killer that they would do anything to please them. That usually means a man and a woman and I don't think we have any suspects who fit the criteria, do we?"

"We don't have any suspects at all," grumbled Lazarus, "I was convinced it was Crabtree, trying to hide his shame, then Janet Riley came to our notice and we thought she might have dosed the girl in error. But neither was really credible, especially after the Soffley woman was shot with a bow and arrow."

"That could have been Crabtree," Stonier reminded him.

"I suppose so," agreed Lazarus gloomily, "Do we have the list of all those who take part in Allingham's competition?"

"We do, and it includes practically everyone who moves in their social circle, including Bembridge the vicar, believe it or not."

Lazarus sat up straight in his chair, "Did you say Bembridge?"

"Yes, but surely you don't think the vicar?"

"Don't I? Give me that list."

He scanned the names but none other leapt out at him like Bembridge's.

"Let's examine the evidence carefully," he said after a moment, trying not to show his growing excitement. The more he thought about it, the more prime the vicar was as a culprit.

"Go ahead," said the doctor, obviously interested and not inclined to dismiss the inspector's suspicions out of hand.

Lazarus pointed to his fingers as he counted down the reasons for his theory,

"One, the man showed no forgiveness towards Mollie, even after her death. He evidently felt she had deserved death for her sins. Two, he can use a bow and arrow. Three, he was present on the evening that Lady Stafford-Naylor was gossiping about Josette Bennett and her lover. Four, he has access to the vicarage kitchen because Mrs Waters doesn't live in."

"Interesting," admitted Stonier, "But how could he cook and have visitors without the curate knowing about it?"

"The curate is a dreamer. You've seen him yourself, Tom. He hardly knows where he is most of the time. I'll bet he could sleep through anything – anyway it would be easy enough for Bembridge to dose him with some sleeping draught on the nights he wants to carry out one of his dastardly murders."

Lazarus slapped the table, sure that he had found his man. Scattergood and Stonier looked less than convinced.

"How are we going to prove it?" asked Stonier.

"I need to get into his study. We need to prove that he knows about poisons and I'll bet my life one of the books on his shelves tells him all about toxins. I presume your information came from some tome or other, Scattergood?"

"It did. I can give you the name of the book you'll probably find there."

"Good. Come Stonier. We finally have something to work on!"

CHAPTER FORTY-TWO

Disappointment was Lazarus' over-riding emotion when he called at the vicarage to try and see Bembridge's library. The vicar himself was not at home, but the curate was only too happy to allow the inspector to look around, though he looked bewildered as to the reason why anyone should want to.

He happily led the policeman directly to the book Dr Scattergood had named as the most likely source of information. It was an ancient tome, in Latin, and covered with a layer of dust which spoke of it's not having been moved off the shelf for a month at least, probably longer. That meant nothing of course. The plan could have been made long ago and the killer had merely waited for the time to be right to strike, but somehow Lazarus felt that was unlikely.

The kitchen also defied logic. Mr Holbrook assured Lazarus that his bedroom was directly above the kitchen and that he was an exceptionally light sleeper. He was sure that he would hear the clatter of pans or the sound of voices, should anyone ever use the room late at night. Beside which, though Mrs Waters did not live in, the scullery maid did. A middle-aged woman, she had very obvious mental retardation, but was bright enough to answer Lazarus' questions about the coming and going in the house, and she assured him that she had never seen or heard the vicar or the curate set foot in the kitchen with the purpose of cooking – and in the case of the vicar, at all. Lazarus could well believe that Bembridge had never lowered himself to visit the nether regions of his home.

This, of course, did not preclude the curate being complicit, but there was something about his open, simple face which made Lazarus believe him.

He left the house frustrated. Yes, Bembridge owned the book on poisons and he had access to a kitchen, but something did not fit and try as he might, Lazarus could not imagine bringing such flimsy evidence before his superior and expecting him to allow an arrest. He needed more.

He also had other tasks to perform. Young Crabtree had to be warned that his life might well be in danger and reaching him was going to be easier said than done. The inspector felt that he had no choice but to call in a favour from Lord Allingham. The elder Crabtree was his friend, after all, and he would surely heed a warning from a friend rather than from a police officer who had been trying to arrest his son only weeks before.

As always he was reluctant to approach the old man directly, so he called on Constance in the hope that she might agree to act as go-between.

Not only was she pleased to do so, she happily suggested that they bypass Lord Allingham completely and that she would go to see Lawrie herself and have a quiet word with him.

If Lazarus could have foreseen the result of this call, he would have forbidden Constance to make it, but sadly he was not possessed of second sight. How could he know that she would meet again a young man who had been pursuing her for months, but who had been too bashful to make his intentions plain?

Edward Moncrieff would have been recognized by Lazarus as the young fellow who was too tall and thin for his suit at the Stafford-Naylor ball, but he would hardly have recalled his name. He had been part of a group of youthful friends of Lawrie and Arabella and had frequented parties, routs and card games purely so he could moon longingly at Constance.

For her part, Constance was suddenly ready to look at him with different eyes. She knew she had been foolish to fall in love with a man she believed to be happily married now she was determined to be sensible. When he stuttered a small compliment to her over tea at the Crabtree's, she smiled and encouraged him to talk to her about his family and his future ambitions. Within an hour he was chatting delightedly to her, within a week he was asking her uncle for permission to pay court to her.

Sir William took her warning seriously and arranged for Lawrie to go off to London to stay with his maternal grandmother, though the young man protested that he would die of boredom.

"Better to die of boredom in London, than a knife between your ribs in Braxton," said Sir William severely, "Allingham has nothing but praise for the work Inspector Lazarus does – if he thinks you are at risk, then by God, you will listen to his advice and get yourself out of danger!"

Another week passed and nothing more happened. Josette was still hanging on to life, but she was growing weaker. Lawrie was safely in London; Moncrieff was a frequent caller at Constance's home and she was now able to take his visits for she had a companion to add an air of respectability.

Letters had flown between her and her newly-discovered relations and within a very short time, Eliza Jane Wakefield had joined her for a visit. Jane, as she was known to her family, was Constance's mother's sister's daughter. She was slight, with blond ringlets and the bluest eyes, the colour of summer skies and the most joyful person Constance had ever met. She lived life with a relish which her cousin wished she could emulate. How wonderful it must be to be so eternally happy and to desire only to bring some measure of happiness to others.

One evening when they sat before a fire, lit because autumn was drawing on and the nights were getting chilly, Constance bravely confided in her cousin about her feelings for the Inspector. For the first time since they met, Jane's sunny countenance clouded with worry.

"Oh, my dear, you must stop seeing him at once. Nothing but heartbreak and scandal could ever come of such a friendship!"

"I know, but oh, Jane, I do love him so …" Constance broke into sobs and her cousin could do nothing but hold her close and wait for the storm to subside.

The following day when Lazarus called it was Jane who saw him, after sending Constance upstairs, "Leave this to me, dear Coz, I will tell the inspector, in the nicest possible way, that you are no longer able to see him."

Constance sat tensely on the edge of her bed, straining to hear what was being said in the parlour, but able to make out nothing but the rise and fall of conversation. She was relieved that voices were never raised, but part of her was disappointed when Lazarus seemed to take his dismissal with no protest whatsoever.

When she heard the front door close, she ran down the stairs and burst into the parlour, "What did he say, Jane? Did he seem …" she trailed off, aware that she should not care how he seemed, nor be interested in what he had said.

Jane merely looked puzzled, "He is quite a strange man, isn't he?" she asked diffidently.

"Why? What on earth happened?"

"Well, I told him that we felt that perhaps he should not call on you anymore and he said that was quite understandable."

"That was all?"

"No. He added that it was time things were put on an official footing and that he would see your uncle."

It was Constance's turn to frown, "What on earth did he mean by that I wonder?"

"I have no idea. He then asked me if I was happy here and if you and I were finding enough to occupy us, so I told him about how we had been coerced by the vicar into helping out in his soup kitchen."

"What happened then?"

"He suddenly looked as though I had said something revelatory for he asked in a very excited voice if we cooked the soup here and I said, no, of course not. We use the range in the odd little scullery at the back of the church hall. He clapped his hands together so hard that I was almost startled out of my wits. 'By God,' he said, 'I've found the kitchen!' then he made his excuses and left."

"How very odd," said Constance.

"I thought so," agreed Jane.

* * *

Stonier was not quite as excited about the discovery of the kitchen as Lazarus had hoped.

"I concede that it is an interesting find, old friend, and it does solve the mystery of how our killer could cook his poisoned food, but how did he entice his victims there? And more importantly, who is it?"

"Bembridge, of course. Who else?"

"The curate, any one of the half dozen or so ladies who help out with the soup kitchen and the dozen or so servants who help the ladies," suggested Stonier wearily, "they all have equal access to the range."

Lazarus paced the floor, "Of course you are right, dammit! And how would someone as lacking in social graces as Bembridge persuade young people to join him for a late night meal?"

"He could only do so by offering a solution to their dilemmas. Let us go through this one step at a time."

Stonier nodded, willing to allow his companion the benefit of the doubt. It was true that the place where the food was cooked had been their major stumbling block, so let Lazarus postulate and maybe he would hit upon the correct interpretation of the facts.

"Go on, I'm listening."

"Well, we have Mollie, pregnant and terrified. Eliza told us that she had taken to spending more time at the church, so we'll assume that for all his bluster, Bembridge was able to convince her that he could help her. Perhaps he told her that he would give her the money to leave town, to go somewhere she was unknown. He may even have told her that he had arranged for her baby to be adopted by some childless couple. She is sworn to secrecy and told to meet him at the church hall where he will give her a sustaining meal before seeing her onto the early morning stagecoach."

"It's sounding plausible so far. But why did she go home afterwards?"

"I'm only guessing – perhaps he had some other tale for her – but it could be that she began to feel unwell and he advised her to go home, rest, and try again the next day. She would have no idea that there would never be a tomorrow for her."

"Poor lass," said Stonier with a sad shake of his head, "all she ever wanted was to be loved and she trusted all the wrong people because of it."

"Lawrie Crabtree has a lot to answer for. If he had behaved like a gentleman, none of this need have happened."

"Precisely. Now, what about the Sofffley woman. Are we agreed she was killed because she stepped in front of 'Liza Dunne?"

"I believe so. He wanted 'Liza dead because he knew that sooner or later we were going to question her again and she was going to give him away, even though she had no idea that she held the information. We kept on going back to her, so he panicked and started to believe that Mollie had told her more than she had."

"Why do you suppose he used the bow and arrow?"

"I suspect he doesn't have a gun. Not many vicars do, to be fair. If he had been the sort who lived in the countryside and hunted, then he might have held a shotgun, but why would a cleric who lived in town need a weapon? He couldn't get near to 'Liza because he thought she knew who he was and if he had approached her, she would have recognized him and screamed blue murder. The only way to get rid of her was to shoot her from a hidden spot near the shop. He probably wandered around, looking for a suitable vantage point – who would question a vicar on his daily round of visits to the sick and dying?"

"You're right. He could have hidden the bow and arrow days before and waited for his chance to kill her. But what about the other two? Josette and her lover?"

"He may have told them that he sympathised with their plight, that he wanted to help them run away together."

"And he transported their bodies how?"

"The vicarage trap. He can use it whenever he likes without question."

Stonier looked as though he was processing this information carefully before he gave a grudging grunt of approval, "I think you may have something, Danby, but I can't for the life of me work out how the devil we are going to prove any of it."

"I know that. So far he's been too clever to get caught and it does no good to know how he did it if we can't pin it on him."

"So how do we catch him out?"

"I'm damned if I know, Tom."

CHAPTER FORTY-THREE

PRESENT

The photos were scattered on the coffee table and Matt stood and stared at them until Libby, deeply embarrassed, gathered them up and stuffed them back into the envelope.

"Do you want a drink?" she asked.

"Yes – a large one," he said, then shook his head as common sense reasserted itself,

"No, forget it. I have to drive back and the last thing I need now is to be caught drinking and driving. That really would put the tin hat on it!"

Under normal circumstances her response to that comment would have been a cheerful offer of a bed for the night, but that was hardly appropriate so she shrugged and said, "Well, I hope you won't mind if I have one!"

"Knock yourself out," he grunted, "Do you mind if I sit down?"

"Be my guest," she said with an expansive gesture of welcome and went off to pour herself a large glass of wine.

When she returned he had taken the pictures out again and was scrutinising them, the policeman in him had obviously woken up and taken over from the hurt and pitiful lover, she thought a trifle bitterly.

"I thought maybe they'd been photo shopped," she suggested hopefully. He looked up at the sound of her voice and shook his head, "I don't think so. They look pretty genuine to me, but what I don't understand is why someone has bothered to follow us around and take pictures. What the hell is going on, Libby?"

"How should I know? I'm as shocked as you are. It's not like we are actually having an affair, so why have we been made to look as though we have?"

He scanned the pictures again, pulling them close to his face so that he could be sure not to miss a single thing, "I think they've been taken with a long lens. Now that's the sort of kit used by paparazzi or private detectives. Not many ordinary folk have access to expensive camera equipment."

"Well since neither of us is famous enough to warrant tabloid interference, that only leaves a private eye."

"I agree, but PI's don't work for nothing. Someone is paying for this – but who?"

"You're sure it's not Tess? Not to be critical or anything, but you are a good bit younger than her and she is somewhat paranoid after her injury last year."

He shook his head, "I can't see it, I really can't. Everything you say is true, but its just not the way me and Tess are with each other. We've both sworn that if we ever want out, we just say so. She knows I wouldn't cheat – there's no point. I can walk away any time without recriminations."

As a woman Libby was well aware that very little of what Matt was saying was actually true. There wasn't a woman alive who would agree to the terms he had just laid out – oh, they would promise it alright, but follow it through? Not a chance. However, she was certainly not going to say so aloud, so she shrugged and said amiably, "Okay, we'll cross Tess off the list for the moment. Anyone else? Past wife, girlfriend, lover? Anyone upset that you are now seeing Tess?"

"Hey, just a minute," he protested, "These pictures are all about you, not me! Don't forget they show you and some other guy as well as you and me."

"Dan," said Libby absent-mindedly, distracted by the truth of what he was saying.

"What?"

"Dan, his name is Dan."

"Forgive me, but I don't care!"

"Alright! Keep your hair on. I was just saying."

"Look Libby, can we just keep to the point? I'm sorry if I

snapped, but my whole life is going down the pan and I'm not really interested in your love life other than in the way it affects me!"

Libby gave him her most quelling look, "You're going the right way to get a smack in the mouth, pal! Dan is not my lover any more than you are. What is the matter with everyone? Why am I suddenly being painted as some scarlet woman?"

Matt seemed pretty angry for a second, then he regained his sense of humour and grinned, shrugging his broad shoulders in a gesture of surrender, "You're right, I'm sorry. Someone is playing silly buggers with both our lives and we need to stick together and trust each other to sort it out. Now, let's start again. If we're agreed Tess isn't behind this, then who else? Could your husband have a suspicious mind? Have you done anything to worry him?"

"No, never! David trusts me, I swear he does."

"Didn't you say he's just walked out on you? Doesn't sound terribly trusting to me, if you don't mind my saying so."

"Yeah, thanks for the reminder! If you must know he's mad about other things, and these photos are the proverbial last straw."

The policeman digested this in silence, then appeared to make a decision, "We can't be certain that it wasn't your husband either, but I'm inclined to discount him. Why would he spend money on a PI when he can cause a row with you and walk out any time he chooses? As indeed he just has! His only possible reason would be money. Is he likely to sue you for your inheritance if you're caught in the wrong?"

Libby grimaced and shook her head, "Considering that one of the things we just had words about was me offering to bank roll his business if he loses the Allingham account, I'd say that was a no, wouldn't you?"

He evidently found this convincing enough to move on, "Okay, we'll discount David too. Now you asked me impertinent questions about my past, what about yours?"

"I may have asked, but you didn't answer," she pointed out reasonably, "But since we are being frank, I'll admit that the only person I know of who would play this sort of mind game is Brendan – but he's in jail and I'm assuming he's not able to hire private detectives from the clink."

There was another stunned silence, then Matt said carefully, "Who told you he was behind bars?"

"You did!"

"That was weeks ago. Haven't you had a visit from someone in uniform telling you that he's out?"

It was Libby's turn to be knocked breathless by an astounding revelation. Her mouth dropped open and it was several seconds before she recovered sufficiently to say, "What are you talking about?" in a small voice, as though asking him to repeat it would give a different answer.

"I'm really sorry, Libby," said Matt as gently as he could, "It's obvious that there has been a huge cock-up somewhere. Brendan was released a few weeks ago on bail, pending his appeal. They were supposed to send a family liaison officer to see you and explain that though he was out, he had been warned to stay away from you. I can't believe they didn't do it."

"Why the hell didn't you tell me?" she snapped, her stomach twisted into knots of fear and anguish at the thought that she had been happily running around, not knowing that the loony who had tried to kill her was free and could have come after her at any point in the last few weeks.

"I can only apologise again. I honestly thought you knew."

"You're an idiot!" she yelled, suddenly furious, "and the rest of the police force is bloody useless! That maniac wants me dead! And he still has my house keys. That was why my furniture had been moved around the other day!"

He held up a hand as though he were directing traffic, "Whoa, back up! What did you just say?"

She explained quickly about the morning she and David had found the sitting room re-arranged and how later it had all been put back, though David had denied doing either. She blushed to the roots of her hair as she admitted that she had thought she was being haunted by a poltergeist, by an angry Decima Watkins, perhaps.

"Was that what that newspaper story was all about then?" he asked, and fortunately for him he managed not to grin. He had read the article and thought her just the tiniest bit hysterical, though he hadn't said so, because Tess had found the whole thing fascinating and was already planning a story along similar lines.

"Yes, it was. That journalist, Joanne what's-her-name caught me on the day it happened and I was still freaked out, which was why she found it so easy to pump me for information. If I'd known Brendan was out, I would have changed the locks and none of this would have happened."

"I can't believe you didn't change the locks last year when it all kicked off in the first place," he said mildly.

"Oh, just fuck right off, smart arse!" she growled back, well aware that he was right, but not wanting to hear it just now.

He began to laugh and she glared at him until the sound of his mirth finally won her over and she began to grin, "What's so funny?" she asked.

"You. Have you any idea of the shaven-headed, cauliflower-eared tough-nut who was the last person to swear at me like that?"

She had to admit he had a point, "My turn to say sorry," she giggled, "It wasn't very lady-like, was it?"

"Not your finest hour," he said wryly, "Now, shall we stop abusing each other and get back to a spot of detective work?"

"Okay. What have you got, Sherlock?"

He picked up the envelope once more and examined it.

"You know, I'm beginning to think I might just know who our private dick is. This post office frank is local. Now if you are taking a package to be posted, you generally wrap it up at home then take it to your nearest post office."

"I'm agreeing so far," said Libby, suddenly interested.

"Now, I just happen to know that we only have one registered PI in the Braxton area."

"Are you sure there's only one?"

"Positive. It's a relatively small district anyway, so there's hardly enough work for more than one person, but the guy I'm thinking of likes to believe he's scared off all the competition."

"Hard is he?"

"Nope, he's a big old softie, actually, but his name is Pietro

Bonaminio and he puts it about that he has Mafioso connections."

"And does he?"

"Does he hell! His mother is a typical doting Italian mama and his dad was a baby-photographer in a department store before he retired. Pietro is about as likely to know any Mafia as I am – but it doesn't hurt his reputation any, does it?"

"And you think this might be his handiwork."

"If it's not, I'll bet he knows whose it is."

"How do we find him?"

Matt grinned, "Oh, I know where to find him – and it's a good job I decided not to have that drink, isn't it? Because it looks like I'm driving."

It crossed Libby's mind that it wasn't the best idea in the world to be getting into Matt's car, when they were supposed to be trying to convince the world they weren't having an affair, but a large glass of wine had knocked out most of her good sense and she shrugged and threw caution out of the window, along with her dignity and what was left of her reputation.

Since it was just coming to the end of office hours, they found Pietro Bonaminio tidying his desk and about to close up for the night. He recognized Matt at once and greeted him with a smile and an offer of coffee.

"You just caught me," he said in a friendly way, but there was an underlying nervousness which told Matt he knew exactly why the policeman had called on him.

"Coffee would be good," said Matt, ushering Libby into the room and pulling chairs across the room to the desk for both of them.

Libby watched him as he went across to the coffee machine. He was tall, well built – a little too well-padded if the truth were told, and his near-shaven head and goatee beard certainly fitted the image of the quintessential private dick. His swarthy complexion spoke of his Italian antecedents, but his accent was wholly British.

Fortunately there was still a little coffee left in the pot. It was lukewarm and stewed, but Libby drank it feeling she needed to sober up quickly if she was going to follow everything that happened from now on.

While his back was turned Matt took out the photos and tossed them on the desk so that they were the first thing the PI saw when he came back to sit down,

"Ah," he said, "I see there's no fooling the great detective. Okay, I hold my hands up, it was me – but I've not broken any laws."

"No one said you had," answered Matt reasonably, "but there's a good chance your client has. Who is he?"

"Come on, chum, data protection and all that," said Pietro, holding his hands out in a helpless gesture, "I'd help you if I could."

The policeman leaned forward threateningly, "You'd better help, Bonny lad," he said sarcastically, "or in the words of the old movies, I'll see you never work in this town again!"

Pietro slowly took his wrap-around sunglasses from his top pocket and put them on, "I think this conversation just ended, mate," he said, "I'd like you to leave now, before I decide that I need to call some friends of mine to show you the error of your ways."

Matt simply leaned across the desk and took the glasses off, before bending them in two until they snapped, "Don't come it with me, Bonaminio, we both know the nearest you get to the Mafia is eating your mother's spaghetti. Now who hired you?"

"Can't tell you," blustered the younger man, but he was clearly rattled by Matt's coolness.

"Alright, I can accept you have your professional ethics to think about, so I'll say a name and you can stay silent. But I expect some indication as to whether I'm right or wrong."

Pietro nodded.

"Brendan Tulliver," said Matt.

"Never heard of him," said the PI.

"What? Really?" said Libby, unable to keep her mouth shut any longer. She was viewing all this macho pretend gangster speech rather disdainfully.

"Not even the right sex," Pietro assured her.

"You were hired by a woman?" asked an astonished Matt.

"Yep," was the succinct reply.

"I bloody told you it was Tess!" raged Libby, but the detective shook his head.

"Not Tess Brookes?"

"Not unless she used a false name."

Matt and Libby exchanged confused looks, "Then who the hell is it? Ordinarily I would suspect my sister Maddie, but she's hardly likely to be playing silly games with me just at the moment. It wouldn't suit my mother to break me and David up either."

"Nice family," commented Pietro, but Libby quelled him with a glare.

Libby thought for a moment longer. Who had been around recently who had displayed enough spleen to serve her a nasty turn?

"Ilsa!" she said suddenly.

Both men looked bewildered.

"I'll bet it's Ilsa," she said again.

"Not the name I was given," said the PI.

"No, but then she wouldn't give her own name, would she?"

"Have you got a picture of her?" asked Matt suddenly.

A regretful shake of the head was halted half way through when Libby recalled that, yes, actually she did. Ilsa had been so made up at being treated to a day in Hanbury Spa, she had insisted on asking one of the staff to take a picture of them both in front of the magnificent old building on her phone. She had sent a copy to Libby the next day. Please god, don't let me have deleted it, thought Libby, as with shaking hands, and thumping heart, she scrabbled in her bag for her phone and searched its memory.

"Yes!" she shouted in triumph, "There she is. Is this the woman?" she asked Pietro, thrusting the phone under his nose. He took it from her and held it at a more usable angle.

"Brassy blond with an attitude, snotty to the point of rudeness, yes, that's her."

"But why?" asked Matt, "Isn't she supposed to be a friend of yours?"

"Let's find out," said Libby decidedly. She took the phone back and dialled Ilsa's number.

Ilsa was obviously surprised to hear from her but she hid it well. After the exchange of greetings, Libby put her on loudspeaker and lay the phone on the desk.

"I wasn't expecting to hear from you, Libby. Is there something wrong?"

"Yes, actually, there is. David just walked out on me. Some interfering bitch apparently hired a private eye to follow me around and take incriminating photos of me with various men."

"Really?" The tone didn't quite convey the required level of shock and Libby smiled grimly at her two companions.

"Yes, really, so my question is, Ilsa, why did you do it?"

"Me?" the laugh was false and somewhat nervous, "Don't be silly."

"Don't bother to deny it. The detective has just identified you from your picture on my phone."

"Oh."

"Well, you at least owe me an explanation."

"It was a favour for a friend," said Ilsa shortly, since it was evident there was not much use in continued denials.

"A friend called Brendan by any chance?"

The call was cut off.

"I think that tells us all we want to know," said Libby between gritted teeth, "The question is, Matt, does that give you enough to arrest him for breaking his bail conditions?"

"Probably, but leave it with me. In the meantime, I think it would be wise not to go back to your place. I'll ask Tess if you can stay with us for a couple of days."

Libby laughed mirthlessly, "I can't see her agreeing to that, can you?"

"Of course she will, when I explain everything."

"Good luck with that, then," said Pietro with deep sarcasm, obviously tired of not being the centre of attention.

"I think you are in enough trouble, pal, without pissing me off any further," said Matt dangerously.

They headed for the door, but Pietro couldn't resist one last barb, "You owe me a pair of sun-specs," he said.

"I'll buy you a pair of ray bans if you promise to repeat all this in court," said Libby.

"Done. Oh, by the way, here you go – have this and enjoy." He handed them an old plastic ice cream tub.

"What is it?" asked Libby suspiciously.

"Cheesecake. I make it myself. It's a bit of a speciality of mine."

She took off the lid and unceremoniously stuck her finger into the creamy top,

"God, that's delicious," she said as she licked up every smidge.

"Told you," said Pietro smugly.

Matt looked pityingly at him, "You really need to keep that hobby quiet if you want to be taken seriously as a hard man," he advised.

"No shit, Sherlock," grinned Pietro back.

CHAPTER FORTY-FOUR

The words were printed on the card in his hand and Lazarus re-read them, but he still couldn't quite believe what he was seeing.

He looked up when Stonier came into the office, and the older man felt a wrench of pity twist his insides when he saw the expression of shocked pain on his old friend's face.

"You've had one, too?" he asked softly.

"What is she doing, Tom? What the devil is she thinking of?"

Tom lowered his bulk into the chair opposite his boss and smiled encouragingly, "Come on, old man, it can't be that much of a surprise to you?"

"Yes, yes, it is. I was going to go and see Allingham, to tell him that I intended to ask her to be my wife."

Tom hadn't quite realized things had gone that far, though he had been aware of a growing affection between Lazarus and Constance. This made it impossible to say anything at all to take away the hammer blow of the young woman's engagement to Edward Moncrieff.

Suddenly anger took over from shock and Lazarus crumpled the embossed invitation and threw it across the room, "Dear God, I'm an idiot for trusting another woman! Be damned to her and all her ilk."

"You are not going to the ball then?" Tom asked diffidently, knowing that he was going to have to take Meg and wondering how such betrayal would sit with his obviously furious superior.

"No, I'm bloody not! Do you think I can smile and wish her well, when all I want to do is shoot him and watch her suffer agonies of grief and shame?" Even as he spoke the words – and by God, he meant them! – Lazarus wondered where this flood of emotion had come from. He had been growing closer to Constance, enjoying her company, sharing jokes with her, finding that looking at her gave him a pleasure he had forgotten existed, but he had no idea until he had seen the news of her engagement in black and white, that he was in love with her. Lost in thought he had to drag his attention back to Stonier, who was still speaking.

"I can understand that, but I warn you that my life will not be worth living if I don't take Meg."

Lazarus merely grunted, "Do what you like," he said bitterly, "Now if we could take our minds off your social life for a moment, we still have a couple of murders to solve."

Stonier was well aware that they were no nearer to bringing their suspected murderer to justice, but he sat and pretended to think about their dilemma anyway – he certainly wasn't going to risk the wrath of the already fulminating Lazarus.

"I've wracked my brains, Dan, and I can't think of any way of getting our man than to trick him into action. We have found the evidence that he had the book which gave him the wherewithal to commit the murders, but nothing to tie him to the killings."

"You're right. There is no discernible motive, that's our problem. This man is killing simply because of some twisted idea of moral justice that we can have no way of understanding. If we could work out who his next victim might be, then we might have a chance."

The sergeant nodded in agreement, but had no useful notion to offer to his superior.

"The scraps of paper were bible quotations, which is why we are setting our sights on the vicar, isn't that so?" he reiterated, merely to get things straight in his own confused mind.

"Yes, I suppose it is –- and because of his attitude towards the unfortunate Mollie."

"But her mother was just as harsh in her judgement."

"She was, but her anger seemed to be directed just towards her daughter, because of the shame she had brought upon the family. She might just have poisoned Mollie, to rid herself of a bastard grandchild and fallen daughter, but I don't see her continuing to kill others for similar sins."

"Umm," grunted Stonier thoughtfully, "Do we know what sort of paper the quotes were written on?"

Lazarus looked thunderstruck, cautiously wondering if his assistant was somehow quite brilliant.

"Quality of paper might tell us quite a lot," he admitted, rising to his feet and walking to the cabinet where the few clues to this mystery were stored.

The messages, when held up to the light, bore a watermark, which was unfortunately not complete, because the paper had been neatly cut with scissors to reduce it to the size required.

"We need to get back into the vicarage study," said Lazarus with determination, "I need to see if there is any matching paper in there."

"How do we do that without alerting the man to our suspicions? The last thing we need now is to let him know we are on to him. He'll simply stop his little games and we'll never catch him."

"We'll have to go in when there is no-one there."

"You are suggesting we break into a vicarage, aren't you, Dan?" asked Stonier in a tone of deep resignation.

"Not exactly," said Lazarus, "We'll go to the house when we know Bembridge is out and tell the housekeeper that we'll wait. She'll show us into the parlour, but there is nothing to keep us in there!"

"How is wandering around someone's home uninvited, any different than breaking and entering?"

"We won't be breaking anything," answered Lazarus with a grin.

* * *

Nothing, of course, is ever as easy as it sounds. Lazarus and Stonier lurked in bushes and took turns to go to the local alehouse for a drink and a bite to eat, but Bembridge and Holbrook spent the entire morning happily ensconced in the house. The inspector was on the point of sending his sergeant to draw them out with some spurious excuse or other, when they finally came out of the wrought-iron gates together, trotting along in the dog-cart and obviously with somewhere important to go, judging by the cracking pace they set.

The two policemen waited until they were out of sight and earshot before approaching the house and ringing the bell.

Rather to their surprise it was the maid who finally answered their summons, after a painfully long wait, during which they both cast nervous glances towards the gate, fearful of the premature return of their prey. They had concocted some plausible excuse to see the men of the cloth, should they be caught in the house, but it sounded a poor reason to them both and they would have been reluctant to use it.

"No Mrs Waters?" asked Lazarus brightly, his smile warm and reassuring.

The girl shook her head, "She's not well, so Mr Bembridge and Mr Holbrook have gone off to see her and bring her some fruit from the conservatory."

Danby and Tom exchanged a triumphant look, then gently brushed the girl aside, "That's a pity, because we need to see the vicar rather urgently, I think perhaps we had better wait for him."

"But he might be a long while," she protested mildly.

"Don't you worry about that," said the sergeant kindly, patting her gently on the shoulder, "You just show is into the study and we'll wait for Mr Bembridge to come back."

"Do you want tea?"

"That would be very nice," said Tom and they followed her down the hall and into the study.

Once alone Lazarus hissed at him, "What the devil did you ask for tea for? She'll be back in a minute, and precious time is wasting!"

"We want this to look like an innocent visit, don't we? Well, what could be more innocent than two fellows accepting a drink while they wait?"

Lazarus was unconvinced, but he let the matter drop. It was too late now, anyway, for they could hardly troop through the house to find the girl and cancel the tea.

Luckily she was more speedy with the tray than he had feared and within minutes, he and Stonier were opening and closing drawers and riffling through papers on the desk.

They found the paper they sought inside a mahogany writing box on one of the shelves which lined the walls.

It was not all that they found. Another one of the little messages was there, printed as all the others were in thick black ink. This epistle was different than the other for it held a message that told them exactly where they might find the next victim.

"SUFFER NOT A WITCH TO LIVE"

The two men exchanged a glance, "Janet Riley," said Lazarus.

"The witch in the wood," agreed Stonier.

They put everything back where they had found it, drank their tea, then rang the bell for the maid.

"Unfortunately we find we can't wait any longer for Mr Bembridge," said Lazarus formally, "But if you would kindly tell him that we called?"

She nodded, lifted the tray, and left them to show themselves out.

It took them over an hour to arrange for a horse to be harnessed to the trap and to get themselves out to the cottage where the witch in the woods plied her trade. Both men feared they would find the worst when the reached her, but apparently Bembridge was not yet ready to kill again, for she was happily pottering around her garden, dead-heading and harvesting her herbs.

They quickly told her of their fears for her safety and she regarded them with calm blue eyes, the slightest hint of a smile on her full, sensuous lips.

"You really believe I'm in danger, gentlemen?"

"We do," Lazarus assured her, as emphatically as he was able without sounding like a bad actor in a melodrama. What he was telling her was unbelievable enough, without adding a metaphorical swishing of a black opera cape.

"Do you have somewhere you can go for a few days, until we have this man in custody?"

She looked thoughtful, "As it happens, my husband is due back into port in the next few days. Perhaps I could take myself off to Whitby for a little while."

"Do so, I urge you," said Lazarus seriously, "Tell no-one, just go, preferably today."

She gave him a long, slow smile, "Very well. Thank you, Mr Lazarus."

"If we catch our man on your premises, it will be us who have to thank you, Mrs Riley," he answered.

As he heaved himself back into the trap, the whole vehicle dipping violently under his bulk, Stonier asked, "What now, Danby?"

"We set a man to watch the house, day and night. The constables will have to draw lots as to who does the night shift, but by God, we are keeping this place under surveillance if it takes a month or more!"

"The superintendent will love that," grumbled Stonier, aware that he was more likely to get his ear-bashed than Lazarus, who was currently the golden boy, due to the patronage of Lord Allingham.

"He can go and play dice with the devil for all I care," said the inspector, clicking to the horse to quicken its pace. They needed to get out of the vicinity swiftly, for there was no knowing who might be watching them and he was desperate now not to alert the killer to their plotting of his downfall.

Stonier excused himself when they reached Braxton. He didn't want to say so, but he needed to go and hire a suit to wear to Havering Hall for Constance's betrothal ball. Meg had made it very clear that they were honoured guests and she would stand for nothing less than his very best behaviour in both garb and demeanour. If Lazarus knew where he was going and why, he made no comment. He merely gave his orders to the uniformed division regarding Mrs Riley's house, then wended his own weary way back to Mrs Baker's lodging house. He toyed with the idea of leaving Braxton for a few days and going to visit his daughter until the wretched party was over and done with, but somehow he could not drag himself away.

The rest of the week passed without incident. Bembridge called at the police station to find out why the inspector had called upon him and Lazarus gave him some convoluted story about wondering if Miss Soffley had ever been to see him or confided in him in any way, as they were having trouble finding any relatives for her. He couldn't help but went away seemingly satisfied that they had consulted him for a genuine reason and were not merely engaged in rifling his study.

As they talked, Lazarus had scanned his features as closely as he could without being obvious, wondering how the chubby, jowly-faced old hypocrite could manage to look not only innocent, but positively cherubic, with his plump, smooth cheeks, bland blue eyes, and oddly small button nose, which Lazarus had only just really noticed.

Was this man really responsible for three particularly painful deaths? And was that perhaps why he chose the methods he did, to keep his hands clean? Poison and an arrow were, after all, killing at a distance. If he chose to, the man could avoid all contact with the dead bodies. All his victims had still been alive when he saw them last. Mayhap he could live with the consequences of his actions simply because he could tell himself that once he had done his worst, the final end was actually in the hands of God. Poison was always a hit and miss affair – one could never tell if the victim would live or die. So much depended upon how much was ingested or indeed vomited up afterwards. And in fact, Josette Bennett had survived so far. Even the arrow could have been said to be vulnerable to a stray gust of wind which might have deflected it from its target. Yes, if the mind was sick enough, any excuse could be made for the reign of death.

Even so, Lazarus could not bring himself to shake hands with Bembridge when he finally left the office. The inspector shuffled some papers busily and pretended not to see the outstretched hand. Bembridge accepted the rebuff as an error and left without further delay.

The policeman could not help but wonder if he was on his way to the little cottage in the woods.

CHAPTER FORTY-FIVE

Constance had never looked or felt prettier. Arabella and Jane had both helped her to dress, and her uncle had spared no expense in both dressing her and arranging the party, so delighted was he that she was finally showing some sense and honouring the family with an exceptional marriage. He had even forgiven the presence of her maternal cousin, for Jane had charmed him as she did everyone, though she had privately begged the others not to leave her alone with her host that evening. She felt very unpleasant emotions emanating from his overbearing, arrogant demeanour and was quite afraid that once he had a drink or two inside him, he could become somewhat uncontrolled.

Her dress was pale blue silk, with a deep lace trim, exposing rather more of her shoulders and upper chest than she would normally have tolerated, but Arabella had been in charge of ordering the dressmaker and she was insistent that for once in her life, Constance was going to be the belle of the ball. She herself was in yellow and white, with Jane in pale green. They were all in tightened stays, giving them a waist at least an inch smaller than usual, and Constance dreaded the dancing, feeling breathless simply standing and waiting for the guests, and quite sure that she would faint before the evening was over if she had to exert herself too much.

They all had their hair dressed with real flowers and they wore elbow-length gloves with a pretty new fan attached by silken cord to one wrist and an embossed dance card dangling from the other. Arabella had treated them all to the fans, and they had giggled as they practised the age-old method of sending messages via various flicks and holds, showing each other how to tell the gentlemen to "come hither" or "leave me, pray, kind sir".

Constance said, with mock severity, that she would not need to know how to tell anyone to "come hither" since she now had a fiancè.

"Looking as you do tonight, Constance, you will have to tell lots of men to 'leave me alone, kind sir'," said Jane admiringly. She was astounded by the change in her cousin, for she had sat with her for many an evening now, as she wept and lamented over Inspector Lazarus. She had advised her not to invite the man, but Arabella had insisted, though she had not explained the reason to anyone other than her darling papa.

Jane had been openly relieved at his refusal to attend, but Constance was still undecided how she felt about the rejection. She knew he was right to stay away, but she was only human, and would have enjoyed seeing his expression when he saw her looking so lovely.

A few special guests had been asked to attend early and eat dinner with the family, then the ball began. Before she knew it, Constance was being swept around the dance floor by a procession of young men, who had seemed to suddenly find her attractive now that she was no longer on the marriage mart. Moncrieff, as only a proud winner could, was delighted to allow his friends to dance with her – dance only mind! Should any one of them overstep the mark, they would find themselves taken outside and have their claret drawn, or so he loudly told them all, as they drank too much and watched the ladies dance with carefully hidden lasciviousness.

Meg was having a wonderful time, with no glowering Lazarus to put a damper on Tom's enthusiasm, she was dancing every dance until her cheeks glowed and her breath came in short gasps.

One gasp which escaped her lips, however, came not from breathlessness, but from the advent of a latecomer, whom no one was expecting.

A sudden silence fell over the company when Lazarus walked into the ball room and ignoring everyone, even his host, he made his way straight to Constance and executing a low bow he held out his hand, "May I have this dance, Miss Allingham?"

The pink in her cheeks owed nothing to dancing and everything to his presence. She hesitated, longing to refuse, but her heart wouldn't let her have this one last chance to be in his arms, and she took the proffered hand, "Good evening, Mr Lazarus, I thought you weren't coming."

"Thought, or hoped?"

She waited to answer that quietly spoken question until the music began and he swept her across the floor.

"I thought you didn't dance," she said coolly, trying not to sound breathless.

"You know what thought did? Followed a dust cart, thought it was a wedding," he said lightly. But the mention of a wedding was obviously a sore point and his grip tightened a little as he moved so that she couldn't see his face.

"Why have you come, Danby?" she whispered into his ear.

"I was invited," he said.

"That was Arabella's doing," she said, anguished, "I would not have put either of us through this."

He again shifted his position slightly, but this time so that he could look down into her eyes, "Why have you put us through it, Constance? Why in God's name are you going to marry that idiot instead of me?"

It took all her self control not to slap him. How dare he come here to her party and insult her betrothed, when he knew fine well that they could never be together. The only indication she gave of her fury was her tightly folded lips, through which she hissed, "And how would your wife feel about that, Mr Lazarus? Is she not with you tonight?"

He was so astounded he stopped dancing for a fraction of a second and it was only due to the skill of the couple behind them that an embarrassing pile-up did not occur.

"My wife?"

"Yes, your wife!"

"I think we had better go outside for some air, Miss," he said with soft menace. She wondered what she had said that had angered him so. Did he still honestly believe that she was unaware of his marital status? Had he been hoping to keep her in ignorance until he had made her his mistress?

They found a quiet spot on the terrace, away from the other people who had come out to cool down after the heat generated by so many guests and the hundreds of candles which lighted the whole house.

"Who told you I was married?" he asked bluntly, as she sank onto a stone bench by the balustrade.

"You did!" she said stiffly.

"I did?" he was genuinely puzzled, "When did I ever tell you such a thing?"

"After your blow to the head. I asked you who Rosamund was and you said she was your wife."

"'Was' is the right word, Miss Allingham, my wife is dead. She died three years ago, giving birth to my daughter."

Her mouth fell open and for the first time she felt that she really might faint. There was a loud buzzing in her ears and she felt her stays gripping her body as tightly as a vice.

"No," she breathed.

"Yes." he answered shortly, "Perhaps you could explain to me why you would think I was the sort of cad who would agree to be alone with an unmarried young woman if I had a wife at home waiting for me?"

She didn't blame him for being angry. She had thought all the worst of him and he had never behaved in anything less than an gentlemanly way from the very first.

"Why didn't you tell me?" she managed to say, when her breathing eased to a more normal level.

"How the devil did I know what you were thinking? I thought everyone knew. I feel waves of pity wash over me wherever I go, so how was I to know you were not feeling the same? Poor Lazarus, left with a motherless child. I must be kind to him!"

"I was never kind to you," she refuted hotly, sensing how he had hated being the object of everyone's solicitude.

"I'll say!" he snapped, "And never crueller than when you threw my regard in my face and elected to marry a mere boy because of the status he can bring to you! How many kinds of fool was I to think you and I …"

He trailed off and she tried to deny his accusations, but it was obvious he was too angry to listen to her. He gave her one last look of contempt and made to leave, but she grasped his arm, "You cannot go like this, Danby. You must let me explain."

Moncrieff came to the French window and called her name. Desperately she clasped at him, "Please, my dearest one, do not believe the worst of me, though I know now I deserve it. We must talk about everything. Come to my house tomorrow night. I'll make sure I am alone and we will discuss what we must do next. I cannot bear to lose you."

He looked down at her and seemed convinced that she was indeed contrite and deadly serious.

"I'll be there at ten o'clock," he said gruffly, "Now, go to your fiancè before he takes offence and calls me out, for I'll not be responsible for my actions if I have to face him with a loaded gun." There was a ghost of a smile and she laughed with relief.

"Until tomorrow?"

"Until tomorrow," he agreed softly.

* * *

Jane was inclined to baulk at the idea of retiring early so that her cousin could have a private assignation with a man. Constance explained very carefully that Lazarus was not, after all, a married man, but as Jane pointed out, "That may very well be the case, Constance, you, however, are an engaged woman."

"I know, I know, but I have to see Lazarus. All will be well when I have seen him."

Feeling she had very little choice, Jane agreed, but resolved to at least stay awake and be there should her relative have need of her assistance.

Lazarus arrived at ten o'clock precisely and Constance let him into the house herself, having rid herself of Sally as well as Jane. The servant was given an unexpected night off to go and visit her mother.

Lazarus took a seat in the pretty parlour and waited for Constance to speak. He had no intention of making things easy for her. He had been torn asunder as though by a physical wound at her defection and it would take more than a few amenable platitudes to pacify his tortured soul.

"Can I get anything for you?" she asked nervously, suddenly aware of how very difficult the conversation was going to be. She was assuming so much and had so little that she was sure of, how could she put into words such a jumble of emotions?

"Nothing, thank you," he said severely.

She paced a little and wrung her hands in her agitation, "Oh dear me, I hardly know what to say to you!"

"You called me here, begged me to come! You must have something to say."

She flung herself down at his knees and looked up into his face, "Danby, I have made the most dreadful mistake and I do not know how to correct it."

"Are you asking me to get you out of trouble, Miss?"

"I suppose I am."

"And what do you want me to do?"

She lowered her head in shame, "I want you to tell Mr Moncrieff that I cannot marry him because I am going to marry you."

"I haven't asked you," he said and she quickly lifted her head, tears welling in her eyes.

"No, you have not, but I very much hope that you will."

He took hold of her chin and spoke very softly and calmly to her, "Constance, I have had time to think about all this – indeed I've thought of little else, and I must be at pains to point out that there is no easy solution."

"I know that," she whispered.

"Do you? Do you really?" he rose swiftly to his feet and left her almost sprawled on the floor, "I cannot emphasise too strongly that this is not merely a romance between two young people. I am considerably older than you, my dear, besides which I am not a wealthy man, far from it. As if that were not enough, I also have a child to think of. I could not even consider marrying again unless my little girl was going to be a welcome part of any new family."

"Of course. I would have it no other way."

"But do you understand what it means to live on a policeman's salary? I could not even consider a house as large as this one, as for servants…" he gave a short 'huh' of bitter laughter, "I'm sorry, Constance, but I cannot see you washing and cleaning as Meg does, your hair tied in a scarf and your hands red with hot water from the copper in the scullery."

"But we need not live quite so impecuniously," she protested, "I have a small inheritance from my mother's family. My uncle has kept it in trust for me until I marry."

"There, then, we have another problem, for I could not live off a woman."

She struggled to her feet, impeded by her voluminous skirts, which rather spoiled the dignity with which she tried to bring to her voice as she remonstrated with him, "How is it that you feel you cannot allow me to lower myself to your station in life, but you also refuse to be elevated to mine? That is hardly fair, is it? I am willing to clean and scrub for you, if you insist, but you will not serve me the same turn."

"It is not the same thing at all," he began, but she had saved her trump card for last.

"And, of course, in keeping yourself so low, from pure pride, you are also condemning that lovely daughter of yours to penury too. What sort of a father would do that?"

He was silent for a moment, unconsciously taking the head of the household position with his feet apart in front of the fire.

"Well, can you not lower yourself to marry me for your daughter's sake, if not your own?" she asked.

He grinned and held out his hands to take hers, "You possess irrefutable logic, my love. All that remains now is to tell Mr Moncrieff that he has lost you to a better man."

She looked appalled up at him, "Oh, Danby, you must do it, for I cannot!"

"I hope that is on account of your kind heart and not from wretched cowardice!" he said severely.

"It is both," she admitted frankly.

She saw him to the door but as they parted, passion overcame them both and she fell into his arms. As he kissed her for the first time, Danby knew true happiness. There were many obstacles to overcome, but together they would prevail.

CHAPTER FORTY-SIX

PRESENT

"Where next?" asked Matt as they drove off.

"Your place," said Libby, through a mouthful of cheesecake.

"What?" Matt was startled enough to pull over having barely started the car and earned himself a blast of a horn from the car behind.

"Your place. You want to sort this out with Tess, don't you?"

"Of course, but I hardly think turning up with you half-pissed and full of cream is going to solve anything."

"Nonsense. Believe me, no woman could taste this stuff and not fall straight into a forgiving mood and who better to tell her we're not having an affair that the 'other woman'?"

"Stop eating it all, then," said Matt resignedly and pulled back out into the flow of traffic.

Tess had obviously had time to think about things, because she gave Libby and Matt no more than a raised eyebrow before gesturing them into the house.

With a jerk of her head she indicated to Matt that he should open more wine whilst she listened to Libby's rambling account of Mad Brendan and the Private Eye.

It was the photo of Dan which finally convinced her, had Libby but known it. As it happened she knew Dan well, since he was her invaluable contact at the police museum when she needed something special researching. Dan was a canny young man and was hardly likely to play about with a married woman. He had enough evidence of where that sort of game could lead every day of his working life. She reckoned at least half the exhibits in the Black Museum would have been from 'crimes of passion'.

Besides, even though she barely knew Libby, she liked her and of course she loved Matt. It just didn't equate with her idea of how two people having an affair would behave – if anyone knew that, she did – she was a romantic novelist, after all.

Libby generously offered her some of the mangled cheesecake, which she had to admit did look good, even after the drunken Libby had been at it. Before Matt had time to come back with an uncorked bottle and three glasses, the two women were dipping into dessert and giggling.

"I think I preferred it when you were fighting," he said grumpily.

"Get used to it," said Tess, "And by the way, Libby is staying the night. I'm not letting her go home until she's changed her locks."

"Good idea," said Matt, "And in the meantime, I'll get onto the station, bollock them for neglecting to inform Libby about Brendan being at large, and tell them to put out a call for him to be brought in for questioning."

"Ooh, you gunna put out an APB on him, then," sniggered Libby.

"No, because I'm not appearing in an episode of CSI Miami," said Matt, with infinite patience, but he was quietly delighted to have everything back to normal – or almost everything. From what Libby had told him, Brendan hadn't lost any of his brooding anger towards his ex-girlfriend. Matt was now convinced that he had tried to kill her once, and it looked as though he were quite capable of trying again. Libby wouldn't really be safe, even with new locks, until Brendan Tulliver was back inside.

Once Matt had made his call, the evening turned quite convivial. Tess and Libby had plenty to discuss about how far Libby had progressed with her Lazarus mystery.

"You mean you still don't know 'whodunnit'?" Tess questioned her when Libby admitted that the book was very nearly finished.

"Not a clue. I know who Lazarus suspects, but I've held off from reading the last few pages until I'm ready to write the end. I think it will give the story an immediacy that I couldn't get any other way."

"I'll say!" said Tess, half in admiration and half thinking Libby was a complete basket case to leave it to the fates the way she had. She still didn't know if Lazarus solved his case – and what the hell was she going to do if he failed miserably? She couldn't invent an ending if she was going to pass the story off as an accurate historical account.

Almost as though she had read Tess' mind, Libby swiftly changed the subject. She didn't want to lose her confidence at this late date and to hear any criticism would do just that. She knew she was taking a risk, but somehow she trusted Lazarus. She just knew he had found his man in the end.

She turned the conversation to Sir Horton Brookes, and without even being aware that she was being manipulated, Tess was soon quite happily telling Libby what she had found out about the lawyer. She had some more information about Decima Watkins, which engrossed them both so much that they hardly noticed when Matt bade them goodnight and went upstairs to bed.

It wasn't until after he was gone that Libby confided how hurt she had been by Ilsa's double dealing.

"Why do you think she did it?" asked Tess, with heartfelt sympathy. She knew how it felt to have those close betray you in the worst possibly ways.

"I suspect Brendan has been pouring his poison again. He's very plausible and if he managed to persuade her that I was at fault and had let him down then had him thrown in clink for nothing, before long, he would have had her eating out of his hand. She always was a sucker for a handsome face. I can't tell you how many no-accounts she's been with over the years. She's just plain dumb when it comes to men."

"A lot of us are," said Tess.

"Yeah, but some of us actually learn by our mistakes!" countered Libby.

*   *   *

Being less used to over-indulging than Libby, Tess lay in next morning and Libby was alone, forcing down a slice of toast and a cup of coffee when Matt joined her.

"Feeling delicate?" he asked unsympathetically.

"A little," she admitted, "Could you possibly give me a run home this morning. I have some stuff I need to do."

"Of course. I'm in work a little later anyway, so I'll drop you on the way. Feel free to have a shower or whatever. We'll go in about half an hour, okay?"

"Fine. Thanks."

"Why don't you ring a locksmith now, and arrange to meet him at your place. Best to get it over and done with as quickly as possible."

She looked vague, and waved a dismissive hand, "Yes, I'll do it when I get home. Listen Matt, I really think you ought to do me a favour, now I've done one for you."

He lifted a brow at her, "Oh, I think you've had plenty of favours," he said, "but go on, I'm listening."

"Couldn't you go and see David for me, today, and explain about the photos? I mean, I came here and sorted it all out with Tess for you."

One look at her deliberately puppy-dog eyes and he knew he had lost the argument before it began, "Oh, alright. I suppose I could give it a go. Where will I find him? But I'm warning you, if he takes a swing at me, you're in deep doo-doo!"

"I'm sure he won't – and he said he was going to sleep at the garden centre in the office for a couple of days."

"Alright. I'll drop you off and go and see him."

* * *

Libby laid her plans carefully. She figured she had about two hours at most before David came home to kiss and make up and she wanted everything done and finished with by then.

He knew her so well that it wouldn't take him long to work out that she was up to mischief.

She made a large pot of coffee and took the tray with milk and sugar into the sitting room. There she settled herself into an easy chair facing the door, with a rug over her knee to cover the shotgun that lay heavy in her lap.

She had never really understood until this moment why she had elected to keep Aunt Lil's gun and licence it properly after Maddie had used it to knee-cap Brendan last year.

She hated guns. But she knew Aunt Lil did too, but she had felt safer knowing it was in the house.

Now she was going to use it for its real purpose – to defend her castle against invaders – or one invader to be precise.

She knew Brendan was somewhere about, watching her every move. He had used the Private Eye to take pictures, but he hadn't needed him to keep track of Libby's movements, he was doing that himself.

And now that he thought his little plan had worked, that he had managed to drive David away and leave Libby alone and defenceless, now he was going to turn up like the bad penny he was. But Libby wasn't quite as defenceless as Brendan was hoping and if Libby should happen to accidentally shoot him, thinking he was a burglar or a rapist, then what the hell! She'd do two years at most. And what was two years, compared to knowing that she would be safe and protected for the rest of her life?

She didn't have long to wait.

Brendan, love, you are so predictable.

* * *

Matt had trouble finding David; he wasn't in the office and none of the staff seemed to know where he was.

The policeman had almost given up the search when he walked in through the double doors.

"Where've you been, boss?" asked young Jamie, the work-based learning student, who hadn't quite grasped the idea of respect for his elders yet, but was dedicated to the cacti, for some bizarre reason.

"At the bank, trying to keep your job for you," said David shortly. He then caught sight of Matt and his expression became even more truculent than it had been in the face of Jamie's cheek.

"You've got a nerve, I'll give you that," he said, with a sneer.

Matt reined in his own temper and shrugged, "I've nothing to hide, mate and if you showed a bit of common sense, you'd know it."

"Maybe. But when I want lessons in life, I'll ask, thanks."

"Can we talk?"

"Do we have anything to say?"

"You may not, but I certainly do."

It was David's turn to shrug. He walked off towards his office and Matt assumed he was free to follow.

Once in the room, David casually began folding the blanket which was thrown over the settee which was supposed to be reserved seating for important visitors.

"Comfy, was it?" asked Matt sarcastically.

"It was alright," said David, but Matt thought he detected a slight wince at remembered aches and pains.

"Why not sleep in your own bed, next to that nice little wife of yours tonight?"

David's hand bunched into an automatic fist, "If that's your idea of a joke, pal ..."

"Calm down. I didn't mean to hint I knew how nice she is, except as a friend. Look she sent me over here to explain things and I'm here because she did the same for me last night."

"I rang her, she wasn't home last night," said David, obviously more bothered by this fact than he was trying to show.

"I know. She was with me and Tess – you should have tried her mobile."

"I did. It was switched off."

"Oh. Well maybe she wanted you to suffer a bit. I can't say I blame her."

David looked at him as though weighing up how far he could be trusted, "Is that true?"

"What?"

"She really spent the night at Tess Brookes' place?"

"She did. In the spare room, whilst I cuddled up to my woman in my own comfortable bed."

David sank into his chair behind the big desk – the big desk which he and Libby had once used in the height of passion in the days when they couldn't keep their hands off each other.

"What the bloody hell is going on, Matt?"

Matt sat opposite him, "Can't you guess? Brendan Tulliver is what is happening. He's out and he's wanting revenge. I'm sorry to say the probation service and the police have failed your wife miserably by not letting her know he'd been released. He's been playing with your head and hers for weeks."

David sat forward, his face white, "Where's Libby now?"

"Gone home to call a locksmith and have your house secured."

David leapt to his feet, "Want a bet she's not called a locksmith?"

Matt frowned, "What are you talking about?"

"Libby, against my advice and wishes, kept Lil's shotgun. She was scared to be in that house alone, so if she went home before the locks have been changed, then she's got a plan."

"What sort of a plan?" asked Matt slowly, but he was very afraid he already knew.

"Got any blue, flashy lights on your car?" asked David, heading for the door.

CHAPTER FORTY-SEVEN

There was the sound of a scuffle outside the office door and Lazarus heard raised voices, which wiped the silly grin of his face.

"I want to see him, now! Where is that damned Inspector fellow?"

He should have known that his precious peace would not have lasted very long. Resignedly he rose to his feet and opened the door, almost causing Moncrieff, for it was he, to fall into the room.

The indignity of his advent wrong-footed the young man for a moment, and the colour rose in his cheeks, but Lazarus was undecided as to whether this was due to anger at seeing his rival or embarrassment at his clumsy entrance.

"Good morning Mr Moncrieff," he said in a calm voice which belied the tangle of thoughts which assailed him. It was more than likely that the boy knew of his imminent loss, but the inspector could not be sure of that so he searched for something to say which would not give anything away, whilst appearing to be solicitous. It was the least he owed the young man, after his behaviour of the evening before. Constance may have agreed to an engagement whilst labouring under a misapprehension, but it was an engagement nevertheless, and must be treated with all seriousness.

"What's good about it, I'd like to know!" muttered the boy, showing his youth in those few sulky words.

"Would you like to step inside?" asked Lazarus, dismissing the two constables who had been endeavouring to hold the interloper back with a jerk of his head.

"I'd prefer to step outside, so that I can dust your jacket for you!" said Moncrieff, regaining his equilibrium and recalling exactly why he had made this trip to Braxton Police Station.

"I don't think that's a very good idea, do you?"

"I've never had a better one!"

Lazarus had to hide a smile, recalling how hot-headed he had been at a similar age. This obviously needed careful handling.

"Come in and sit down, sir," he said gently, "Let's discuss this in private, like gentlemen. You don't want the lady's name to be bandied about by all and sundry, do you?"

Apparently this had the desired effect of making the young man rein in his temper. Whether it was due to deference to Constance, or for the sake of his own manly pride, Lazarus had no idea, and frankly, by that point, he hardly cared. He just wanted the mess cleared up as quickly and painlessly as possible.

Moncrieff threw himself into a chair and glowered at Lazarus across the expanse of the desk, "Well, you absolute bounder, what have you to say for yourself?"

"Might I be allowed to know my offence first?" Lazarus was still playing for time. He had no intention of handing the boy any ammunition.

"Do you deny that you went alone to Miss Allingham's last evening and on the doorstep you …" Evidently Moncrieff would not or could not bring himself to use the word kiss, for he stopped speaking and actually, audibly, ground his teeth in fury.

This was entirely unexpected to Lazarus, who had thought that Constance had been abroad early and had visited her erstwhile betrothed and told him the affair was at an end.

"Who told you that?" he asked brusquely, forgetting all his good intentions of speaking kindly to the boy.

"Never you mind who," spat Moncrieff, "Someone who has my best interests at heart, unlike you!"

"Oh, give it up, boy," said Lazarus irritably, far too intrigued now by the fact that he and Constance were being spied on to find any compassion for his young rival, "Why the devil would I have your best interests in mind? Have you never heard the expression, 'all's fair in love and war'? I've as much right to woo the lady as you have!"

Mouth open in a shocked 'o', Moncrieff took a good few seconds to find something suitably cutting with which to respond, "But, but, you're old!" he spluttered. Nothing he could have said would have infuriated Lazarus more, since his age had been one of his own concerns when he was debating declaring himself to the woman he loved.

"I'm thirty-six," he protested, "And Miss Allingham is twenty-seven. And you are, what? Nineteen?"

"I'm twenty-two," said Moncrieff with as much dignity as he could muster, lying by a year, but the inspector would never know that.

Lazarus raised a sceptical eyebrow, "Too young for a mature woman," he stated bluntly, "I know it seems harsh, my good fellow, but you'll get over this, I promise. You'll have set your sights on some other young filly before the year is out." Lazarus could scarcely believe the words were coming from his own mouth, 'young filly'? Who the hell was he turning into? Lord Allingham? Spend five minutes with the aristocracy, he thought bitterly, and you started spouting nonsense as if you had spent your youth at Eton and Cambridge!

It seemed Moncrieff found his comments quite as offensive as he had, for he turned a deeper shade of red than Lazarus would have thought possible.

"You cad! You only showed an interest when Constance transferred her affections from you to me. What sort of a chap plays fast and loose with a girl like that?"

"She hasn't transferred her affections, Moncrieff, she has far too much sensibility to tell you herself, but there was a misunderstanding between us, which has now been explained. Her engagement to you has been an error for which we are both more sorry than you can ever know – but it was an error!"

Moncrieff looked as though he might burst into tears, he leapt to his feet, "Do you think I would take your word for anything? I'll see her myself and hear it from her own lips – if it is true!"

Lazarus also rose, "Do that, by all means, but I warn you, do not harass or distress the lady, or you will have me to answer to!"

The younger man was fortunately prevented from replying to this threat by the door opening so violently that it bounced off the wall, "Lazarus! Come out here, now!"

"What is it?" asked the inspector, brushing past the boy and following his sergeant out into the corridor.

"Bembridge! We've arrested Bembridge on his way to Janet Riley's cottage."

"What? The devil you have," responded Lazarus with a triumphant grin, "What did I tell you, Tom? I knew she would be the next victim."

He barely noticed that Moncrieff stormed off, evidently in high dudgeon that he should have been so summarily dismissed. It was only after the boy had gone that he recalled he had wanted to force him to give the name of the spy who had reported the late-night kiss on Constance's doorstep. He toyed briefly with the idea of sending one of the constables after him for a name, then shrugged. They had Bembridge, so anything was of little importance just at the moment.

He followed Tom into the room at the end of the corridor where they had seated the protesting vicar. In deference to his position they would not put him into the cells – yet!

If Moncrieff had been crimson, Bembridge was puce. As they entered the room, he threw Lazarus and Stonier a glare that should have turned them both to stone.

"What is the meaning of this outrage?" the older man hissed, between gritted teeth, struggling with a mix of emotions he had never felt in his life before. Never had he been insulted, infuriated and frightened all in the same moment. He had nearly had an apoplectic fit when a crowd of policemen had emerged from various hiding places and forced his trap to a standstill on the road to Little Lowton. That shock was bad enough, but then to be arrested and forced to walk into Braxton Police Station in shackles was the supreme indignity. He swore Lazarus was going to pay.

Alone in that small room, however, reality hit and he began to grow fearful. Of course he had committed no crime, but the inspector obviously thought he had some evidence to the contrary – what would happen if Bembridge could not convince the police that he was innocent of whatever it was they imagined he had done?

When the two plain clothes men entered the room, he had to

restrain himself from either hitting them or begging them to let him go. Since neither action could be said to be dignified, he managed to remain seated, but he could not quell the feeling of utter hatred that swept over him when he saw the man whom he considered to be the author of his misfortune. He had felt a mutual animosity with Lazarus from the first moment they had set eyes on each other, and he could not help but believe that this was mere malice on the part of the policeman.

"I don't think there's any need for the handcuffs, Sergeant," said Lazarus mildly, and Stonier immediately stepped forward to release the vicar from his bindings.

Bembridge automatically rubbed his wrists, though in truth the restraints had not hurt at all, "I should think so," he said gruffly, but he could not help but feel slight gratitude that Lazarus was at least prepared to behave like a gentleman.

"I do apologise, sir," continued Lazarus, "I feel my men were more than a little over zealous. I'm sure that you would have come quietly if they had only asked politely."

"Of course I would," conceded the vicar, "If only I knew why they wanted me."

"This arrest really is a complete mystery to you, Mr Bembridge?" asked the policeman.

"Of course it is. Don't be so ridiculous, my man! I have never knowingly committed a crime in my life."

"Do you think you might have done so unknowingly?" asked Lazarus, feigning interest in the possibility that the man might now claim to have done murder whilst under some sort of brainstorm that wiped his memory clean.

"What the devil are you talking about?" demanded the now thoroughly roused man of God, "How could anyone commit a crime unknowingly?"

"I was about to ask you the same question. Do you think it is possible to commit – shall we say a murder, for arguments sake? – and not remember that one had done it?"

"Are you due for Bedlam, or am I?" snapped Bembridge, "I have no idea what you mean."

Lazarus held out his hand to Stonier and had the file on the case placed there. He opened it and produced the slips of paper containing the bible quotations.

"Do you recognize these, Mr Bembridge?" he asked.

Bembridge glanced at them, "No, I'm afraid I don't. What are they?"

"One was found in your study."

Ever conscious of his elevated position in the community, Bembridge immediately latched on to what Lazarus considered the irrelevant part of this sentence.

"And how did it find its way from my study into your hands, may I ask?"

Since he did not have a satisfactory answer to that pertinent query, Lazarus chose to ignore it.

"The other two were found clasped in the hands of the two young murder victims, both of whom, I understand, were known to you."

It was at this point that light began to filter. Bembridge found his heart suddenly pumping furiously as the import of those few words began to sink in.

"What are you saying?" his voice came out as a harsh croak and he was furious with himself for letting the inspector see his fear, but it couldn't be helped. Now he really was afraid. The police obviously thought he had killed Mollie Waters and Josette Bennett's lover.

"Two young people are dead, Mr Bembridge, another lies gravely ill. Paper was found on their bodies which matches paper found in your study. You have, from the first, shown a callous disdain for those who fail to live up to your high standards of behaviour. Both parties were fed poisoned food – you have access to the church hall kitchen, which gives you ample opportunity to prepare food without being observed by anyone else. Now, I'd like to know what you have to say to those facts."

"I want to see your superior," gasped the older man.

"I don't think being a Mason will help you now, Mr Bembridge."

"How dare you? I had no intention of calling upon the brotherhood! I have no need! You are speaking absolute nonsense and I refuse to listen to another word."

"Are you denying killing these young people?"

"I most certainly am!"

"Then perhaps you could explain away all these questions I have asked? It is a simple enough request. Tell me how all these things can be resolved and I will release you without further ado."

Bembridge was slowly calming down and gathering his wits. He took in a deep reviving breath and said with icy contempt, "You have not asked me any questions, Mr Lazarus. All I have heard so far have been accusations."

Stonier and Lazarus exchanged a glance and Stonier gave an almost imperceptible nod. The man was right – Lazarus had not asked anything, only stated his case. It was time to give the man an opportunity to defend himself.

"Very well." said Lazarus, "Do you recognize the writing on the papers?"

"No. But such plain printing has obviously been used with the intention of disguising the handwriting of the person, wouldn't you say?"

"Probably. Do you accept that the paper is the same?"

Bembridge looked at it indifferently, "It may be. But it is not mine in any case. Where exactly did you find it?"

"In a dark wooden writing case, in your study."

"Then it most certainly isn't mine. I own no such item."

"Who in the household does?"

"I have no idea. It could have been left there by the last incumbent, or it could belong to my curate."

Lazarus frowned, "You seriously expect me to believe that you do not know the contents of your own study?"

"I'll be frank with you, Lazarus, I scarcely ever go in there, except when I have visitors. Holbrook uses it more than I."

"What about when you write your sermons?" asked Lazarus, by now thoroughly confused.

"What's the point of having a dog and barking yourself?" The vicar laughed unkindly, "What use do you think I would have for a curate if he didn't take over the bulk of the parish duties?"

Lazarus and Stonier once again exchanged another glance, but this time the underlying message was one of startled dismay.

"When you say the bulk of the work, Mr Bembridge, what exactly do you mean?"

"What, besides the sermons, you mean?"

"Yes."

"He takes care of the visits to the poorer parishioners – of course I make calls on the benefactors of the church – but Holbrook does the rest. He takes confession from those poor souls who are troubled. And of course, as you know, he helps the ladies in the soup kitchen …"

"Then why were you on your way to see Janet Riley?"

"Because I was told that she was meddling in church matters and I felt it my duty to confront her and warn her that she is treading a path that will imperil her immortal soul."

"And who told you to go there today?"

"Holbrook, of course. He had heard of her activities and felt I should try and stop her."

Stonier and Lazarus didn't bother to listen to any more. They both headed for the door, "Thank you for your time, Mr Bembridge, and apologies for the error in bringing you into the station. One of the constables will see you safely home."

"I beg your pardon …" began the vicar, but the two were gone.

In the corridor Lazarus turned to Stonier, "We were wrong, old friend, taken in by a charming exterior, just like everyone else. Holbrook is the man, not Bembridge."

"And where do we find Holbrook?"

Lazarus shook his head, "I don't know," he muttered, wracking his brains to think where the murderer might strike next, "He's always one step ahead of us."

"It's as though he has eyes everywhere," said Stonier, clearly frustrated.

"Eyes everywhere," repeated Lazarus thoughtfully. Then his face paled, "Oh dear God, I think I might know where he's going to strike next."

"Where?" asked Stonier.

"I'll explain on the way. But we need to hurry. Get me a vehicle, Stonier, for the love of God!"

CHAPTER FORTY-EIGHT

PRESENT

It had been an interesting few days, Maddie had to admit, but now she really needed to get back to Hill Farm and discuss the next move with Libby.

She couldn't wait to tell her little sister the results of the myriad tests which had been going on, unknown to everyone but Maddie and the team from the television programme she had managed to get involved in the bizarre story of great, great, great Aunt Decima and her feud with the Allingham clan.

Maddie was never one to turn away from a fight and the exchange of letters between herself and the Allingham lawyers had grown ever more vitriolic. They had pushed and pushed her buttons until she was ready to burst with frustration. It was bad enough that they had sneeringly refused to supply a DNA profile for comparison with hers and her father's, but when they suggested that the fact that Decima had been hanged for murder might destroy all her claims on the Allingham Estate, then Maddie really set about doing battle.

Of course they had a vague point – it was illegal for a person to benefit from a crime, but it was a stretch to say that murdering her three sisters might have any bearing on the marriage into the Allingham family and the birth of an heir.

It was a good thing that they were finally agreeing that the Wedding Licence was legally binding and the genuine article – they hadn't much choice after three British Museum experts had verified it, and the corresponding entry had been found in a small, isolated church deep in the Peak District.

Never one to be beaten, Maddie had decided that the easiest way to refute their claims would be to prove that Decima was framed. If she could find the graves of those long-deceased sisters and have them exhumed and autopsy any remains, then perhaps she would be able to clear the unfortunate girl.

Luckily enough Great, great, great, great grandfather Watkins was well-to-do enough to have purchased a family plot which contained not only his own mortal remains, but those of his wife and several of their offspring, including the three sisters, since they had sadly pre-deceased him. As with all these things, when money talked, it spoke loud and clear. The television company greased a few palms, promised a few judicious mentions of certain personages who had a badly-hidden longing for their fifteen minutes of fame, and before Maddie knew it, she had permission to disinter and test the three great aunts for arsenical poisoning – filmed, of course, for posterity.

That very morning she had received a large brown envelope in the post which contained the results. She couldn't help the wry smile which adorned her face as she opened it with shaking hands. Funny, but she'd always thought of Libby being the history buff and until last year, she would have sneered at the very thought that she might have any interest in long dead ancestors and how they had met their maker, but now she could hardly bear the suspense.

She scanned the technical guff before she reached the important bits. The bodies showed more decay than would have been expected in victims of arsenic poisoning, since it was an odd side-effect that the toxin acted as a preservative. Since there was very little left of the stomachs of the corpses to test, it was decided to test hair and nails, which would still have traces of the poison.

None was found. Nor were any of several heavy-metal poisons which would have been available at the time, such as antimony or bismuth.

The conclusion was that there was no evidence of poisoning in any of the three women. Libby and Aunt Lil had been right all along. Poor old Decima had been framed and hanged not only for a crime she hadn't committed, but for a crime which had never been committed at all. The Victorian Lord Allingham had taken full advantage of a normal, if tragic, event, where three relatively young mothers had all fallen ill within a short space of time – more than likely of the same food-poisoning bug or even some sort of then-unknown virus – and he had twisted the situation to his own appalling ends. If anyone was a killer, it was Lord Allingham and not Decima, but like many despots, he had employed others to get their hands dirty whilst he had walked away with his reputation untarnished. Well, until now! Maddie fully intended to expose the old bastard for exactly what he was, with the help of a media he could never have dreamed of in his wildest fantasies.

She rang the researcher from the TV company and told her the results, happily agreed to pretend to open the envelope for the benefit of the cameras later in the week, then tried to ring her sister to tell her the good news.

No reply. That was odd. Never mind, she would drive over there anyway. This called for a celebration and Libby was always good for an expensive meal, so guilty did she feel at inheriting Lil's millions.

* * *

She had to admire his coolness, though she despised him. Not many men could have walked into a room to find themselves facing an angry ex-girlfriend pointing a shotgun at them and still manage a grin.

He went to put his hands in his pockets, but Libby shifted in her seat and lifted the gun a little higher so it was directly in line with his heart, "Oh no you don't," she said, "hands up, Brendan, just like in the movies."

"Can I at least sit down?"

"Nope. Don't worry, this won't take long, you won't be standing more than a few minutes."

He shrugged and did as she asked, though the grin was still firmly in place and she realized that he was patronising her. He really didn't think she would fire the gun. For her own satisfaction she had to convince him that she really did intend to kill him. After all he had put her through, it was not enough to simply pull the trigger, she wanted to see him squirm a bit first. She also needed to make sure that she wanted to do it. She needed to weigh the pros and cons for a little longer. How she felt now, facing the slimy creep, would tell her whether he was really worth going to jail for.

"Whatever you say, honey. If there's one thing I've learned in life its never argue with a woman holding a gun."

"This has happened to you before?" she asked in mock surprise, "You astound me. You mean to tell me that there are other women you've pursued and persecuted enough for them to want to blow you away?"

"A couple," he admitted guardedly.

"Doesn't that tell you something about your behaviour, Brendan? Doesn't that tell you that you're a complete nutter? A raging loony who needs locking up in a psychiatric ward, not a prison?"

His lips tightened almost imperceptibly, the smirk slipping for a second. He hadn't liked that, not one little bit.

"Shut up, Libby and put the gun away. You're a silly girl and we both know you don't have the bottle to pull the trigger, so why are we going through this charade?"

It was Libby's turn to grin, "But that's where you're wrong pal. I've got it all worked out. I can kill you, splatter your brains all over that wall behind you, and I'm going to walk away scot-free."

"And how do you propose to do that?"

"Easy – and you helped me get there! You see, your pursuit of me has been enough to send me over the edge. You've managed to convince everyone that I'm the loony, that I'm unbalanced and suicidal. You've made sure everyone thinks I see and hear things that aren't there, so when I shoot you, I'm going to plead guilty but while the balance of my mind was disturbed – and who disturbed it? Why you, of course!"

"They'll still put you away," he countered, but he was beginning to look a little less sure of himself.

"They may – but it won't be for long. Let's face it, I have enough money to hire the best legal team in the country. If they can't paint a picture of a poor, deluded hysteric, driven to the borders of insanity by a stalker, then I'll serve the time and look happy about it. It will be worth it, knowing that when I come out, it will be to a world that doesn't have you in it!"

"You'd really serve time for me, I'm touched," he said sarcastically.

"Well, you know I would, but I still think I won't have to. There is another point that I think you are overlooking."

"Really, what's that?"

"You are currently standing on my property. I do believe that there is a restraining order on you, saying that you shouldn't be within miles of me, let alone in my house. And being the poor, terrified little woman that I am, it would be natural for me to try and defend myself against an intruder."

"Others have tried that," he said dismissively, "murder is murder, even if it is killing a burglar."

"Oh, but I'm allowed to use 'reasonable force' and can I help it if my prowess with a shotgun is so poor that I attempted to fire a warning shot over your head and – oops! I missed!"

She lifted the gun to her shoulder and put her eye to the sight, "Prepare to meet your maker, Brendan, even though he did cock up quite spectacularly when he created you!"

She wished she had both eyes open for the expression of pure terror that passed across his face. She felt a grim delight that she had indeed managed to convince him that she was deadly serious.

"Come on, Libby, you've had your fun and so have I. Let's just calm down."

"I'm perfectly calm," she said, "but I will be a quivering wreck when they find me standing over your bloody corpse!"

"Don't be ridiculous. This has gone far enough. Can we discuss this rationally?"

"No discussion necessary, pal. I'm getting exactly what I want and I don't need to negotiate with you, thanks all the same."

"All right, you win. Give me a few grand and I'll disappear. No court case and you'll never see me again."

"But Brendan, I'd much rather give a lawyer a few grand to get me off and I'll still never see you again! You really don't have much to bring to the table, do you?"

"Do you want me to beg?" he asked, between gritted teeth.

"That would be nice," she answered, "I'd like to see that. Get down on your knees then, hands behind your head, and tell me you're sorry."

She let him grovel for a few minutes before she interrupted the flow of his false Irish charm, "Nah, it's not doing anything for me, shut up and close your eyes. I don't want to have to look into those sparkling green eyes as I pull the trigger – too off-putting."

"Libby …" he licked his lips and she grinned in triumph.

"I've finally scared you back, haven't I?"

"Yes, alright, you've had your revenge. Now let me walk away."

"Nope. I want you dead."

Libby would never be quite sure if she could have pulled the trigger. She was mad enough to, for brief snatches of time during their conversation. She felt such a cold fury when he begged her for mercy that she really felt she could have shot him without a second thought. He had subjected her to such terror, such abject misery and fear, that she wanted him gone from her life forever, but she wasn't sure she could kill, not him, not anyone.

If Maddie hadn't walked in at that moment who knew how it would have ended?

"What's going on here?" asked her sister, taking in the cowering Brendan and the armed and dangerous Libby with one intrigued glance sweeping of the room.

"I was just about to kill Brendan," said Libby calmly.

"Oh, good, can I watch?" said Maddie and Libby grinned with delight at the wild look in Brendan's eyes. He was well aware that Maddie was crazy enough to shoot him. She had already done so, after all. She had only knee-capped him, but she had done it in cold blood, having already threatened to shoot him in the genitals. He had a feeling he had got off lightly on that occasion, he was not sure he would be so fortunate this time.

"Get that mad bitch out of here!" he shrieked, suddenly really panicked. He had been fairly confident of talking Libby down, but Maddie the witch was quite another matter.

"What are you waiting for?" demanded Maddie, "shoot the green-eyed slug, or give me the gun and I'll do it!"

While Brendan snivelled and Libby and Maddie enjoyed his discomfiture, Matt sneaked up behind Brendan and slapped a none-too gentle hand on his shoulder, whereupon Brendan screamed like a girl and nearly fainted with fright. Meanwhile David entered the room behind him and frowned at Libby.

"What the hell do you think you're playing at?"

"Getting a bit of my own back," said Libby calmly.

"Well, now you've had it, so put that bloody gun down, you mad cow!"

"You've no right to tell me what to do," she snapped back, "You lost any say in my life when you walked out!"

"Yes, well now I'm back. Now do as you're told."

"Am I still a mad cow?" she challenged him.

"Yes, but you're my mad cow," he took the gun off her and dragged her to her feet so that he could kiss her more easily.

"Thank God, you've arrived in the nick of time. That loopy bitch was about to kill me!" said Brendan to Matt.

"Really?" said Matt, "Because all I see here is a stalker who's been allowed out of jail on the understanding that he doesn't come within miles of a law-abiding citizen. You're under arrest, mate."

Brendan's mouth dropped open, "You've got to be kidding me! You're arresting me after what she's just done? She threatened me with a shotgun, for God's sake!"

"A perfectly legal one, I think you'll find. Mrs Wright is a fully licensed gun holder since her aunt's death, when she took over the ownership of her late uncle's shotgun."

"So that's how it's going to work, is it?" asked Brendan bitterly.

"It certainly is. Aren't we policemen just absolute bastards?"

CHAPTER FORTY-NINE

They found Jane and Moncrieff in conversation, but no sign of Constance.

"Where is Miss Allingham?" demanded Lazarus, whilst Stonier cast his eye about the room, then went to the kitchen to quiz Sally.

"Why the deuce should we tell you?" asked the young man rudely, "You can just go and play dice with the devil!"

The inspector forced himself to remain calm, much as he wanted to slap the youthful Moncrieff and force an answer from him, "Mr Moncrieff, much as I would love to spend my morning in verbal jousting with you, I'm very much afraid Miss Allingham is in deadly peril and I need to find her immediately."

Jane's hand flew to her throat in horror, "Mr Lazarus, is that true?"

"It is, ma'am."

"But how can that be, when Mr Holbrook is with her?"

Despite his mad dash to find her, part of Lazarus had been hoping that he was mistaken, that Holbrook had some other victim in mind. To have his deepest fears confirmed was almost enough to knock him off his feet.

"Oh, sweet Jesus," he whispered under his breath.

Jane looked shocked at the blasphemy, but it merely drove home to her, more strongly than anything else could have, that Lazarus was in earnest and Constance really was in danger.

"Where did they go?" asked Lazarus, but he could barely speak, his mouth suddenly dry.

She was almost weeping with terror, "I don't know. She would not say. He had warned her most strongly that she must tell no-one that she was seeing him. She only confided in me because she was concerned that I might worry about her."

"What exactly did he say to her?"

"He offered a way out of her troubles. She was so distressed at the situation in which she found herself. She was devastated that she must cause Mr Moncrieff pain, but she knew she must follow her heart. I know Mr Holbrook approached her and offered her consolation. He told her that he had a plan which would end all her problems for her, but that she must on no account let anyone know that he was helping her. He said he would get in the most dreadful trouble from Mr Bembridge if it were known that he had offered succour. He said Mr Bembridge had the strongest possible objection to him interfering in affairs of the heart because his own moral code was so very unbending."

"He must have used the same beguiling offer to all his victims. No wonder not one of them breathed a word."

"Constance would not have done so, either, had she not had me here to worry about. What did he mean, that he could help her find a way out of her troubles?" The hesitant way she asked the question told Lazarus that she knew full well what the answer was, but wanted him to deny it for her. He wished with all his heart that he could do so.

"Let us endeavour to track them down so that we never have to find out," he said grimly. He took his pocket watch out and flipped open the cover, "It's now nearly eleven. I suspect that he will offer her something to eat at lunch time. We have little more than an hour to find them. Are you positive she gave no clue where they might be headed?"

"Not a word was said as to their destination, I'm sure of it."

"Did he come in the gig or did they perhaps take a cab or the omnibus?"

"No, he came in the gig."

Lazarus rubbed his chin with his hand, trying to put himself in the shoes of the maniac curate. Where would he go? If he did indeed intend to make an attempt on Constance's life, he needed to take her somewhere isolated. Unfortunately he could not be relied upon to use his usual method of killing, by using poison, for he had already proved that he had no particular aversion to murder by other methods. The only thing Lazarus could know with a fair amount of certainty was that he would not lay hands on the young woman. This was a man who killed only at a distance. Or at least he had until now. Lazarus felt sick when he thought of Constance in the company of the madman, all unaware of the danger in which she stood.

Stonier came back from the kitchen, shaking his head to Lazarus' questions about Sally's knowledge of her mistress's whereabouts.

"All Sally knows is that they went off in the direction of the church, but there are a dozen turnoffs they could have taken once they were out of sight."

"We have no choice but to try there first. He may think we are still interviewing Bembridge, after he so carefully sent the man into our trap."

As Stonier took the reins and clicked the pony into a smart trot, he asked his superior to explain the situation more fully. He felt as though he had missed out on several large chunks of information whilst Lazarus had been in possession of certain facts which gave him the advantage.

The inspector explained impatiently, then gave in to his deeper emotions, much to Stonier's surprise, who had known his friend was fond of Constance Allingham, but had no idea they had fallen in love with each other and that the Moncrieff engagement was all but over.

"Tom, I can't believe I have been such an idiot. How could I be taken in by that façade of pleasant simplicity that Holbrook hid behind?"

"Don't blame yourself for that, old man," said Tom kindly, "we all were taken in by him, including his victims. What I don't understand is why he did it. What prompts a man to kill a procession of innocent people?"

"That's the whole point, isn't it? In his eyes, they weren't innocent. God knows why he should feel it was his duty to do away with 'sinners' but he has and we have to make sure he doesn't kill another."

"But why Miss Allingham? I understand that she has broken her betrothal but that is no real crime, is it?"

"I don't think it is the broken engagement that has incensed him, but the fact that she thought I was married and has probably confessed that to him. I was foolish enough to allow my feelings to overcome me the other night. I kissed her in plain view on her doorstep – and I now know that he spent a great deal of his time creeping about the town and spying on those he suspected of immoral behaviour. His twisted mind would naturally assume that we had been together in the house indulging our passion."

"And were you?" asked Stonier, forgetting himself for a moment and becoming a policeman and not a friend.

"Certainly not!"

The church hall was not deserted, as Lazarus had been assuming, but in full use by the ladies of the parish. Of course they were still providing their charitable soup kitchen, he thought, almost amazed that life was still going on in the ordinary way, whilst he was engaged in a frantic search for the woman he loved.

Bembridge was back at the vicarage, but he too had no idea where they might find his curate. His astonishment that they should suspect the amiable Holbrook was bordering upon the comical.

"Really, Mr Lazarus?" he said in his most condescending tone, "Holbrook a murderer? Don't you think I might have been aware of his comings and goings?"

"If you were, sir, and said nothing, you will still have charges to face," responded the policeman grimly, which had the desired effect of pricking the older man's pomposity.

"Where now?" asked Stonier, "I can't think of anywhere else."

"What about the empty house where he hid when he shot Miss Soffley?"

They retraced their path and found the house as disappointingly empty as it had ever been.

"Damn, damn, damn!" exclaimed Lazarus, "They must be somewhere. Come on, Tom, think. Where is there an empty, isolated house?"

"The only place I can think of that is isolated is the cottage in the woods, where Janet Riley lives. We sent her away remember."

Lazarus looked at his companion as if he thought he might just be in the presence of a genius, "Of course, that's it! He imagines it will be the last place we will look because we were there to arrest Bembridge, and so we have ticked it off our list. He must be there. He has planned everything down to the last detail. He hoped to kill Mrs Riley, but we managed to prevent that; though unfortunately we also alerted him to the fact that we were closing in on him. That was why he persuaded Bembridge to go to the cottage. He knew damn well we would assume the vicar was our man."

"He's been clever, I'll grant him that."

"He's been careful to throw dust in our eyes right from the first. There has always been someone obvious for us to suspect. Young Crabtree was the first sacrificial lamb, and had I managed to bring him to the gallows, well, I would simply have been doing Holbrook's work for him, in punishing a sinner – though his was the sin of fornication, not murder."

"So it was 'Liza Dunne he was trying to kill when he hit Soffley with the arrow?"

"Of course. She knew Mollie was spending lots of time at the church, though she didn't know who with. When we continued to question her, Holbrook started to panic, thinking the girl would give him away. Miss Soffley, because she could not resist asserting her rights and loved giving vent to her grievances, stepped in front of Eliza at just the crucial moment and paid with her life."

Tom looked thoughtful, "In using a bow and arrow he gave us a great long list of possible suspects, since toxophily is a local pastime in which half the county indulges."

"Absolutely," agreed Lazarus, "Even the vicar takes part in the Allingham summer garden party competition!"

It seemed to take a dreadfully long time to reach Janet Riley's cottage and when they did it was already past twelve o'clock. Lazarus found himself praying that Constance had partaken of a large breakfast and had therefore refused any food or drink Holbrook might offer her.

The door was unlocked and they walked into the low-ceilinged kitchen to find Holbrook and Constance sitting quite companionably at the table. Constance looked up and was astounded to see Lazarus, but still she smiled happily, if a little shyly.

"Mr Lazarus, what are you doing here?"

"Looking for you, my dear. Are you well?"

"Of course. Why do you ask?"

"Has Mr Holbrook given you any food or drink, Constance?"

She looked even more astonished, "Yes, as a matter of fact he has, but what is going on, Danby?"

Holbrook was watching this exchange with interest, but no other apparent emotion.

Lazarus tried to remain stoic, but his heart was pounding and his mouth was dry, "Constance, my love, I need you to come with me, right now."

"She's going nowhere," said Holbrook suddenly vicious and Constance threw him a bewildered look. She had never heard him behave in anything other than a mild and pleasant manner and this change of tone to a man of purpose and determination was so out of character that she began to worry.

"Please will someone tell me what is going on?" she asked, but the three men ignored her and she could feel the tension in the room grow with every passing second.

"Holbrook, you have the situation wrong this time. I need you to know that Miss Allingham has done absolutely nothing wrong."

Holbrook laughed cruelly, "You of all people would say that, Lazarus! How does your wife feel about your philandering?"

"My wife died three years ago, Mr Holbrook," said Lazarus gently, "I repeat and I emphasise that Miss Allingham has done nothing wrong. She is as unblemished as the day she was born. Do you understand what I am saying to you?"

The colour drained from the younger man's face, "I don't believe you," he said hoarsely.

"I promise you that it is true. This time you have chosen your victim ill, and God will judge you harshly for it!"

Holbrook seemed to take several long seconds to digest what the policeman was saying, then he made his decision.

"Stonier, I trust you. You are a good man. Is the inspector telling me the truth?"

"He is, Mr Holbrook. I have known Mr Lazarus for nearly fifteen years. He would not take advantage of a young lady. If he says there has been no wrong between him and Miss Allingham, then it is the unvarnished truth."

"Then you must get Miss Allingham to a doctor immediately. Tell him she must empty her stomach as soon as is humanly possible."

They never knew whether it was the shock of realising she had been poisoned, or the effects of whatever it was Holbrook had given her, but Constance suddenly slid to the floor in a dead faint. Lazarus gave an animal groan of despair and rushed to her side. Hoisting her up into his arms he shouted to Stonier, "Keep him here, Tom, I'll have to take the trap and get her to Dr Scattergood."

"Go, old friend, go now!" answered Stonier.

Within seconds Lazarus was lifting the insensible Constance into the vehicle and was whipping the poor pony into the fastest gallop it could manage.

Holbrook watched them go then turned to Stonier, "He has about twenty minutes, I hope Scattergood is nearby."

"I hope so too, but if he isn't at home, you will have killed her!"

"I know it and I'm sorry. But you must understand that I'm not sorry about the others. They were demons in human form. Their black souls will burn in hell forever."

"They were just people, Holbrook, with flaws like any other. What right did you have to be their judge and executioner?"

Holbrook looked at Stonier as though he were speaking a foreign language, as though what the older man said had no meaning to him at all, "But I am sent here for this purpose, my friend. God set me this task, unsavoury as it might have been. How could I refuse to do as my Lord and Master commanded me?"

"Are you telling me that God spoke to you and told you to kill those young people?"

"Of course."

"Well, you will have to face a judge and jury here on earth before you face your Lord and Master," said Stonier grimly.

Holbrook smiled, "No, I won't. Miss Allingham was not the only one to partake of my little repast."

With dawning horror Stonier realized what the man was telling him. At first he despaired, thinking that he would have to sit here and watch the young man die, since he had no way of getting him to a doctor in time. Then he glanced about the kitchen and saw that there might yet be a chance to save the situation. Before Holbrook could protest, Stonier took out his handcuffs and pulled the curate's arms behind his back. Once the man was shackled, the policeman busied himself pouring a large amount of salt into a glass of water.

"Head back, Holbrook, I have a little concoction of my own and by God, you are going to drink it!"

When the curate realized what Stonier intended, he struggled wildly, but bound as he was, and half as broad in the shoulders as the policeman, he soon found his head forced back and the brine poured down his throat. Within minutes he was vomiting very profitably.

Stonier grinned with grim satisfaction, "Seems harsh, I know, to bring you back, just to see you dangle in the magistrate's picture frame, but that's justice for you!"

CHAPTER FIFTY

PRESENT

"It's pretty good," said Dan as he read the last of the pages Libby had given him, "but when are you going to finish it."

"It is finished," said Libby.

Dan looked aghast, "What do you mean? You can't end it there! Did Constance survive? Did she and Lazarus get together? What happened to young Will Carter?"

Libby shrugged, secretly delighted at his reaction, which was just what she wanted to hear. What better way to know if one has hooked the reader than by such a volley of protests? "I don't know. The diaries and papers seemed to end there. I don't know what happened next."

"Well, bloody well find out!"

"That's where you come in, my old friend. I'm being nothing less than truthful, the stuff I've got really did fizzle out and I don't have a very clear idea of what went on after. We've got to do some digging if we want an end to the story."

He leapt to his feet, "Let's get digging, then. I can't stand this, it's like torture! How could you get me interested in these people then leave me on a cliff edge?"

"It's not my fault," she said waspishly, "How was I to know there wasn't a full story."

"You would have known if you'd done what any normal person would do and read the stuff first before trying to fictionalise it!"

"If I'd done that," she pointed out, "Then I wouldn't have written what I have so far."

"Exactly!" he said emphatically, "And I wouldn't now be wondering what the hell happened a hundred and fifty years ago, when it really shouldn't matter, because everyone is long dead and gone! Really Libby, I could strangle you sometimes!"

After two hours they had searched every archive, box file and shelf they could think of and came up with nothing.

"What the hell are we going to do now?" asked Libby, brushing a damp tendril of hair from her sweaty forehead.

"Your guess is as good as mine," said Dan moodily, "I thought we held all the local police history here in the museum, but I now find there's a huge gap. Probably the best we can do now is look up the names on the next census after your period and see if any of the names still appear. It won't help us much, but we may at least find out if Constance died of poisoning and if she lived, did she marry Lazarus?"

"We could look up and see if Will carter ever appears again too."

"We can, but this is all very unsatisfactory, Libby."

"Well, I'm sorry, but how could I know it would turn out like this?

The look he gave her answered that question very fully without him saying a single word.

She glanced at her watch, "Oops, I've got to go. Maddie rang and invited herself over this afternoon, said she had something exciting to tell me. She's probably had the results of the DNA test or something. Can I leave that with you, then?"

"You cheeky …"

She grinned, "Now, Dan, you know you are far better at all this than I am. Give me a ring as soon as you find anything." With that she was gone and Dan realized he could either stand about fulminating at her gall or get onto the internet and start trying to trace a few dead people.

Surprisingly Maddie was not alone. Libby's mouth dropped open in an extremely unattractive gape when she saw who was accompanying her sister.

"You!" she breathed, for the first time in a long time too stunned to say anything else.

He grinned disarmingly, "That's a nice welcome I must say."

"I can't think of any reason to be welcoming to you," she

answered rudely, "And I'm astounded to see you in the same room as Maddie."

"Now, Libby, stop being so uppity with my fiancè," said Maddie with a grin, knowing full well that this was going to risk Libby dying of an apoplexy.

"What!?"

David stepped forward and offered his hand to his old friend with a wry smile,

"I suppose congratulations are in order, Rick, but I must say that's not exactly the word I would use to any man volunteering to join this family."

Richard Allingham accepted the handshake and the sentiment with equal placidity, "Thanks mate. I appreciate that. I expect your wife will come round eventually." He nodded towards Libby, who had sunk onto a chair and was still rendered speechless, merely looking from her sister's face to Rick's as if trying to detect a vague hint that they were perpetrating some elaborate hoax.

Finally finding her voice, after a painful few seconds, during which everyone stared at her, waiting for her reaction, Libby finally said rather bitterly, "Don't bother with the congratulations, David, this is a total wind-up. There's no way these two are getting married."

Maddie was affronted, "Oh yes we are. Why don't you believe us? Think you are the only member of the family who can catch herself a husband?"

Libby knew that Maddie had been furious that her younger sister had been married before her, but she hadn't thought it rankled enough to make her consider this drastic solution but she could hardly say anything of the kind, so she went for the kinder comment, "Well, for a start, I can't see Rick's boyfriend being too happy with the arrangement."

"Oh, Paul and I split months ago," said Rick, his insouciant tone hiding a wealth of unhappiness, "Mother finally drove him away, though he always swore to me she wouldn't manage it."

Maddie reached out a comforting hand and squeezed Rick's arm, "To be fair to him, love, it can't have been easy withstanding the constant carping."

Libby and David exchanged a glance. They had neither of them expected this show of affection from Maddie, nor could they believe that Rick had confided so much of his private life to her. There was more to this relationship than was at first evident.

"How long have you two been seeing each other?" asked David suspiciously.

"Rick and I got in touch when the whole thing blew up last year. We've been seeing each other to try and bring about a solution without resorting to lawyers and feuds."

Libby observed her sister with renewed admiration. She had this all planned out, knowing full well that Rick was the soft touch in the Allingham Clan. She would never have beaten his mother, had she fought for a century, but by getting Rick on her side right from the beginning, it was only a matter of time before he was hooked in one way or another. Friendship with Rick was the carrot, the threat of legal action against the Allinghams was the stick. Either way she won. Maddie, as usual, had all bases covered.

"But you are not trying to pretend that you fell in love with each other?" asked Libby, brutal in her inherent honesty. She certainly wasn't going to let either of them think they had fooled her for a moment.

"Not love, no," said Maddie, with a fond glance at Rick, "but brought together for our mutual benefit. Rick's mother is never going to let up on him until he has produced a legitimate heir, and I want justice. It's a no-brainer to bring those two things together."

"But how are you going to make it work?" asked Libby, despairing of ever getting her sister to see just how crazy this scheme was and how it simply spelled disaster for them both.

"How does any marriage work?" asked Maddie flippantly, "I don't see what right you have to judge. Yours wasn't doing too well up until a day ago!"

Libby decided not to rise to that particular provocation and attempted to say what she had to in a delicate manner. She still didn't know Rick well enough to be as graphic as she would have been had she and her sibling been alone.

"Not to put too fine a point upon it, how are you going to manage the having children aspect of the union?"

"I don't think that's any of your business," said Rick, but he sounded remarkably unfazed by the question.

"Never heard of turkey basters?" asked Maddie with a giggle.

Libby blushed to the roots of her hair in response to both these answers and David was unkind enough to laugh and say, "Well, you did ask, Lib!"

"All right," she snapped, "I didn't ask to be salacious, I'm merely trying to point out that this is not quite so simple as you seem to think. You are both single now, but what will happen if one or both of you fall in love with someone else? Where is that going to leave the marriage and any children you may have?"

"We've both agreed that once we have an heir and a spare, we'll be free to go our own ways. We'll stay married, but we'll be discreet."

Unable to find a way to express just how horrified she was by this, Libby could only throw up her hands in despair and say tersely, "I give up! You two deserve each other if you think this is any way at all to behave."

"Oh, come down off your high horse," said Maddie, "When are you going to accept that you are not the arbitrator of acceptable behaviour? Rick and I know exactly what we are doing and we are going into this with wide open eyes. Get it into your head, Libby, we don't care what you think."

"Well said," David interpolated, "Let's have a drink to celebrate. I think I can rustle up a rather good bottle of red."

"No champers?" asked Maddie facetiously, "You are going to have to get used to providing me with champagne, David, I'm moving in altogether loftier circles now, you know."

She went off with him to help find the glasses and Libby was excruciatingly embarrassed to find herself alone with Rick.

He sat down beside her on the sofa and said softly, "I know your heart is in the right place, Libby, and I want to assure you that Maddie and I really do know what we are doing. Would it help if I promise to look after her?"

"It would help a little, Rick, but I don't see how you can keep an oath like that when it may be beyond your capabilities. Maddie likes to give the impression that she's as hard as nails, but I know she would be devastated if you humiliated her by going off with someone behind her back. She would also suffer horrendous guilt if she was tempted into doing the same to you. You both think you are being terribly modern and pragmatic, but I know you are both loving people. Neither of you is going to be able to exist without love in your lives."

"How do you know we don't have a sort of love already?"

"Do you?"

Rick looked thoughtful, "You may not believe this, Libby, but I've never met anyone like your sister. She is strong, determined, quite possibly mad, and I know that I could stand spending a lot of time in her company – which I've never felt about a woman before, I can assure you!"

"And what about her?"

"Be honest, have you ever known her be that into guys that she's spent broken-hearted nights weeping over lost boyfriends?"

Libby thought back over their mutual past and was surprised to realize that no, Maddie had never actually been that interested in the opposite sex. She'd always been far more driven by her work than romance. The only men she had seriously dated had been those who could further her career.

She frowned at her companion, "Are you trying to break it to me that my sister is gay too?" she asked, dangerously calm.

Rick laughed, "I've no idea. I haven't asked her that particular question. I was just trying to point out that not everyone in the world is driven by romance. If Maddie is happy then you should be happy for her, even if you don't approve."

"Well, I don't, and I can't help it. But you are right, I've said my piece and now I'll hold my tongue – but I'm warning you now, if in the future I think either of you is behaving in a way that is detrimental to these theoretical children you are planning on, then I will kick both your arses!"

"Agreed. But I can promise that if we are blessed, I intend to make sure any kids of mine are raised to be happy and fulfilled human beings – in other words, my mother will be allowed very limited access to them!"

With that Libby had to be satisfied.

When Maddie and David returned, bearing a bottle of champagne that David had found at the back of the fridge, left over from their own nuptials and forgotten in the salad drawer ever since, Libby managed to thaw enough to hug her sister and wish her all the happiness in the world, even if she didn't believe the words as she spoke them.

As the bubbles worked their magic, they all visibly relaxed and the conversation became general. Maddie and Rick were only too eager to tell their in-laws of the many plans they had for their home, most importantly telling the future mother-in-law that she was welcome to make use of the London house, but that Derbyshire was basically off limits for her. David was reinstated as the official plant-provider for Havering Hall and the mention of the stately home brought something to the foreground for Libby, which the shocks of the last hour or so had driven from her mind. She debated with herself how soon it would be permissible to ask for access to the Allingham papers. A month? A week? She decided that she would ask anyway.

"Ooh, speaking of Havering, Rick, now that the vendetta is over and we are to be related, please could I have access to the library? I've come to a standstill in my book and I need a bit more info."

"Libby!" admonished her husband, "You really are the limit! Can't you show a bit of decorum and at least let the man get used to being a member of the family before you start demanding favours?"

"You don't ask, you don't get," said Libby succinctly.

"I don't see why not," said Rick, well-mellowed by his second glass of bubbly, "Come over whenever you like, and I'll tell my archivist to let you run amok. In fact, if you are nice to him, he'll probably give you a hand."

"Thanks. I'll go over tomorrow, if that's okay?"

"Fine by me. I think my mother will be gone by then – in fact when we go home now and break the news to her, I shouldn't be at all surprised if she's not on the late train to London tonight!"

"You mean you haven't told her yet?" asked Libby, aghast.

"No, we have yet to face that – and telling mum too," said Maddie, in a far-too light-hearted tone for Libby's liking. Honestly, the woman had absolutely no sense of danger or self-preservation!

"Good luck with that, then," said Libby gloomily, "Let me know if you are still engaged by tomorrow, because if one of our mothers doesn't put an end to it, then I'll be astounded."

"You worry too much," said Maddie and held out her glass for more booze, which sadly had run out.

"Fetch the red," said Rick and he and Maddie fell against each other laughing.

Libby thought about her own mother and the formidable Lady Allingham and reflected that she didn't think the pair of them would be laughing for long.

CHAPTER FIFTY-ONE

Maddie came down the front steps to meet her as Libby drew up outside, a huge smile adorning her face. Libby had to admit she had never seen her sister look happier and as they went into the house together, Maddie never drew breath telling her about all the plans she and Rick had for making the place an even bigger draw for the public than it was already. As she listened, not really taking in anything that was said, Libby realized with quite a shock that Havering was to be Maddie's new project. It was scarcely credible to the highly sensitive Libby, but Maddie really was going to be quite content as the joint owner of this ancient pile of stones, and she would take to motherhood in a similar manner. Suddenly Libby could see her with two boys and perhaps even a girl too, arranging riding lessons and overseeing piano practice, with a couple of setters leaving their hairs everywhere. Maddie would set about all this in the same businesslike way as she did everything else in life. If she did take a lover, it would be well away from home and she would be in the driving seat, dictating when it began, when it ended and how the affair was conducted. It wasn't the way Libby would want to live her life, but who was she to inflict her morals on anyone else?

Maddie took her to the library, saying, "Take as long as you like. We'll have tea together when you're done if you like. The butler will know where to find me."

The butler, thought Libby, now I really have heard it all! Of course she hadn't, because it happened that not only did Havering Hall boast a butler and a full compliment of indoor and outdoor staff, just like the "good old days", but Rick also employed an archivist to make sense of three hundred years of family and estate papers.

He rose as Libby entered the room and walked across to greet her.

He was tall with blond hair, just a little grey at the temples, which just served to make him look erudite, and his naturally solemn expression immediately lightened into the most charming smile Libby had ever seen on a librarian. She had to quickly remind herself that she was happily married.

"Hi," he said, proffering his hand, "I'm Dave Allen, I understand you are Libby Wright, Maddie's sister?"

"That's right – you mean Dave Allen as in the Irish comedian from the 1970's?"

He grinned and held up his spread fingers, "Yes, the same, but I have all my digits, as you can see." Libby barely remembered Dave Allen, but when he said that she recalled that he had indeed had half a finger missing – her father had been a huge fan.

"Are you funny?" she asked teasingly.

"I'll let you be the judge of that. Now, what can I do for you? Rick mentioned something about the Lord Allingham of the 1850's onwards?"

"He's the one – though I ought to warn you, I'm not very fond of him. In fact I think he was a grade one bas… evil person!" she corrected herself hastily.

"I agree, he was – and I think you'll find that Rick feels that way too. He was not a nice fellow. Come and sit down and we'll try and furnish you with the information you need."

Libby felt quite nervous about sitting on chairs which she was more used to seeing festooned with red silken cords to prevent members of the public using them. She wondered anew how her sister could ever feel comfortable or at home in a place so huge and packed with priceless antiques. The table that stood between her seat and Dave Allen's was worth more than she had earned in her first year at work.

Dave soon set her at her ease though by embarking straight onto the subject which had grown to be so important to her in the past few months.

"So what exactly is it you want to know about Lord William Allingham and his family?"

Libby gave him a swift rundown on what she had learned so far, but when she reached the part where Arabella's peccadillo came to light, he raised an eyebrow and gave a silent whistle of surprise, "Wow! She managed to keep that quiet. According to the family history I've read Arabella had a serious, unspecified illness which required a long convalescence by the seaside."

"I can assure you she never went anywhere near the sea," said Libby grimly, "she might just have seen a couple of stray seagulls circling over the river Mersey, but that's about it."

"Interesting," commented Dave, "but in the end it made very little difference. It sounds as though Lord Allingham nearly broke his neck his to keep it all hushed up because he planned a hugely advantageous marriage for her and couldn't risk any breath of scandal. However, his second son died shortly afterwards and Arabella was sacrificed on the altar of family duty."

Libby was immediately intrigued, "Really? How so?"

"Naturally you know about the older son, Richard, being killed in the Crimea?"

"Of course, it's through him that we have a claim on the estate."

Dave grinned, "And what ructions that has caused! Not that I'm complaining. It's partly through you that I have a job. Why do you think it has suddenly become so vital to archive the family history? I think they were hoping against hope to find something to refute your case."

"Did they?"

"Not a thing – quite the contrary. Everything I have dug up has merely strengthened your case. Lord Allingham wasn't particularly lucky where his children were concerned. First he lost Richard, then his younger brother William junior."

"What happened? He hasn't really been mentioned in the stuff I've been reading. In fact not at all. I didn't know he existed."

"Not surprising. In the early 1860's he was away at Oxford University and behaving fairly reprehensibly if the reports written at the time can be believed. Basically he was whoring and drinking his way through Uni, as is perhaps not entirely surprising. He had lost his older brother and was faced with the prospect of inheriting a vast estate, the responsibility of which must have been somewhat daunting. Small wonder that he was determined to enjoy what he probably saw as his last chance of freedom."

"So, did he catch something nasty?" asked Libby, trying to relish the idea of Lord Allingham's suffering should that have been the case.

"No, he was stabbed in a brawl over a prostitute, whilst in his cups, as the old expression used to be."

"So he was basically bladdered. Was she worth it?"

"Apparently not. She was forty-seven and reportedly toothless."

"What a loser," said Libby with contempt, "What a complete waste of a life. So what happened next?"

"That left Arabella as Allingham's only surviving child and he was determined that his direct descendants would inherit, so she was married off to her cousin, who would have been the next male heir."

"Couldn't he just have left everything to her?"

"No chance. The entail was tied tighter than the knot on a miser's purse strings. The only way Allingham could pass on his genes was through his wayward daughter. And from all accounts she wasn't much improved by the stability of marriage. She produced the heir and a spare then went her own wild way. She died of a heart attack at the age of fifty two in the arms of a twenty year old lover, having drunk and eaten herself to obesity."

"Oh dear," said Libby, suitably repressed by this sad tale. She had been envisioning Arabella as a pretty but silly little thing, capable of rousing pity from Stonier and Lazarus, but this made her realize how swiftly life passed and how things could all go so terribly wrong – still, at least the lover had been only twenty. There was always a plus side if you looked for it. That thought, however, raised another horrifying scenario and she added almost reluctantly, "She didn't end up crushing the lover to death or anything dreadful like that, did she?"

Dave Allen laughed, "If she did, it wasn't reported."

"Thank goodness for that. Now what about Constance? Did she marry Inspector Lazarus?"

He looked across the table at her for a few seconds before he said, "I have found some papers that will interest you, but I'm pretty sure the Allinghams wouldn't want you to see them."

"But you are going to give them to me anyway?" she answered hopefully.

"I really shouldn't. In fact, Lord Allingham didn't want anyone to see them. He left instructions for them to be burned when he died, but for some reason they were shoved to the back of a cupboard instead. I only found them the other day and from the layer of dust, I think it's quite likely they haven't been touched since his death."

"Well, you absolutely have to show me now!"

"I should ask permission."

"Now you know as well as I do what the answer would be – and if this stuff was supposed to be burned, then presumably the present family don't know about it?"

"That's true – but academic!"

Libby turned tragic eyes upon him, "Please, Dave, don't leave me in suspense! I promise I'll never breath a word about where the info came from. And I also promise I won't write anything derogatory about the family. After all, they are about to become my family too, so I'm not about to slag them off."

He pretended to consider her request for a few more seconds, but they both knew he had been won over by her personality.

"You did say you were married?" he asked.

She grinned, "Yes, I'm afraid so – very happily."

"Let me know if that ever changes," he said and went over to one of the many cupboards which lined the bases of each of the ceiling high bookshelves. He scrabbled in the back, pulling out other objects and piling them behind him, until he found the thing he sought and handed her a dusty box, which was marked only with his own fingerprints and evidently really hadn't been handled for a long, long time.

"I really need some time to look over this stuff. Can I take it home?"

He looked startled, then shrugged resignedly, "Might as well be hung for a sheep as a lamb," he quoted, "I suggest we meet back here tomorrow at the same time so you can hand them back."

"Them?" asked Libby, "So there's not just a letter or something?"

"Lord Allingham's personal journals," he corrected, "And no wonder he didn't want anyone to read them!"

Now Libby could scarcely wait to get out of there and home to peruse her treasure. She forced herself to take her leave in a calm and polite manner. The last thing she wanted to do right now was cause offence to her new best friend!

As usual life took over and scuppered her plans. She drove home just barely inside the speed limit so eager was she to get to work, but when she arrived it was to find the other David in her life waiting for her, having prepared a special lunch.

"I thought it was time we had a talk," he said, "We need to get back on track, don't you think?"

Libby thought she ought to be allowed to cuddle up in her favourite arm chair with a glass of wine and something playing quietly on the music centre whilst she read someone else's private thoughts written over a hundred years ago, but she realized that to voice that desire might very well kill the present stone dead, and satisfying though it might be from an historical point of view, she couldn't risk it.

She forced a smile to her lips, "Can't think of anything I'd like more," she said, hoping she didn't sound insincere. Of course she wanted to sort out her marriage – just not right this very minute!

David had prepared all her favourites and once they were seated opposite each other and the first glass of wine had begun to go down, she found Lord Allingham fading into the background.

"You know I'm sorry, don't you, Libby?" asked David, once their first hunger was a little sated, "I was too fixated on how all this mess of your sister's was affecting me, and I never gave a thought to what you were going through with that bloody madman Brendan."

"I understood, David, really I did. You thought Brendan was safely locked up, just like I did and I know it has taken you a long time to build up your business. All you could see was Maddie destroying it in one fell swoop for a principle which must have seemed just this side of pure madness to you."

"She did seem to be spitting into the wind," he admitted, "How was I to know that she actually had enough of a case to scare the

Allinghams into action?"

"Hey, don't beat yourself up about it. I thought she was bloody crazy too. I think I still do. How can she bring herself to marry Rick, knowing what she knows?"

David shook his head half in despair at his sister-in-law's latest escapade and half in confusion as to what was driving his friend into joining her, "Don't ask me. I don't understand either of them, but I'm more concerned with our marriage right now, let them take care of theirs!"

She toyed with her wineglass, trying to formulate her next question in such a way that he wouldn't immediately blow up, "What did you really think when you got those photos, David? You didn't honestly believe I'd been playing around behind your back?"

He grinned a little shamefacedly, "I hate to admit it, but my first marriage has left me a little touchy on the subject of betrayal. In my saner moments I know you are not the deceitful sort, but when I opened that envelope, the green-eyed monster took over. I wanted to smash Matt Piper's face in. Then I saw the second picture of you and – what's the guy from the Museum called?"

"Dan," Libby supplied.

"Yeah, Dan. Then I started to have second thoughts. That was Brendan's mistake really – the overkill. I could just about see you getting sick of me and seeing one other bloke – but two? That was never going to happen."

"Oh, thanks for that vote of confidence," said Libby with deep sarcasm, "You saying I don't have the wherewithal to attract two fellas?"

"No, I'm saying you don't have the energy," he said frankly.

That she had to admit was nearer the truth and they laughed.

"That's the first time we have had a laugh together in months," said David rather sadly.

"Not quite months," protested Libby, but she knew he wasn't far wrong.

"So what are we going to do about it?"

"Just let me finish this book and then I'll devote myself to you entirely," promised Libby.

David gave her a long appraising look, "Do you think you won't have an idea for a new book the minute this one is finished?"

She met his eyes with a challenge of her own, "I'll make you a deal," she said, "I'll devote less time to writing if you devote less time to the garden centre."

"Okay," he said, raising his glass to drink to the oath. She clinked glasses with him.

"How long do you think that will last?" she asked.

"Oh, about a week," he said.

"But what a week it will be!"

CHAPTER FIFTY-TWO

Allingham found Lazarus pacing Constance's parlour floor, a glass of brandy untouched on the occasional table, his face white with strain.

"How is she?" asked the uncle, dispensing with the formality of greetings in his agitation.

"Not good. Scattergood is with her. If anyone can save her, it is he."

The peer sank into a chair and without thinking picked up the brandy and swallowed it in one gulp.

"What the devil has been going on, Lazarus? Why did that maniac target my niece? I understood he had been killing those whom he felt had transgressed the laws of the church in some way, so what possible reason could he have for murdering my precious heifer?"

The inspector bunched his fist, but managed to restrain himself from planting it squarely on his companion's nose by telling himself that the idiot actually believed that he was using a pet name when he called his brother's child a 'heifer'.

"He was mislead," he answered shortly, loath to confide in the obnoxious old man. He certainly wasn't going to admit his own part in the misunderstanding.

"Mislead in what way? I don't understand any of this."

Lazarus contemplated the empty fireplace. He was going to have to make some sort of an admission, but it was vital it was not one that Allingham could use for his own purposes. He might be in shock now, but he wouldn't remain so for long and once the truth had sunk in, the man would have no hesitation in destroying the reputation of both Lazarus and Constance, if it suited him.

"The curate thought that I was still married. When Constance broke off her engagement and seemed to transfer her affections to me, Holbrook thought he was saving her from making the error of becoming a married man's mistress."

It took a few seconds for Allingham to process this information, but obviously something was not quite making sense to him.

"But why should he imagine you were married? What gave him that impression? You are not hiding a wife from us all, are you?" This last was supposed to be an attempt at humour, but there was a sharp look to accompany the sally which Lazarus didn't miss.

"My wife has been dead these three years," said Lazarus grimly, "In fact she died not long after Decima Watkins."

At the mention of that name Allingham went a shade whiter, as Lazarus had suspected he might. So there was a guilty conscience buried somewhere deep in the miserable old sinner's soul then?

"Yes, I seem to recall something of the sort," he muttered, "I apologise."

"For what? Killing Decima or my loss?"

As quickly as the colour had drained it now rushed back into the older man's cheeks, he leapt to his feet, "Damn it all, I wasn't responsible for the law then, no matter how much you want to blame me!"

"Really?" drawled Lazarus, as though bored by the protestation of innocence, "You deny you have every Mason in your pocket from here to Yorkshire? Probably beyond."

"If you think just because I am Grand Master that I can manipulate the law …"

"Save your breath to cool your broth," interrupted Lazarus, "I'm not interested in hearing your excuses. You know as well as I do that Decima Watkins was innocent."

"Then you should have saved her," he retorted cruelly, "You were the policeman in charge of the case."

"In charge? Hardly that, with your Mason cronies defeating me at every move. Poor Decima didn't stand a chance, as you well knew. And if you think I have forgiven myself for letting her down, you are mistaken. I still lie awake at night to the vision of her poor ravaged face when they told her she was to hang. Have you lost a minute's sleep over her, you ruthless bastard?"

The aristocrat in him reasserted itself, "Watch your mouth, Lazarus. You are only tolerated because of the service you did my daughter, but my gratitude will not carry you far."

"I don't want your gratitude. I don't want your assistance in any way. Do your worst and then I shall do mine. The choice is yours."

Allingham was spared the necessity of responding by the entrance of Dr Scattergood, who looked drained but triumphant.

"She'll recover, thank God. That was a nasty poison she was fed. She's going to be ill for some days to come, but provided she has careful nursing, there should be no long term effects."

For once Lazarus and Lord Allingham were united. They both gasped a heartfelt thanks to the Creator and the doctor for Constance's deliverance, though in slightly different words.

"May I see her now?" asked her uncle, when he had gratefully wrung Scattergood's hand.

"No. She wants to see the inspector, no one else."

At that Lazarus was gone, racing up the stairs, leaving the doctor and the uncle alone together.

"Do you think she will see me when she has spoken to Lazarus?" asked Allingham, and for the first time in his life Scattergood felt sorry for the great landowner. He had little enough reason to sympathise with the man in the past, since it was to keep his coffers filled that good men and women strove and starved, and produced child after child to send out to work to keep a roof over their heads and food in their bellies. Now the man looked every moment of his years. He was evidently fonder of Constance than anyone had supposed.

"I wouldn't waste your time waiting around, Allingham," he counselled, but kindly, reaching out and briefly touching the older man's shoulder, "She's really not fit for visitors and only wants the man she loves with her. Try again tomorrow."

Allingham nodded in defeat and shuffled away, suddenly a very old man, not merely an aged but fit one.

Scattergood left the house with him and saw him into his

carriage, with its doors emblazoned with the Allingham crest.

All the money in the world wasn't going to help with the pain of that rejection.

As the carriage jerked into motion, Allingham stared blindly out of the window, unaware of anything but his own thoughts. He could scarcely believe that his lovely little heifer was actually contemplating marriage with that damned policeman. How could she lower herself so? He knew a moment of discomfort when he recalled the reason Lazarus had given for her leaving, but his ego soon overpowered any hint of blame lying with himself. He had been right to chastise the girl. She had been given the charge of her young cousin and had failed. A horsewhipping should have been the least she would have expected and he swore to himself that when the beating was over and he had been overcome with remorse, that when he bent to kiss her poor abused shoulders, she had shuddered with desire beneath his lips. She felt as he did, he was sure, and only their relationship held her back from expressing her affection. They must go abroad, that was the solution. He would take her to Europe. The French had much more modern ideas about these things than the starchy English. She had settled on Lazarus because she felt she had no choice, but when he explained everything to her, she would come to realize that her place was with him.

Let the engagement remain for the moment, but when the time was right, he would take her away from everything that was holding them back.

He could not know then that within a day he would be on his way to Oxford, to identify the body of his second son.

* * *

Jane Wakefield was by the bedside when Lazarus entered, but she discreetly sidled away when he approached, holding his hand out to take Constance's pale fingers.

"Are you feeling better?" he asked.

"Not really," she answered hoarsely, her throat still raw from the vomiting the good doctor had induced, "Something like a wrung out dishrag."

"Yes, that's pretty much how you look," he agreed with a grin. If she had possessed any strength, she would have hit him, as it was he escaped without reproach.

"Is Holbrook dead?" she asked, "He took the same poison as me – though, of course, I didn't realize he was trying to kill me. I can still hardly believe it. What on earth was he thinking?"

"Forget about Holbrook. I left him with Stonier and I have no idea what happened. I've been here pacing the floor, waiting for you to live or die. It's not something I want to think about."

"Nor I. So, what happens next?"

"If Holbrook survives, then he'll go to trial and eventually, I hope, he'll hang."

"I didn't mean with Holbrook, I meant with us."

"Us? Well, that's a complicated question."

"It is not. It is a very simple question," she retorted, with as much emphasis as her poor damaged throat could manage.

"Really? What question is that?"

"Its one you have to ask," she said coyly.

"I can't imagine what that is," he teased.

"Yes, you can! Will you marry me?" she supplied.

He grinned, "This is so sudden, Miss Allingham, may I have time to think it over?"

This time she did find the strength to hit him, albeit none too hard, on the arm.

"You are incorrigible!" she said, "Now go away, I'm tired."

"I'll be back tomorrow."

"You'd better have a ring with you," she warned.

Downstairs Lazarus found Miss Wakefield had a caller of her own. Captain Andrew Hughes, late of his majesty's army, had been captivated the week before at Constance's betrothal ball and had called to see that all was well with the ladies when he heard of the arrest of Curate Holbrook.

Lazarus shook his proffered hand and gave him a cynical smile, "I'm sure the ladies will be fine, Mr Hughes, now that the murderer is in custody. How did you hear of that, by the way?"

"Mr Stonier brought him in several hours ago and the news soon spread through the town. It's one of the most exciting things that happened around here for years, everyone is full of it."

"I'll just bet they are," said Lazarus, suddenly realising how long he had been at Constance's house, waiting for her to recover, cocooned from the events unfolding at the police station and in the town itself.

"Damned fine show, by the way, Inspector, working out what the demon was up to. He'd covered his tracks well from all accounts."

"Thank you, sir," answered Lazarus, "but a little sooner and I could have saved Miss Allingham some considerable discomfort."

"Better than being dead, though, eh, what?"

"Infinitely better," replied the policeman, "well, if you'll excuse me, I really ought to show my face at the police station. Can't have Stonier taking all the credit."

"Absolutely not. Nice meeting you, Inspector."

"And you, Mr Hughes. Good afternoon, Miss Wakefield."

"Nearer to evening, Inspector," said Jane primly, "And that makes it time you too were on your way, Captain Hughes. There has been enough gossip in this town and I don't intend to add my name to the list!"

"Absolutely," blustered the captain hastily, evidently it was his favourite word, "cheerio, then, until we meet again."

Lazarus hesitated at the gate long enough to ensure that the captain was going in a different direction to himself. He was too tired now to endure the long walk back to the station accompanied by a garrulous companion.

Stonier was waiting for his return, impatient to be off, but determined to hear all the news of how Constance was doing before he went home.

"Scattergood worked his usual magic," Lazarus assured him, "And I believe you did the same for Holbrook?"

"Probably not quite as subtle as the good doctor," said Stonier grimly, "I simply poured salt water down his throat until he brought the whole lot back up. The cure nearly killed him!"

"Serve him right," said Lazarus with deep feeling, "I'll see him now."

Stonier put up a restraining arm, "That you'll not. Superintendent's orders, you are to be kept well away from the prisoner."

"Why?" demanded the inspector, "I'm the senior officer in this case."

"You are also the lover of the woman he tried to kill. We want him in one piece for his trial, thanks, Danby!"

The younger man seemed inclined to argue, but rapidly became aware that the ban was probably the safest route. The more he thought about Constance, washed out and sickly, the angrier he became. He really could not be sure to control himself if left alone in a cell with the cherubic curate, whose angelic face and friendly demeanour had indeed hidden the mind of a demon.

"What's more, you've been granted a few days off. Meg suggested that it might be politic to go to Sheffield and bring back Lucy to meet her future step-mama."

"Meg, is, as usual, right," said Lazarus thoughtfully. This would be the final barrier to be cleared so that he and Constance could be together. If his daughter and his future bride took an instant dislike to each other, who knew what would happen next? A wedding would seem unlikely.

* * *

It was six months later that he was called to the death-bed of his uncle-in-law. Arabella, now married, met him in the hall and sent Constance upstairs alone. She took Lazarus by the arm and drew him into the library, "I must talk to you, Danby," she whispered urgently.

"What is it, Arabella? Much as I have no desire to see Allingham, my place is by my wife's side."

"I shall not keep you for very long, but I have to tell you this before you see my father."

"Very well, tell me then."

She looked up at him, very troubled, "You know how this happened, don't you, Danby? That my father has been in decline ever since William died and that he suffered a stroke three days ago and will not recover?"

"Yes, yes," he said impatiently, "I know all that, But what has it to do with me?"

"It was I who found him collapsed, but what no one knows is that he managed to speak to me before he sank into oblivion."

"And he mentioned me?" asked Lazarus, bordering upon incredulity. He could hardly credit the idea that Allingham's last words would be directed to himself, considering the enmity in which they had existed for the past five years at least.

"Not exactly," said Arabella, "but what he did say frightened me. I don't think I can live in this house anymore."

"What the devil are you talking about?"

"Danby, when I came into the room, my father was staring at something that I could not see. He was gasping for breath, clutching his chest and staring, his eyes bulging in disbelief. I asked him what was that matter and he managed to speak, his voice coming as though he was being strangled."

"And said what?" asked Lazarus, still unimpressed by these histrionics. If he wanted melodrama he could go to the theatre.

"He said, 'By God, Lazarus was right, she is haunting me. Do you not see her, Bella? There she hangs, swinging in the wind, that brat of hers in her arms. She's dead, but her eyes are open, looking at me, cursing me.' Then he choked and said not another word, though he has tried often enough."

The inspector repressed a shudder of horror. This was ridiculous, an illusion dreamt up by a sick mind in a dying body.

"What did he mean by it all, Danby? Is this house really haunted?" Arabella might wear a wedding ring, but she showed her extreme youth in her agitation at the thought of a ghost.

"Calm yourself, you silly girl," he said soothingly, "You must remember that your father was ill. If he saw anything it was a result of many years of accumulated guilt. He has done much in his life that would shame any man. There is no ghost."

"But he said it was Decima. I know about Decima. She was in love with my brother Richard and they made him go to war and he was killed. She went mad with grief and did dreadful things. I'm not supposed to know about it, but servants talk and I overhear them sometimes. I'm afraid to be here if Mad Decima is haunting this house. I won't stay here, I won't!" her voice rose to a higher pitch and he hushed her hastily. The last thing he wanted was an hysterical cousin-in-law and a crowd of interested servants and family. There was a gathering of the clan for Allingham's final hours and the house was full to bursting.

"There's no ghost," he said firmly, "Now, I have to pay my respects to your father. Put the incident from your mind. And remember, you actually don't have to live here, if you'd rather not. You are mistress of your own destiny now."

This had evidently not occurred to her and she looked thoughtful as she preceded him out of the room. If only he had known what future troubles his words would hold for Arabella Allingham, when she finally became mistress of her own destiny.

* * *

Libby closed the final journal and looked about her with a slight shudder. She thought she knew what the vision of the hanged Decima Watkins-Allingham looked like.

She had seen it herself in this very house.

But Decima could rest in peace now, finally vindicated and with her blood-line in the place it belonged.

If you have enjoyed reading this book,
Suzanne's other titles can be ordered post free
www.countrybooks.biz

THE DEVIL DRIVES A JAGUAR
Paperback 210 x 148 mm 340 pages
ISBN 978 1 898941 75 3
Price £8.95

BLOOD AND STONE
Paperback 210 x 148 mm 338 pages
ISBN 978 1 901214 36 9
Price £8.95

AN EMPTY-HANDED TRAVELLER
Paperback 210 x 148 mm 345 pages
ISBN 978 1 901214 90 1
Price £8.95

COUNTRY BOOKS
COURTYARD COTTAGE · LITTLE LONGSTONE · BAKEWELL
DERBYSHIRE DE45 1NN
Tel: 01629 640670
e-mail: dickrichardson@country-books.co.uk